An
UNEXPECTED
Earl

ANNA
HARRINGTON

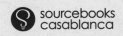

sourcebooks
casablanca

Published by Sourcebooks Casablanca, an imprint of Sourcebooks
P.O. Box 4410, Naperville, Illinois 60567-4410
(630) 961-3900
sourcebooks.com

Printed and bound in the United States of America.
BVG 10 9 8 7 6 5 4 3 2 1

Dedicated to Rachel Taylor,
my former student turned friend
and one of the best future nurses in the world.

One

THAT DRESS WAS PURE SIN.

Brandon Pearce, Earl of Sandhurst, raked his gaze over the woman standing on the other side of Lord Torrington's smoke-filled ballroom. No matter that her back was to him, she was still delicious to drink in. Red satin shimmered like brimstone as it draped over her curves, cinched tightly enough at the waist to highlight her full hips and cut low enough in the back to expose a delectable stretch of flesh that was rivaled by her bare shoulders. Only a hint of gauzy straps dropping over her upper arms gave assurance that the dress wouldn't fall down at any moment of its own wanton volition and reveal every inch of soft flesh beneath.

"Wouldn't that be a damn shame if it did?" Pearce mumbled against his glass as he lifted it to his lips.

Sweet Lucifer, he wished she'd turn around so he could confirm that the front of her was just as much a creation of the devil as the back.

Her face would be hidden, of course. This was one of Torrington's infamous masquerades, which meant that all the gentlemen in attendance wore the most expensive finery Bond Street could offer and all the women wore masks. As Torrington had told him when he arrived, "Makes the competition all the more interesting."

Apparently, that's what tonight was about. Gentlemen behaving badly. Anything which encouraged their debauched behavior was welcome. Including masked women.

And *this* masked woman had transformed his otherwise boring evening into something interesting.

After all, he was attending the party only to gain more information about Scepter. Certainly not for the entertainment. Although he'd have to admit that it was certainly not the usual society fare. He slid his gaze across the ballroom to watch a pair of half-naked female acrobats grab each other by the ankles and roll head over heels across the room, while no one else seemed to notice except for a violinist whose bow paused straight up in the air when they went rolling past.

Marking the approaching end to Parliament's session, Torrington's annual party was the most anticipated event of season's end. All of London's most influential, powerful, and wealthiest men clamored to attend... Well, all the influential, powerful, and wealthy men who wanted to spend the evening at what amounted to little more than a drunken orgy with some gambling tossed in.

Which was how Pearce secured an invitation. As a new earl, he ranked high enough socially to gain Torrington's notice, and because he was a former brigadier, Torrington was certain he shared the same crude tastes in entertainment.

Torrington was wrong. Tonight, Pearce was here as bait.

Of all the gentlemen at the Armory, he was the only one whom Scepter might approach to bring into their fold. So he had to make himself visible at events like this where he was certain their members would be in attendance.

He watched the acrobats roll back across the floor and blew out a hard breath. Even if events like this irritated the hell out of him.

Marcus Braddock, Duke of Hampton and former general, had gathered together the men who had served with him on the Continent to stop the criminal organization. The men worked out of a renovated armory north of the City, but the old building had also become a sanctuary, a place where they could go when they needed to be around men like themselves—all former soldiers struggling to adapt to postwar life. For some of them, fighting Boney had been easier. Only joining together to stop Scepter had given them a path forward.

What they'd discovered was that Scepter functioned like an octopus, with tentacles reaching from London's underworld to men at the highest ranks of the aristocracy and into all kinds of criminal activity. Including, most recently, what appeared to be the assassination of several government officials, all made to resemble accidents or suicide. Sir Alfred Wembley, War Office Paymaster, who stepped in front of a speeding carriage. Mr. John Smithson, Chancellor of the Exchequer, who drowned by falling drunkenly into the River Avon. Lord Maryworth, Master of the Mint, who shot himself with his own dueling pistol. And Sir Malcolm Donnelly, who died from falling off his horse...and who made the men of the Armory realize that the deaths were more than they seemed. Because Donnelly had never been astride a horse in his entire city-dwelling life.

Twelve deaths of prominent officials, twelve deaths now considered murder. All gentlemen of various backgrounds and positions, with no connection to each other except that they'd held government appointments. And that they'd all been quickly replaced in their positions, sometimes within a fortnight of the funeral. Pearce would have bet every penny of his newly acquired fortune that Scepter was responsible.

After all, the organization was already amassing great power and murdering those it needed to silence. Wholesale slaughter of government officials to further their agenda was absolutely possible.

But no one knew Scepter's endgame or the men behind it.

Pearce frowned as he glanced around the party. At this rate, nothing new would be forthcoming tonight either. Certainly not from the gentlemen gathered here, who were all foxed out of their minds or well on their way to it, losing great sums of money in the card room and doing their best to wiggle their hands beneath the skirts of every woman in the place.

He'd been ready to leave and call it a night. But then he'd seen that flash of red and stopped in his tracks.

"Who the devil are you?" he murmured.

The longer he stared at her, the more convinced he was that he needed to introduce himself and do the gentlemanly thing of offering to help her out of her dress at the end of the evening. With his teeth.

Even from across the room, he could see she wasn't like the other women in attendance tonight. Those women treated sex like a commodity, to be bought or sold to fit their needs. They were courtesans auditioning new protectors for the long term, less skilled light-skirts chasing the monthly rent in exchange for a few hours of bed sport, and society wives and widows escaping their normally boring lives with an evening's adventure. All safely hidden behind the anonymity of masks.

But the lady in red didn't seem to be here for any of that. Even when talking to the men, she kept herself apart in a way the other women didn't. She didn't lean in when they spoke to her; she leaned away. She didn't tap them flirtatiously with her fan; she held it between them like a shield. And she didn't view the other women as competition, giving no territorial signs toward any of them. No, she was distant. Cool. Wary. She didn't belong here, despite that dress.

Sinful *and* a mystery. And becoming more interesting with every passing moment.

Apparently, though, not just to him. His eyes narrowed on the Earl of Derby as the man ignored the dismissive way she turned away from his advance, slipped his arm around her waist, and yanked her back against him.

Immediately, she smacked the earl on top of his head with her fan, hard enough that the ivory guard bounced against his skull.

Pearce choked on his drink.

Good Lord, he'd never seen *that* before at one of these parties. Neither had Lord Derby, based on his stunned expression and the bruise undoubtedly forming on his crown.

Yet the little minx had the nerve to feign surprise at what she'd done, followed by a mumbled apology even as she attempted to sashay away.

But the earl pursued. This time, when he grabbed her fully into his arms, she gave him a hard push that sent him rocking onto his heels. Derby only laughed, still determined to find his way beneath her skirts, and grabbed her once more into his arms, this time too tightly for her to fight her way free.

Pearce's grin melted into a grimace. He snagged a glass of champagne from the tray of a passing footman and sauntered forward. That red flash of temptation not only beckoned but now also needed to be rescued.

"Scarlet," he called out. "There you are!"

Derby looked up, startled.

Seizing on the distraction, the woman shoved her way out of Derby's arms. She wheeled around to face Pearce.

At the sight of him, her green eyes flared from behind the mask that covered everything except for her sensuous lips, and she froze like a doe startled by hunters. But then, so did he...except for his gaze, which dropped deliberately over her from head to slippers.

Sweet Lucifer. The back of her might have been pure sin, but the front was simply soul-stealing.

Her hair cascaded over one shoulder in a riot of golden curls that teased seductively at the swell of her breasts, visible above the low-cut neckline of her tight bodice. But for all that the shimmering satin of her dress captivated him and those silky tresses had him longing to brush his hands through them, what struck him was the gold locket she wore around her neck on a little blue ribbon. The schoolgirl innocence of that single piece of jewelry undercut the sinfulness of the red gown in startling contradiction.

More. The sight of the locket jarred something inside him, knocking loose from the past a memory he couldn't quite place yet one so familiar that it begged to be remembered... Damnation, did he know her?

He sent her a far too intimate smile. "I leave you alone for two minutes and you slip away, sending me on a merry chase to find you."

Her brilliant eyes grew wider, but wisely, she said nothing.

"Shame on you." He winked at her. *Trust me...* Then he glanced past her to Derby, the man standing so close at her side that surely he could see right down her dress to her navel. His smile tightened. "Ah, you've been making friends."

"Pearce," Derby bit out with his own forced smile. Like half the peers in the Lords, he refused to acknowledge that Pearce was now one of them by not using his title.

The man probably considered the slight an insult. Pearce considered it a compliment.

"Derby." Pearce stepped forward and took the woman's arm to gently but possessively move her safely away from the earl and to his side. "I see you've met my Scarlet."

"Yes." Derby's mouth twisted. "I didn't realize that you'd already claimed her."

"*Claimed?*" Pearce clucked his tongue in chastisement, then lifted her hand to kiss the backs of her gloved fingers. "Can any man truly claim a woman like this?" He saw her arch a brow above her mask at that blatant whopper of a flirtation. "God knows I'm not man enough for her."

At that, her other hand flew up to her lips to stifle a shocked gasp. Or a laugh. With this bold woman, it could have been either.

"Something in your throat, my dear? Here." He held out the glass. "The champagne you requested."

Her eyes sparkled as effervescently as the bubbles in the wine. "How thoughtful," she mumbled as she accepted it, playing along.

"Anything for you, darling."

Her mouth fell open. She covered her surprise at his audacity by quickly raising the glass to her lips.

Biting back a grin at her expense and unable to resist, he leaned over to place a kiss to her ear. She trembled but didn't fling the champagne in his face. *Good.* He'd take his victories however he could get them.

He wrapped her arm around his. "Shall we dance?" Not giving her the chance to refuse, he led her toward the dance floor and tossed dismissively over his shoulder, "Goodbye, Derby."

The earl said nothing. But as he turned and stomped away, Pearce was certain the man was cursing him, his ancestry, and every stray French bullet that had somehow managed to miss killing him during the wars.

The woman began to slip her arm away.

"Not so fast." He placed his hand over hers to keep it on his jacket sleeve. "I helped you. It's only fair that you now help me."

She stiffened with wariness. "How?"

"Help me put a positive end to a very boring evening by dancing with me. That's all." When that didn't seem to mollify her, he gestured toward the dance floor. "It's for your own benefit."

"That's a novel approach for a lord to meet a woman," she drawled, her voice so low and throaty that he suspected she was purposefully attempting to disguise it. But she couldn't hide the sardonic laughter that colored it.

He crooked a grin. "I'm not an average lord." When she began to give him the cut that bit of arrogance deserved, he interrupted. "Everyone will see us together, so you can tell every other unwanted man who comes too close that you belong to me for the evening." His gaze fixed on hers. Sweet Jesus, a man could happily drown in those emerald pools…ones that seemed so oddly familiar. "They won't dare touch you then."

"You're awfully sure of yourself."

When it came to making men fear him… "I am."

She hesitated at his offer—one dance for the opportunity to be left alone for the rest of the evening. He felt like the devil himself bargaining for her soul.

She must have realized it, too, because when she glanced toward the dance floor, she murmured in a voice that was little more than a purr, "I don't think what they're doing is dancing."

He followed her gaze. Couples who hadn't yet left to find more private spaces where they could be alone danced across the floor. But this wasn't a London society ball. Instead of bouncing through quadrilles or reels, these couples completely ignored the music to move to their own wanton rhythms. They touched fully along their fronts from hips to shoulders, with the women clasping glasses of brandy and port in their hands and the men clasping breasts and buttocks in theirs.

"No, indeed," he agreed. But for some reason he couldn't name, he wanted a dance with her. He wanted the chance to have her in his arms if only for a few minutes, to find out who she was beneath that mask and why she was here…and why he felt increasingly certain he knew her. "But the musicians won't mind playing for a couple who want an old-fashioned waltz."

"An *old-fashioned* waltz?" she asked, her voice breathless with irony. "Is there even such a thing?"

He called out to the lead musician and tossed the man a coin. "There is now." When the first flourishes of a waltz went up, he held out his hand with a formal bow. "Lady Scarlet, our dance." He arched a brow. "I promise to keep my hands where you can see them at all times."

An ironic smile tugged at her lips. "With a request like that, how could a lady refuse?"

Pearce took her into position and twirled her into the waltz, making certain to maintain a proper distance as he led her through the steps.

She followed lightly in his arms, just as he'd suspected she would. Refined and polished to the bone, she gracefully placed every step, including the perfectly positioned tilt of her head that showcased her elegant neck. Just another reason he knew she didn't belong here tonight. She was far too good at waltzing to be someone who made her living on her back, and she lacked the hard-edged bitterness that marked the society ladies.

So who the devil was she? And why couldn't he shake the suspicion that he knew her?

He led her into a half turn. "Now that I've rescued you from Derby, tell me... What's your name?"

She stared at him in surprise, as if he should know her. And damnation, if he didn't feel the same. "Apparently, it's Lady Scarlet."

He turned in the opposite direction, hoping to catch her off-balance. "Your real name."

She hesitated, then dodged. "You first."

"Pearce."

She sized him up with a sliding glance in his direction. "Just Pearce?"

"Just Lady Scarlet?"

"Yes." The determined sound of that told him she'd obstinately cling to her defenses even as she teased, "But my friends call me Red."

He laughed, a warmth stirring inside him. He wasn't making any headway in solving her mystery, but heavens, she was amusing.

"And what do your friends call you?"

"Brigadier."

She missed a step and stumbled, but he caught her, solidly righting her again.

Her eyes darted to his. She repeated in an incredulous whisper, "Brigadier?"

He *knew* her. He was certain of it now. But from where?

"Brandon Pearce, current Earl of Sandhurst and former brigadier in His Majesty's army, Coldstream Guards." He lowered his mouth to her ear as he spun her through a tight circle and started back across the dance floor. "But most people call me Pearce."

"Pearce." The soft sound of his name curled heatedly along his spine. And around another more sensitive place.

His memory couldn't place her, but his body somehow knew what he didn't. He'd been intimate with her. He would have wagered in the book at White's on it. But when? Where?

Beneath his concentrated stare, she nervously cleared her throat and looked away over his shoulder. "Do you often go around rescuing women?"

"Constantly," he drawled dryly. "Do you often need to be rescued?"

"Never."

He arched a disbelieving brow.

"I would have handled Lord Derby just fine on my own."

His brow inched higher.

"I'm handling *you* just fine, aren't I?" Her green eyes gleamed mischievously, sparking a yearning desire in his gut. "And you're a brigadier."

He grinned at her cheekiness. They weren't dancing. They were dueling. And he was enjoying it immensely. She was the kind of woman who could easily keep a man on his toes, or leave him lying in the dust without a second thought if he couldn't keep pace.

"I'm not like the other men here tonight." He hid the gentle warning of that behind a tease of arrogance.

She smiled, just as he'd hoped. "So I've gathered."

He changed direction in their waltz. And in their conversation. "And you're not like the other women."

She tensed in his arms, her smile tightening. But this time she didn't miss a single beat and continued to match his steps, her eyes never leaving his.

"So why are you here tonight, Lady Scarlet, when you so obviously don't belong?"

"Why are you?" she countered, sending back the next shot in

their volley. But the husky tone of her answer told him that he'd rattled her.

"So I could rescue you." He had no intention of answering that honestly. "Why are you here?"

"Apparently, to be rescued."

He smiled grimly. Their waltz was coming to an end, and so was his opportunity to learn the truth about her. "You're not a light-skirt looking to make rent, and you're not a courtesan searching for a protector." His eyes searched what little of her face he could see beneath the mask, looking for answers. "You're also not some jaded society widow looking for an evening's entertainment."

"I might be." The trembling in her voice undercut whatever assurance she'd aimed for. "You don't know."

"But I do."

To make his point, he stepped forward and brought the front of his body in full contact with hers.

She stiffened immediately with a surprised gasp, her hand at his shoulder flattening against the kerseymere of his jacket as if catching herself before she pushed him away. Or before she cracked him over the skull as she'd done to Derby. No courtesan or light-skirt would have done that. Just more proof of how far out of her element she was.

His point made, he shifted away to a respectable distance. Regrettably. The part of him that remembered her desperately wanted to rekindle old acquaintances.

"So why are you here?" He frowned as the last notes of the waltz floated away. "If you're in some kind of trouble, I can help." When she hesitated to reply, he added, "And I won't even ask your real name."

She paused a moment before muttering, "You *do* rescue women, don't you?"

"A man needs a hobby," he replied, deadpan.

When her shoulders eased down and she bit her bottom lip, he knew he'd won her over, if grudgingly. "If you truly want to help…" As the orchestra fell silent, she stopped dancing and searched for any sign that she could trust him. Either convinced of his trustworthiness—or simply desperate—she said, "I'm looking for Sir Charles Varnham."

His eyes narrowed on her. "Why?"

"Business."

And none of yours. The unspoken words lingered on the air.

She dropped into a curtsy, which seemed as out of place at Torrington's masquerade as the formal waltz had been only moments before, and the curious stares she drew confirmed it. "I need to talk to him. Alone." She held his hand lightly in her fingers, but urgency pulsed in her touch. "Have you seen him?"

The dance had ended. He'd saved her from Derby and any other man who wanted to prey on her tonight. She was no longer his concern.

Yet he couldn't stop himself from attempting to rescue her again. What could she want with Varnham? If rumors were to be believed, Sir Charles was here only to keep watch on his younger brother, Arthur.

"Please, Pearce."

The familiarity of that soft plea pierced him. Damn the world that he couldn't place the distant memory it stirred in the dark corners of his mind, couldn't put that voice into a context that would tell him who she was.

He also couldn't refuse. Reluctantly, he told her, "Varnham was lingering in the stair hall a few minutes ago. He might still be there."

"Thank you." Her eyes shone with gratitude. "It was a pleasure seeing you, Brigadier."

He suspected she'd wanted to say something more but thought better of it. Instead she slid her hand from his sleeve.

He reached for her arm, stopping her. "Who the devil are you? Your real name."

"You said you wouldn't ask if—"

"How do we know each other?" Her eyes flashed from behind the mask in an eruption of alarm and suspicion, yet he pressed. "Tell me."

"I–I can't… We don't—" Unable to hide the immediate quickening of her breath and the pounding pulse at her wrist beneath his fingers, she forced out instead, "I have to go."

Unexpected jealousy swirled up his spine. "Whatever you're planning with Varnham, it isn't a good idea. Going off alone with any man in a place like this—"

"Thank you," she repeated and persisted in pulling away, yet something about her reminded him of a rabbit caught in a snare. "But as I said, I don't need to be rescued."

She turned to leave.

Oh no. She wasn't getting away that easily. Pearce started after her—

"Sandhurst!" His name carried in a loud shout across the room. "Lord Sandhurst—Brandon Pearce!"

He ignored the calls and chased after her. Just as he was about to reach for her elbow to stop her, a man stepped into his path and blocked his way.

He slid to a halt to keep from slamming into the nodcock.

The woman glanced back at him as she fled. When she saw the man standing in front of him, she stumbled. Her hand went to her face, to check that the mask was still in place, still hiding her identity. But she never slowed in her flight.

Pearce tried to follow, but the man grabbed his hand to shake it, stopping him before he could take another step to pursue her.

"Frederick Howard." The man pumped his hand hard in that irritating American fashion that had become popular in certain circles in London. "We've met before."

Vague recollection flashed at the back of Pearce's mind, but he was too preoccupied by the woman in red to immediately recognize the name. "Not now," he growled and began to move around Howard, only for the man to step in front of him again.

"I was hoping for a word with you tonight." The man forced a too-bright laugh. "How fortunate that I found you."

Biting back a curse, Pearce leaned to the side to look past him—

The woman was gone. She'd vanished into the dimly lit townhouse as mysteriously as she'd appeared. He'd lost her.

Damnation. He rolled his eyes. Tonight was proving to be frustrating in all kinds of ways.

Blowing out an irritated breath, he slid his narrowed gaze at the dandy in front of him, who didn't seem to realize—or care—that he'd just interrupted something important. Although what it was, exactly, Pearce couldn't have said, except that he'd wanted it to continue. He'd barely scratched the surface of Lady Scarlet's mystery, her identity still unknown.

But she was gone, and all chances of learning more right along with her.

"Howard, you said?" Pearce ground out. After all, it was only polite to learn the name of the man he was about to pulp.

"Yes. *Frederick Howard.*" Irritation pinched his face that Pearce didn't recognize him. "Our families knew each other years ago. In Birmingham."

Unlikely. Pearce's parents died long before he was shipped off to his innkeeper uncle in Birmingham, and this man didn't seem the sort that frequented inn yards.

"You recently inherited the Sandhurst estates, and we now have neighboring properties." As if realizing he was stirring up more acrimony than memories, the dandy changed tack. To bluntness. "I want to discuss a joint business venture."

"Business?" Pearce repeated, unwilling to believe that he'd been stopped for something so unimportant.

"Exactly." The man smiled tightly. "The best kind, too—capital development!"

"No such thing as the best kind of business." He peered past the man, still hoping to catch a glimpse of red satin. No luck. "All business is—"

"Turnpike."

That caught Pearce's attention, if only for its unexpectedness. He blinked. "Pardon?"

"I intend to put through a new turnpike, and you're the perfect man to help me realize it."

Oh, he sincerely doubted that.

"A turnpike has the potential to leverage all kinds of possibilities for property that is otherwise worthless. Imagine the funds that…" Beneath Pearce's stone-cold stare, Howard's voice trailed off. Realizing that he was losing the battle, he cleared his throat. "If I could set up a time to call on you—"

"Fine." Pearce dismissed the man with a wave of his hand. He couldn't care less. He had more important concerns at that moment. The woman had been after Varnham, and Varnham was in the stair hall. Maybe he could still catch her there. Pearce stepped around the man before he could stop him again and strode toward the front of the house.

He hurried through rooms that were all piled into each other like Russian nesting dolls. She should have been easy to spot in that dress, but a sea of jewels and satin filled the rooms—

A flash of red slipped through the front door and out into the night. "Scarlet!" He chased after her.

Pushing his way through the crush, he stumbled through the handful of men gathered at the front door and out onto the footpath. He stopped to glance down the rain-drizzled street. His breath clouded on the cold night air, and his heart pounded as loudly as the rumbling of horse's hooves over the stones. He *had* to find her—

There. Her dress showed a muted blood-orange in the yellow lamplight as she hurried across the wide street toward a waiting carriage.

He started after her.

Without warning, a phaeton turned onto the street at break-neck speed, so fast that it lifted off its rear right wheel, careening nearly uncontrollably behind its racing team. The rig hit a rise in the pavement and jumped into the air, sending the team darting to the left—right toward the woman, who froze in fear.

"Look out!" Pearce shouted and sprinted across the street.

He grabbed her around the waist and hurled her forward with him. The wheel of the phaeton spun past so close that it shaved against his calf.

Momentum propelled them forward. Just before they crashed into the building on the other side of the street, Pearce turned so that his shoulder slammed into the stone wall instead of her soft body, so that his arms protected her from the blow.

The jolt came so hard that it ripped the air from his lungs. Yet he held onto her, even though his grasp had loosened, even though she'd fallen against him, momentarily stunned and breath-less. Her hair had escaped its ribbon and now spilled freely around her shoulders. The mask slipped, revealing her face.

Recognition slammed into him as hard as the stone wall.

"Amelia?" he whispered hoarsely. *Good God*…he was staring at a dream.

She pushed herself out of his arms and ran.

Two

"Hill Street, Berkeley Square," Amelia Howard called out frantically to the jarvey of the waiting hackney. She allowed herself only a fleeting glance over her shoulder to make certain that Pearce hadn't followed her before ducking into the carriage. "Hurry!"

She closed the door. As the carriage jerked into motion, she rested her head back against the cracked leather squabs and shut her eyes.

Of all the men to run into this evening, and dressed like this, no less—what a nightmare! Even now, her heart pounded a fierce tattoo because he'd seen her face, because he remembered her...

But then, why wouldn't he? After all, she'd never forgotten him.

"What happened?" Her maid's concerned voice reached out to her in the darkness. "What's wrong?"

Unable just yet to squelch the shock of seeing Pearce again and open her eyes, Amelia simply shook her head.

"Oh, I knew coming here was a bad idea!"

Her maid, Maggie, who was almost ten years older than Amelia, had refused to let her venture out alone tonight and insisted on waiting in the carriage. Now guilt prickled in Amelia's belly that she'd upset the woman.

"Nothing's wrong," Amelia assured her, finally finding her voice. *Except that I saw a ghost...*

"You spoke to him, then?"

She meant Sir Charles Varnham. Amelia's purpose for going to tonight's masquerade. "No."

Her shoulders sagged at her dashed plans. She'd borrowed the red dress and mask so she could speak to Charles Varnham without

any servants or society gossips—and especially her brother—
knowing. After all, there was no proper way for an unmarried lady
to talk privately to a bachelor gentleman of Sir Charles's rank and
the leading member of the House of Commons's Committee of
Privileges, no less. No way to send him a message without risking
that servants or his secretary would read it. And no way to keep
Frederick from finding out. So when Freddie had mentioned that
Sir Charles would be at the masquerade, Amelia had seized the
night as the only opportunity she would have to approach him.

But it had turned into a complete disaster.

"I couldn't find him in the crush," she admitted in defeat.

Her maid unleashed a string of curses beneath her breath.
"Then we're back to where we began."

"Yes." With no more information than the little she already
knew. That her brother, the Honorable Frederick Howard,
Member of Parliament for Minehead, was being blackmailed.

By whom, over what, why—she had no idea. All she had was a
note of extortion that mentioned Sir Charles Varnham's name and
a brother she couldn't confront about it, who was behaving even
more erratically than usual. More suspiciously. More...desperately.

She'd discovered it all by accident. A crumpled note had been
forgotten in the pocket of her brother's jacket, one he'd been so
foxed while wearing that he'd gotten sick on himself—or one of
his cronies had—leaving the garment too soiled ever to be worn
again. Maggie had given it a last once-over before tossing it onto
the pile for the rag-and-bone man, found the note, given it to
Amelia...

She had no idea what her brother had done—the unsigned
note wasn't specific. But if he didn't continue to cooperate, then he
would be exposed... *You can be assured that I will reveal everything
you have done, and the consequences will be far worse for you than if
Charles Varnham learns of your illegal activities. Please do not force
me to destroy you...*

If Freddie's recent behavior was any indication, the threat was very real.

She pressed her hand to her belly. Just thinking about it made her sick! But she hadn't dared speak to Freddie yet. What good would it have done? She loved her brother and knew him well, which meant she knew his character. Moral fortitude, unfortunately, wasn't part of it. If she confronted him, he'd simply deny everything, accuse her of meddling where she didn't belong, or outright lie, just as he had to his prefects at school whenever he'd been caught breaking the rules and to Papa whenever he'd done far more than that. Worse, because if he suspected that she was stirring up trouble—or if he *had* done something illegal that he didn't want her to discover—he had the power to close down her charity shop.

She could never let that happen. The war widows who worked there depended upon her for their livelihood, and she depended upon them for giving her a reason to rise from bed every morning. Her throat tightened. What would she have left to live for if she lost her charity?

Eventually, she would have to confront Frederick, she knew. But not yet. Not until she had more facts, at least enough to force him into telling the truth. Even if it meant having to dress like a courtesan to hold anonymous conversations about blackmail in order to get them.

Sweet heavens, *how* had her life come to this?

"So why were you running?"

"I—" She bit down the sting of guilt at lying to the woman who had been with her since she was eighteen. "Frederick saw me."

A new string of Irish curses poured from Maggie, even more creative than the ones before. "Did he recognize you?"

"He only saw me in my mask, only for a moment." And mostly as she was running away. "No, I'm certain he didn't."

But the other man who'd seen her had recognized her

immediately. Brandon Pearce… Good heavens, what was *he* doing there?

It had been over a decade since they'd last seen each other. Since that horrible night of her sixteenth birthday when he'd come to her bedroom, crawling in through her window just as he'd always done since they were children to give her his present—a little gold locket that he'd saved up all his money to buy. The same night when he'd come close to taking her innocence. *Very* close. She would have let him, too, if Papa hadn't burst in upon them.

Even now her cheeks heated with the humiliation of it, their friendship abruptly over and both of them banished—Amelia to school in Scotland by her father and Pearce into the army by his cousin, the Earl of Sandhurst, who'd called in favors to quickly purchase an officer's commission for him. Neither man wanted the scandal that would befall both their families if anyone learned of what happened. Or risk the possibility that it might happen again.

Her father's plan had worked. Not one mention of scandal was ever raised about the two of them, and they never saw each other again.

Until tonight. When the sight of him had ripped Amelia's breath away.

Twelve years… Could it truly have been that long since they'd last been together? But her heart knew it was so. The foolish thing had kept count.

He'd changed over the years. The gangly eighteen-year-old she'd known had become a man, leaving behind almost no trace of the boy he'd once been. Yet she would have known him anywhere despite the fine wrinkles that age now crinkled in the corners of his blue eyes and the wide breadth of the muscular shoulders that army life and hard work had given him. Gone, too, was the restlessness she remembered, transformed now into a confidence that radiated from him like his rich scent of port and cigars. So heady and powerful, and just as masculine.

When he'd approached her tonight, she felt as if time had folded in upon itself and those years apart had never passed. The ache in her belly came so swiftly and fiercely at seeing him that for one excruciating moment she'd been transported back to Birmingham, when her world hadn't yet crumbled around her. When she'd still believed that she would always be with him.

An earl and a brigadier—wouldn't her father have laughed his wig off to know that this was what Pearce had made of himself, against all odds?

But then, maybe not. Gordon Howard had never possessed a strong sense of humor. Nor did he hold any love for Pearce, a young man he'd viewed as a threat to his daughter's proper future as the wife of an aristocrat. A worry that had proven worthless in the end.

"You'd better hope that Mr. Howard didn't see you," Maggie warned, "or it won't be Sir Charles you'll be dealin' with but a husband. He'll see to that!"

Amelia choked down an ironic laugh. *That* could never happen. After all, not even her brother possessed the power to force a husband upon her when she already had one. *Somewhere.*

But she also couldn't let the scandalous things she suspected Freddie might have done become known. Because if her brother's sins ever came to light, then so would hers. And those of her absent husband.

"Help me out of this gown and into my dress, will you?" She scooted to the edge of the seat, hoping to change subjects while she changed clothes. The last thing she needed now was Maggie's worry. Or her prying. "We're almost to Mayfair, and Freddie's servants cannot see me like this."

"*I'm* one of his servants." Maggie's lips pursed in chastisement. "And I don't think undressing in a hired hackney is at all proper, not for the sister of an MP and a respectable lady who depends upon her reputation."

In other words, a lady who had nothing but her reputation and the good graces of her brother to survive upon.

But those graces were now under attack, and she simply wouldn't sit by and let their lives be destroyed.

Oh, Frederick could certainly be weak-spined and self-serving, but he'd also supported her in those dark days seven years ago after Aaron Northam had wed her and then abandoned her before the ink on the parish register was even dry, stealing her fortune and shattering her heart. Freddie had hired all manner of lawyers, accountants, and investigators in a desperate attempt to find Aaron and force him to return—and to return her money. But Aaron had fled to America, and once there, he'd vanished, leaving no trace.

After two years, Amelia agreed with Frederick to give up the search. No one except the two of them—and Aaron—knew that she was married, and she'd go to her grave keeping it that way. Because Freddie had also protected her from being a social pariah by covering up all traces of her reckless elopement.

True, Freddie had also been protecting himself by helping her; even then he'd had political ambitions, and the brother of a socially ruined woman could never have a career in the Commons, especially when the seat he'd been given had been granted by influential friends who would gladly rescind it to keep his family's tarnished reputation from tainting theirs. And true, as well, that even though he'd taken her under his roof and provided her with an allowance, he'd never let her forget how foolish she'd been.

Yet Freddie hadn't had to help her at all. Now that he was in deep trouble, just as she'd been, how could she turn her back on him?

"Yes, you're a Howard servant, but you're also my friend." Amelia's eyes heated with desperate emotion. "And right now Frederick and I both need your help." She presented her back to her maid. "Please."

Maggie grudgingly switched benches to sit beside her and began to unbutton Amelia's tight bodice.

"Thank you," Amelia said over her shoulder as the dress loosened enough that she could shimmy out of it. "I couldn't do this without you, you know that."

"What I know is that both our gooses will be cooked if your brother ever catches wind of what you did tonight."

Amelia smiled at the lack of venom in Maggie's scolding. "Then he won't find out. Even if he does, I'll protect you. I promise."

Pearce's words flashed through her mind—*So I could rescue you.*

If he only knew the truth! Stripping out of a gown designed for a courtesan in a hired hackney rolling through Mayfair...she wasn't certain that even a brigadier turned earl could rescue her from the mess her life had become.

Or if he'd even want to. They hadn't exactly parted well all those years ago, their childhood friendship coming to a crashing end. Papa had made certain that they'd never see or contact each other again by threatening to have Pearce court-martialed and her married off immediately to any son of a peer he could find if they ever tried. Neither of them dared attempt it for fear that it would ruin the other. In that, at least, their lives had still been entwined.

And in that, she also knew that Pearce had loved her. Because he'd let her go.

Losing him had been sheer hell, but she would never begrudge him the outcome. After all, because of that night, he was given the chance for a grand life in the army, a life he deserved—or at least that was the lie she told herself in order to survive the pain. And she'd planned to marry, to have a house of her own, a family... all those things she'd hoped would replace the emptiness Pearce's leaving had created. Only once had she attempted to rekindle their friendship. After Papa died and was no longer an obstacle between them, she'd sent off a series of letters to Pearce, confessing her feelings and asking for a new chance at a future together.

But he'd never replied. Not once. Apparently, by then he no longer wanted her.

Soon after, she met Aaron and determined to have the life with him that fate had denied her with Pearce. She'd done her best to put the past behind her and move on.

Only tonight, when she was waltzing in his arms, did she realize how much she'd truly missed him. The pain had been simply brutal.

With her buttons undone, Amelia stood as tall as she could in the swaying carriage and gripped the ceiling for support, one hand at a time, so that Maggie could remove her gown. In the darkness, no one could see into the compartment and glimpse her in her stays and chemise, but unease fluttered butterflies in her belly—or perhaps that was a result of the evening. Surely not all of the swaying that gripped her was because of the rocking carriage.

Would she even know him now? Was any of the boy she'd loved still left inside the man Pearce had become?

Things were so different before, when they were children. They'd been brought together only because of the proximity of her father's town house to his uncle's inn. He'd been raised there by his uncle after he'd been orphaned, and she'd been allowed to wander unsupervised from the house after her own mother died. After all, Papa had no care or use for her then. That was before he'd made his fortune and came to society's notice. Before he needed a daughter to marry the son of a peer and launch the Howards into the aristocracy.

Back then she and Pearce had been nothing more than two misfits who belonged nowhere except with each other. Companionship turned into friendship and eventually into affection. For Amelia, it became love. She'd wanted nothing more than to be with him for the rest of her life.

But it had all come crashing down, and nothing could ever be the same between them again.

Maggie slid the blue muslin dress over Amelia's head and tugged it down into place around her hips and legs. Amelia sank onto the bench.

"You didn't have the chance to learn anything more at all,

then?" the maid pressed as she reached to button her up. "About what Mr. Howard's been up to?"

"No." Although after seeing Pearce, her brother had been the least of her concerns.

Maggie pulled pins from her own hair and began to twist Amelia's into a chignon. "What do we do next?"

"I don't know." But surrender was not an option, not when her brother's career hung in the balance. If Frederick truly had done something illegal—and what MP hadn't these days?—then he might very well be ruined, thrown out of Parliament, perhaps even arrested and put into prison. And her life would be ruined right along with his. A victim of proximity. If he fell, she'd go tumbling after, and the women her charity helped right along with them. "Don't worry. I'll think of something."

Ignoring the painful hopelessness that panged inside her, she kicked off her red slippers and pulled on a pair of sturdy half-boots. Her normal, not-so-glamorous fare. She turned toward Maggie and pulled her long sleeves into place. "How do I look?"

The woman gave her an assessing glance. "Plain and boring."

"Perfect." After all, she had to look as if she'd spent the evening at one of her bluestocking meetings. She trusted no one inside her brother's house except for Maggie, not knowing where the black-mailer had gotten his information. And if Frederick ever discovered what she'd done tonight and why...God help her.

"Anything else you want to tell me about tonight?" Maggie asked as she folded up the gown and tucked it into the bag in which she usually carried her knitting. They would have to smuggle the dress into the house, then back to Madame Noir, the brothel owner who had lent it to Amelia. For a hefty price, of course. Madame was nothing if not mercenary. "Seems to me that you're awfully upset just to have run into your brother."

"Doesn't Freddie upset everyone he runs into?" Amelia muttered.

The woman shot her a chastising look.

With a long sigh, Amelia admitted, "I saw someone else there... an old friend."

"Oh?" Maggie arched a curious brow.

"Not *that* kind of old friend," she corrected. Heavens! The last thing she needed was Maggie thinking of love matches for her. No, those kinds of hopes had been dashed long ago. "A childhood friend from Birmingham. I hadn't seen him since I was sixteen. It was a bit of a shock."

"I can imagine." Maggie pursed her lips together suspiciously. "What kind of friend of yours would attend a masquerade like that?"

A brigadier. That's what Pearce would have answered, what he was certainly most proud of. Not some silly title that was handed down like old linen, but something he had to work to earn. Something that proved his worth.

"A very successful one," she answered sincerely.

The carriage turned onto Hill Street, and her brother's town house came into view. The three-bay terrace house perfectly symbolized her brother—aristocratic tastes on a tradesman's allowance. She'd always wondered how he'd managed to afford the house, belong to so many clubs, frequent the best tailors, and spend nearly every evening at cards, drink, and women on the meager income their father had left him. She'd never dared to question him, knowing that she should be the last person to question how he managed his money, given how foolishly she'd lost hers.

But since finding the blackmail note, she'd begun to wonder... Had he been taking bribes? Was that why his friends had worked so hard to place him into the Minehead seat when he didn't have the money to buy it himself? Had that been how he funded his lifestyle? Or was he involved with something even worse, like smuggling?

Certainly, there were gambling debts and prostitutes. He'd never cared about hiding evidence of those, despite how he kept all of his other papers under lock and key in his study. Yet there had to have been so much more that he'd been doing that she didn't know about.

But the blackmailer knew, and whatever Freddie had done now threatened to come crashing down on both their heads if she couldn't find a way to stop it.

Amelia rapped at the roof of the carriage to signal for the jarvey to stop. "Ready?"

Maggie gave a conspiratorial nod and recited, "It was an evening of spirited bluestocking discussion among the London Ladies regarding Voltaire. And tea. Lots of tea, although I suspect that Lady Agnes Sinclair slipped whiskey into hers."

Amelia laughed. A perfect alibi!

She squeezed the woman's hand in gratitude, then opened the door and descended to the footpath. If the hackney driver noticed that she'd changed clothes en route, he made no comment, only tugging at the brim of his tall hat when she indicated that someone from inside the house would pay the fare. Linking arms with Maggie, Amelia walked to the front door, rapped the brass knocker, and waited.

The door opened, and the man who served as butler, valet, and footman all rolled into one nodded at her. Another servant whom she now didn't trust. "Good evening, miss."

"Drummond." She smiled. "Would you please pay the jarvey?"

The butler swung his gaze to Maggie, who nervously clutched at her knitting bag so tightly that her fingertips almost glowed white. Under his suspicious frown, the maid began to shake.

But Amelia gave the woman no time to panic as she tightened her hold on her arm and whisked her past Drummond and into the house. She hurried Maggie up the stairs to her room, grabbing a candle from the wall sconce on the first landing to light their way. With a deep sigh of relief, Amelia handed over the candle and sagged back against the closed door.

Thank God this horrible evening was finally over.

Her breathing returned to normal as Maggie moved around the room, lighting another candle on the bedside stand and bending down to stir up the banked fire in the small fireplace. The coals flamed, a soft glow lighting the room.

"You'll have to keep the gown with you tonight," Amelia instructed, pushing herself away from the door. She couldn't risk that the maid-of-all-work might find it in her room, then report to Frederick. "I'll collect it from you after breakfast and return it to Madame Noir on my way to the shop."

"La!" Maggie stood and wiped the soot from her hands. "For what that woman charged, you could have bought a new dress of your own."

No, she couldn't have. Satin was expensive, and the dressmaker would have sent a bill. Frederick monitored every ha'penny she spent and would want to know why she'd bought a ball gown. A red satin one, no less. But Madame Noir survived on the scandalous and knew how to keep her confidences. That was what Amelia had paid so dearly to obtain—not the woman's dress but her silence.

Madame Noir ran a brothel on King Street where she sold women to society gentlemen, ironically only a few doors down from Almack's, where marriage-minded mamas sold their own daughters to the same society gentlemen. Amelia knew about Madame's business because Frederick had received bills from the woman for services rendered. *Discretion guaranteed*, the invoices read.

Amelia had taken her up on that promise.

"It was the only way," she sighed.

She took the gown from the bag and held it up to look covetously at it one more time. Such a beautiful dress! She'd felt beautiful in it, too, especially when Pearce's eyes darkened when they'd swept over her in a way he'd never looked at her when she was younger. As if he'd wanted to devour her. A shiver sped through her just thinking about it.

"It is a shame, though, that I only wore it once," she murmured, watching how the firelight shimmered across the material. "How grand it would be to be able to wear something like this to the opera or—"

"Amelia!"

Her heart lurched into her throat as her brother's voice boomed through the town house. The dress slipped through her numb fingers to the floor.

Frederick was home early. And most certainly because he'd seen her at the masquerade.

Three

"AMELIA, WHERE ARE YOU?"

As her brother called out for her again, Amelia snatched up the dress and shoved it back into the knitting bag. She yanked the bag closed and buckled the straps, swallowing down her panic.

"I need to talk to you—now!"

With shaking hands, she shoved the bag at her maid, who had gone pale. "Go upstairs to your room. He probably just wants to make certain I arrived home all right." But even she didn't believe that. "Everything will be fine."

Maggie's jerking nod did little to bolster her courage.

Amelia hurried downstairs before her brother could send up another shout that would wake both the dead and the neighbors on both sides. She paused outside the study to take a deep breath, then plastered on a smile and stepped into the room. "Frederick, you're home early."

"And according to Drummond," he mused as he poured cognac into a crystal tumbler from the drink tray, although he'd clearly had more than his fair share of liquor already, "you were out late."

"Well, you know how the London Ladies are." She clasped her hands behind her back, more to hide their shaking than in contriteness. "We often become carried away when we have our discussions, and I lost track of time."

Did he know she was lying? She couldn't tell from the way he smiled and returned the stopper to the decanter with a soft clink. His hand shook. Something was bothering him. *Please, God, don't let him have seen me!*

He asked over his shoulder, "Voltaire again?"

She forced a long-suffering sigh to hide her nervousness. "Voltaire always."

He raised the glass to his mouth to take a healthy swallow. "Be careful when you're out." His voice was scratchy, the sound a combination of too much drink and snuff. "You know I worry about you."

Yes. Since Papa died, he'd kept a close eye on her. The only time he'd slipped was when she'd eloped with Aaron without a marriage contract in place, and they were both still paying for that mistake.

"Which is why I always take Maggie with me," she assured him. "Besides, what's the worst that could happen among bluestockings—someone mistranslates the Latin and insists that Caesar said, 'I came, I saw, I ate crumpets'?"

He laughed at her quip, far too happily for a man who was being blackmailed and certainly only because he was foxed, and growing more so with every sip he took. Even now he swayed unsteadily on his feet as he crossed to his desk. As he brushed by, she could smell the odor of expensive brandy and cheap perfume that lingered around him like a cloud.

"After tonight, we might not have to worry so much anymore," he said sotto voce so that he wouldn't be overheard. Apparently, Freddie didn't trust his own servants any more than she did. "I succeeded at my purpose for the evening."

She fought to keep her shoulders from sagging in relief. He hadn't seen her after all. *Thank God.* "And what purpose was that?"

He grinned stupidly, placed his hands flat on the desktop, and leaned toward her. "The turnpike trust!"

She froze, except for a cold dread that coiled its way up from the backs of her knees like a slithering snake. "We've discussed this before," she replied calmly, forcing herself to remain stoic. "I told you that I am not interested in allowing a turnpike to be built on my property."

His smile faded. "We don't have a choice this time." He reached for his drink. But his hand shook uncontrollably, forcing him to set down the glass before he spilled it. "I've gotten myself into a bit of a predicament."

"Oh?" She held her breath. He meant the blackmail.

Not looking at her, he began to pace behind the desk in short, jerking turns that reminded her of the caged animals at the Tower Menagerie. He scrubbed his hand over his face and gave a strangled laugh. "Seems there's someone who has a grudge against me."

That was an interesting definition of blackmail. But she knew not to interrupt. Let him divulge what he would, let him lay out just enough rope to hang himself...and then she would demand answers. And the truth.

"You know all those government positions that have been coming open lately? Well, the man's demanding that I use my influence to put the men he wants into them." He gestured wildly in the general direction of Westminster. "Of course, I had to agree or—or I would lose power in the House."

"Extortion?" she asked ingenuously, dangling the end of the rope...

He gave a quick, curt nod. "Yes, that's—"

"Or blackmail?"

He jerked up straight, halting in his steps. When his bloodshot eyes darted to hers, she *knew*—with that look, he'd formed the end of the rope into a noose himself.

Deflecting her concern, he gave a dismissive shrug. "Is there a difference?"

"Yes." A huge one. Extortion implied quid pro quo...yours for mine. A deal that could be broken if both parties were willing to live with the consequences. But blackmail was one-sided, happening after the fact, when crimes had already been committed... *Oh, God*, what had he done?

"All right, then I'm being blackmailed." He announced that by lifting his glass in a mocking toast. "Cheers!"

She grimaced. *None* of this was amusing. "Since when?" The

crumpled note clearly wasn't the first threat. No, it had been issued simply as a reminder to keep following orders.

"The start of the session."

Six months. Her stomach roiled at how long this had been hanging over their heads without her knowing. "Over what?"

Taking his time to swallow down a mouthful of brandy, he shook his head, then wiped the back of his free hand across his mouth. "So far I've done what he's asked," he explained, evading her question. "I've placed all the men just as he's wanted. I've managed to keep him happy enough not to enact his threats."

"Who?"

Another shrug. "The entire Tory party, half the men in the Whigs, anyone who wants my seat for himself… Your guess is as good as mine."

He was right. Too many men disliked him to narrow the choice down to just one who might hate him enough to do this. "What exactly has this man threatened?"

A guilty pause filled the silence. "To tell Sir Charles Varnham what I've done. He leads the Committee of Privileges and would love to make an example of someone like me." He muttered bitterly, once more lifting his glass, "The son of a factory owner, the upstart in their ranks…"

Her heart thumped painfully against her breastbone. "And what have you done, exactly?"

He scowled and jabbed the glass at her to make his point. "Nothing that the rest of Parliament hasn't, including Varnham. We *all* use our positions for our own gains."

She pressed quietly, "Illegal gains, Frederick?"

"Yes! Yes, I did illegal things, all right?" The angry snarl reminded her of a wild animal who had been cornered. "But nothing that others haven't, I promise you that." He set the glass onto the desk so hard that cognac splashed over the rim. "But it's enough, if the House rules of conduct are taken strictly—"

"And English law," she interjected beneath her breath.

He shot her a quelling look. "Nothing the others haven't done," he repeated forcefully. "But enough to remove me from the House." Then a long, ragged sigh tore from him, and he turned away from her to stare out the dark window. He said almost to himself, "And wouldn't some of those pompous old bastards just love to get their hands on my seat? Minehead's a jewel, the best of the pocket boroughs. Lots of men all over England are simply drooling to put their hands on it…"

His voice faded off. But the drawn and haggard expression marring his face showed exactly how serious his situation was, how much was at stake.

"There's no reason to think the blackmailer will expose you," she reminded, attempting to calm him, "since you've done everything he's asked."

"So far."

The two small words chilled her to her bones. "What do you mean?"

He faced her. "I mean that he's asking for three more appointments, but I've already used up every one at my disposal. The session's ending in a few days, and there aren't any other positions coming open that require Parliamentary approval." His obvious desperation took her breath away. "Except for a turnpike trust. There's still time to propose one and for Parliament to enact it."

"No," she whispered, finding the resolve to speak out over the dread seeping through her. She was grateful to Freddie for all he'd done for her, wanted to help him however she could, but… "Not that."

He slammed his palm onto the desk. She jumped with a small gasp, her hand going to her throat, her fingers grazing her locket.

"Damnation, Amelia! It's the only way out of this mess, don't you see that? To do what he's asking, one last time—to save everything—" As if realizing he was showing a lack of control, he cut himself off, inhaled deeply, and then blew out a hard, cognac-scented breath. "A trust of this size needs five trustees to oversee it. The most important landowners take two, with three slots left for any named trustees we want. Three slots for those last three men I have to place. If I find positions for them, then the black-mail stops."

"Turnpike trustees?" she repeated incredulously. He was beyond drunk and into lunacy. "You said you were being forced to find government appointments."

"I am finding them! That's what these are." He raked his shaking hand through his hair in frustration. "Don't you see? It's filling the *positions* that matters, not the position itself. A trust will do that, and we'll be free from this mess."

His mess. She ached for him, but the rest of her wanted to shake him hard for allowing this to happen.

And now he wanted to free himself by taking all that was left of her inheritance. That small piece of land was the only part of her fortune that Aaron hadn't absconded with the morning after their wedding. A turnpike would cut right through it, with the trust claiming the greater part of it under their rights of access. There would be no useful portion left for her to control.

"Parliament and Prinny want turnpikes and improved roads across England because they understand the importance of devel-opment," he explained, as if she were a child. But it was difficult to sound authoritative, she supposed, when slurring one's words. "And our property is right in the middle of a grand route between Birmingham and the Severn. Don't you see? Not only would the last men be placed and the threats against me stopped, but we'd also be set up financially. Turnpikes are gold mines! We'd be fools not to take advantage of that."

He'd be a fool, he meant. She doubted that he planned on shar-ing the profits, not that she wanted any. She'd much rather keep control of her land.

"Parliament's doubled the number of turnpike trusts just in this session alone," he told her. "They'll agree to mine."

"Trusts take control," she reminded him. They'd fought this battle before. "They take it away from the private owners and keep it for themselves."

"Trusts collect the tolls and maintain the roads. They do all the work but ensure all the profits for landowners who are smart enough to capitalize on improving their property." He snatched up the letters that Drummond had left on his desk on a silver salver, as if needing to keep his hands busy, and tossed an unwanted one away with a flick of his wrist. "But I don't expect you to understand the complexities of money, given how easily you lost yours."

Expecting that jab, she'd steeled herself so she wouldn't give him the satisfaction of showing any visible reaction. But that didn't stop the slice to her heart.

"So you plan to put a road across Bradenhill." She watched as he took another sip of brandy. Oh, what she wouldn't have given for a strong drink herself right then! "And build posting inns, taverns, warehouses…" *Brothels, gin palaces, gambling hells…*

Another flick of his wrist, another unwanted letter sent flying. "And so much more." He smiled triumphantly. "It will be a fresh start."

No, a fresh hell. "Unfortunately, there seems to be a problem with your plans. Bradenhill belongs to me," she said quietly, playing her trump card. The one that had always stopped him in the past from going beyond merely contemplating the idea. He couldn't put through a turnpike without her permission.

"But your charity doesn't."

Her gaze flew up to his. She understood his words exactly as he meant them—a threat.

"You only have that shop in the first place because of me, remember."

Panic gripped her until she couldn't breathe. "The Bouquet Boutique supports itself. It pays its bills and—"

"Only because I took out the lease for you, because I agreed to sign onto your bank accounts—accounts that I control, that *I* can close down."

Her blood turned cold. *Because I am a woman…*and banks wouldn't let unmarried women open their own accounts or sign leases. They had to have the cosignature of a man. She'd had no choice three years ago but to ask for Frederick's help to start the shop. She'd always believed he'd done it because he knew how important it was to her and how much she needed the purpose it gave her. At the very least, how much it kept her busy and out of his way.

But he'd never before held it over her head like this.

She whispered, unable to prevent the fear from creeping into her bones, "You wouldn't dare."

"To save us? In an instant." He slapped the letters down, his hands flat on the desk, and leaned toward her. "If I don't put these last three men into some kind of appointments—*any* kind of appointments—my career is over. I'll be publicly exposed, most likely arrested—I'll be thrown into prison. Is that what you want?"

"No! Of course I—"

"If that happens, then your charity shop *will* close, and you'll find yourself out on the street with all those war widows who work there." His eyes flared as brightly as the coals in the fireplace behind him, reminding her of the devil himself. "So you need to make a choice, Amelia." A devil who was attempting to take her soul. "Either support me in this trust, or lose everything, including your charity." His red eyes fixed on hers, and what she glimpsed in their dark depths frightened her. "Which will it be?"

Damn him for putting his mess upon her shoulders! Afraid her voice would break beneath the churning fear and anger inside her, she said quietly, "Forcing me to place Bradenhill into the trust won't do you any good. You know that." She folded her hands behind her so he wouldn't see them shaking. And so she wouldn't be tempted to scratch his eyes out. "You might have both our properties then, but that small stretch won't make for a turnpike."

"That's where you're wrong." He straightened to his full height. "Joining your share of Father's property to both mine and to the property abutting it puts us over halfway across the county. Parliament will see the wisdom of constructing a turnpike across the rest and gladly enact a trust." He smiled and clawed at his cravat to pull loose the knot at his throat. "And tonight, I spoke to the neighboring landowner. He's willing to listen to my plans. Seemed very interested, in fact."

She tensed with dread. *That* was why Freddie had been at the masquerade. Not because of the blackmail. Not because he'd caught wind of her plans to speak to Varnham.

"You knew him once." He sank into the chair behind his desk, most likely too far into his cups to remain on his feet. "A man I think you should get to know again, and well enough to convince him that a trust is a brilliant idea."

Her heart slammed violently against her ribs. Because she knew, even before he spoke the name—

"Brandon Pearce." He leaned back in the chair and closed his eyes. "Your old friend."

No. If Pearce agreed to the trust, then he was her new enemy.

Four

PEARCE SLAMMED THE METAL DOOR CLOSED BEHIND HIM WITH a teeth-jarring clatter.

The Armory needed a better—and quieter—way inside, but Marcus Braddock, former general with the Coldstream Guards and now Duke of Hampton, insisted that the two sets of metal doors remain in place. Because he wanted to pay homage to the building's previous life as a true armory. Because the doors rattled loudly enough to wake the dead in St. Paul's crypt, notifying everyone within that someone was entering.

"Because he wants to drive me into Bedlam," Pearce muttered and winced as the inner door clanged shut.

He passed beneath the archway and the shield bearing the Armory's motto... *Ubi malum timet calcare.* Where evil fears to tread. A reminder to all who entered this place of the purpose for which it existed and the new life's purpose it gave to its men.

But tonight, Pearce came here seeking solace of another kind.

He rubbed at his nape. Amelia Howard. After all these years.

He could hardly believe it. But the woman in red was her. He'd have bet his life on it. Those green eyes, that golden hair... He remembered her smile, too, even though a sadness lingered behind it that hadn't been there before. Now he knew why she'd seemed so familiar, why the locket had jarred a memory. Because he'd given it to her. For God's sake, she'd even kept the blue ribbon he'd used to tie up the box.

But what the hell was she doing at one of Torrington's masquerades? And why on earth would she need to speak to Sir Charles Varnham from behind a mask?

None of it made sense. Including why she'd fled.

True, they hadn't exactly parted as friends. Gordon Howard had nearly killed him after finding him in his daughter's bedroom and on the verge of compromising her. Pearce had been unable to fight back—oh, he could have dropped the old man with a single punch; God knew he'd won enough fights back then to pulp him with barely any effort. But that would have destroyed Amelia, and Pearce couldn't have lived with himself if he'd brought her any kind of pain. Which was why he hadn't attempted to contact her after he'd been tossed from the house, for fear that her bastard of a father would make good on his promises and force her into marriage with a man she didn't love. Worse—a man who might treat her with the same contempt as her father.

But the past was long dead, and they were no longer the children they'd once been. Certainly not Amelia. Not with the way she'd looked in that dress. *Sweet Lucifer.*

Shoving down a fresh ache, he strode into the main room of the Amory to the sound of clashing sabers.

Clayton Elliott and Merritt Rivers slashed in fierce strokes as they chased each other through the octagonal central room. Their blades flashed beneath the blazing light of the gas chandelier that hung from the medieval-looking tower overhead, and each strike of metal upon metal echoed against the stone and walnut-paneled walls. The fencing match must have started in the adjoining training room, then run amok to encompass the rest of the old building that had been turned into a gentlemen's club of sorts by Marcus Braddock.

Pearce ignored them and strode straight through the room toward the sideboard and its dozens of liquor bottles. The two men fought around him, with Merritt using him as a shield at one point to change his feint into an attack that had Clayton retreating over the brocade sofa.

Pearce shrugged out of his greatcoat and tossed it aside with his hat and gloves onto one of the leather chairs, just missing the end of Merritt's blade.

"His shoulder drops before he lunges," he called out as he snatched up a crystal tumbler from the silver tray on the sideboard.

"Thanks," Merritt answered as he blocked a thrust.

Pearce opened the cabinet doors and pulled out a bottle of cognac. "I wasn't talking to you."

Clayton laughed and attacked by leaping over the tea table.

Ignoring the fighting behind him, Pearce pulled out the stopper and splashed the caramel-colored liquid into the glass—

Rattling metal against stone jarred up his spine. His hand jerked, and brandy spilled onto the table.

Biting back a curse, he glanced over his shoulder to see Clayton's saber on the floor at his feet, with the tip of Merritt's blade pointed at his throat.

"Apologies," Clayton called out to Pearce, breathless from exertion. He put up his hands and stepped back in a gesture of surrender, and Merritt lowered his saber with a grin. The two men shook hands and slapped each other on the back, already critiquing the match.

Pearce scowled into his brandy as he took a long, welcome swallow and dropped into one of the leather chairs in front of the massive fireplace where a warm fire blazed against the unseasonably cold and damp night. He gestured at the footprint one of the pair had left in the middle of the sofa. "The general will have your hides if he finds out that you've been fighting in this room."

Marcus Braddock had spent a considerable portion of his personal fortune renovating and redecorating the old building. The general had turned it into a property that could rival any gentlemen's club in London, but also into a training facility that bested Gentleman Jackson's salon, filling the adjoining room with all kinds of equipment and weapons which the men of the Armory could use to maintain their fighting edge. And more importantly, into a sanctuary. Here, men who had witnessed the horrors of war could gather to take comfort in knowing that they understood one another and what they had been through. Here, there was no judgment. Only acceptance, honor, and a new way to serve England.

But the general had also been absent a great deal of late, spending time with his family and new wife. Pearce couldn't fault him for that, even if he were damnably jealous.

"We had to do something to kill time while we waited for you," Merritt commented, carrying the two sabers back into the training room.

"But you're back early." Clayton slumped into the chair across from him and kicked his boots onto the low table between them. "You must have learned something tonight."

Yes. That twelve years could disappear in the blink of an eye.

But Clayton meant Scepter.

"The exact opposite." Pearce swirled his brandy. "I discovered nothing new. So I came here to report it."

He also came here because he couldn't yet bring himself to go home. That was the sad truth. The encounter with Amelia had rattled him to his bones, and he needed the sanctuary of the Armory and the company of his friends to put him at ease.

All kinds of ghosts haunted him tonight. Not only Amelia and the terrible way they'd parted all those years ago, but others as well. He could feel one creeping up inside him again right now, that old restlessness that had shadowed him since he was a boy. Lately, it had followed him everywhere, making him feel antsy and unsettled, but he'd managed to keep it contained. Until tonight.

Seeing Amelia again had yanked the cork right out of the bottle.

He tossed back a large swallow. "I made it clear to anyone who listened that I was interested in pursuing ventures of all kinds, including unscrupulous ones," he muttered. "If Scepter was interested in bringing more peers into its fold, they would have jumped at the chance to have me join them. But they didn't."

"No bites at all?" Merritt asked as he strode back into the room and snatched up the decanter of cognac as he passed the side table.

"Only one." He blew out a breath and tugged at his cravat. The damnable thing was choking him. "But I'm certain it had nothing to do with Scepter." He grimaced as Merritt refilled his glass before topping off his own. "Frederick Howard." A bitter taste covered his tongue at the thought of Amelia's family. Oh, he definitely recognized the man now, but wished he didn't. "He wanted to discuss developing a property I own near Birmingham."

Merritt froze in midpour, his gaze darting to Clayton. The two men exchanged a solemn glance.

Suspicion gnawed at Pearce's belly. "What's wrong?"

"The reason I stopped by tonight wasn't to let Merritt skewer me with a saber." Clayton leaned forward, elbows on knees. He reached beneath his waistcoat to pull out a piece of paper, then handed it to Pearce. "A list of gentlemen recently given Parliament-approved appointments."

Pearce scanned the list of names, only recognizing about half of them. The half he knew had replaced the men who had been murdered. He handed it back to Clayton. "These names don't mean anything by themselves."

"Then it's a good thing that they're not by themselves," Merritt interjected as he stepped up to the fireplace. "Because they all have one thing in common."

"Yes. Their predecessors were murdered by Specter."

"No." Merritt met Pearce's gaze. "The Honorable Frederick Howard, Member of Parliament for Minehead."

That bit of information shocked through him like a jolt of electricity, yet he somehow kept his face inscrutable. "Explain."

"Howard bought his way into a pocket borough a few years ago, and since then, he's formed political allies among both Whigs and Tories, putting himself into a position of increasing political power." Clayton tucked the paper back into his waistcoat. "Each man on this list received his appointment due to Howard exerting his influence."

He scoffed. "Influence peddling? Every MP does that." Pearce desperately wanted that to be true. For Amelia's sake, he prayed that her brother was nothing more than a typical Westminster politician. "That doesn't mean he has connections to Scepter or the murders."

"No. But he did have close associations with the Earl of Hartsham, whom we know without doubt was involved with Scepter. I'm not willing to take a chance that influence peddling is all he's been doing."

Merritt interjected, "And he wants you to consider a business arrangement with him?"

"Nothing that involves murder, that's for sure." He tossed back the last of his cognac and frowned at the bottom of the glass. "He wants to build a turnpike across our adjoining properties."

The two men exchanged another look. But this time, Merritt grinned.

"What is it now?" Pearce half growled. He was a step behind. But then, subtle strategy had never been his specialty. His expertise had lain in blasting the hell out of the enemy once plans had been made. Even now, the old restlessness that gnawed at him demanded action.

"It takes an act of Parliament to create a turnpike," Merritt explained. "A bill to empower a trust has to be passed to allow for the confiscation of land and to oversee the road's creation, the collection and disbursement of tolls, and ongoing maintenance."

"I know," Pearce grumbled. He was part of the Lords now, whether he liked it or not. "I've voted on over two dozen of the things since May."

"Then you also know that all trustees have to be approved by Parliament. Which technically makes them government appointees."

"Technically," he repeated for emphasis, not yet wanting to admit to himself that Amelia's brother was involved with Scepter.

"But there's a grand difference between turnpike trustees and the types of government positions that Scepter's willing to murder for." But saying that didn't alleviate his growing unease. "This doesn't mean Howard's involved with Scepter. Just opportunistic."

"We can't be certain of that," Clayton reminded him.

For Amelia's sake, Pearce prayed they could be.

He shoved himself out of the chair and crossed the room to the side table, ignoring the bottle that Merritt held only a few feet from his chair. He needed to move. Pouring himself a whiskey was simply an excuse to do so. "Howard's involvement aside, we're dancing around the most important question. Why should Scepter care about government appointments in the first place, and enough to kill for them?"

"To put their men into positions of power," Clayton answered.

"*Turnpike* trustees?" Incredulity colored his voice. "No one in the history of England has ever associated turnpike trustees with positions of power."

"Never in the history of England has there been an organization like Scepter," Merritt echoed quietly.

That was the God's truth. If what Clayton and Merritt were saying was true, then Amelia's brother had been swept up into a hornet's nest. "But a *trust*? Scepter murdered at least half a dozen men to free up those positions on your list." He gestured at Clayton with his empty glass. "Maybe more. If they're willing to do something like that, why on earth would they settle for trustees, men who don't even earn a sinecure for serving?" He yanked the stopper out of the decanter and refilled his drink. "If Scepter's intention is to put men into positions of power, they've gotten this one all wrong."

"Maybe not," Clayton considered. "The Home Office and Bow Street have been investigating the deaths as murders. If Scepter has an informant inside the Home Office—and we have to assume they do—then they wouldn't want to draw any more attention to themselves and what they've been doing. They'd find other ways to create openings. Perhaps even settling for something as innocuous as turnpike trustees."

"And now we're back to my original question." The stopper clinked softly as he returned it to the crystal decanter. "What does Scepter want with these positions, especially if they're willing to accept such low ones?"

Merritt grinned. "That's why we have you. To find out exactly that."

Christ. Pearce tossed back nearly half the whiskey, but it did nothing to wash the acid from his tongue.

Clayton asked, "Howard made you a formal offer?"

"He suggested that we meet to discuss the possibility."

"Then I think you should, to see what you can discover."

Scepter and turnpikes? Pearce bit back a laugh. They were chasing down the wrong path.

Instead of returning to his chair, he began to pace. His agitation didn't bloom because this would prove to be a grand waste of time, just as all the other leads on Scepter had during the past few months. No, it was because of the Howards themselves. No matter that the old man was dead now, or that Amelia had clearly claimed the life in society she'd been destined for. The thought of becoming close with them again rattled him to his core, especially if Amelia planned to be involved with the trust.

Was that why she was at the masquerade tonight, to assist her brother in working to convince him to partner with them? Did Howard also want to make Varnham a trustee?

No. He'd seen the way she'd reacted when her brother approached him. She'd been startled, enough to flee into the path of that phaeton.

So why the devil *had* she been there?

"What do you have to lose?" Merritt collapsed into Pearce's vacated chair. "If Howard's working for Scepter, then we'll use him to gain more information on the organization's leaders. If he's just an MP peddling his influence, then you'll be the proud father of a new stretch of turnpike and all the benefits it brings."

"Wonderful," Pearce drawled sardonically. "Just the heir I need."

Clayton shot him a hard look, one that had made subordinate officers and infantrymen quake in their boots during the wars. The same look that now brought quickly into line the men who worked beneath him at the Home Office. "Howard's the link we've been hunting for," he said with absolute certainty. "He might not have had a direct hand in the murders, but I'd bet a box of the finest American cigars that Fribourg & Treyer sells that he's working for Scepter."

Dread seeped through Pearce. He didn't give a damn about turnpikes and land development. But if Howard was involved with Scepter, then Amelia was in danger, and he would still do anything he could to protect her.

He drawled out his agreement. "It seems I'll be calling on Howard in the morning, then."

And on his sister.

He set down his glass, picked up his coat, and left.

For once, nighttime London was quiet as he made his way from Mayfair to Wapping in the hackney he'd hired, having sent his own town coach home. How he preferred to spend restless nights like this wasn't the business of his coachman, and his own personal safety wasn't a concern. After all, God help the footpad who attempted to rob him when he was in a mood like this.

Sweet Jesus...Amelia Howard. Apparently a lot more had transpired in the past twelve years than he'd been aware of to bring a sweet girl like her to an event like Torrington's.

But then, hadn't everything changed for him as well?

That night of her sixteenth birthday had broken his heart. He'd loved her, it had been that simple. She was kind, brilliant, and lovely, inside and out. His best friend. How could he deny himself the chance to finally be that close to her? But they were discovered, and all hell had broken loose.

As he'd left her father's house, bloodied and bruised after their private *conversation* in the man's study, Peace hadn't even been able to take a last look over his shoulder at all he was about to lose. Because she would have been there, he knew, standing at her upstairs window, watching him go.

Yet leaving had been for the best—for both of them. He'd hated the reason, but because of that night, he'd been given an officer's commission in the army and a new life that allowed him to put his energy and restlessness to purpose and gave him the chance to prove his worth.

He'd always known that Amelia belonged with someone else. Someone better. An aristocrat who could give her the life of status and luxury that she deserved. The one she would never have had with him. It had always been only a matter of time anyway until he left Birmingham for a better job and she found her way into society and marriage. Attempting to have any other future but the one fate had thrust onto them would have been pointless.

He just hadn't expected that leaving her would be so damned painful.

When the hackney reached the main street in Wapping that ran between the Thames and the row of warehouses that fronted it, he pounded his fist against the carriage roof. "Here!"

The hackney stopped. Pearce bounded to the ground, tossing a coin up to the jarvey.

The driver glanced around at the damp and deserted street that was rapidly filling with fog. "You sure this is where you want me t' drop you?"

"I'll be fine." Pearce slapped his hand against the side of the rig to send it away and strode quickly down the street toward one of the old abandoned warehouses. *More than fine.*

Tonight, he needed to come here the way other men needed air to breathe. He needed to push Amelia from his mind and punish his body until he turned numb, just as he'd done all those years ago when he'd taken up his commission with the 1st Battalion of the Coldstream Guards. Fear and physical pain had done a damnably fine job of it then, too. He'd been able to focus on his command to the exclusion of all else, and as a result, he'd proven himself on the battlefield, saving as many men as possible and earning promotion after promotion. By Waterloo, he was a brigadier. The army had become his life, and he'd been more than happy with it.

Then, while the Coldstream Guards were still in Paris, no longer fighting the war but keeping the peace, everything changed. The Earl of Sandhurst had died without warning and without a close heir. The House of Lords's Committee for Privileges had to search all the way down the family tree to its roots to discover that the next viable heir was Pearce. He could only imagine the shock that must have rung through both Wythburn Manor and his uncle's inn in Birmingham when that news arrived on their doorsteps. It was the same shock, certainly, that had slammed into him.

Good Lord. A more screwed-up system of awarding fortune and privilege he couldn't imagine. But here he was. Earl of Sandhurst. Now saddled with estates, houses, a fortune to manage, and an officer's rank that had become obsolete with the peace.

Twelve years after leaving Birmingham, he was starting over again, but this time, there was no clear path. All he knew was that he wanted his life to mean something, and being a peer wasn't enough. The need for purpose lived inside him as a physical yearning, one that burned in his muscles and left him restless, sleepless, on edge. Always had. Like a tightened coil ready to spring. Being in the wars had helped to mitigate the tension, but now that he'd returned to England, it had crept back.

And he had no idea how to end it.

He ducked into an abandoned warehouse. Inside, the building

was alive. Lamps blazed throughout the large ground floor, which was crowded with working-class men and women who had gathered illegally for tonight's boxing match. All kinds of bets were being placed, prostitutes bargained for, gin guzzled from tin mugs and other alcohol from flasks.

In the center of the old warehouse, an eight-by-eight-foot square had been roped off, where one man who stood bare from the waist up and bruised from previous rounds waited for the next challenger. His bottle man and knee man waited nearby while the referee shouted into the noisy crowd, antagonizing them to produce a challenger so the matches and gambling could continue.

There were no takers tonight. Their champion was too big, too muscular for the usual fighters among the sailors and porters who worked the docks.

But he was perfect for Pearce.

He stepped up to the rope and began to strip off his clothes, to bare himself down to his breeches. "Me," he called out, tossing a coin to the referee to secure his own bet on the match and slipping inside the square. "I'm next."

The brute charged toward him with a ferocious growl. Pearce dropped his shoulder and swung.

Five

"Such a beautiful dress. One of my favorites." Madame Noir held up the red gown in the late morning sunlight that fell through the diaphanous curtains of her boudoir. She slid Amelia a conspiratorial glance over her shoulder. "Did you look absolutely *wicked* in it?"

"Well, I—" The way Pearce had stared at her… Heat began to simmer low in Amelia's belly, and she fought down a thrilled smile as she answered secretively, "I believe so."

Madame laughed and tossed the dress over the back of a chair.

She glided across the room to the tea table and the tray that she'd requested for them. Amelia had only wanted to drop off the dress and leave, afraid that Varnham or one of the other MPs might see her here. Or worse—Frederick. But Madame had insisted that she come up for refreshments, and Amelia knew from all the hard work she'd done to establish her shop that she couldn't afford to offend anyone. A person never knew when an acquaintance might prove helpful. Even a brothel owner.

Madame Noir picked up a saucer and teacup. "I will admit I was rather surprised when you told me that you wanted to borrow a dress, and that one in particular." She carefully poured the tea. Amelia was coming to realize that Madame did everything exactly like that. *Carefully.* Every move she made was measured and exact. "You. The sister of an MP."

"Which is why I came to you." Amelia accepted the tea, then waved away offers for sugar and milk. "Discretion is what keeps you in business."

"Yes, but *you* are not in the business of discretion."

Amelia boldly met the woman's gaze. "There are times when we all must do things we don't want to simply in order to survive."

Madame smiled as if the two women understood each other perfectly and poured a cup for herself. Instead of joining Amelia where she sat on the settee, she remained standing. Also a calculated posture of imperialness and power, although Amelia wasn't certain the woman was conscious that she was doing it. Running the King Street brothel named Le Château Noir—which had earned her the nickname Le Chat Noir, the Black Cat—had taken a spine and skill that most women didn't possess.

But then, Madame wasn't an ordinary woman.

Her chosen profession aside, an uncompromising air lingered about her, even dressed casually as she was in an emerald-green silk dressing gown with her black hair piled loosely upon her head. In the diffused light filtering through the gauzy curtains, the fine lines around her mouth and eyes showed her age. Yet her figure still possessed youthful curves, and her complexion remained fair, belying the hard life she'd undoubtedly led. Her presence fit perfectly into this room, the boudoir decorated as exotically as the woman herself...purple silk draping the walls, gold brocade settee and chairs dominating the space, mahogany mirrored dressing table, Chippendale writing desk.

Around them, the brothel was quiet, as if pausing to catch its breath between visits by the men who left at dawn but would descend upon the place again at nightfall. Like locusts.

Madame took a soft sip of tea, eyeing Amelia curiously. "So you run a charity."

She stilled. Had the woman been asking around about her? "A shop, actually. It's called the Bouquet Boutique, and we sell all kinds of luxury goods—hand-painted fabrics, linens, porcelains, baubles... anything with a garden theme." She smiled. "Our specialty is roses."

"But it's more than just a shop," Madame murmured from behind her cup. "Isn't it?"

Amelia stiffened. She meant the war widows who worked there. So she *had* been asking around. In detail.

"Yes." She returned her cup to her saucer. "I found women who'd lost their only means of support when their husbands were killed in the wars and invited them to work for me, both learning to work the shop floor and to create some of the goods we sell—the fabrics, the jewelry, the lace. Whatever skills they might have are put to use, and in return, they're paid a fair wage and given room and board. They're also taught how to manage their money properly." So no one could steal it from them, the way Aaron had so easily stolen hers. "When they're ready, they find better employment elsewhere and move on, giving their space to another." She shrugged. "So both a shop and a charity."

"You've no need to be modest with me, Miss Howard. It's far more than that." The woman's green eyes gleamed like the cat she was named for. "It's survival."

Amelia swelled with pride that someone recognized that, even if that someone was a brothel owner. "Yes. I suppose it is." How had Madame noticed what Frederick had always failed to understand? Surprise sparked inside her at finding the most unlikely of confidantes, and she admitted, "I teach them how to be independent so that they never have to rely upon a man again." Then, feeling the old chagrin at her own foolishness, she added quietly, "So they never have to be at a man's mercy."

"The way you feel at your brother's." Not a question. Thankfully, before Amelia could pale at that, Madame continued, "I wonder if you might have room at your shop for two more women. Not war widows, but then, now that the wars are over, there will be fewer of those, will there not?"

"I hope so." *If God listens to my prayers.*

"There are two ladies in my employ who are finding life here at Le Château…difficult." With a frown, she traced her fingertip around the rim of her teacup. "They've been in my employ for several years, so I want to help them find a new path for themselves."

In other words, they had grown old, and gentlemen no longer

wanted to seek pleasure in them. Or they had the pox, and their symptoms had become too visible to hide beneath powders and perfumes.

Amelia's heart wept for them. Only by fortune of birth had she been the daughter of an industrialist, with all the luxuries and privileges of life handed to her, when others had landed in the filth and poverty of the streets through no fault of their own. But the government—and those with means—did little except to complain that the poor were simply lazy and turned a blind eye to the fact that there was no way out of poverty for most of them, having neither the skills nor education to advance beyond hard-to-find jobs that paid pennies in return for hours of work.

"Yes," she answered, despite the emotion that tightened her throat. "I have positions for them." *Somewhere.* She had no idea where, but she would find them. "Please tell them to come to the Bouquet Boutique and ask for me."

"Thank you." Madame set down her tea and moved to the little writing desk in front of the window, where she unlocked the middle drawer and withdrew a stack of banknotes. "I find your charity quite admirable, Miss Howard, and would like to make a donation."

A sizable one, Amelia observed as Madame counted out the notes. More than enough to cover the living expenses of the two women until they were able to find their feet and move into good positions. Or to pay for kind nurses to help them into heaven.

"An anonymous donation." Madame held out the banknotes. "Discretion, you understand."

"Of course." Amelia placed them into her reticule.

Madame crossed to the dressing table with its large and ornately carved gilded mirror and sat on the velvet stool. She assessed her reflection, turning her head from side to side, then reached for a little enameled jar of rouge.

As Amelia watched her ready herself for the afternoon, a

thought struck her. A wild and utterly desperate idea. One that would test all the discretion and newfound trust oddly springing up between the two women.

"You must know a lot of society gentlemen," she commented casually, despite the spiking of her pulse at what she planned to ask.

"I do." Madame tapped the red color faintly onto her cheeks.

"Is there anything you can tell me about one who might—"

Madame's gaze darted to Amelia's in the mirror, silencing her in midsentence with a look so imposing it could have cut glass.

Amelia caught her breath.

Madame turned her attention back to her reflection and the color on her cheeks, then sighed out her capitulation. "It would depend, I suppose, on who you have in mind." She set down the rouge pot. "And why."

"An acquaintance of my brother." Amelia sat forward on the edge of the settee to seize this unexpected chance to gather information about the man who held the power to bring down her world. And the only lead she had to find her brother's blackmailer. "Sir Charles Varnham."

"Hmm." Madame applied the powder puff to her nose, then leaned toward the mirror to examine her work. "Arrogant, paunchy, judgmental, entitled...like any other English lord, I suppose."

Amelia's hopes plummeted. "Nothing out of the ordinary about him?" She set her teacup on the table before her trembling hands could spill it on the Turkish rug beneath her feet. "Nothing at all?"

"Not that I know of. But then, what were you hoping to hear— that he's a wolf in Bond Street clothing? A devil in disguise?"

Exactly that, actually. Because it meant the man might have a connection to the blackmailer. Or be the one doing the blackmailing himself.

"I'm afraid I can't be much help to you. Sir Charles has never visited Le Château." She carefully applied charcoal to her eyelids, giving them a smoky effect that made her look even more cat-like.

"His younger brother, Arthur, however," she mumbled, sitting back, "does business here several times a week. He's easy to satisfy, from what I've been told. Prefers curvaceous blonds. And whips."

Amelia blinked. *That* wasn't at all the kind of information she was hoping for!

As if reading her mind, Madame smeared a bit of the red rouge across her bottom lip with her pinkie. "Tell me…why do you want to know about Sir Charles?"

"I think it's important to know about the men Frederick works with."

If Madame read that for the lie it was, she graciously said nothing. Instead, she rolled her lips together to spread the color and began to take down her hair.

"Don't you have a ladies' maid for that?" Amelia asked, glancing at the suite door that remained shut, expecting one to come scurrying in at any moment.

"I do. I run a fully staffed town house, just like any other in St James's." Madame smiled a bit patronizingly. "But I also have an appointment with my solicitor in an hour and so need to dress while we talk, and I'd rather keep our conversation private. Wouldn't you?"

Absolutely. "Then at least let me help you."

Amelia rose to her feet and came forward.

Surprise shot across Madame's face, the first uncontrolled emotion Amelia had seen from the woman. But her shoulders eased down in acquiescence as Amelia approached from behind, took the pins from her hands, and unwound her hair.

As she picked up the brush and began to smooth out the woman's locks, this new intimacy of helping with her hair sparked a boldness that made it seem perfectly fine to ask, "What do you know about blackmail?"

"Quite a bit, actually." Madame didn't even blink at that unexpected question. "You'll need to be more specific."

Amelia bit her bottom lip. "How does one make it work?"

Madame laughed, a throaty and amused sound. "You'll never be able to blackmail anyone, Miss Howard." She glanced at their reflection in the mirror as Amelia finished brushing her hair and set the tortoiseshell brush down on the dressing table to reach for a set of silver pins. "You have too much kindness in you, too much sympathy."

Amelia grimaced, certain she'd never received such a complimenting insult before. "I didn't mean—" Good Lord! She'd never have the courage to do something like that! "Not me, of course."

"Of course not." Disbelief colored Madame's smile. "Which is good. Because in order to be successful at blackmail, you have to care not at all about the people involved. You have to be willing to hurt them. And severely. That's the secret to it, you know. The trick that makes it work. The person you want to control must believe that you'll do exactly as you threaten. If they suspect for one moment that you won't carry through, you've lost."

Which was why she and Frederick were at the blackmailer's mercy. The man would do exactly as he'd threatened. They both knew it.

"Best to leave blackmail to the professionals," Madame murmured, watching in the mirror as Amelia began to twist her long hair into a simple chignon.

"Becoming involved with it was never my intention," she muttered on an earnest breath.

Without moving her head, Madame knowingly arched a brow. "Gotten yourself into a sticky spot, then, have you?"

"I haven't gotten myself into anything." Freddie had. This was all his mess, but one that she'd been forced to clean up. Yet the way out—

Her stomach sickened, knowing she was trapped. Surrender Bradenhill to the trust and save Freddie from blackmail, thus also saving herself and her shop, or save her land by stopping the trust and risk that all Freddie had done would be revealed, destroying both of their lives and the war widows who depended upon her right along with them… *Dear Lord, is there any way out of this?*

Freddie thought so, with Pearce as his preferred solution. But she hadn't seen him in twelve years, didn't know if the man he'd become could be trusted… In his desperation to find a savior, had Freddie tossed their lot in with the devil?

"And the Earl of Sandhurst?" Amelia asked as nonchalantly as possible. "Do you know anything about him?"

"Ah, Brandon," Madame purred, as if privately delighted that Amelia had mentioned him. "I do know him. Quite well."

Brandon… Madame's use of his given name implied intimacy. The unexpectedness of that nearly took Amelia's breath away. She mumbled, "Do you?"

"He's a war hero, you know. Wellington would have lost Waterloo if not for Brandon and his men."

Amelia's throat tightened. "No, I didn't know that."

When he hadn't answered her letters, she'd stopped reading about him in the papers, stopped asking about him with old acquaintances in Birmingham…just *stopped* everything to do with him. She'd set her sights on completely forgetting about him, even if her nightly dreams hadn't cooperated.

But she wasn't surprised to hear that about him. He'd always been courageous, even in his youth when he'd so rashly thrown himself into fights, seemingly at every chance he had. Constantly, his face had carried bruises and cuts in all stages of healing, which had somehow only made him more dashing. Even then he'd been a natural-born fighter.

"He's a good man. A *very* good man." Madame smiled knowingly as Amelia began to secure the pins and fought an immature urge to yank the woman's hair out. "One with secrets." Her gaze darted to Amelia's in the mirror. "But I'm not certain they're worthy of extortion."

Her cheeks flushed. "No! I didn't mean Pearce when I—"

"If you see him, tell him that I miss him." She took the last pin from Amelia's startled hand as it froze in midair and slipped it into place. "He hasn't been by to see me in far too long."

Gracefully, Madame stood with a swoosh of her green silk dressing gown and crossed the room to a small jewelry box on her dresser. She opened one of the tiny drawers and withdrew a bauble—an emerald and gold bracelet that dazzled in the sunlight.

"I have this because of Brandon. I acquired it the last time I saw him." She held it out to Amelia to fasten around her wrist for her. "A beautiful little prize, don't you think?"

With a tight smile, Amelia forced out, "Yes." Whom Pearce chose to spend time with was none of her business, even a woman like Madame Noir. So drat it, why did the backs of her eyes begin to sting? Had he changed that much in manhood that he'd seek pleasure at a place like this? "Quite beautiful."

Steeling herself, she fastened the bracelet in place and forced down by sheer will the unbidden jealousy now pulsing through her in waves.

Madame reached for a day dress tossed over a nearby chair. "If you'll excuse me, I have to dress now." She pulled free the tie on her dressing gown, then stopped. "I'd let you stay and watch, but I charge for such pleasures." Her lips curled in amusement. "Business, you understand."

"Perfectly." Accepting that unusual request to end their tea, Amelia collected her shawl and reticule and moved toward the door. Despite the jealousy and resentment roiling in her belly, she knew she couldn't afford to offend Madame and said, "Please visit the Bouquet Boutique whenever you'd like."

Then she remembered who this woman was and the hard life she'd undoubtedly led, remembered why men sought her out—

If Pearce *had* come to her, it had surely been nothing more than a physical encounter. But he'd once wanted intimacies with

Amelia because he'd loved her. That much, at least, she'd never doubted.

Her jealousy dissolved into pity, and she added sincerely, "I'd be happy to show the shop to you."

Madame's expression changed into one of gratitude and womanly connection. A look that left Amelia wondering as she slipped out the door if Madame had any friends who didn't work for her at Le Château Noir. Or any true friends at all.

She made her way downstairs and out the rear kitchen door, safely out of sight from King Street. She couldn't risk being seen leaving a brothel, even in broad daylight.

The hackney waited at the end of the alley where she'd left it, having dearly paid the jarvey to wait for her. When she approached, he stirred and tugged at the brim of his hat.

"Marylebone," she called out as she stepped into the compartment. She needed to go to her shop to find space and time to catch her breath, calm her nerves, and plan out what to do next. "Montagu Square."

She leaned back against the seat and closed her eyes. Her fist pressed against her chest in a futile attempt to slow the frantic pounding of her heart and the pain that had lodged itself there. The thought of Pearce with someone like Madame Noir seared her insides.

She groaned softly in disgust at herself. What a goose she was! To care anything about whomever Pearce had given his body to, or gifted expensive jewelry, or granted his affections—He was a grown man, for heaven's sake! An army officer and a peer. A war hero. Women would be no novelty to a man like him, including courtesans.

But blast it, she *did* care. Because in a secret part of her heart, he still belonged to her. And always would.

Yet her conversation with Madame Noir proved that she needed to find a way to purge him from her thoughts. And completely from her life, because she couldn't risk that he might agree with Frederick to petition for the trust. After all, what aristocrat would decline the opportunity to increase his wealth and influence?

Pearce had said that she could trust him, that he wanted to help her and keep her safe. But Aaron had said the same thing, even pledged so in front of a priest, only to take her money and abandon her. How could she be certain that Pearce wouldn't also betray her? After all, she'd thought she'd known Aaron, thought he'd loved her, too, the way Pearce had…

A soft sob tore from her throat. She'd already lost so much to men who had claimed to love and protect her. She couldn't bear to lose what little she had left.

And Pearce could never, *ever* find out about Aaron. The humiliation would simply end her.

Damnable heart! The mess her life had become was all its fault. Because it had made her want to be loved—

The door jerked open wide.

With a leap, Pearce swung into the compartment and landed on the bench across from her with a simple "Hello, Amelia." He settled casually back against the squabs. His eyes glinted as they swept over her. "Or should I say…Lady Scarlet?"

Then he banged a fist against the side wall, and the carriage started forward.

Six

HER EYES WIDENED, AND FOR ONE FLEETING MOMENT, PEARCE would have sworn he saw her old affection for him in their green depths. But then they narrowed in anger…and with something else he couldn't quite identify.

"Stop this carriage." Beneath her icy request, the temperature inside the compartment surely dropped twenty degrees. "Please be a gentleman and go away."

"I can't do that, Amelia."

"Then *I'll* leave." She pounded her tiny fist against the side of the carriage to signal to the driver to stop, her gaze never leaving his. As if she didn't trust him not to vanish into thin air. Or pounce. From the mix of emotions swirling across her face, he couldn't have said which.

Damnation. He'd known from the way she'd fled last night that she wouldn't be happy to see him today. What had happened on her sixteenth birthday had certainly humiliated her, and she'd probably blamed him for it ever since. She wouldn't be wrong. After all, he'd certainly blamed himself for being so careless that her father caught them together, for not having the control to keep himself away from her.

But her anger bothered him. More than he wanted to admit. A part of him had stupidly hoped that she'd be happy to see him again. God knew he was thrilled to see her. At that moment, he wanted nothing more than to pull her into his arms and hold her close, to prove she was real and not merely fantasy.

Apparently, though, all Amelia wanted was to flee. She put her head out the window and called up to the jarvey. "Please stop!"

"He won't listen to you," Pearce told her calmly as the team drove on.

Ignoring him, she pounded her fist once more against the compartment wall, harder than before.

"You're going to hurt yourself." Biting down an aggravated curse that she wanted to be away from him so badly, he gently took her by the wrist. "And what a damned shame it would be to bruise such tender flesh."

She gaped at him, stunned.

He shamelessly took advantage of her breathless reaction by raising her hand to his lips so he could place a lingering kiss on the backs of her fingers. After so many years of not seeing her, of not knowing what had happened to her, he simply couldn't resist even this small taste of her.

That caused her mouth to fall open in an O as round as her big eyes. In that reaction, Pearce glimpsed the girl he remembered, the one who had never been good at hiding her emotions. He nearly grinned. The Amelia he'd known still lurked beneath the facade of the beautiful woman she'd become. *Thank God.*

He could barely believe that she was here. But the nervous trembling of her fingers against his lips was certainly real.

So was the wariness in her eyes.

When she slowly pulled her hand from his grasp, he resisted the urge to snatch it back. Instead, he leaned against the leather squabs and casually angled his long legs across the small compartment, hoping he looked relaxed even though his heart drummed against his ribs.

"The driver has orders to ignore you," he explained.

"Why would he do that?" Her voice emerged surprisingly husky, and thankfully more curious than angry.

"Because I paid him to."

"You…" She blinked. "Why would you do that?"

"Because we need to talk," he explained. "And I couldn't be certain after last night that you wouldn't try to run away." *Again.*

The undulation in her throat from her nervous swallow proved him right. She would have done just that. "We have nothing to talk about."

"A great deal." He leveled his gaze on her as the carriage rocked around them, swaying them in their seats. "Starting with why you were at Le Château Noir this morning."

Her fingers tightened around the reticule she held in her lap as she defensively tossed back, "Why were you?"

"I'm a former soldier turned peer. Visiting brothels is practically a requirement." He couldn't tell her the truth. That he'd followed her there. Not until he'd learned how much she knew about what her brother had been doing. But instead of drawing a smile, that teasing comment surprisingly darkened her expression. So he continued cautiously, "What I'd like to know is why would a respectable lady and the sister of an MP?"

"Don't confuse the two," she countered dryly. "They're not necessarily inclusive."

His lips curled in amusement. The sharp woman who'd verbally fenced with him last night had returned. "Why were either of them at Lord Torrington's masquerade, then?"

"The dancing," she quipped, dodging his question. "I'd heard the waltzing there would be unparalleled."

"It was. Damned shame that your brother got in the way."

Her eyes locked with his. "We were finished."

Her quiet words slapped him. She didn't mean the waltz. He said quietly, "Not due to my choosing."

"Wasn't it?"

He knew better than to answer. She was picking a fight, the way she used to as a girl to worm her way out of uncomfortable situations, most likely in hopes that he'd grow angry, stop the carriage, and leave.

But he wouldn't be so easily deterred. "Why were you at the masquerade?" Unbidden jealousy made him ask, "What would you want with a man like Varnham?"

"What would you want with a woman like Madame Noir?"

He sat up. Her question came out of nowhere, taking him completely by surprise. "Nothing, I assure you."

"She showed me the emerald bracelet you gave her." Controlled iciness dripped from her voice. "How thoughtful of you to give her a bauble that matches her eyes."

He went completely still, his gaze locked with hers across the compartment. This wasn't simply another attempt to stir up a fight. "I did not give that woman any jewelry."

"She seems to think you did."

"I did not give that woman a bracelet, emerald or otherwise," he said as firmly but calmly as possible. "The *only* woman I've ever given jewelry to…" *Damnation.* His eyes lowered to the gold locket at her throat.

Her hand rose to grasp the locket, and her voice trembled with uncertainty as she asked, "Then why would she say so?"

He grimaced. "Knowing Madame, just to see if she could draw a reaction from you. Did you give her one?"

"No." She stared at him intently for a long moment, as if trying to reconcile the lad she knew with the man sitting before her. Finally, she whispered, "I believe you about the bracelet."

"Well then," he drawled. "Good to know you'll take the word of a brigadier over a brothel owner."

A faint but uneasy smile pulled at her lips, and she released the locket, her hand dropping away. "Barely."

He chuckled. She was just as sassy as he remembered. And in more trouble than she knew.

His amusement faded, and he leaned forward, hands folded between his knees. "Tell me—why were you at Le Château Noir this morning?"

She hesitated, her doubt over trusting him visible on her face. But then she admitted, "I was returning a dress I'd borrowed. Why were you there?" She swept an assessing gaze over him, hiding behind her sardonic teasing to keep from having to hold a meaningful conversation. And to keep from having to answer his questions. "I doubt she has anything in your style."

He couldn't resist volleying back, "It's not the cut of the gown that matters—"

"But how a man wears it?"

He grinned. She'd read his mind, just as she'd used to do.

Sweet Lucifer, being with her felt like old times. The sensation emerged with a vengeance, forming a hollow ache deep inside him. He hadn't realized until that moment exactly how much he'd missed her. The way a desert misses the rain.

"And speaking of cuts…" She tilted her head, studying him. "What did you do last night after you left the masquerade?"

He admitted truthfully, "The usual. Got drunk, stripped off my clothes, and ran around the city half-naked."

"Just another evening in Mayfair, then?" she asked dryly.

"Terribly dull life."

"Hmm. Well, *this* wasn't there last night when I danced with you." She reached across the compartment to touch the bruise on his jaw.

He stilled immediately beneath her fingertips. Except for his heart, which leapt into his throat, and his cock, which flexed shamelessly in his breeches. "You noticed something as small as that?"

"We waltzed," she reminded him, her fingertips brushing gently across his brow. "How could I not have noticed when you were that close? Or that your jaw has mysteriously turned black and blue overnight?" Her eyes softly searched his face for more evidence of what he'd been up to last night, yet he found the sensation oddly soothing, as tangible as her touch. "Or that you have a cut—just there—at the corner of your left eye?"

"I like to spar occasionally," he admitted. "After I left the masquerade, I went to a match."

"Still getting into fights," she murmured and traced the features of his face to soothe his wounds. "Just as you used to in Birmingham with the men from the factories."

Her touch stirred a forgotten familiarity whose ache seeped into his bones. He rasped out, suddenly hoarse, "You remember that, from so long ago?"

"I remember everything about you." Then, as if realizing who they were and what she was doing, she dropped her hand away and pulled back against the squabs. "As they say..." Sadness laced her trembling voice. "Know thy enemy."

Her words cut him. "I'm not your enemy, Amelia. I only want to protect you."

Slowly, careful not to startle her, he leaned toward her. But damnation if she didn't draw further back into the squabs, not at all convinced by his reassurances.

"I told you." Wariness flared in her eyes. "I don't need to be protected."

"More than you realize," he said solemnly.

Her lips parted in surprise.

Frederick Howard was playing with ruthless men. Amelia wasn't part of it—he didn't want to believe that of her. But he also needed to discover the truth. Yet how much could he tell her to ease her fear without exposing her to additional risk? "Your brother has been illegally using his influence to secure government appointments. He's placed at least twelve men so far."

"Isn't that what all peers and MPs do? Peddle influence." She casually threw his earlier words back at him. "It's practically a requirement."

"Except that most of the appointments he's secured are simply titular, a few have limited power, and none are able to provide political favors in return," he explained. The carriage was circling Berkeley Square now, with Hill Street only a few minutes away. He was running out of time and had no more answers than when he'd jumped inside. "Not the kind a young MP on the rise could draw on to improve his political leverage or his bank funds. So why is he doing it?"

"I don't know."

A lie. He could read it in every inch of her. What the devil was she hiding from him? "Is Varnham involved? Is that why you wanted to speak to him?"

"No." This time, the lie was accompanied by a telltale fidget.

"Your brother is involved with dangerous men, Amelia," Pearce said bluntly. The time for sparring was over. "Ones willing to commit murder to get what they want."

Her face paled. *Good.* Maybe she'd understand now how serious he was. How much danger she was in.

"Were you at the masquerade because of them?"

"No! I went there because—" She choked off, her confession unfinished.

In that unguarded moment, he saw beneath the facade she'd erected, and it wasn't anger or annoyance he glimpsed in her now. It was fear.

The realization washed over him like ice water. That's what he'd seen when he first stepped into the carriage, what had flashed over her face last night when she'd fled. Her earlier anger had been nothing but a shield to keep him away.

But why? He'd given her no reason to be afraid of him. *Never.*

Had she been threatened by Scepter? Was that why she'd been at the masquerade? Had she been coerced into helping her brother?

"Amelia, you can trust me," he entreated, moving to the edge of the seat to bring himself closer. "You don't have to be afraid of—"

"I'm not afraid of you!" She forced a stiff laugh at the absurdity of that, but her reaction didn't ease the apprehension that pulsed from her. It hovered around her as tangibly as her rose-water perfume.

"Good. Because I want to keep you safe." His shoulders eased down under the weight of the past. "That's all I've ever wanted. You know that."

She stared at him, saying nothing. But her lips parted tentatively, as if she ached to confide in him but couldn't yet bring herself to do it.

"But you have to help me."

"How?"

The word was little more than a breath, yet it stirred hope inside him. "By telling me the truth. Why were you at the masquerade?"

Her hands clutched tightly at her reticule, as if physically fighting back the urge to trust him. Good Lord, he wished she would!

When she didn't answer, he offered gently, "Let me help you."

"As I told you last night," she rasped out quietly but resolutely, as if attempting to convince herself as much as him, "I don't need your help." Yet her face darkened with that ever-present fear that he now couldn't help but see in her, no matter how much bravery she attempted to exude. Dread, panic, apprehension, distrust—a kaleidoscope of it shone in her eyes. "Forgive my bluntness, but in my experience, when a man says that he wants to help me, what he really means is that he wants to use me."

He sat back, her words landing like a punch. Did she mean her father? Gordon Howard certainly hadn't hidden how he'd planned to use her as a stepping-stone into the aristocracy. Or did she mean her brother?

Pearce had no answers, but at least he could assure her, "I am not one of those men."

"Aren't you?" The wounded whisper emerged as pure accusation.

"No." But the forcefulness with which he said that didn't register any visible trust in her.

The hackney turned onto Hill Street and stopped in front of a row of terrace houses. When she glanced out the window, relief flashed over her face. She was home.

And he was out of time.

He reached across the compartment to place his hand over hers to keep her with him a few moments longer and tried not to let himself notice the way she flinched at his touch.

"Whatever's wrong, whatever trouble you're in, I can help you. But you can't keep secrets from me." Ignoring the ball of lead-like dread forming in his gut, he pulled in a deep breath and forced himself to ask, "Have you been assisting your brother with the appointments?"

Her gaze shot back to him. "Have I—" Then a shocked laugh fell from her lips as she pulled her hand away from his. "I could ask the same of you!"

He jerked up straight. "Me?"

"Frederick said that you supported the idea of putting a turn-pike across our properties." Her voice shook from the churning emotions that visibly gripped her. "He was practically crowing this morning over how excited you seemed to be about it. Said that you couldn't wait to start."

Bloody hell. Pearce couldn't deny it. He'd sent her brother a message just that morning claiming exactly that—that he was interested and wanted to know more about Howard's plans and the men who would be made trustees.

But it wasn't for the reasons she thought, and he couldn't defend himself without giving away what the men of the Armory planned to do. He would never betray their faith in him.

"You're wrong about me," he said instead, the only answer he could give.

"Oh, but I don't think I am." Her voice was raw and intense, just like the gleam in her eyes. "You see, unlike others in your new life as a peer, I know you. I know how restless you are, how driven…how compelled to keep moving forward. At all costs." A slight pause, so small no one else would have noticed, yet he heard it. A world of accusation lived there. "That's why I can't trust you, Pearce." The quiet fierceness with which she uttered her next words cut him like a blade—"And *that* is why you're my enemy."

Seven

AMELIA WATCHED HIM STIFFEN, SURPRISED. AND STUNNED JUST long enough for her to open the door and bound to the street before he could stop her.

She had to get away. *Now*, before he could see her own surprise at the things he'd been asking about—or her desperation to keep them hidden. Or worse, how the affection and attraction she'd felt toward him when they were younger now bubbled inside her again.

Something else ached inside her, too. Something hotter... He'd always been charming and dashing, even all those years ago when he'd been on the brink of manhood. But the passing years had made him broad and tall and oh so very solid, put lines of experience at the corners of his eyes and mouth, placed depth behind the mischievous gleam in his eyes.

Now he was simply breathtaking.

He caught her before she reached the front portico, taking her elbow to keep her from running away. The touch was meant only to slow her, yet it sparked an electric heat all the way down to her toes.

She rolled her stinging eyes in frustration. Damn him for reappearing in her life right now, when everything was such a mess that she couldn't give him the setdown he deserved for ambushing her in the carriage. Damn him for not answering her letters, for never once attempting to contact her in all the years they'd been apart.

And damn herself for remembering how wonderful it had been to be with him.

She moved her arm to pull free, but he held firm. She couldn't yank herself away without causing a scene in the busy street, in front of her own house, no less, with all of her neighbors and their servants watching. He gave her no choice but to let him escort her to the door.

"I am *not* your enemy," he half growled under his breath.

"You are certainly not my salvation," she countered. No matter what Frederick thought.

"Well then." He leaned down, bringing his mouth close enough to her ear that his breath fanned across her cheek. Close enough that she could feel the knowing smile of his lips. "Good thing we're in hell together."

Her head snapped up. "We are not togeth—"

"Because I've been here before," he said enigmatically, ignoring the perplexed look she gave him as he turned his gaze solemnly up at the town house and rapped the brass knocker. "And I can show you the way out."

She blinked hard, her lips parting as she stared at him. Dear God, if only that were true!

"So tell me, Amelia, and no dissembling this time," he murmured, keeping his gaze straight ahead on the door. "Exactly what kind of trouble are you in?"

Her heart lurched. For one desperate moment, she wanted to confess everything about Frederick and the trust and the blackmail—

Drummond opened the door.

Thank God.

She darted past the butler and into the house, heading straight for the stair hall. Sweet escape. Finally. The weight lifted from her shoulders, and she heaved out a breath of relief so large that it pulled all the way through her.

Only for cold dread to slither back up her spine when she heard Pearce's deep voice. "Is Mr. Howard at home? I'm here to call on him."

She spun around, her mouth falling open. Pearce stood inside the entry as if he belonged there, removing his hat and gloves and handing them all over to Drummond. Oh, that devil's audacity!

"Brandon Pearce, Brigadier," he announced with the confident air of the battle-hardened soldier he was. "Earl of Sandhurst."

Drummond sketched a bow. "Of course, your lordship." He gestured toward the stairs and the formal drawing room above. "If you would wait—"

"No," Amelia interrupted. *Oh no, no, no!* Letting him into her home—back into her life—was the *very* last thing she should do. Too many secrets could be revealed, so much could be destroyed... She hurried back to him, gesturing at Drummond to remain right where he was. "We are not accepting visitors today."

"Is that true?" Pearce asked the butler, who glanced in confusion between the two of them, not knowing whose orders to follow. "Perhaps you should ask Mr. Howard himself." He smiled confidently. "Tell him that Sandhurst is here to discuss turnpikes."

He blinked, confused. "Sir?"

"*Turnpikes*," Pearce repeated deliberately, slipping out of his greatcoat and tossing it over the butler's arm. "I'll wait here."

With a stilted nod and a wary glance at Amelia, Drummond quickly disappeared into the house toward the study. There was nothing she could do to stop him from announcing Pearce's arrival to her brother.

Panic twisted down her spine. "What do you think you're doing?"

He casually shrugged a shoulder, which rolled exasperation through her. "Discussing turnpikes with the neighboring land-owner. Should be pretty easy to establish a trust since he's an MP and I sit in the Lords now, don't you think? Damned title ought to be good for something." Pearce's eyes slid to Amelia, a faint gleam of challenge lingering in their depths. "Unless you know of a reason why I shouldn't. One you want to share with me." He paused to give time for that quiet threat—and its only means of escape—to settle over her. "A *good* reason."

"Please don't do this," she whispered. Desperation blossomed in her belly. "You don't know what you're getting yourself involved with."

"Then tell me."

Damn him! He was forcing her into a corner. "I can't."

"Then I have no choice." He folded his arms, doing a fine impersonation of an immovable mountain. "If you won't give me answers, Amelia, then I'll get them from your brother."

A laugh strangled in her throat. She'd fallen in over her head, and the current was pulling her under. "He won't tell you! He's more afraid of what could happen to him than he'll ever be of you."

"What do you mean?"

She kicked for the surface, frantic to save herself—"That you're right," she admitted quickly, glancing over her shoulder in fear that Drummond might return at any moment. "Freddie *has* been using his influence to put men into government positions."

His eyes narrowed on her. "Why?"

She bit her lip. She couldn't tell him the truth. The further she kept Pearce away from this mess—and from her—the better. She couldn't risk that anyone else might find out what illegal activities her brother had done.

Or that Pearce would find out about her husband.

"Freddie has three more men he needs to place." She offered up this little bit of information to evade a more dangerous answer. "He thinks this trust will allow him to do that."

"You don't agree with what your brother's been doing?"

"Of course I don't." She swallowed hard, her gaze darting into the house toward Freddie's study, and lowered her voice. "And I certainly don't want the trust."

"Why not?"

"The turnpike requires Bradenhill, the property Papa left me when he died," she rushed out. With every desperate second that passed, she knew she was running out of time to convince him to decline her brother's plans. "It's just a few acres, nothing much at all, but it lies between Freddie's land and yours. He thinks that if he has all three properties lined up for the turnpike that Parliament will force the trust through for the rest of the county, and he'll be able to place these last three men as trustees. He's promised me that this will be the last of it."

"But you don't want a turnpike?"

"I have other plans for that land." Once she freed them from this mess, she could move ahead with creating a training school and workshop at Bradenhill, be self-sufficient and away from all the gossips and problems of London. It would become the one part of her life that no man would ever be able to touch or harm. Not Freddie, not Aaron…not even Pearce.

"So why not tell your brother no? Tell him in no uncertain terms that you don't want the turnpike." His eyes narrowed on her, studying her reaction. "After all, it's your property to do with as you'd like."

Refuse the trust, force the blackmailer into exposing Freddie, watch as her life came crashing down around her… She nearly groaned. "It isn't that simple."

"So you want *me* to tell your brother that I've decided against the turnpike?"

"No!" Good Lord, if Freddie thought she had something to do with that decision, he'd have her hide! And the blackmailer would have Freddie's head. "I'm not saying that. Just—just put off making a decision." She grimaced, biting her bottom lip. "For a month or two."

"What good would that do?"

"It will delay the trust." A delay was all she needed. Just long enough that the blackmailer would think Freddie was cooperating, just long enough for other positions to come open. Then the need for the trust would vanish, and the threat to Freddie's career and her charity right along with it.

He shook his head, unconvinced. "Why is your brother doing this?"

She wouldn't tell him that, *couldn't* risk it. If she put her faith in him, only to once more be manipulated and used by a man for his own advantage—

But Pearce had never hurt her, except for leaving her. He'd only ever been kind to her, bringing her flowers and handmade gifts, teaching her how to shoot and ride and swim just like the boys, talking with her on blankets beneath the stars about all his future dreams. Her best friend and first love who went so far as to defend her with his fists when other men made crude comments about her—men twice his size and age. He knew her better than anyone else in the world, even her own family.

But twelve years... Was any of the boy she'd once trusted still left inside the man?

Gambling on her heart's intuition, she sucked in a deep breath for courage. "You said you wanted to help me, so help me." In desperation, she reached for his arm. The hard muscle flexed invitingly beneath her fingertips. "Pretend that you're interested in the turnpike and let Freddie line up the trustees, but delay it so that the act doesn't go through before Parliament ends. Make the bill wait, then change your mind right before the next session begins."

His face remained inscrutable, but his eyes searched her face for answers she couldn't give. "Why should I do that?"

"For me," she choked out and dropped her hand away. *Because you once loved me...* "Because we were once friends."

Footsteps echoed from deep within the house, growing louder as they drew closer. Urgent and eager—

"Please, Pearce." She blinked hard to clear the hot tears of panic from her eyes. "If I ever meant anything to you—"

"Sandhurst!"

Frederick strode into the entry hall, his hand extended toward Pearce in greeting. He beamed a thrilled smile and slid between the two of them, ignoring Amelia in his eagerness to get to Pearce.

But Pearce solemnly made eye contact with her over her brother's shoulder as the two men shook hands.

"What a pleasant surprise," Frederick gushed. "I'd planned on calling on you myself this afternoon, but how wonderful that you've anticipated me. Proof that you're a man who knows his mind when opportunity strikes." He placed his hand on Pearce's shoulder to nudge him in the direction of his study. "Let's discuss business, shall we? I have a special bottle of brandy that I think you'll enjoy."

But Pearce didn't move. "I'm not certain about the trust."

Hope fluttered inside her. Was he going to help her after all?

Frederick froze. "Pardon?"

"I'm not certain that a turnpike is the best use of my property," Pearce explained. "I want to consider all options."

"But—but a trust *is* in all of our best interests, I assure you." He gestured toward Amelia. "Tell him, Amelia, about all the new business to be made with a turnpike, the industrial development that can happen."

She caught her breath as both men looked at her expectantly—Frederick, for her to use whatever charms he thought she possessed over Pearce to sway him to their side, and Pearce, for her to give him the answers he wanted.

But she couldn't do that. Not without raising Frederick's ire and his suspicions that she wasn't doing everything she could to support the turnpike. And not when Pearce now held power over her.

She was cornered. "I—well, I—" she stammered, praying an answer came to her.

"We can talk about that between us," Pearce told her brother, rescuing her once again by mercifully giving her an escape from the conversation. "I'm certain Miss Howard doesn't want to be bothered with men and their business."

She breathed out a silent sigh of relief. "Quite true." She was already far more involved in all of this than she wanted to be. And desperate for a way to stop it. Meeting Pearce's gaze, she said, "I know you'll do what's in my best interests, Lord Sandhurst."

Pearce's eyes gleamed, recognizing that for the lie it was. She wasn't at all certain that she could trust him again, and he knew it.

"Good," Frederick chimed in as he once more took Pearce's shoulder and practically turned him toward the back of the house. "Let's adjourn to my study, shall we? We have lots to discuss, and no better time than the present." He led the way toward the rear of the town house. "First, we need to consider the properties. Bradenhill is too small and worthless, of course, for anything else…"

As the two men walked away, Amelia saw the hopeful bounce in her brother's step. She leaned back against the wall as all the tension drained from her, replaced by churning confusion, fear, and doubt.

Her hand rose to clasp her locket, and she closed her eyes against the hot tears of frustration threatening at her lashes. How much could she trust Pearce? Twelve years ago, he'd left Birmingham without a fight because he'd wanted to protect her, only to ignore her letters two years later. And ignore *her* ever since. Until now.

And now, when presented with all the profits that a trust could bring, would he decide to protect her? Or would he, too, take her property and cast her away when she was no longer useful or wanted, the way Aaron had?

Once more she'd been trapped by a man. But this time, it might just end her.

Eight

"THIS ISN'T A GOOD IDEA," MERRITT RIVERS MUTTERED AS HE jumped onto the narrow bed in one of the upstairs rooms of Le Château Noir and stretched out across the mattress, boots and all.

Pearce pulled back the curtain and gazed down at the street. "I think it's a grand one."

Beneath the drizzle of rain that had begun to fall an hour ago when the sun set over London, King Street was surprisingly quiet, yet just enough traffic prowled the street to make their visit to the brothel seem commonplace. The man standing guard at the front door had barely blinked an eye when the two of them arrived and asked to see Madame Noir. Alone. Of course, the coin Pearce had handed over helped to ensure that.

"If we're seen here, I can most likely forget any chance of taking silk," Merritt grumbled and reached for the bottle of whiskey and the glass sitting on the bedside table that had been left there for clients, courtesy of Madame.

"Then best not get caught." Not spotting anything unusual on the street below, Pearce dropped the brocade curtain back into place and leaned against the wall. He couldn't help but notice that for all of Merritt's complaints about how dangerous it was for a potential king's counsel to visit a brothel, he'd been quite eager to help when Pearce dropped by the Armory and told him his plans. "It's only reconnaissance, after all."

On cue, a wailing moan of female pleasure echoed down the hall. Pearce rolled his eyes at the unconvinced look Merritt shot him over the rim of his glass.

"Madame Noir owes me a favor," Pearce explained.

"Oh?"

"Not that kind of favor," he half growled, then immediately regretted his snap.

But damnation, he was on edge. Had been since this morning when he spoke to Amelia—no, since before then. When he first saw her at the masquerade.

Now he was in a brothel, his frustration not helped by thoughts of Amelia in that red dress and the sounds of wanton pleasure rising around him. She hadn't been the first girl he'd ever kissed, but he'd been the first man to kiss her. Her first kiss, her first touch… If they hadn't been caught that night of her sixteenth birthday, he would have been her first everything.

He began to pace, but the room was too small, the distance between the red-velvet-papered walls too short to take more than three decent strides. None of his frustrations were helped by Merritt, who lay on the bed, calmly sipping whiskey and watching him as if he were a lion at the Tower Menagerie stalking in its cage.

"Something's on your mind," Merritt called out. "If I had to guess I'd say…a woman."

"Not a woman." *A girl.* The girl to whom he'd once given his love, even when he'd never been good enough to deserve hers.

Orphaned tavern rats like him weren't meant for beautiful daughters of wealthy industrialists. They might as well have tried to invert the world order as to think they could continue to be together. Even as children, they'd both known that their friendship would eventually have to end, that he would go off to work and she would marry a better man.

Now, though, he *was* that better man. Fate had turned him into the kind of successful and wealthy gentleman she'd been meant for. Yet, apparently, it still wasn't enough for her to leave the past behind and trust him again.

The door opened. Madame Noir paused in the doorway, sliding her left arm up the jamb while her right dangled at her side and curving her body sinuously into the frame. But of course she did.

The woman had distinguished her brothel from the hundreds of others in greater London by her clever use of the dramatic. Based on the diaphanous gown she wore under her open dressing robe, whose sheer material revealed every secret beneath, she hadn't yet lost her flair.

Or her figure.

"Brandon," she purred. "How thoughtful of you to visit." Her cat-like eyes traveled slowly to Merritt, who didn't bother getting off the bed at her arrival. "And you've brought a friend." Her red lips curled. "How delicious."

Merritt grinned and lifted the glass to her in a toast.

At the pair's antics, Pearce bit back a harsh breath. "We're here on business, actually."

She shrugged, and the robe slipped down to reveal a bare shoulder. "Everything in my world is business."

She stepped into the room and closed the door with a throaty little laugh.

"I haven't seen you in far too long," she commented as she slipped past Pearce, running her fingers down his bicep.

In truth, she hadn't seen him at all inside her brothel. Not since he'd first returned to London after the wars ended, when he'd been forced into the life of a peer. He'd been just restless and foolish enough during those dark days to buy his way into pleasure, and Madame had been happy to oblige by introducing him to a young widow named Patrice who was discreet in all things and desperate for funds.

But for all her beauty and knowledge about how to satisfy a man, Patrice hadn't been able to tamp down his rising restlessness. Only those boxing matches in the East End had been able to do that.

"And who are you, pet?" She extended her hand toward Merritt, who climbed to his feet and greeted her by bowing over her hand. She trailed her gaze over him, shamelessly lingering at his breeches. "I daresay that Brandon needs to bring his friends by more often."

"Merritt Rivers." He smiled at her warmly and folded his long fingers around hers. "Barrister with the Honourable Society of Lincoln's Inn. A pleasure to make your acquaintance, Madame."

"A barrister?" Her expression hardened, and she slowly pulled her hand free in disgust, as if she'd put it into filth. Her eyes not leaving Merritt, she called out to Pearce over her shoulder. "You've brought a snake into my henhouse, Brandon. How discourteous of you."

With an annoyed tug, she yanked her robe shut and tied it, covering both the sheer gown and the temptations beneath. She took the glass from Merritt's hand.

"Customers only," she explained, all the warmth she'd shown him earlier now gone.

Merritt tsked his tongue. "Don't be like that. Just because I have the power under the Disorderly Houses Act to have you arrested and put on trial, your brothel closed and property confiscated, and you transported if found guilty—why shouldn't we be friends?"

With a dark laugh, she tossed back the remaining whiskey in the glass. "What do you want? I should warn you that if you're looking for bribes, my business isn't as lucrative these days as one might think." She muttered as she refilled the glass, then kept it for herself, "Damned religious reformers think they have the right to tell the rest of us how to live."

"Keeps *me* in a living," Merritt drawled ingenuously as he leaned back against the wall with a shrug.

"Yes," she purred icily, "I'm certain it does."

Merritt had the audacity to grin.

"I need information," Pearce interjected, bringing the conversation to the business that had brought them here. "A member of Parliament is selling his influence. I need to know if he's doing it willingly or being blackmailed."

"How interesting," she purred, delighted at the scandalous nature of their conversation. "That's the second time today that someone's asked me about blackmail. Must be a veritable plague of it gripping Westminster."

Pearce didn't believe in coincidences. "Who?"

"I'm afraid I cannot say. Discretion is my business."

"Odd," Merritt interjected, looking up at the ceiling. His half-veiled threat emerged as innocent musing. "I thought prostitution was."

She slid a murderously narrowed glance at him but didn't deign to reply. She turned toward Pearce and answered, "Miss Amelia Howard."

His blood turned cold. "What did Miss Howard want to know about blackmail?"

"Apparently, how to do it. But the poor thing is in over her head. You really need to give her lessons, Brandon." She gestured her glass at Merritt as an example. "After all, you're very good at extortion."

He smiled tightly at that backhanded compliment. "I'm here about her brother." Amelia would never blackmail anyone. She was too good a person. "Frederick Howard."

"Ah, so someone beat her to it." She traced a fingertip around the rim of the glass. "What a shame. The Honorable Mr. Howard is one of my best customers."

That didn't surprise him. "What would someone use to extort him?"

She feigned ignorance. "What makes you think I would know?"

"I hear Australia's lovely this time of year," Merritt commented to the room at large.

"*Bore!*" she snapped at him over her shoulder. Then, with a long sigh, she faced Pearce and admitted, "He visits frequently and prefers small blonds with large breasts. His favorite is Marigold. You met her when you came in. She led you upstairs."

Yes. A very pretty and vivacious blond who asked all kinds of questions of him and Merritt.

"Overall, his proclivities are tame and nothing unusual. I've heard that he likes to brag about how politically powerful he is, how well connected. How the laws do not apply to men like him. I've no hard evidence, of course, only hearsay, but he's talked of questionable activities—bribery, smuggling, bank schemes, fraud. If it's true, then he's done more than enough to be blackmailed for." She waved her hand dismissively at the brothel around them. "But you know how most men are when they're with women. Always attempting to make themselves seem more masculine and important than they truly—"

"And Scepter?" Pearce pressed.

Her face paled, her hand freezing in midair. Of course she knew about the organization. She couldn't be in the business of London prostitution these days and not hear of it, so ubiquitous had the group become.

The amusement she'd worn like a mask melted away. She lowered her hand to her side. "I have nothing to do with them."

"Does Howard?"

"Not if he knows what's good for him."

He fixed his gaze on her. "What do you know about them and their plans?"

"Just enough to stay away," she answered sincerely. "And I have no intention of learning more."

To punctuate that, she set down the empty glass on the side table with a soft thud.

The mask returned as easily as her smile. "Now that we've concluded your business, is there anything I can do to help you find pleasure?"

"Yes."

Her eyes lit up hopefully.

"Leave Amelia Howard alone."

She stiffened territorially. "I won't pass up a good business opportunity, no matter how small."

"And the bracelet you told her I gave you?"

"Bracelet? I said no such—Oh, *that.* I never said you gave it to me." She laughed at the misunderstanding. "But truly, though, I only have it because of you."

Merritt's brow inched up.

Pearce bit out, "You and I have never—"

"What a shame that is, too." Another long sigh, this time accompanied by her hand going to her bosom and toying with the fold of the robe lying between her breasts. "I'd bet that you would be utterly magnificent."

At that, Merritt's brow nearly shot off his forehead.

Christ.

"In fact, I *have* bet on you—which is how I got that bracelet. I bet on you to win a fight about six months ago." She ran her fingers up his arm. "I came across the bout quite by accident, but there you were, stripping down and stepping into the square. Of course, I had to linger and watch."

"Of course," Merritt echoed earnestly.

Pearce tightened his jaw in aggravation.

"No one else knew who you were, but I did." She squeezed his bicep, and the hard muscle tensed beneath her fingertips. "How could I not wager every ha'penny I was carrying that you'd win?"

"I might have lost."

"Not you," she purred knowingly. "You never lose at any-thing—or anyone. Do you, Brandon?"

His breath hitched. She didn't know about Amelia. Couldn't possibly have known what had happened between them all those years ago and was so carefully covered up by Gordon Howard. Yet the irony of her comment bit into him.

He stepped back, putting his arm out of her reach.

She let her hand fall away with a soft laugh of victory that she'd pricked him.

"Unless there's something else I can help you gentlemen with—" Her gaze traveled back to Merritt and teasingly lingered at his crotch as she reached down to slowly unfasten her robe and let it fall open again. Like a shop merchant displaying her goods in a window to entice customers to buy. "Anything at all." She decadently licked her lips, then turned away with a disheartened sigh at the futility of what she was offering. "Then I must return to my business. You may see yourselves out."

"Madame Noir." Pearce's call stopped her as she opened the door. "Thank you."

"This conversation never happened, do you understand?" Her hard gaze moved between the two men. "If anyone asks, you paid me to service both of you, which I did eagerly and with so much relish that you felt generous enough to leave an extra sovereign."

She lifted her chin in challenge.

Pearce grudgingly tossed her the coin. She certainly knew extortion, all right.

"And if Amelia Howard ever asks to borrow another dress from you," he warned, "you'll tell her that you've nothing in her size."

Madame's eyes glinted with amusement. "Of course." She palmed the coin and sashayed from the room. "It was a pleasure doing business with you."

She left with a throaty laugh, and for several long seconds, the two men stared after her, saying nothing.

Then Merritt drawled, "Amelia Howard, hmm? Frederick Howard's sister."

Pearce grunted noncommittally.

"Borrowing dresses from a brothel owner. And you upset about it." Merritt slid a sideways glance at Pearce. "Do I even want to know?"

"No."

Wisely, Merritt let the subject drop and asked instead, "Do you want me to assign men to follow Miss Howard?"

"No, I want you to put them on her brother." Pearce strode from the room. "Amelia is all mine."

Nine

AMELIA DID HER BEST TO PRETEND THAT SHE WAS LISTENING TO Frederick as he paced the rear room of her shop, and directly behind her as she was attempting to work at her desk in the slant of afternoon sunlight falling through the window. But sweet Lord, he was bothering her to no end! And right when she was so terribly busy, too, with inventory to take, window displays to arrange, a plan to formulate for convincing Charles Varnham to overlook whatever Freddie had done, and Pearce to avoid at all costs.

Especially avoiding Pearce. He'd already come far too close yesterday to learning the truth. At one point, she'd almost capitulated and told him everything, a part of her longing for the protection he'd offered. The thought of being able to confide in him stirred a comforting warmth in her belly, a familiarity of being with him that colored memories of her childhood and made her ache once again for that same closeness. And *that* was dangerous, because she still didn't know if she could trust him with her secrets.

But all that Frederick could think about—

"It's a *turnpike*, for God's sake!"

He paused in pacing to smack his hand in frustration against the desk where she was attempting to update the account ledgers. Her quill jerked and streaked a line across the page.

She bit back a curse, heaving out an irritated sigh instead, and reached for the blotter to clean up the mess.

"How could Sandhurst not be interested? The man should be turning cartwheels of joy that I'd suggested it to him."

"You met with him yesterday," Amelia reminded him. For over an hour. She knew because she'd kept herself carefully hidden in the dining room the entire time, hoping to overhear important information as Pearce left, but garnering nothing except his part-ing appreciation for Freddie's choice of cognac. Now she feigned disinterest when the voice inside her head screamed for details. "What did he say, exactly?"

"Nothing. I couldn't pin him down. All he did was ask questions—who the trustees will be, why I chose them, why I would want a turnpike trust in the first place…" He scowled. "Damned suspicious, if you ask me."

"What ulterior motive would Lord Sandhurst possibly have for delaying?" she murmured as artlessly as possible, not daring to lift her eyes to look at him.

"I don't know." He turned hopefully toward her. "You two had a moment alone together in the entry hall before I arrived. Did he say anything to you about not wanting be part of it—anything at all?"

"Not one word." The God's truth. He hadn't said anything to the contrary…but only because she'd been the one doing all the talking. If Pearce had any compassion in him, he would find a way to continue to evade a concrete decision until after Parliament ended. If only for her sake.

"Are you certain?"

"It's all new to him. He just needs more time." *To string you along until the blackmailer is no longer a threat.* "You're asking the man to place a large chunk of his property into someone else's con-trol for what could be uncertain profits." *And asking me to hand mine over for a complete loss of control and no profits at all.* "Give him time to consider it."

"We don't have time." As he began to pace again, he gestured in frustration in the general direction of Westminster. "The session's going to end in less than a fortnight."

Dear God, she hoped so! Yet she calmly reminded him, "But the trust will remain viable, that's what matters." Knowing she would never be able to figure the last of the columns with him here, she patiently put down her quill and closed the ledger. "You might have to wait until the next session before the act can be passed, but whoever is forcing you to make these appointments knows it, too. The blackmailer will give you the time you need to put forward the bill next session."

He slowed in his pacing, only to shoot her an aggravated grimace.

"Pearce will be less likely to decline because he'll have the chance to think it through thoroughly." *And then decline it.*

Frederick faced her. "Do you truly think Sandhurst will be persuaded?"

"I believe so." *Persuaded to decline.* She wasn't certain at all, but every ounce of her soul prayed for exactly that.

She stood and crossed to the worktable, where she fussed with several yards of cream-colored silk that the women who worked in her shop had hand-printed with wooden blocks and paint, the way the silk weaver in Spitalfields had taught them to do. They'd picked up the skill quickly, creating lengths of beautiful silk that could be used for all kinds of projects—wallpaper, pillows, bedding… Amelia could barely keep the fabrics in stock because the society ladies who shopped at the Bouquet Boutique snatched them up as fast as they could be produced. This one of a red damask rose was particularly exquisite and—

"I want you to charm him."

The fabric slipped through her surprised fingers and piled on the table. "Pardon?"

"Sandhurst. You and he were once quite fond of each other, as I remember."

Guilt pinched her stomach. Oh, that was a lovely way of stating that they'd behaved scandalously and gotten caught!

But Frederick had been away at school the night when Papa caught Pearce in her bedroom, and she would have sworn that Papa wouldn't have told him for fear that her brother would have revealed it to his cronies during some drunken rout. No, he must have figured out on his own how much she and Pearce had once meant to each other. Dear heavens, had they been that obvious?

She leveled her gaze on him. "What, exactly, are you asking of me?"

"Oh, don't pretend naivete with me." He cut her an accusing glare. "Surely, he still has an attraction for you. After all, beneath the uniform and finery, he's still just a former tavern rat."

"Frederick!" *How dare he!* To insult Pearce like that—

"Use your feminine charms, Amelia! Men like Pearce fall for that sort of nonsense all the time." When her eyes narrowed to slits, he added, "You don't have to let him do anything untoward, of course."

"Well, thank goodness," she drawled sarcastically, so furious that her hands trembled as she picked up the cloth and shook it out. "Someone more mistrusting might think you wanted me to compromise myself."

He placed his hands on his hips in aggravation. "Why can't you be serious?"

She'd never been more serious about anything in her life. Her world was about to come crashing down around her—again. But this time, no one would be there to help her pick up the pieces.

Except possibly for Pearce. *If* he'd truly been sincere in his offer to help her.

"Smile at him, flatter him, laugh at his comments, twist your hair around your finger—"

"*Twist* my hair?" The calmness of that question belied her simmering anger.

"Just be nice to the man, will you?" Exasperated, Freddie ran a hand through his hair. Fitting. Because she wanted to yank it out of his head. "For God's sake, half the wives in the *ton* pretend for their entire lives that they like the men they're married to. The least you can do is pretend to like Sandhurst for the next fortnight."

No. That wasn't the least she could do. The least she could do was let Frederick go to the dogs.

But that meant letting herself—and the shop—go down with him. She could never do that.

"I will try," she half-heartedly promised.

"Good. Because I hope to see him tonight at the Black Ball."

She let out a surprised squeak. "*Pardon*?"

When Frederick had purchased tickets to White's grand gala six weeks ago, she hadn't known that Pearce was back in London, let alone would be attendance. As the sister to an MP, her presence was expected—mandatory, if Freddie had any say in the matter. But seeing Pearce again was the very last thing she wanted. She'd come too close to confiding in him yesterday. If she saw him again, if old memories stirred—

No, she *had* to keep away from him. Avoiding him completely was the only way to ensure that he wouldn't learn Freddie's secrets. Or hers.

"The earl is attending?" Trepidation panged hollowly in her belly. "Are you certain?"

Her brother grunted in answer, clearly distracted by thoughts of cornering Pearce at tonight's ball. But from everything she'd discovered about him since the masquerade, he wasn't the type of man who let himself be trapped. Several thousand dead French soldiers proved that.

"I'll pull him aside at some point and demand an answer," Freddie mumbled to himself. "Perhaps in the game room when he's distracted by cards and drink." He waved his hand dismissively and once more began to pace. "You know how these evenings are for gentlemen."

She sighed a bit mockingly. "No, not really."

"*Don't*, Amelia." He leveled a quelling look at her. "Do not minimize the importance of this. Everything we have is at risk."

"I am well aware of that." For heaven's sake, she was standing right in the middle of it. War widows who depended upon her charity to survive were most likely out in the shop at that very moment, whispering about the two of them and this latest argument they'd gotten into.

"Good." He tugged at his cuffs, then at his waistcoat. That same nervous gesture that Papa had done whenever he wanted to remind himself that he was a wealthy businessman who had risen so far in the world that he nipped at the heels of the aristocracy. One of her brother's inherited traits which she despised. "Then we've come to an understanding. You'll do whatever you can to bring Sandhurst over to our side."

No. She hadn't agreed to anything of the kind.

He picked up the silk cloth she'd been examining. "You have a lovely shop, Amelia, you truly do." He released the panel and let it fall to the table. Then he wiped his hands together, as if ladies' things disgusted him. "But you won't be able to save it if I'm ruined."

Was that a threat? All the tiny muscles in her stomach twisted, and for a moment, she feared she might cast up her accounts. Wouldn't it be a shame if she ruined his shiny new shoes?

"I mean it," he warned as he moved toward the door. "Do not do anything to dissuade Sandhurst."

"I wouldn't dream of it," she mumbled as he left.

When he was out of sight, she hung her head in her hands and let her shoulders sag, gulping down mouthfuls of air to calm her roiling stomach. For this one moment only, she let the anguish sweep over her about the mess life had become, the loss of control, that despised feeling of helplessness that was once again descending…

But only a moment. She'd learned long ago that feeling sorry for herself solved nothing.

Gathering her strength with a deep inhalation, she ignored her trembling fingers as she reached for two of the silk panels and spread them out across the table.

That was it—lose herself in her work, just as she'd always done...when Pearce was forced away, when Papa died and she'd been left to suffer Frederick's anger about the will, then again when Aaron left her. Plans for a better future had always sustained her. Just as they would now.

After this mess was over, once her charity and Bradenhill were both safe, she would *never* let herself be under another man's control again.

"Which is better, hmm?" Talking to herself, she turned her attention back to deciding which of the silk pieces to keep in stock and which to rotate out of inventory. "The red roses with their green leaves or the pretty peonies?"

"I prefer the roses myself."

With a surprised gasp, she wheeled around. Her eyes landed on Pearce as he stood in the doorway, leaning casually against the frame.

"But then," he drawled with a shrug of a broad shoulder as his gaze wandered over her, "I've always been fond of scarlet."

The silk slipped through her fingers and puddled on the floor at her feet.

Like a cake of a girl, she stared at him, all dusty and rumpled from riding, his posture both rakish and defiant. *Good God...* he so easily took her breath away.

The dark-green jacket that stretched over his shoulders only served to make him look more dashing than usual, impossibly broader and more muscular, from his shoulders all the way down over the tan riding breeches hugging at his hard thighs. Unlike how other gentlemen dressed, he wore no hat or neckcloth, as if he couldn't be bothered with unnecessary bits of clothing or dandyish fashion trends. The slightly open shirt collar that just peeked out from beneath the plain tan waistcoat scandalously revealed his bare neck, making him look like nothing more than a common worker or ruffian drifting in from the docks. He knew it, too, based upon the defiant gleam in his eyes.

But of course Pearce would snub both fashion and decorum. When had he ever followed society's rules? That he was part of it now would make no difference.

She swallowed hard as he shoved himself away from the door and stepped into the room, uninvited. His eyes left hers only when he stopped in front of her and bent down to pick up the silk. But the reprieve was short-lived, and heat streaked through her when he rose to his feet, his gaze traveling slowly up the length of her and lingering in all kinds of places it had no business being.

She would have told him so, too, if he hadn't left her speechless. And aching.

"Good afternoon, Amelia." His deep voice played like warm fingers down her spine.

"Pearce," she forced out breathlessly. The world was spinning beneath her, and she reached out to grasp the edge of the table to keep from falling away. "What are you doing here?"

"I went to your brother's house. The butler said you were both here." He cast a leisurely glance around the room before landing his gaze on her. "I'm not surprised you run a shop. Your father was one of the most successful businessmen in England. It must be in your blood."

"No, it's not." She laid the silk panel aside. She *never* wanted to be compared to Gordon Howard. "And it's not a shop."

"Could have fooled me," he mumbled dryly, reaching for a small vial of perfume containing a new scent that one of the women had recently concocted and which Amelia was considering offering for sale.

"It's a charity." She sounded defensive, even to her own ears, but she couldn't help it, feeling like a mother protecting her child. "I give employment to women who otherwise have no means of support."

"That doesn't surprise me either. You always were caring."

He removed the cork and wafted the scent beneath his nose,

then curled his lips in an appreciative expression that spun through her all the way to the ends of her hair. The same way he used to look at her when they were younger. Right before he proposed some wild scheme that undoubtedly ended up casting them into trouble. Like the time they'd sneaked into the Twelfth Night celebrations and drunk so much punch that she'd gotten sick. Or when he'd asked her to go sailing on the boat he'd made, only for it to sink in the middle of the river, forcing them to be rescued by the ferryman. And all those times when they'd gone off alone into the fields for picnics or stargazing, lying on a blanket in each other's arms… She'd thought they'd always be like that, always going from one adventure to the next. Together.

But fate had never been her friend.

Slowly, she took the bottle out of his hand and replaced the stopper. She had no time for memories of a past now best left to the shadows.

"Freddie's not here. He left about ten minutes ago, most likely for Boodle's. So you don't have to stay just to be polite." She set the bottle aside before he could see her shaking hands. "I'm sure you have more important things to do than visit a ladies' charity shop."

Instead of leaving, though, he folded his arms and leaned a hip against the table beside her in a pose of such masculine confidence that her belly tightened with desire. The memories of giving him her first kisses as a girl, and other intimacies, came flooding back unbidden. And mercilessly.

"We were interrupted in our conversation yesterday," he said. "I think we should finish it, don't you?"

No. Finishing that conversation was not at all what she wanted. Instead, she smiled, dismissing his concerns by turning to show him out of her shop. "I asked you to help me by delaying and declining the trust, and you agreed. So there's nothing more to—"

"I didn't agree."

She stopped. Holding her breath in a silent prayer that she'd misheard, she looked at him over her shoulder. "What did you say?"

"That I didn't agree to scuttle the trust."

Dread rushed through her as she turned to face him. "But you did. That's why you haven't given Freddie your decision yet, because you're delaying." *For me.*

"I haven't given my decision because I need more information." He tilted his head slightly to the side, studying her. "About your brother's reason for wanting this trust so badly, about the trustees he's picked…and you, Amelia."

"Me?" Instead of the squeak she'd expected, the word emerged as a throaty rasp. Drat the man for having this effect on her! "I don't want that turnpike."

"I know. What I can't figure out is why."

He pushed away from the table and straightened to his full height. Good Lord, she'd forgotten how tall he was, how she'd had to tilt back her head to look into his eyes whenever they'd stood as close as they were now. And to let him kiss her.

Clearing her throat, she stepped away. "I told you. I have other plans for Bradenhill."

"What plans, exactly?"

"For my charity." She would surrender this small bit to keep the rest hidden. Sometimes the best place to hide was straight behind the truth. "I want to expand it by starting a trade school and workshop at Bradenhill where women from all over England can learn skills. Weaving, lace-making, pottery—whatever we can teach them, and give them a safe and quiet place in the country to live while they master those skills." She couldn't hide the pride she felt in her charity, or the determination to make it even better by helping more women. And by helping them, help herself by giving her life a purpose. "That's why I don't want a turnpike across my land. I'd rather dedicate it to helping people than making a profit." She quietly added another truth beneath her breath, "But these days, apparently, Frederick cares only about himself."

Nothing visibly changed in his expression, but she felt a tension rise in him. A familiar pang sent it pulsing through her, the same way she'd been able to discern his moods when they were children. As if he were merely an extension of her. Apparently, to her foolish heart, he still was.

"I didn't realize that charity work meant so much to you," he murmured. His eyes roamed over her as if attempting to reconcile the girl he'd known with the woman she'd become.

"You wouldn't have." She gave him a reprieve from any self-blame. If any of the boy she'd known still lurked within the man, he'd be chagrined at not knowing about that part of her life when he'd always had access to the rest of it. "I was only able to dedicate myself to it after we moved to London."

"After your father died."

"Not immediately after," she answered, reaching past him to fuss with the silk. "He died unexpectedly when I was eighteen. We were still in Birmingham then. I had just returned from Scotland and—"

"Scotland?" Genuine surprise colored Pearce's voice. "I was told you went off to school."

"I did. In Scotland. Papa banished me all the way to Aberdeen, as far away as he could." She smiled grimly. "If Calcutta had had a boarding school for aristocratic young ladies, he would have put me onto the first ship bound for India." She picked up the silk panel and shook it out, holding it in front of her like a rose-covered shield. He stood far too close for comfort. "I thought your uncle would have told you."

"My uncle was glad to have me gone and no longer his responsibility." To her surprise, no bitterness came from him. Just acceptance. "His letters were few and far between."

And most likely not at all concerned with the whereabouts of the daughter of a neighboring factory owner, not knowing the reason why the Earl of Sandhurst had so graciously—and expeditiously—bestowed Pearce with an officer's commission. Her father had made certain that no one but the four of them knew what had happened that night, including Pearce's uncle.

"I wish *you* had told me where you were," he said quietly.

I wanted to, so very much! "I couldn't. If I tried to contact you, Papa would have punished both of us. You know that." That old feeling of helplessness came flooding back. Dear Lord, how she hated it! "Even if I'd dared try, I had no idea where you were, what regiment you were with… I didn't know how to reach you."

"And after your father died?"

She flinched, unable to steel herself against the pain. Or keep her hand from rising to her throat and to the locket dangling from its blue ribbon, which she'd replaced five times over the years when it had worn and frayed from wear. He waited for her answer, but her throat tightened too much for her to find her voice.

"That was ten years ago," he pressed gently. "Why didn't you try to contact me then?"

The desolation of that time flashed over her with a vengeance, so strongly that she had to hide her face by turning her head away. To hide her shame of having to beg Frederick to help her find out what regiment Pearce was in, to beg him to help her write to him. "I did… I wrote you letters…" *And letters and letters*—Dear God, so many confessions of her love and pleas for him to return to her! Not one of them answered. In little more than an aching breath, she scratched out, "You never replied."

He went deathly still, holding his breath as what she was revealing registered inside him.

"I never received them." His voice was strained, suddenly hoarse. "The wars… Mail was sporadic. I didn't even know that your father had died until last year." A drawn and bleak expression darkened his features. "We were constantly marching across the

Peninsula back then, from battle to battle. Supplies could barely keep up—"

"I know." She cut him off gently, unable to bear the truth that swept through her like an icy wind. He *hadn't* refused her letters, hadn't simply thrown them away into the fire as she'd always believed. She pressed her fist against her bosom, to keep her heart from shattering anew. All these years…

He simply hadn't known.

"I wish you had tried again," he said quietly.

The agony of all she'd lost enveloped her until she could barely breathe, until she could barely force her numb lips to form the soft confession, "I would have, but…"

But by then, when she'd considered pressing Freddie a second time for help, she'd already met Aaron, and she would *never* tell Pearce what happened after that. The way he would look at her if she did, with such pity at her utter stupidity in trusting so blindly, at so desperately wanting the life she'd been denied with him that she'd allowed herself to be robbed and abandoned… She couldn't have borne it.

"I'd moved on," she whispered, those three words encapsulating the grandest mistake of her life. One that still punished her every day. Even now—*especially* now—it ate at her. "And so had you. You had a new life in the army, a wonderful future ahead of you. The last person you needed to be bothered with was me."

Desperately needing to believe that so she wouldn't break down in tears, she picked up a red paper poppy that one of the women had made to decorate a hat and tucked it into the first buttonhole of his waistcoat with a light pat of her trembling fingers. To dismiss the past and its mistakes. To make him believe that she'd been fine. And conveniently, so she didn't have to look into his eyes.

She stepped around him, circling to the other side of the table to pick up a long wooden rolling pin. She laid the silk across the table and placed the roller on one end. Work—work had always gotten her through. It would help her survive this new pain, too. So she focused on the cloth and carefully began to wrap it around the roller so that it could be stored without being folded. If the silk were folded, then the paint would flake off and—

"That's why you think I'm your enemy, isn't it?"

His deep voice came from directly behind her and sent a hot shiver of remorse curling inside her. She stilled, except for her hands, which tightened on the rolling pin so hard that her knuckles turned white.

"Because I never returned your letters."

She turned to look at him over her shoulder, only to find him standing behind her. *Right* behind her. His nearness tingled across her skin and raised goose bumps in its heated wake.

Her gaze dropped to his mouth, which lingered so close to hers that the warmth of his breath tickled her lips. She could kiss him simply by lifting onto her tiptoes. There would be solace there, she knew, an easing of the pain that made her long to simply lean back and bring herself into his arms. That's all it would take, just a simple shift of her body. Not even turning around… And if she did, she would be lost.

"Because of the turnpike," she corrected softly. "If you join Freddie in advocating for it, I'll lose Bradenhill."

She held her breath, waiting for him to assure her that he would do exactly as she'd asked of him—

"If the trust is causing so much tension between you and your brother, then let him have the property and build your school elsewhere."

Her shoulders sank in equal measure disappointment and exasperation. Was he going to help her at all? Had she completely misread the man he'd become? Desperation scratched her voice. "Bradenhill is all I have."

"But your father was wealthy. Surely, he left you other property that—"

"Gordon Howard was a mean and spiteful old man who caused trouble right up to the end, even from the grave." She turned to face him and steeled herself against showing any unease at finding herself less than six inches from his chest, his hips even closer. And his mouth…*sweet heavens*. "Instead of leaving his fortune to Frederick and an allowance to me, he left the fortune to me and gave Frederick the allowance."

Surprise crossed his face. "Your father left you everything?"

"Except for the land, which was divided between us." Which was why she was now in this mess. "Papa believed that a man needs land in order to be a proper gentleman, so he gave part to Freddie, and that I would need it to find an aristocratic husband, so he gave Bradenhill to me."

"Then you have enough money to buy more land and put your charity wherever you'd like."

"No, I don't."

"Why not?"

Not wanting to answer that, she tried to politely move him aside, so she could step away and clear her head. But the man didn't budge. "Pearce, please—"

"Amelia." He took her chin and gently lifted her head, making her look directly at him. "Tell me."

She blew out an exasperated breath and rolled her eyes to the ceiling. "I found myself in a spot of trouble," she admitted, hoping he would accept that whopper of an understatement. Because she'd *never* tell him the truth. He looked at her now as if he longed to kiss her, as much as she longed for him to do just that.

But if she told him about Aaron, how would he look at her then?

A frown of concern wrinkled his brow. "What kind of trouble?"

"Financial," she answered vaguely. In the end, though, wasn't that what it had been? The ramifications of losing her fortune had certainly lasted longer than her marriage. "It happened right before I turned twenty-one, when Freddie was still acting as my guardian and in control of my money."

"Being passed over in his inheritance for his younger sister, then having to manage it all for her," he mumbled, his eyes gleaming with amusement at Frederick's expense. "Your brother must have hated that."

"He resented it. Quite a bit, for a while. But then—then there was an unexpected problem." She refused to give specifics and prayed that Pearce was too much of a gentleman to press. "I lost everything except for Bradenhill."

Concern darkened his face. "Did Howard do something foolish and cost you your fortune?"

"No." Her voice lowered to a whisper as she dared to put this small part of her trust in him. "It was all my doing. But Freddie stepped in after to take care of me. The town house is his. He lets me stay there, employs my maid, and grants me an allowance. He even helped me start my charity shop. I couldn't have done it without him." Guilt clawed at her belly. He had done so much to help her... "I owe him everything."

"So you would now do anything to help him."

"No." She fixed her eyes directly on his. "I won't give up Bradenhill." Not to Freddie, not to a trust... She pulled in a deep breath. "Not to anyone."

A frown creased his brow as he stared down at her, but an inexplicable sensation sparked through her that he admired her for her resolve. Nothing he said told her that, no change in his expression...but it resonated through that connection they'd shared since they were children, like a ribbon that wound around them and joined them even now.

"At least tell me this," he conceded, letting her keep her privacy. "Are you all right now?"

She warmed at his concern. "I will be, once I know that Freddie won't build his turnpike."

He stood close. *Far* too close. Needing space and air, she put her hands on his shoulders and pushed to make him step back.

But he didn't move, except for a flexing of his muscles beneath her fingertips. Electric tingles raced up her arms and landed heavily in her breasts. As a young man, he'd been tall and slender with lean muscles that had made him seem so solid then—but nothing as solid and hard as this. She remembered the strength of his young arms when they'd wrapped around her. How would they feel now that he was a man in his prime?

She dropped her hands to her sides, afraid she'd stop pushing him away and instead pull him toward her to find out.

"That's why you were at the masquerade," he concluded. "Because you've been trying to put a stop to the turnpike?"

"Yes."

"And you knew your brother planned to approach me that night?"

"No," she admitted, her voice exasperatingly breathless. "You were a complete surprise." That was the God's truth. "I thought I was seeing a ghost."

"Me too." He reached up slowly and caressed her cheek. The tender touch rushed liquid heat through her, all the way down to her toes.

"But you *are* real." She forced herself to keep from leaning into his touch, into the comfort and warmth she remembered. "So is Freddie's plan for the turnpike."

"So is the threat to you," he warned gently. "The last thing I want is for any harm to come to you."

If only she could believe that! She wanted to trust in her memories of him, in his assurances now to protect her… But Aaron had made assurances, too, only to destroy her life. She couldn't open herself to wounding like that again by another man. Especially not Pearce. If he did, it would end her.

"I'll only be hurt if the trust goes through." Despite the emotion stinging her eyes, she found enough strength to smile, although shaky. "But with your help, Parliament will never enact it. Freddie can find other appointments to fill, and he can stop selling his influence." The blackmail would stop. They could go on with their lives—

"What your brother is doing is much worse than that," Pearce murmured grimly. He rested his hands against the table on both sides of her, surrounding her but not touching. Yet he made her heart race just as fiercely as if he were. "Howard is working with an organization called Scepter."

She didn't recognize the name. "My brother's involved with lots of organizations."

"Not like this. They're a criminal group with contacts at all levels of society and in all types of crime, from smuggling to prostitution and everything in between. Including murder." He paused to let that wash over her. "What contact have you had with them?"

She gaped at him. "You think that because I was at the masquerade and Le Château Noir that I—" She choked off in surprise, then bit out indignantly, "I have *nothing* to do with any criminal group. I assure you that Freddie doesn't either."

"But he does. So does every man he's helped into an appointment during the past few months. And most likely, so will the men he presents to be trustees for the turnpike. Which is why he wants the trust. Not only because of the money a turnpike will bring in, but because it also gives him three Parliament-approved positions he can fill." His gaze bore into hers. "Your brother is involved with dangerous men, Amelia. Men whom the Home Office believes murdered nearly a dozen government appointees just so your brother could replace them with their own."

"No..." Her fingers clamped hard onto the edge of the table to keep herself from slipping to the floor. Oh God! What on earth had Freddie done? "No, you're wrong," she breathed out. "We've had nothing to do with any murders."

"No. Just with blackmail."

Her stomach fell through the floor. "How—" She swallowed hard to clear the strangling knot from her throat. "How do you know that?"

He ignored her question, countering with one of his own. "Who's being blackmailed, Amelia? Your brother into forcing through the trust, or you into stopping it?"

This time when she shoved at him to push him out of her way, he moved—so quickly she gasped with surprise. He slipped his arms around her waist, lifted her into the air, and set her on the edge of the table, blocking her with his broad body so that she couldn't leave.

"I need answers." He slowly lifted a hand to brush his knuckles across her cheek.

She closed her eyes against the sweet torture of his caress.

"And I need you to trust in me, just like you used to."

A soft sound of frustration rose at the back of her throat. To have an ally in this mess, to have someone to confide in—how perfect if she truly could trust in Pearce—

"Freddie's being blackmailed," she admitted in a rush, and with that confession came a flood of relief. "You're right. He's being forced to place men into government positions, into whatever appointments he can."

Another caress, stroking his thumb over her bottom lip. This time in reward. "By whom?"

She opened her eyes and stared boldly at him. "Why do you care? None of this has anything to do with you."

"More than you realize," he murmured enigmatically. When she opened her mouth to press for answers of her own, he interrupted, "What has your brother done to be blackmailed?"

"I don't know."

"Does it have to do with your lost fortune?"

"No," she whispered, the word barely a sound on her lips.

"Then how did you lose it?"

She couldn't tell him that. Would *never* tell him— "It's not important." But the quaver in her voice easily gave that away for the lie it was.

So did the disbelieving lift of his brow. "A lost fortune, the head of the House Committee of Privileges, a brother who's being black-mailed by a criminal organization into replacing men who have been murdered, a sister who's doing everything she can to protect him... Seems to me that everything about this is important."

Breathe. She forced herself to remain calm, to keep her breath steady and the tremors that gripped her from becoming visible. To keep him from discovering more... *Just breathe!* "Not that."

"One."

She blinked, confused. He was making her head swim! "Pardon?"

"That's your first lie."

Her confusion dulled into quick anger. "How dare you accuse—"

"Two." When her mouth fell open, he drawled, "Now you're lying about lying."

Her mouth snapped shut, and she pushed once more at his shoulders. This time with both hands. She had to leave. *Now.* "We're done with this conversation. I want you to leave. I don't want to see you or talk to yo—"

"Three."

His mouth came down upon hers.

Ten

PEARCE GROANED AT THE BITTERSWEET TASTE OF HER KISS. Sweet Lucifer, he'd forgotten how soft and warm her lips were, how yielding and supple beneath his. The memories came rushing back of the hours spent kissing her when he'd still been nothing more than a green lad, when she'd been eager to learn how to kiss and actually asked him if he minded if she practiced on him.

If he minded… Laughable! What he'd minded was having to stop. Even back then, a dark part of his soul suspected that she would never be completely his. That teaching her that last and most important lesson of intimacy would belong to another man. But he'd selfishly taken whatever else she'd been willing to give, including kisses and caresses that had left her trembling. Just as she was trembling now.

Yet those kisses had been nothing like this.

True, she still tasted of vanilla and sugar, like a decadent dessert just waiting to be devoured. Still tilted back her head to mold her lips perfectly to his. Still ran her hands over his chest as if she couldn't touch him enough to satisfy herself. But now a hesitation tempered the longing inside her, one that held her back when it never would have before.

God help him, but he wanted her to surrender to the moment and let him give her the kind of passionate kiss he'd been longing for since he laid eyes on her at the masquerade. No—since long before that. Since that night twelve years ago when he was forced to leave her behind.

With a growing need to deepen the kiss, his lips teased at hers to coax her to open her mouth and invite him inside.

"Pearce," she whispered, half an entreaty to be given more, half a plea for mercy. But then she did as they both wanted and welcomed his kiss by parting her trembling lips.

Joy surged through him. He cupped her face between his hands and slipped his tongue between her lips in a silken glide. With sweeping plunges and little licks, he slowly explored her mouth in an attempt to rediscover her.

When a soft sigh escaped her, he couldn't resist the urge to take her bottom lip and worry it gently between his teeth.

This time, it wasn't a sigh that came from her but a whimper, one that stirred aching heat in his loins. When she slipped her arms up to encircle his neck and pull him down to her, giving herself over to the old affection and rising yearnings stirring between them, he couldn't stop his own sound of pleasure.

Kissing her felt like coming home.

He moved his mouth away from hers to bury his face in her hair. He breathed in deep the delicious scent of her and drank in the softness and warmth of her body pressed against his. He could barely believe she was real. He slid his hands over her shoulders and down her back, needing to feel her to prove that she wasn't a dream.

But she turned her head away when he leaned in to kiss her again. "You…have to stop." Yet she belied her words by fisting his lapels in her hands as if she were afraid he'd do as she said and vanish like smoke.

He nuzzled his cheek against hers with a smile. "*I* have to stop?" The tip of his tongue darted out to delve into the corner of her mouth and capture the sweetness waiting there, and she bit back a soft mewling of longing. "I think you're a willing party to it."

"Pearce…"

At that plaintive whisper, he relented and shifted back, but he didn't release her. He couldn't. Her hands were still tangled in his jacket front, still keeping him with her. Besides, letting go of her at that moment would have killed him.

"Why stop?" He caressed his thumb entreatingly over her bottom lip. "We used to be quite fond of kissing each other."

"A lifetime ago." Yet she leaned into his touch, like a rose bending toward the sun. "That was all before…"

"Before what?"

"Everything," she whispered, with so much desolation that he ached for her.

Wanting to comfort her, he leaned in to brush his lips in featherlight caresses against hers. For a moment, she capitulated, surrendering to the solace she found in him. She returned his kiss with the same need and longing, slipping her hand up his front, as if to encircle his neck and bring him down even closer—

Suddenly, she tore her mouth away, and the hand at his shoulder pushed hard to move him away. Then her other hand did the same. This time to keep him away.

"Amelia?" he murmured, confused. "What's wrong?"

She turned away from his touch, her eyes squeezing shut. As if she couldn't bear to look at him.

"You need to go," she whispered, her eyelashes glistening wet with unshed tears.

The sight of her grief tore into him like a razor. "What's the matter?" He cupped her face between his hands. But she refused to open her eyes and look at him, her nose and lips both turning dark pink as tears threatened. "Tell me."

"Please—go. I can't…" She shook her head between his hands, her shoulders sinking with distress. "It's too much. I can't…bear it."

Slowly, he dropped his hands away, instinctively knowing not to touch her. "What can I do to help?"

"You can't," she rasped out, her voice bleak. When she opened her eyes, a single tear slipped free, sliding slowly down her cheek. "It's too late."

"It's not. I'll keep you safe, I promise."

She pressed the back of her hand against her mouth like a

shield, as if she were afraid he'd attempt to kiss her again. "It's too late for that, too," she murmured through her fingers.

He stared down at her, helpless to understand and give her the comfort she needed. Did she think he would purposefully hurt her? That he'd changed so much since they last knew each other? No. It was more than that, he could read it on her face—

It was betrayal.

"I told you," he said quietly. "I didn't receive your letters. You can't blame me for that."

"I don't. That's not—I don't blame you," she whispered, as if she knew her voice would crack with emotion if she dared speak any louder. "All those years, I thought about you...wondering how you were, where you were, if you missed me, if you were happy. I never forgot you." Twelve years of anger and anguish overwhelmed her, and a wounded sound tore from the back of her throat. "You were my best friend. I wanted to spend the rest of my life with you."

Her words cut him to the quick, and he could barely breathe out, "So did I."

"But things are different now," she admitted, the words tearing from her. "We can't go back into the past. Do you understand? I *can't*."

"I'm not asking for that."

She whispered, her shoulders slumping, "Now who's lying?"

Slowly, she slipped down from the table, stepped out of his arms, and walked away.

Knowing better than to stop her, he raked his empty hand through his hair, but the gesture did nothing to alleviate his mounting frustration...at her, at himself, at the entire situation—*Christ!*

"I would appreciate it if you didn't try to see me again. If you would just...leave me alone." She swiped her hand at her eyes but refused to look at him, her watery gaze glued to the doorway where she wanted him to go. "There's nothing left between us now."

That was a damned lie. Based on the way she'd kissed him, there was a bonfire left between them.

And he certainly had no plans to leave her alone. Whether she liked it or not, he planned on dogging her every step, if for no other reason than to keep her safe. If Scepter knew she was attempting to stop the turnpike, they'd kill her to stop her interference.

"Please go now." Turning her back to him, she busied her hands with the other silk panel, as if their conversation about murder and blackmail hadn't just happened. As if they hadn't just kissed. But she couldn't hide her shaking. "I think we've said all that needs to be said."

Not by a long shot. But pressing her right now wouldn't garner any more answers. Or forgiveness. She was too upset. Knowing Amelia, she would only dig in deeper.

"All right," he agreed quietly. "I'll go. But we're not finished."

"Actually, we—"

"Not with this conversation." Heated promise laced through his voice. "And certainly not with that kiss."

She wheeled around, surprise lighting her face. And more—a raw yearning he recognized in the depths of her eyes. Because he was certain he wore the same longing for her in his.

He stepped forward and dared a slap by taking one last touch of her cheek. She trembled beneath his fingertips.

"Before we're done, Amelia," he warned, bringing his lips to her temple in a lingering caress, "you'll share all your secrets with me."

Not giving her the chance to say something that both of them might regret—and before he could no longer resist the urge to grab her into his arms and hold her there until all her pain vanished—he turned on his heel and strode from the shop. Every step he took away from her twisted a knife into his gut, but he couldn't stay. Years of warfare had taught him that sometimes the best method of advance was simply waiting for the enemy to retreat on its own.

When she did, he would be waiting for her.

He jogged across the street to his carriage. "Home," he ordered his coachman, then yanked open the door—

Only for a curse to explode from him.

Marcus Braddock, former general with the Coldstream Guards and now Duke of Hampton, waited inside, along with Clayton Elliott. A perfect ambush at the completely wrong time.

"You're fired," he called up to the driver, only for that empty threat to be answered by a grin from the former sergeant. Pearce settled onto the seat across from his two friends and scowled. "What do you want?"

"Told you he wouldn't be happy to see us." Clayton slid a sideways glance at the general and drawled sardonically, "A man doesn't like to be interrupted in his shopping."

Pearce rolled his eyes. He was in no mood for this.

"Something tells me that it wasn't mercantile goods he was interested in." The general leaned across the compartment, plucked the paper poppy out of Pearce's buttonhole, and held it out to him.

Pearce snatched it out of his hand. "Merritt was too busy for you two to bother, so you decided to annoy me?"

"Merritt isn't tracking Miss Howard," Clayton reminded him.

"Neither am I, apparently," Pearce grumbled. Or at least not successfully. She'd given him answers, but not nearly enough of them, leaving him with even more questions than when he'd arrived. And not all of them about Scepter. "Madame Noir was right. Amelia's involved with her brother's blackmail."

"She confirmed that?" Clayton pressed.

He gave a short nod. "Howard's being blackmailed into using his influence to place men into government positions. Which means he's not willingly working with Scepter." Which meant that the amount of information the men of the Armory would be able to gain through Howard about its leaders would be limited. At best.

"And his sister?"

"She's never heard of Scepter, and I believe her." Pearce remembered Amelia's reaction when he'd mentioned them—she didn't know who they were. *That* hadn't been a lie. He'd always been able to tell when she was lying, even as a child, and the blank look on her face proved that she had nothing to do with them. Yet. But if she kept attempting to thwart her brother, he feared she soon would. "She's only involved with the trust to protect Howard."

Marcus Braddock mumbled, "That makes sense. Who else does she have but him?"

Me. But Pearce didn't dare utter that aloud. "Her shop. That's how she got caught up in this mess. As long as Howard's being blackmailed, her charity's under threat." He stole a glance out the window at the storefront. They were still in front of it, the carriage not yet moving, most likely on the general's orders. "She loves this place. She'd protect it like a mother would a child." He grimaced at Amelia's lack of trust in him. "But she also knows more than she's telling."

"Any ideas what, exactly?"

"None. But I'm going to find out."

"Then you'd better hurry," Marcus interjected. "I just came from Westminster. Late yesterday afternoon, Howard introduced a bill to create your turnpike."

"It isn't *my* turnpike," he grumbled, his jaw tightening. But he wasn't surprised that Howard had acted already, and without Pearce's consent. If Amelia was right, her brother was desperate. "The bill's not going anywhere. Parliament dismisses in less than a fortnight. He doesn't have time for it to go through all the steps necessary to be enacted."

"Apparently, he does. The second reading is expected in two days."

"*Two days?*" Surprise rang through Pearce, followed immediately by dread. Amelia had no idea what her brother had done, or how quickly he was moving to push it through. "A bill usually waits two weeks between readings."

"There's not expected to be any debate, so no reason to hold it up. It's only a turnpike trust, after all. We've passed over two dozen of the things just this last month," Marcus muttered. "He's made clear to the other members that he's eager to have it approved and given royal assent before the session ends."

Pearce's chest constricted with a sickening jolt as he remembered the look of betrayal he'd glimpsed on Amelia's face earlier when she spoke about losing Bradenhill. Hearing this news would devastate her.

"He's announced the names of the five trustees," Clayton informed him. "You and himself, of course, along with Sir George Pittens, Mr. James Markham, and Sir Robert Graves."

Pearce scanned the list. "Are we certain they have ties to Scepter?"

"Not yet," Clayton answered. "But we can't take any chances and have to assume they do."

"Do we know anything about their connection to Scepter's leadership?" Frustration filled his voice. Not all of it because of Scepter. "I thought the Home Office was supposed to be good at espionage."

So far, Clayton's men at the Home Office and the Bow Street investigators who teamed with them had turned up next to nothing specific about Scepter and its plans, and what reports they had discovered contradicted each other. It was as if Scepter knew it was being tracked and was purposefully leading a campaign of misinformation and confusion.

"Damnably hard to track down Scepter when we're busy cleaning up Prinny's latest mess," Clayton grumbled defensively, kicking out his long legs. But the casual pose belied the aggravation seething inside him that the Home Office was increasingly playing nursemaid to the Regent these days. "And none of our usual channels have been able to provide anything concrete about who might be leading the group or their motives." His expression turned grim. "Right now, your connection to them through Howard is the best chance we've got."

"So you'll keep after Howard about the turnpike," Marcus said. An order. Not a request.

"Yes, General," Pearce answered, as if they were still in the field with Marcus still their commanding officer. To the men who'd served with him, he always would be.

"And Miss Howard?" Clayton interjected. "Do you think there's any worth in pursuing her?"

Pearce grimaced. Wasn't *that* a damnably ironic question?

"I think," he drawled, "that I won't let her out of my sight."

Eleven

"DO YOU SEE SANDHURST ANYWHERE?" FREDDIE CRANED HIS neck as he led Amelia inside Devonshire House. They handed over his coat and her wrap to the footman waiting at the door, along with their tickets.

"No." But then, she wasn't exactly looking. She only wanted to leave.

She would put in her obligatory appearance in the ballroom on Freddie's arm, then she would feign a terrible malady of some kind or other, helped along if necessary by a vial of a noxious concoction that Maggie had slipped into her hand when she'd finished dressing her. Guaranteed to cause sickness, her maid had assured her.

Although as nervous as she was at the prospect of seeing Pearce again after their earlier encounter, she didn't need any help on that score. She was more than uneasy enough to cast up her accounts all by herself.

"He's been avoiding me," Freddie complained as he led her through the circuit of reception rooms, not to see what entertainments were lined up for tonight but to hunt for Pearce. "I searched for him all afternoon, but he was nowhere to be found." He smiled and nodded at an acquaintance in the crowd. "We're running out of time."

She knew that more than he did.

"You'd better help me with him, Amelia."

"I wouldn't dream of doing otherwise."

He slanted her an assessing look, as if uncertain if she were being sincere.

Around them, the party was already in full swing, proving itself to be the last great event of the season. In only a few days,

Parliament would end, and the *ton* would flee for their country estates, for fresh air and hunting. But tonight they were still in the city, and the cream of society who had been well connected enough to gain tickets were all gathered here, all of them dressed in pure black as required on the invitation.

The Black Ball. An ironic pun on White's selection ritual in which existing members tossed a ball into a bowl in order to vote on new members—a white ball for acceptance, a black one for rejection. It took only a single black ball to deny someone membership. Amelia contemplated the men in the crush around her. How many of them had been rejected by a black ball yet paid dearly to attend tonight, as if never having received that insult?

But not Pearce. Certainly, he had his choice of clubs. As a new earl and a war hero, he'd been welcomed into society with open arms, even if being in their embrace wasn't at all what he'd wanted.

He was here, she could feel it—dressed in black like everyone else, meandering through the house that had been decorated throughout in white. The rooms had been tented in white sailcloth, complete with white silk curtains and sashes draped from windows and white sheets on the floor, and giant bouquets of white roses, daisies, and baby's breath in white porcelain vases were scattered throughout. The terrace doors in every room were opened wide to let the guests drift between the house and the gardens, where white silk sashes hanging from the trees danced on the evening breeze like ghosts. All the servants wore white uniforms as they moved through the party, right down to the men who stood in the drive and directed the long row of carriages winding up to the front door. Among all the white, the guests contrasted starkly in their solid black silks and satins, their pearls and diamonds sparkling beneath the chandeliers.

The whole place looked as if a group of funeral mourners had stumbled into a snowstorm, then decided to linger for drinks and dancing.

"Stay here." Freddie maneuvered her to the side of the ballroom as several dozen pairs of dancers faced off for a quadrille and thrice as many people lined the walls to watch. "I'm going to find the master of ceremonies to learn where the devil Sandhurst is. I'll be back. Don't wander off."

"Why on earth would I do something like that?" Amelia mumbled beneath her breath as he hurried away. With a long-suffering sigh, she turned her head to look across the room—

And straight into Pearce's eyes.

Her breath caught in her throat. *Good heavens.* The man was mesmerizing.

Even in this crowded room, he stood apart with a dashing and dangerous look that was simply captivating. His dark-blond hair shone like gold beneath the chandeliers, his tailored finery accentuating the solidity of his broad shoulders and muscular arms. Unlike the other men at the party who'd dressed in solid black, he'd cheekily chosen a diamond-patterned satin in black-and-white for his waistcoat, daring to break the black-only rule. But of course he would. Even here, amid the gentlemen and peers where he now belonged, he wanted to prove that he was different. Yet hadn't he always stood out from the crowd, regardless of dress?

Little of the boy she once knew was physically visible in the man who now boldly returned her stare. Except for his smile, which curled slowly at his lips and warmed her through.

He rakishly lifted his glass to her in a toast, accompanied by a long perusal over her, from the upswept curls crowning her head to her slippered toes just edging out from beneath her hem. A blatant and sexually predacious look, as if he could see right through her clothes to her naked flesh beneath. And very much enjoyed what he saw.

All the tiny muscles in her belly contracted in a primal response to his presence that came so swiftly, so fiercely that it took her by surprise. So did the pulsating ache that followed on its heels. Under the heat of that brazen stare, she knew— She wanted him. More than she'd ever wanted a man in her life. Not just for physical pleasure, although as she shamelessly let her own gaze travel over him the way he'd done to her, she very much wanted that.

No, she wanted even more. She wanted *him*. In every way. Friend, confidante, hero, lover…

But that simply could never happen.

With his gaze pinned to hers, he lifted a brow. His sensuous lips twisted with private amusement to acknowledge her own lingering look.

Caught. She flushed and turned away, snagging a glass of champagne from the tray of a passing footman so she could lift it to her mouth and cover the expression of embarrassment blossoming on her face.

"You're Miss Howard, aren't you?" A beautiful auburn-haired woman sidled up to her from behind, catching her by surprise.

A second woman flanked her other side. This one younger, with a sprinkling of freckles across her pert nose. "Frederick Howard's sister, correct?"

"We are so pleased to make your acquaintance." The first woman smiled warmly and linked her arm around Amelia's.

Amelia's mouth fell open as she recognized the woman. The new Duchess of Hampton. "Your Grace."

But when Amelia attempted to curtsy, the duchess would have none of it and held firmly to her arm, keeping her straight up. "Please call me Danielle. And this is my sister-in-law, Mrs. Claudia Trousdale."

"A pleasure to meet both of you." Amelia managed to squelch her surprise—and bewilderment—at the way the two ladies had descended upon her.

"You'll forgive us that we forewent the stuffiness of a formal introduction and simply introduced ourselves, won't you?" Claudia pressed.

Introduced themselves? No. They'd *pounced*. There was no other word for it. "Of course. But I don't—"

"We have a friend in common." The young duchess glanced across the ballroom toward Pearce and smiled. "The Earl of Sandhurst."

Ah. Of course. The fog of confusion was beginning to clear. But when Amelia hardened her gaze on him for setting up this sneak attack, he didn't look at all pleased. Downright miffed, in fact. So did the Duke of Hampton standing next to him.

Apparently the two women had taken it upon themselves to approach her.

"I understand that you've known each other for years." Danielle wiggled her gloved fingers at Pearce in greeting. "From before he entered the army."

"We knew each other as children in Birmingham." Yet something told Amelia that the two women already knew that and were here to uncover other, more intimate details. So she threw the conversation back at them. "How do you know Sandhurst?"

"Marcus," both women answered at once. Testimony to how close they were.

"My husband Marcus, Duke of Hampton," Danielle explained. "That's him there at Pearce's side, scowling at us in dark irritation. He's awfully good at it."

Amelia had already lost the course of the conversation. "At being a duke?"

"Heavens no!" She laughed lightly. "At scowling with dark irritation."

"An expert," Claudia agreed. "That's what made him such a good general."

Yes. Amelia had heard about the man. His leadership had been rated second only to Wellington's in the fight against the French. And looking at him now, she had to agree that he certainly possessed an imposing air that would have brooked no resistance when giving orders.

But standing next to Pearce, the man seemed a bit…lacking. Of course, she might have been biased, but Pearce appeared so much more untamed and dangerous, so much more muscular and solid. So much more dashing because of it.

"We're quite fond of Pearce," the duchess commented. "Marcus thinks of him as a brother, in fact."

"So do all the men who served with him in the Coldstream Guards," Claudia interjected. "He's a true war hero, you know. Saved his men's lives on several occasions when all should have been lost. He was a great brigadier."

Amelia raised the glass to her lips to cover the proud smile lingering there. Of course he was. He was born for battle.

"But not so much an earl."

Amelia froze, the flute at her lips, not at all expecting that. "Pardon?"

Even though Danielle's voice lowered so that they wouldn't be overheard by anyone in the crush around them, her concern rang clear. "He's having difficulty adjusting to being a peer."

"Oh?" Amelia couldn't have told that from the way he looked tonight. Just as handsome in his evening finery as the other gentlemen filling the room, his presence just as commanding and confident. As if he'd never belonged anywhere else.

"He's restless." Danielle's pretty brow creased. "He's having trouble with being thrust back into London life. Even being responsible for the earldom isn't enough, not when he has an army of accountants, solicitors, and servants to run it for him." Her frown deepened. "Marcus went through that at first, too, when he was granted the dukedom."

"Yes, but Marcus had you," Claudia reminded the duchess. "You gave him new purpose." An overlong, intentional pause… "Where will Pearce find *his* purpose, do you think?"

With that, the fog vanished. Amelia's mouth twisted. Clearly, the two ladies already had an answer in mind.

"Pearce and I haven't seen each other in years," she clarified. "We're barely friends anymore. What you're suggesting is…" Ludicrous. Preposterous. Outlandish.

Impossible.

A piercing thud jarred along her spine. Amelia raised her glass to her lips, to hide whatever stray emotions might be visible on her face. And her pain.

"Oh, no! We're not suggesting anything of the sort," Danielle protested quickly.

"Nothing at all like that," Claudia agreed. Then another long pause… "But would it be so terrible if we did?"

Amelia choked on her champagne.

"I mean, just look at the man." Claudia gestured at Pearce with her wineglass, not attempting to hide that the three women were obviously talking about him. "He's been captivated by you since the moment you walked into the ballroom."

Amelia's face flushed in embarrassment. How on earth had she gotten into this peculiarly personal conversation with these two women whom she barely knew? "That isn't—"

"He hasn't been able to drag his eyes away from you for a moment." Claudia cast her a knowing look. "And he isn't at all looking at you as someone he once knew as a childhood friend and now holds in fond affection."

"No," she had to agree, with full chagrin, or risk being called out for a liar. "He isn't." He stared at her as if he were a wolf who wanted to devour her. And shamelessly, she very much wanted to let him.

"Now, Claudia," the duchess scolded lightly, "you know we shouldn't play at matchmaking."

Yet something told Amelia that the two women planned on doing exactly that.

"If Miss Howard says they're only acquaintances, then we have to respect that."

Relief surged through Amelia. "Thank you, Your—"

The duchess added beneath her breath, "It doesn't mean we have to like it, however."

Oh bother. Amelia rolled her eyes—

Just in time to see Freddie return to the ballroom in his hunt for Pearce.

"But making certain Pearce has an old friend in town—a *dear* friend," Danielle continued, although Amelia only half paid attention, "well, there's no fault in that, is there?"

"None," Amelia murmured, distracted.

She watched as her brother stopped and scanned his gaze around the ballroom. He knew Pearce was here, and it was only a matter of time until he found him. After all, Pearce wasn't exactly inconspicuous in the crush, towering a good half-foot over the rest of the men. And judging from the resolute expression on Freddie's face, he planned to force Pearce into making a decision about the trust tonight, potentially ruining her plans for delay if he agreed or forcing the blackmailer into going to Varnham if he refused.

Icy dread chilled her. Both outcomes would destroy her.

"And if you two happened to be able to spend more time together—say, at small private outings and dinners—wouldn't that be best for him? And for you?"

Amelia mumbled some sort of preoccupied agreement and caught her breath when Freddie spotted Pearce, then made his way toward him in a beeline. There was nothing she could do to stop him.

"After all," Claudia added, "you two are dear, old friends. There's no harm in two friends spending time together and getting to know each other again. Perhaps walks through the park or carriage rides…"

Amelia winced as Freddie interrupted Pearce's conversation with the Duke of Hampton and another gentleman flanking his other side whom Amelia didn't recognize. Oh, so rude! Made worse by the way he stuck out his hand in eager greeting to Pearce and largely ignored the duke and his friend.

Pearce smiled wryly and shook his hand anyway, letting Freddie's discourtesy pass unacknowledged. But she also noticed that Pearce didn't introduce her brother to his friends.

"…seats in our box at the theatre and Vauxhall…"

"…renting a boat down to Greenwich or up to Hampton Court…"

"Yes! With a picnic…"

Amelia didn't hear the two women, so focused was she on her brother as he gestured toward the door. An invitation to Pearce to converse somewhere more private, and Freddie's opportunity to corner him about the trust.

Pearce nodded his agreement and stepped aside to let Freddie lead the way. Giving his apologies over his shoulder to his friends— and sliding one last parting look at her—Pearce followed after.

"Oh no," Amelia mumbled in dread. Everything was going to be ruined!

The duchess stiffened. "If you don't like the idea of a picnic, then perhaps just dinner at our town house."

Her attention snapped back to the two women, who were both staring at her as if she'd just sprouted a second head. God only knew what she'd agreed to during the conversation, while they'd been plotting out her courtship and she'd been focused on her brother.

"No, that's not—I mean, I enjoy dinners—and picnics—" she stammered, her eyes trailing after the two men. They were leaving, and she needed to know what they were going to discuss, what decisions they would come to about the trust. And somehow find a way to stop them. "It's just—I can't…"

Her Grace's eyes narrowed on Amelia with concern, and she reached a gloved hand toward her arm. "Are you unwell?"

"Yes!" Amelia seized upon the excuse and waved her fan

like mad. "I'm feeling unwell. Too much champagne, I'm afraid. If you'll both excuse me—" As she dipped a curtsy, she threw a glance after the two men. "I need to find the retiring room." They disappeared from the ballroom. "*Now*."

Mumbling a string of apologies, she hurried away, leaving the two women staring curiously after her.

Twelve

"YOU DON'T SEEM TO BE EXCITED ABOUT THE TURNPIKE," Howard commented as the man helped himself to a glass of cognac in the small room where they'd gone to speak privately. The space had once been the Duke of Devonshire's private closet where he could escape when he was forced to be in London rather than in his country gardens. Pearce didn't blame him. He certainly wanted to be anywhere else at that moment.

"I wouldn't say that." What Pearce *would* have said was that had Howard been any other man, he would have given him the set-down he deserved for interrupting his conversation with the general and Merritt Rivers.

But since both men knew why Howard had approached him, Pearce had willingly gone off for a private conversation.

"Then why haven't you fully committed?" Howard eyed Pearce over the rim of his glass as he took a sip, the liquid golden in the lamplight.

"I haven't yet come to a decision."

"Why not?"

Because any decision would destroy your sister... Because I still care about her... Because the look on her face when she told me how much my leaving had devastated her twelve years ago cut me like a knife... Because I never want to see a look of fear, sadness, or betrayal in her eyes ever again...

He shrugged. "It might not be the right investment for my property."

Howard nearly choked on the brandy. He sputtered, "Not the right investment? Are you joking?" He gestured wildly with his glass. "Do you not realize how much money can be made from a turnpike?"

"I've got more than enough money now. I'm not concerned with making more."

Howard's mouth fell open, flabbergasted. He had no idea how to respond to that.

"What I *am* concerned about, however, is your sister." Pearce darted his eyes toward the door and the flash of movement there. "I won't press Amelia into agreeing to the turnpike if she doesn't want it."

"Of course she wants it!" Howard laughed stiltedly, as if that were the most ridiculous thing he'd ever heard. "That land is her only property. Why would she not want to capitalize on it?"

"She has other plans for it."

"That silly idea of hers to build a trade school?" Howard scoffed. "Once she sees how much money a turnpike can generate— money she can then spend on her worthless war widows—she'll be all for it."

His soldier's blood turned to ice. He repeated in a menacingly low voice, "*Worthless* war widows?"

Howard paled instantly, realizing his mistake. Pearce wouldn't have been surprised to see a puddle form at the man's crotch, given the terrified expression that gripped his face. "I didn't mean that the way it sounded."

Pearce crossed his arms and pinned his gaze on him, every bit of the brigadier inside him rising to the surface. "Then exactly how did you mean it?"

"I meant—I meant the war, of course. That the war itself was a terrible waste. Of worth." The words tumbled out so quickly that his tongue tripped over them. "Not the women themselves, you understand."

Pearce said nothing, letting the man stew in his own juices.

"Or the war—good Lord, I'd never say that the war itself was without merit. Never that! But wasteful. A terrible waste of life and resources. So very destructive, and it—"

"I saw thousands of men die during the wars," Pearce finally interjected, reaching his limit with Howard's nonsense. "Some standing right beside me on the battlefield. The best men I've ever met in my life. Brave men, not pompous dandies who think it matters what they wear." His gaze darted to the glass in Howard's now trembling hand. "Or drink. Those men left behind mothers, fathers, wives, and children in order to fight for the Allies, to give their lives for a cause far greater than themselves."

"Of—of course—"

"As far as I'm concerned, we should all be like your sister, giving all that we can to help the families those men left behind. If she wants to turn her land into a school to help them, then I will support her." He paused, making certain that the seriousness of his point sounded loud and clear. "If she wants to do nothing with it at all but let it go wild and fester into weeds, then I will support her in that, too. Understand?"

"Yes—yes, I do." Howard took an ingratiating step forward. "But you should also—"

"I will not force Amelia into handing over her land. If she doesn't agree to the turnpike one hundred percent on her own, then I won't go through with it."

"I assure you that she will agree."

Most likely because Howard would threaten her into it. Or already had. Pretending to her brother to go along with the trust while asking Pearce for his help in stopping it might be the only way she had to directly avoid Howard's wrath yet keep her charity safe.

"If you harm her in any way," Pearce said somberly, the threat clear, "you will regret it."

"I would never harm my sister. I have always had her best interests at heart."

Pearce stared at him silently for a moment, weighing the truth in the man's words. And finding it absent. "You should also know that I hold enough sway in Parliament myself now to make certain that you won't be able to force through the trust on your own."

Howard said nothing, but his eyes narrowed murderously.

Good. Let him be furious, and furious to the point where he decided to throw a punch. Pearce longed for it, in fact, because he would drop Howard to the floor before the man landed a single fist.

"This trust will happen, I assure you." Howard set the glass down, the rest of the cognac unwanted. "Amelia understands what it means for us. As long as we assure her that she'll have the funds to do her charity work, she'll go along with whatever we say. Mark my words."

And pigs flew. Did Howard know his sister at all?

"Can I count on your support, Sandhurst?"

"Ask me again in a few days."

Howard laughed darkly. "I don't have a few days."

"Why not?"

Howard's head jerked up as he realized he'd let slip information he shouldn't have. His panic reminded Pearce of a green soldier surrounded by the enemy on his first sortie.

"Parliament, of course. The session ends in a few days. I've— I've gone ahead and introduced the bill." Frustration shook visibly through him. "Had no choice. There's barely time to escort the bill through debate and voting as it is."

Pearce glanced at the screen near the door, then drawled, "So we put it on hold until the next session."

Howard froze, his face paling. "You might not be in a hurry, Sandhurst, but I have obligations that need to be met. As soon as possible."

In other words, his obligations to the blackmailer.

"I can't wait until next session." He rubbed at his forehead and the headache that was undoubtedly forming behind his eyes. "It has to be now or never."

Never and lose the chance for the men of the Armory to use Howard as a way to find out more about Scepter and its leaders. Now and risk that Amelia wouldn't understand why he was pressing forward with the trust.

Damnation. He was trapped.

"Tomorrow, then," he assured Howard. "I'll give you my answer by noon."

The man's slender shoulders sagged with relief. "You won't be disappointed, I promise you."

"Something tells me you're right." Then he nodded toward the door. "I'll return to the party in a moment." He grinned. "Rumors say that Devonshire keeps a bottle of forty-year-old Kopke port in this closet, and you can't blame an old army officer for ransacking the place to find it."

The joke broke the tension. Somewhat. Howard laughed stiltedly, but Pearce could still sense his desperation.

"Close the door when you leave, will you?"

Howard did as ordered, without another word.

Glad that conversation was over, Pearce leaned back against a side table positioned between the two tall windows, crossed his arms, and kicked one ankle over the other. The pose of a man completely at ease.

Until he called out, "All clear, Amelia. You can come out from hiding now."

She stepped out from behind the paneled screen in the corner near the door and glared at him, hands on hips and chin lifted high into the air, eyes blazing. A fighting stance if ever he'd seen one.

The battle was about to begin.

———

"You agreed to give him an answer by *tomorrow noon*?" Amelia demanded, her hands clenching into fists against her hips. Because if she didn't let anger overtake her, then she'd most likely break down in tears. Already her nose and throat were burning.

"Howard was demanding an answer, and I had to tell him something," he explained calmly. "I bought us more time."

She almost laughed. "Little more than twelve hours!"

"During which I'll have thought of another way to stall him. Besides," he reminded her grimly, "he's already introduced the bill. The wheels have been set in motion, whether we like it or not."

"And the rest of it?" she pressed. "The part about not going ahead with this unless I willingly agree?"

"I meant every word." His blue eyes softened. "I would never betray you."

Her shoulders deflated, the anger slowly easing out of her. She wanted to believe him, so very much…but could she?

"Perhaps it's time that we stop arguing," he suggested, "and start working together."

A ball of heat formed at the base of her spine. "What do you mean?"

He shrugged, and the rakish movement started a liquid burn twisting up her spine, coiling its way through her and replacing all residual traces of her anger with tingling warmth. "You want to save your charity, and we both want to find out who's been blackmailing your brother. Working separately has gotten us nowhere except speeding up the creation of the turnpike trust."

"I know." But *together*… Could she truly do it? Warily, she asked, "What do you propose?"

"A compromise. You tell me everything you know about your brother and his blackmailer."

When he didn't continue with the second half of his terms, she prompted, "How is that a compromise?"

"I didn't say it was a compromise for *me*."

She folded her arms across her bosom and coolly arched a brow.

"But it will work to keep you safe." His eyes twinkled in amusement. "And out from behind screens."

Oh, that devil! Before she could give him the setdown he deserved, he shoved himself away from the table, took her upper arms in his hands, and placed a kiss to her forehead, very effectively silencing her in surprise.

"Wouldn't it be so much better if we were working together rather than at odds?" he murmured against her temple before returning to his perch on the table, in that same raffish pose as before. "Think of all the war widows we could help then."

With a capitulating sigh, she dropped her hands to her sides. The rascal knew exactly how to attack her defenses to get what he wanted. Always had. Apparently, some things never changed.

"All right," she agreed cautiously. "We'll work together. I'll tell you everything I know about the blackmail and what Freddie's been doing with those appointments." She wagged a finger at him. "But in return, you promise not to agree to anything else regarding the turnpike until you talk to me first." She had no choice but to add, "And you'll understand that other parts of my life are out of bounds, that you won't try to pry if I don't tell you everything about them."

"And how is that working together if you keep secrets from me?"

She tossed his words back at him. "I didn't say it was a compromise for *me*."

A slow grin crossed his face at her cheekiness, one that stole her breath away. "All right, I agree. You?"

An excited tingle began to lick at her toes. "Agreed."

When his eyes gleamed into hers with a look that told her that he had completely different ideas of *together* and *compromise* than she did, the tingle turned into a jolt of electricity that shot straight out through the top of her head. Dear heavens, what had she just gotten herself into?

"So all terms have been agreed to and business concluded for the evening, then?" he asked.

"I suppose so. Freddie thinks you'll—"

"Good. Then we can skip from business to pleasure."

She laughed nervously. "I don't believe that was mentioned in any of our negotiations, do you?"

Ignoring her question, he murmured instead, "You are simply stunning."

"Stop that," she scolded. But she also couldn't help the ribbon of pleasure that wrapped around her at his compliment. "We should return to business, then. What you said about the trust—"

"You were beautiful the night of the masquerade. But tonight..." His gaze slowly drifted over her black dress, lingering in places that simmered heat low in her belly. He mused in a tempting purr, "Tonight, you're glowing."

"Stop that," she repeated. This time the scolding emerged as a throaty rasp, lacking all bite. She was certain that she did glow then—with a scarlet flush.

When his gaze slid over her bosom, she could almost feel the solidity of his hand caressing her flesh. "I saw it in you at your shop, how special you've become. Every inch of you confident, strong...glorious."

This time, she couldn't find the breath to say anything at all.

"It's true." He pushed himself away from the table and stalked toward her. "I always thought you were pretty, always knew that you'd grow up to be beautiful." He reached up to stroke her cheek. "But I had no idea exactly how exquisite you would become."

Cupping her face against his palm, he leaned down to kiss her—

"And I had no idea how much of a silver-tongued devil *you'd* become."

He paused, his mouth barely a hairsbreadth from hers and so close that she could feel the heat of his lips tickling hers as they curled into a grin.

"I can show you exactly how much." He followed that wanton challenge with a gentle lick across her bottom lip, a light and teasing caress that elicited a shiver from her. "Would you like that?"

Whatever logical thought had been left inside her scattered like petals on the wind. She made one last, desperate attempt to reclaim them, only for them to fall through her grasp when she curled her fingers into the diamond pattern of his brocade waistcoat. A waistcoat that should have been pure black.

"You broke the rules," she whispered.

"There are no rules for this." He lowered his head and claimed the kiss.

She caught her breath, tensing for a fleeting moment as his mouth found hers. Insistent yet soft, his lips moved against hers in a cajoling plea to surrender to the pleasure of being in his arms.

Unable to stop herself, she did just that. Her hands slipped over his shoulders to encircle his neck and tug herself closer, pressing into his hard front as she melted against him and opened her mouth to his with a soft whimper of capitulation.

Kissing him was utterly divine. Today in her shop hadn't been a fluke. Hadn't been just a trick of her imagination that he kissed as pleasurably as he did. No, it was him and the way he made her feel…feminine and free, special, cherished. As he'd always done. As he was doing now. And God help her, as she knew no other man ever could.

"Pearce," she whispered achingly and turned her mouth away to recapture her breath. But he didn't release her, and the sweet torture of being in his arms began to overwhelm her.

The door handle rattled.

Without warning, he grabbed her around the waist and propelled her behind the screen before she could protest. Then he clamped a hand over her mouth to make certain she didn't when the door opened.

"Be quiet," he urged into her ear from behind her. "You'll be ruined if we're found together."

Breathing hard, she silently nodded.

Two sets of heavy footsteps trod inside the room, accompanied by men's voices. Her heart beat so fiercely that the blood rushing through her ears nearly deafened her, and she took several long seconds to realize that one of the men was Arthur Varnham. Sir Charles's younger brother.

"...saw him coming in here just a few minutes ago," he announced as he crossed the room.

The man who was with him said something that Amelia couldn't quite make out.

"Not for nothing. Cognac."

Another mutter from near the door, this time full of irritation. *Please leave. Please just turn around and go...* The very last thing she needed was to give anyone in the Varnham family more ammunition with which to destroy hers.

"Not that sludge they're serving the guests. *Real* cognac. From the finest French smugglers this side of Ramsgate." His voice grew closer, and Amelia offered up a prayer that they wouldn't be found. "Ha! Devonshire is nothing if not predictable."

She couldn't have missed the derogatory sneer in his voice at that, or the sound of liquid splashing into two glasses, the scrape of boots on the floor moving toward the fireplace, the clank of metal as one of the men picked up the poker and jabbed at the fire to stir up the coals.

Good Lord, they were settling in for the evening! She and Pearce were trapped behind the screen, with no way to escape.

"Are you all right?" he whispered into her ear, barely louder than a breath.

No! But she nodded anyway, only to reassure him. What was one little lie when they would be found at any moment?

"We'll be safe here until they leave." Confident now that she wouldn't cry out and give them away, he removed his hand from her mouth. "They'll finish their drinks soon."

But that assertion did nothing to put her at ease, certainly not when he slipped both arms around her and pulled her against him, her back touching fully along his hard front.

Her heart leapt against her ribs, so hard that she was sure Pearce could feel it. After all, she could certainly feel the pounding of his beating steadily against her own back, just as she felt the hardness of his front against her, the strength of his arms encircling her waist like iron bands. The heat of him soaked into her and turned her insides molten.

She had to put space between them. *Now*. She wiggled in his arms—

He sucked in a mouthful of air and clamped his arm over her hips, forcing her to stand still against him. "*Don't* do that," he rasped into her ear.

"Why not?" she mouthed. His warm breath tickling at her earlobe tumbled a shiver through her. Dear heavens, she needed to move away from him before he realized the wanton sensations his nearness stirred inside her.

In answer, he shifted to bring his pelvis against her. She caught her breath. He wasn't fully aroused, but the hardening bulge pressing into her bottom was unmistakable.

"I'm sorry," she murmured.

"I'm not. After all, if I'm going to be caught, then…" He followed that whisper with a soft suck to her earlobe that pulled through her, all the way down between her legs.

Oh, this was dangerous. So very, *very* dangerous! To be pressed against him like this again, after all these years—

No. This was *nothing* like before when she was a girl and he'd sneaked into her bedroom for long talks into the night, for stolen kisses and embraces. His shoulders were broader than before, his arms more muscular and strong. She bit back a groan. Good Lord, his abdomen was just as hard as his chest! Before, he'd been on the cusp of manhood, still a bit lanky and too full of energy to control himself completely when he was with her. But this—

His hands rubbed deliberately over her hips in a slow caress that burned through her like wildfire. *This* was pure control.

He spread his long fingers wide as he swept them down her thighs and back up to her waist. One scandalously rested against her lower belly, while the other moved slowly upward to place featherlight caresses against the top swells of her breasts above her neckline. So gentle and soft… When he placed a kiss to her temple, the tenderness of it made her shiver.

Less than a dozen feet away, the two men continued to drink and talk, their conversation punctuated by laughter. But Amelia heard none of it. At that moment, her entire world was nothing more than the wonderful circle of Pearce's arms.

His mouth returned to her ear, and the tip of his tongue circled slowly around its outer curl before plunging inside in a swirling lick that twisted all the tiny muscles in her belly into a roiling knot. Right beneath where his left hand rested. The same hand that now started to move in slow circles against her lower abdomen and created an ache between her legs that pulsed in time to his heartbeat throbbing against her back.

When they'd been younger, kissing him had been fun. And forbidden. And even more fun because of that. It had been nice.

But now, of all the sensations he churned inside her, *niceness* wasn't one of them.

"Pearce—"

"Shh," he whispered. "They'll hear you."

She bit her lip. If he kept touching her like this, they'd definitely hear her, when a whimper of longing tore from her.

He moved his hands expertly over her body now, as if attempting to know her again as he once had, to discover the woman she'd become.

She clamped her arms to her sides, fighting back the rising desire to surrender to the past. How easy it would be to give over and let herself indulge in the pleasures he could give, even small ones, even here, trapped behind the screen. This embrace didn't have to lead to anything more—*couldn't*, in fact. They'd missed their chance.

But at this moment, she could allow herself a small bit of pleasure, a reminder of what they could have shared had life not interfered. She could pretend that he still belonged to her.

With a sigh of surrender, she closed her eyes and rolled back her head, her fists relaxing at her sides as she let herself go.

"Yes," she breathed out her permission.

He kissed the side of her neck in an openmouthed caress that sent her spinning. The tip of his tongue flicked against her spiking pulse, and he smiled against her throat at discovering the effect he had on her. Oh, that arrogant devil…that dashing and bold man who now had her trembling as he slid his mouth down her neck to the slope of her shoulder. Who had her foolishly longing for more than these few stolen touches.

When his hand slipped down to cup the fullness of her breast, her nipple tightened into an aching point despite the thickness of the stays that dulled his touch against her sensitive flesh. They'd done far more than this that last summer they were together, but his touch had never felt like this…so pleasing, so confident.

His fingers slipped beneath her neckline to caress her bare breast—

She gasped. So sure of what *she* wanted from him.

Still leaving hot kisses against the side of her neck, he began to tease at her nipple. His wickedly skilled fingers alternated between tender caresses and hard pinches that had her arching her back against him to bring her breast harder against his hand, that had her panting in soft, shuddering little breaths.

She wanted this. And more—she wanted to turn back time and make the last decade vanish, to claim back all those years she'd lost with him. The moment poured over her like a warm summer rain, and she simply couldn't deny herself.

So she took his hand, laced her fingers through his, and slowly slid it down her front. Only a moment's hesitation at her lower belly where butterflies somersaulted beneath the warmth of his palm… then deliberately lower between her legs. Lifting her skirt with her other hand, she guided him beneath to that aching place at her core.

He tensed against her, then breathed out a jerking sigh, as if he couldn't believe that she wanted this intimate caress. *With every ounce of my being.* She slowly moved his hand against her in a gesture of silent permission.

"Amelia," he breathed into her ear, then began to stroke her.

She couldn't stop the shudder of pleasure that swept through her as he teased at her folds, now growing damp and hot beneath his fingertips. Pearce was the only man who had ever touched her like this. That last summer, the month before she turned sixteen— the first time he'd dared to slip his hand beneath her skirt. His fingers had trembled against her then, too, the way they did now. But then the cause had been the eager excitement of a green lad being granted a fleeting and forbidden pleasure. Yet now he trembled from something far more intense. So did she.

Without warning, he froze. His hand stilled between her legs while the other darted up to cover her mouth.

"Shh," he whispered, that soft warning flashing her attention back to the two men in the room with them.

Forcing her pleasure-fogged brain to function, she held her breath and listened. The soft clink of glasses being set aside, the creak of furniture as the two men rose to their feet, the scuffle of boots—

They were leaving. *Finally.* But the relief that sped through her was punctuated by a spike of disappointment when Pearce slipped his hand away from her and let her skirt fall down into place.

The door closed shut with a soft click.

Sanity rushed through her. What she'd been about to do—oh, she simply couldn't! It was all too late for them. For this—

"Let go," she forced out, moving to twist herself out of his arms.

"Amelia—"

"Let me go!"

Immediately, he released her, and she dove out from behind the screen.

Panting hard to catch back the breath he'd stolen, she stumbled backward, putting the distance of the room between them... because she wanted nothing more than to remain right there in his arms. Oh, even closer than that! She wanted him inside her. And that was the one thing she absolutely could *not* allow.

He stepped out from behind the screen, slowly, as if she were a doe he didn't want to startle. "What's wrong?"

Everything. Simply *everything*! "I-I can't—I'm sorry. I thought I could, but..." She pressed her hand against her forehead and breathed deeply to calm herself. But it wasn't working. Especially when he so rakishly leaned a hip against the writing table and waited patiently for her to explain. Although to explain... A dark laugh strangled in her throat. How could she *ever* explain this part of her life to him? "I can't do this."

"But you want to," he challenged quietly in a velvety voice that wrapped itself invitingly around her like a warm cloak on a winter's night. "Why not take what you want?"

The dark temptation of that ached into her limbs and made her breasts grow heavy, knowing he would give her every pleasure her foolish body craved. But that's all it would be, all it could ever be—only physical, only temporary.

She could never belong to him, not completely. Parting with him when they were younger had been agonizing. If she gave herself over to him now, to love and be loved in return, leaving him this time would be so much worse.

It would *end* her.

Mistaking her hesitation for uncertainly, he slowly approached her and slipped his arms around her to draw her against him, then leaned down to kiss—

"No," she whispered, her hand pressing at his shoulder to keep him away.

He stilled, then slowly pulled back until he could stare down at her. The raw yearning she saw in him stole her breath away.

Her heart tore. To surrender and accept the joy that being with him would surely bring—she wanted nothing more. *Nothing* more!

Yet she somehow found the strength to whisper, "I can't—*we* can't." A fierce stinging filled her eyes, blurring his face behind her gathering tears. *Thank God.* Because she couldn't have borne seeing his expression when she breathed out, "It's too late for us."

Thirteen

Amelia hurried back to the ballroom, pushing her way through the crush in her desperation to find her brother. To put an end to all of this. To banish Pearce back into the past where he belonged—

"Frederick!"

She spotted him in the crowd, surrounded by a handful of gentlemen he knew from Parliament. Her blood turned cold. She knew that even now he was pushing for the turnpike, even now using his influence for his own gain.

When she reached him, she inhaled hard for both air and courage. "I need to talk to you." She eyed the men around them and rested her hand on his arm. "Privately."

"Not now, Amelia." He pulled his arm away, then tugged at his jacket sleeves as if her touch had soiled him. "I am in the middle of a conversation."

"This cannot wait."

"It *can* wait, and it will." He jerked his head toward the refreshments. "Go drink a glass of punch and calm yourself. I'll find you later."

The men chuckled at how he'd dismissed her. As if she were nothing more than a child who needed to be scolded by her guardian.

But she wouldn't tolerate it. Not this time. "I will not assist you with pushing through your trust." She took a deep breath and announced, "If you want this turnpike, you'll have to do it without my help."

That made their laughter choke in their throats. Their eyes darted to Freddie for explanation, but he only glared at her, his face instantly red with anger and humiliation.

As she spun on her heel to leave, he grabbed her arm and hauled her to the side of the room, garnering surprised stares from the men and bewildered looks from the other guests.

"What the hell do you think you're doing?" he seethed, so angry that he shook. "I need those men to speed the act through before Parliament ends. If they think you're not behind it—" He forced out through gritted teeth, "For God's sake, the blackmailer will destroy everything, don't you understand? *Everything!*"

"You mean that he will destroy your corrupt career," she shot back, keeping her voice low enough not to be overhead. But anyone in the crowd with eyes could have seen they were arguing. "Not me or my charity—you've never once cared about how the blackmailer could destroy my shop and ruin the lives of all the women who work for me. All you care about is yourself, your own career, your own gain. And you've committed all kinds of illegal activities because of that."

"You don't know—"

"I *know*!" she hissed out in a whisper so she wouldn't be overheard. "All the lying and cheating, the political favors... God only knows what other things you've done that I don't know about. It all ends now. *Now*, Frederick."

There would be hell to pay once the ball was over and they were home, where he could berate her openly, take away what little allowance he gave her, once again threaten her shop—

But she simply couldn't go on this way. God help her, but she'd rather endure Freddie's wrath than Pearce's affections. The anguish would be less.

"If you push on with this trust, then you'll do it without my help in persuading Pearce." She choked as her throat tightened. "I'm done with your games. All of them."

His hand tightened on her arm, and his face twisted with outrage. "Why, you ungrateful, ruined piece of—"

"Miss Howard!"

The Duchess of Hampton appeared at her side, all smiles and flitting fan, but Amelia could sense the underlying tension in her. And the concern.

"I've been looking for you everywhere. And here you are." Danielle's gaze dropped icily to Freddie's hand as he gripped Amelia's arm, and she muttered, "With your caring brother."

With a smile, Danielle slid her arm around Amelia's and gently took it away from Freddie, who had no choice but to release her unless he wanted to create a scene, one involving a duchess no less. But he was livid at being interrupted. Amelia could see it in the way his lips nearly snarled like a dog's.

"You hurried off so quickly before we had the chance to finish our conversation." Danielle turned her attention to Freddie and smiled tightly. "I wanted to invite your sister to Charlton House for dinner next week. Of course, Mr. Howard, we would expect you to escort her."

He straightened at the offer of dinner with a duke. "Of course, Your Grace, I'd be honored—"

"Do you know my husband, Mr. Howard?" She dismissively waved a gloved hand at herself, for foolishly asking that question. "But of course you do. It seems my husband knows everyone from being a general at Waterloo and now as a duke. Simply *everyone*." Her eyes fixed coldly on Freddie. "Given that he seems to know everyone and has a great deal of influence over Parliament and the Regent—and given that *I* have a great deal of influence over my husband—" She laughed, but the warning she was delivering was clear as glass. "I would hate to be one of those men foolish enough to displease either of us." Her smile faded. "Wouldn't you agree, Mr. Howard?"

He paled as he realized the true meaning behind the duchess's invitation. To put him in his place.

"Yes, Your Grace," he returned stiffly. Her point had struck home like an arrow.

The duchess no longer bothered with polite pretense. "Your sister is obviously unwell, and whatever conversation you two were having seems only to have distressed her further." She placed a second hand on Amelia's arm in a private suggestion that she remain silent. But Amelia wouldn't have dreamed of stopping her now. The woman was a force of nature. "I'll see to her care this evening, and the Duke and I will make certain she arrives home safely."

"Your concern is appreciated, but you needn't trouble yourself. I can attend to Amelia and—"

"Absolutely not." The hard look Danielle shot him brooked no argument.

Amelia stared at her, blinking. Good heavens, who needed her husband's army to come to the rescue when the duchess was as capable as this on her own?

Danielle forced a smile that left her eyes cold. "I see no reason for you to leave the party early. I think you should spend the rest of the evening here enjoying yourself. *All* evening." Her voice was soft, but the order to stay away from Amelia tonight was hard as stone. "Don't you?"

Without waiting for an answer, the duchess turned Amelia around and led her away through the throng of people.

"Are you all right?" Danielle squeezed her arm. "When I saw how he'd grabbed you like that—"

"I'm fine, truly." *Now.* She'd come to several realizations this evening, not the least of which was how much she admired Danielle Braddock.

"If he strikes you once you're home—"

"He won't." No, her brother had other means of punishing her. "He's mostly bluster."

Nevertheless, she persisted, "If he does, you have friends in Marcus and me." She paused. "And in Pearce. Please remember that."

Amelia looked away before Danielle could see the emotion darkening her face. It wasn't a friendship with Pearce that worried her. "I think…I should just like to go home, if you don't mind."

"Is someone there to take care of you?"

In other words, someone to come between her and Frederick. "Yes. I have a maid I trust."

"And do you trust me enough to tell me what you and your brother were arguing about?"

"Turnpikes," she admitted with chagrin. "And how I want no part of them."

"I see."

No, she didn't. She couldn't possibly. Yet Amelia appreciated the duchess at that moment more than she could ever have said. "Thank you for what you did."

"It was nothing." Danielle slipped her a sly smile. "Helping women escape trouble is a specialty of mine."

Before Amelia could decipher what she meant by that, they'd reached the front hall, and Danielle gave orders to one footman to send for a carriage and to a second to fetch Amelia's wrap. Both men jumped into action. Moments later, the first man reappeared to escort her to the carriage.

Danielle glanced out the door at the hackney and frowned. "Perhaps we should have one of Devonshire's maids accompany you."

"I'll be fine," Amelia assured her.

The duchess's gaze softened grimly on her. "Will you, truly?"

So much more meaning lay behind that quiet question, and it wrenched at Amelia. "I can't tell you what's wrong. I wish I could, but…" Choking off, she shook her head.

"Then tell Pearce." She took both of Amelia's hands in hers and squeezed them reassuringly. "He'll keep you safe. You can trust him."

She might be able to trust him, but she couldn't trust herself when she was around him.

Amelia slipped on her cloak and left the house. The footman

helped her into the carriage and closed the door. Then the old rig rolled away, down the semicircular drive and out into the street.

As the wheels turned from one street to another, taking her further away from the party and closer to home, Amelia closed her eyes and rested her head back against the squabs. Oh, how she wished she could vanish into the night, like a ghost into the fog—

Without warning, the carriage jerked roughly. The team darted wildly to the side of the street with a clatter of hooves against the pavement, throwing her against the compartment wall. They strained against their harnesses as they tried to break loose from the driver and run, and the carriage tossed violently from side to side behind them.

Grasping the seat edge to keep from being tossed to the floor, Amelia tried to look out the window but could see nothing in the darkness. The carriage halted with a jolt just as she heard men's shouts rise in anger and echo down the dark street.

A loud thump hit the side of the carriage, and she gasped, ducking down in the compartment. *Good God, what on earth—*

A gunshot split the night.

The carriage door was yanked opened. A gloved hand reached in for her. She screamed—

"Amelia, it's me!"

Pearce. The scream on her lips turned into a cry of relief. But from the street outside she could still hear shouts and the noise of fighting. All hell had broken loose around them. "What's happening? Is it a riot?"

"Come on!" He grabbed her around the waist and swung her down to the ground, then took her hand and pulled her away from the carriage before she had time to catch her breath.

She stumbled beside him to keep up with his long strides as he raced with her down the dark street. Their footsteps pounded over the pavement, ringing as loudly in her ears as her pulse. No—not their steps, but those of others.

Her breath choked with fear as she glanced over her shoulder. They were being chased!

Pearce's hand locked with hers, and he darted into the service yard behind the nearest house, pulling her along with him. Amelia sprinted to keep pace with him, terrified of being left behind. And just as frightened of the two men who were pursuing them across the service yard.

When they reached the small stone wall that lined the rear alley, Pearce grabbed her around the waist and threw her over it. She landed on her feet with a jarring thud. He scrambled over after her.

"Are you all right?" he demanded.

She gave a jerking nod. "Yes, but—"

"This way!"

He seized her hand and ran with her down the alley, not giving her time to catch her breath. She didn't dare glance back over her shoulder now. But she heard the two men's pounding steps behind them, closing the distance—

Her toe caught on a bump, and she fell. Her hands and knees slammed into the stones, and she cried out in pain.

"Amelia!" Pearce was immediately at her side, his arm around her shoulders and lifting her to her feet.

Too late. The men had caught them.

"Halt where you are!" the taller of the two men shouted as they slowed to a stop in the alley less than ten feet away. They were breathing hard from the chase, their hands drawn into fists. The taller one pointed at Amelia and told Pearce, "We only want the woman. Hand her over, and no harm will come to you."

"The hell I will." Pearce moved her behind him to shield her. His gaze darted between the two men, and every muscle in his body tensed. Alertness coiled inside him, ready to spring. "Go away, and no harm will come to *you*."

The two men laughed and started forward.

"Run!" Pearce ordered Amelia, then stepped forward to meet the attack.

As the shorter man charged toward him, Pearce hauled back his arm and swung. His fist landed with a sickening thud in the man's stomach. The attacker doubled over as a whoosh of air poured from him with such force that the sound echoed off the stone walls.

But the taller man was quicker. When Pearce swung, he ducked, dodging the blow and countering with one of his own. His fist caught Pearce on the chin. Pearce staggered back a step, then recovered his balance and let his right fist fly, followed immediately by a cross punch from his left.

As he beat the man back, the first man recovered his breath and staggered up from behind.

"Look out!" Amelia cried as the man swung and landed a lucky blow to the side of Pearce's head.

Pearce dropped his shoulder as he spun in a circle, throwing a punch into the first man's face with his right fist and into the second's stomach with his left. The sound of bare knuckles thudded sickeningly with each punch, along with groans of exertion at each flinging swing.

One last jab, and the tall man crumpled to the muddy ground. This time, he couldn't find the strength to climb to his feet and stayed down on his hands and knees. Blood lay splattered across the alley around him.

The other man leaned against the stone wall, a trail of blood trickling from the corner of his mouth as he fought hard to catch his breath and pant down the pain. He glared murderously at Pearce, but he was smart enough to stay back.

Pearce kept his fists clenched, his eyes on the two men, as he slowly moved down the alley to Amelia.

He swiped a trickle of blood from the corner his mouth with the back of his hand. "I told you to run."

She took his hand and laced her fingers through his. "I'm not leaving you."

That stopped him cold for a moment, and his expression softened with relief in the darkness. He bent down to touch his lips to hers—

"They went into the alley!"

Pearce stopped, his mouth hovering just above hers. Biting back a curse, he broke into a run again, once more pulling her along with him.

As they raced through the rabbit warren of streets lying between St James's Square and the river, she could hear men pursuing them, but thankfully, she and Pearce were too far ahead to be seen. In the dark shadows that grew thicker the closer they came to the riverbank and the wharves built up along every inch of it, they were practically invisible. Yet the men remained always behind, like a pursuing pack of dogs nipping at their heels.

They reached the river. Pearce halted at the top of the embankment to glance over his shoulder. She followed his gaze. Three men wearing all black hurried down the street toward them.

Biting back a curse, he led her down to the water's edge. "This way!"

She followed trustingly, staying close at his side as he rushed her down a set of stone steps to the black river below.

A boat waited at the bottom of the stairs, its waterman sitting back in the bow, half-asleep. The man jerked up with a start.

"Downstream," Pearce ordered, helping her quickly into the boat. "*Now*."

Without waiting for the waterman, Pearce yanked the rope loose from its tie and shoved off, pushing the skiff away from the stairs and into the river's fast current. But not quickly enough. The three men reached the top of the steps and hesitated only a moment before scrambling to find another boat.

"Go!" Pearce shouted.

"Aye, guv'nor!" the waterman returned as he took up the oars and rowed them out into the river.

In the darkness, Amelia could just make out the three men as they jumped into a boat and pushed off in pursuit. She clutched at Pearce's hand. "They're coming after us!" Panic rose in her voice. "They'll catch us!"

"No, they won't." He tucked her into the hollow between his arm and his side, then turned to the waterman. "Shoot the bridge."

"At night, comin' on t' high tide?" The waterman paused in his rowing. "Yer fuckin' mad!"

"I'll pay you a sovereign when we come out the other side."

"*If* we come out, ye mean. But it's yer death." The man shot a troubled glance at Amelia and muttered, "Hope the lass can swim."

But the waterman rowed harder now, putting his back into each deep stroke of the oars as he steered them around the hulks and ships anchored in the middle of the swift river, speeding them downstream toward London Bridge.

Fourteen

"Can you still swim?" Pearce asked her.

Amelia stared at the dark bridge as it rapidly grew closer, her hands clutching the side of the narrow skiff so tightly that Pearce could almost see her white knuckles in the darkness.

"Amelia." He took her chin and made her tear her eyes away from the river to look at him. Terror gleamed in their depths. "I taught you to swim when we were children. Can you still do it?"

She nodded jerkily. "I–I think so."

That answer didn't instill confidence in him. So he grabbed up her skirt and ripped it with his hands, tearing off a strip of fabric about six inches wide, all the way around her hem.

She gasped in surprise but thankfully didn't try to stop him. "What are you *doing*?"

He tied one end of the black cloth around his wrist as tightly as he could. Then he dipped it into the inch of water lining the bottom of the boat and yanked on it again to fuse the knot.

"Tying us together," he answered. He grabbed her hand, and in seconds, he'd tied the other end of the cloth strip around her wrist. "This way we won't be separated if the boat overturns."

Or smashed to bits against the stone starlings. Pearce couldn't bring himself to utter that aloud. He was putting their lives at risk, he knew that. But he wouldn't let those men catch her. If they did, she'd be dead for certain. He was gambling that they would make it through the churning water beneath the bridge and that the men chasing after them wouldn't dare follow.

Wide-eyed and stunned into silence, Amelia glanced between him and her tied wrist as she held it up in front of her. She flexed and unflexed her fist, as if she couldn't believe the tie was real.

The bridge loomed closer. Pearce cupped her face between his hands to make certain she was paying attention. "If we turn over, we'll swim to the north bank, understand? Don't fight the current. Let it sweep us downriver, and we'll use it to make our way to the quayside. There are all kinds of ladders and steps there that we can use to climb out. All right?"

But when she nodded, the hard swallow he felt undulate down her throat told him that she wasn't all right. Not at all.

"I'll be with you at every stroke you swim." He rested his forehead against hers. "Just like we did in the River Tame, remember? That summer when I showed you how to swim? I knew someday that you'd need to know how. This is why I taught you."

"No, you taught me because when the water soaked through my clothes, it plastered them to my skin. Everywhere." She bravely forced a weak smile. "I saw how you looked at me. It wasn't because you wanted to teach me to swim."

True enough. He flashed her a rakish grin. "Why do you think I tied us together tonight? So I get first glimpse of you all wet."

But his teasing did little to alleviate her growing fear or stop her shaking.

The bridge was coming on quickly, now less than a hundred yards away.

"Sit in the bottom of the boat." He helped her off the wooden seat and down against the hull. She flinched at the cold water soaking into her stockings and skirt. Before this was all over, though, at the very least she'd be drenched. "And hang on tight."

He sat on the seat behind her and wrapped his legs around her waist to hold her down in the boat.

The man nodded knowingly at Pearce's preparations. "Ye've shot the bridge before, then?"

"No," he answered, keeping his gaze straight ahead at the oncoming starlings and the swirling water funneling through them. His hands tightened their grip on the sides of the narrow boat. "Just charged French cannon at Waterloo."

The waterman put one oar into the skiff and lifted the other from its pin to drag it behind the rear of the speeding boat like a rudder. He turned the oar and pointed the boat toward the center arch, lining it up right between the stone piers.

"There will be rapids when we reach the arches, and a drop of several feet when we come out the other side," Pearce warned her as the bridge sped toward them. "But hang on tight to the boat, and everything will be fine." *Ten, nine, eight...* They barreled at top speed toward the stone starlings. "I'll protect you." *Five, four, three...* "I'll *always* protect you."

She glanced back at him. Only for a moment, but in that pause, he felt the unbreakable connection between them. It was still there, even after twelve years apart, as tangible as the strip of cloth now binding them together.

The skiff hit the rapids beneath the arch and dropped, slamming against the river's churning surface.

Amelia screamed as the tumbling water tossed them ferociously. The skiff rose and fell like a bucking horse. Each plunge lifted them several inches from their seats, only to be slammed down when the hull slapped onto the surface. Water splashed over the sides in great ice-cold waves that drenched them through to their skin. They floated helplessly, tossed by the tide and churning black water like a leaf in a gale.

"Look out!" the waterman shouted as the skiff spun off course and smacked into the stone starling. *Crack!* The boat bounced away, shoved back into the tide by the racing current.

The waterman put his full weight against the oar with a screaming groan of exertion that pointed the boat back toward the middle of the arch.

"Hang on!" Pearce yelled, tightening his legs around her like a vise.

Propelled by the tidal current, the boat shot out from beneath the arch. The little bow plunged away as the skiff dropped over the six-foot-high waterfall created by the water rushing through the narrow arches. For a breathless moment, they were suspended in the air. Then the boat slammed onto the water, throwing them so hard that Amelia nearly bounced out of the boat and the waterman tumbled down into the bottom behind Pearce. The swirling eddies caught the skiff and sent it whirling toward the bank.

Pearce grabbed the spare oar and shoved it into the water to stop the spinning. His back muscles strained as he dragged the paddle deep into the rushing current to pull them back straight and pointed downriver.

"I got 'er!" The waterman took the oar from Pearce and regained his seat. A few expert strokes had them headed smoothly for the north bank.

Amelia lay on the bottom of the boat, still gripping the sides for dear life and shuddering in the layer of cold river water sloshing around her.

Pearce gently lifted her onto the seat next to him. He pulled her against him, cradling her in his arms. She clung to him as she fought to gain back the breath that the wild ride had stripped from her.

"It's all right," he murmured reassuringly. She buried her face against his shoulder but never sobbed with fear the way any other Mayfair lady would have. Not his Amelia. She was far too brave for that. "We're safe now."

She nodded against his waistcoat, her hands clutching at his lapels.

"Congratulations, Amelia Howard." He smiled against her wet hair. "You just shot London Bridge and lived to tell about it."

"Barely," she rasped out hoarsely.

Despite her attempt at humor, concern tightened his chest. He glanced behind them at the bridge and the black, churning water beneath.

They'd lost the men who were chasing them. *Thank God.* But those men were also smart enough to know that the waterman would have to pull up onto one of the steps just past the bridge. The men might still come looking for them tonight. And Pearce needed to have Amelia well out of sight if they did.

"Take us to the Pelican Steps," Pearce ordered the waterman, who had fully regained control of the boat and was using the tide to his advantage now rather than fighting it.

"Aye, sir."

As Pearce worked loose the strip of her hem that tied them together, the waterman guided the boat gradually toward the north bank as they drifted downstream, following the current as the river turned gently at Wapping and curved away toward Greenwich on the opposite bank. Slowly, he guided them across the dark ribbon of water to the set of stone stairs tucked up beside the old Prospect of Whitby tavern.

The boat smoothly slid to a stop at the stone steps, and the waterman grabbed for the piling post to hold the boat in place while Pearce carefully helped Amelia onto the small landing, then climbed out after her. Pools of water formed beneath their feet from their soaked clothes. Amelia wrapped her arms around herself, unable to stop her shivering as the unseasonably cold air engulfed them and chilled them through to the bone.

Pearce knelt down to hand the waterman his promised sovereign.

"Thank ye, sir." The man shook his head. "Wish I could say I enjoyed th' fare."

Pearce held up a second coin. "You didn't see us, and you didn't shoot the bridge. You've been working this side of the bridge all night because you'd heard there was a boxing match set for midnight in the old warehouse on High Street. You know the one I mean." He placed the coin onto the man's palm, which was callused like a piece of leather from years spent working the oars. "Understand?"

"What bridge?" the waterman asked dryly, slipping the coins into the inside breast pocket of his jacket. "Been workin' Wapping all night. Gave no ride to no gentleman an' his lady friend."

Pearce slapped the piling post as he pulled back up to his full height. "My gratitude to you."

"Waterloo, huh?" The waterman shoved the boat away from the steps. "My gratitude to *you*, sir." He gave a small salute. Then he was gone, slipping away into the darkness of the river.

Pearce took Amelia's arm and felt her shivering violently. Guilt gripped him. He needed to get her warm and dry before she froze.

He led her carefully up the steep steps that lined the stone wall of the Prospect of Whitby and toward the street. The old tavern had perched here above the river for three hundred years if the stories the tavern keeper and bar wenches liked to tell were true. Although tonight, judging from the noise coming from inside and the lamplight spilling out through the wide rows of windows, the man and his maids were too busy to tell any tales at all. *Good.* Exactly what Pearce had hoped for. The best place to be lost was in a crowd.

"Your *lady friend*?" Amelia repeated through chattering teeth with a backward glance at the river. "He thinks that I'm—" She lowered her voice despite no one else being in sight. "That I'm your lover."

"Not exactly."

"Oh?" She let him help her over the last step and onto the narrow road above. The welcomed gravel of solid ground crunched beneath their feet, but he didn't ease his hold on her arm. He didn't trust that they were yet safe.

"He thinks you're a prostitute I've hired for the evening."

"He's thinks I'm a—" Amelia halted, coming to a dead stop in midstep. Her mouth fell open as she stared at him. "You didn't correct him!"

"With what, the truth?" Pearce led her toward the tavern's front door. "That we were being chased because your corrupt brother is involved with a criminal organization?"

Her shoulders sagged, and she muttered, "When you put it like that, perhaps the truth isn't such a good idea."

With a grin, he opened the door to the tavern and guided her inside with a hand to the small of her back.

Amelia froze in the doorway as every pair of eyes in the crowded room turned toward them, then raked over her, down her ruined gown and wet hair to her sopping slippers. The room exploded in a series of whistles, lewd cheers, and shouts.

She spun around to flee—

Pearce's hand clamped over her wrist, keeping her in place.

Despite the icy-cold water that dripped onto the floor around her feet, her face flushed with heated embarrassment. "I've changed my mind. I'd rather face the truth."

Pearce arched a brow. "That you're the unmarried sister of an MP who stumbled into a Wapping riverside tavern after midnight with a former soldier?"

"Stop making the truth sound like that!"

He slid her a sideways glance. "You mean like the truth?"

The glare she gave him was murderous.

"We don't have a choice. We have to get off the streets so we won't be seen, and you're freezing cold. This is the best place to—"

She yanked her arm away and spun on her heel.

Oh no. That little hellcat was going nowhere!

He grabbed her around the waist, lifted her off her feet, and tossed her over his shoulder like a sack of grain. He carried her inside the tavern and through the crowded room, where the men nearly fell over themselves with laughter. Fists pounded in amusement on the tables, so hard that tankards of ale and pewter plates bounced on the planks.

Startled, Amelia gave a gasping cry. "Put me down!"

"No."

"This instant!" She began to kick her legs and hit her tiny fists against him as she dangled down his back.

"Stop that." Pearce slapped her bottom to make her behave, which sent up a new round of laughs from the crowd, and carried her across the room to the bar that guarded the stairs leading to the rooms above. "A private room, if you please."

The barkeeper tossed him a key. Pearce caught it in one hand and slapped her on the bottom with the other when she started to kick again.

"Send a messenger boy up to the room immediately," he ordered. Then he fell easily into the local East End city cant he'd come to know since he'd begun to haunt the Tower Hamlets by adding, "Hot splash and good, plenty of both. Toss in a gold watch."

"Aye." Not bothering to hide his laughter at the sight the two of them made, the barkeeper gestured for the bar wenches to jump to it and fetch what Pearce had ordered.

He carried her up the stairs, ignoring the slaps of her hands against his buttocks and clamping an arm around her legs to keep her from kicking him in the stomach. But a well-placed elbow to his left kidney caught him off guard.

"Damnation, woman! Stop that."

"Then put me down!"

"Very well," he muttered, kicking open the door. He strode inside and tossed her onto the bed.

She landed with a stunned bounce, her mouth falling open. "That was not what I meant!"

He shot her a look that told her he'd brook no argument. He was long past the point of tolerance. He yanked at his wet silk cravat to tear the thing away from his neck before it choked him. Then he tossed the black cloth to the floor and peeled off his wet jacket.

Her eyes grew wide. "What are you doing?"

"Undressing." He dropped the jacket away and began to work at his cuffs. "And so are you."

"No, I'm not—and stop that!" She waved a hand at his discarded jacket. "Put that back on!"

His last thread of patience snapped. "Take off that dress, Amelia," he ordered, "or I'll strip it off you myself."

Fifteen

AMELIA BLINKED. HE WANTED HER TO—

"No!" she blurted out and clamped her arms over her bosom. "Absolutely not."

Through gritted teeth, Pearce offered up a curse so fierce that she flinched. "Why the hell not?"

"Why the hell should I?" she shot back, refusing to be cowed. If he thought she would simply take off her clothes and let him have his way—

But of course he thought that. For heaven's sake, she'd done nearly exactly that at the ball.

He pointed at her skirt where the wet material wrapped around her legs like a second skin. "Because you're soaked through to the bone and freezing. I didn't save you from those men tonight just to have you die of fever."

She fought back a grimace. He'd had no intention of removing her clothes to seduce her. Oh, she felt like an utter goose!

Gathering what little pride she still possessed, she lifted her chin. "I'm not cold."

He arched a brow. "I can hear your teeth chattering all the way over here."

Damn those shivers! She sniffed dismissively. "You are mistaken."

Answering that obvious lie with a sharp glance of chastisement, he squatted onto his heels at the fireplace and set to starting a fire.

"You don't need to worry about me, Pearce. I'm not your concern."

"I told you before." He chucked in several logs and stuffed a handful of kindling beneath them, then struck a spark with the tinderbox. Carefully, he coaxed out a flame until it caught on the kindling and bit hold onto the wood, then turned to look at her over his shoulder. "I'm in the business of rescuing women."

What she wouldn't have given to allow him to do just that—to give herself over to him to be protected, to be held safe and sound in his arms.

But she knew better. Because it wouldn't stop with simply being held in his arms.

"And I told you," she reminded him, "that I don't need to be rescued."

Laughing at that, he jabbed at the fire with the iron poker to stir up the flames. "Amelia, I've rarely seen a woman in more need of rescue than you."

She scowled. "I am quite capable of taking care of myself." She shoved herself off the bed. "I'm not some silly girl or one of those society misses who suffers from the vapors and faints at the drop of a hat. I'm nothing at all like those women who are part of your world now."

"Believe me," he murmured with conviction, "I certainly realize that."

The heated look he sent her seared over her. He returned the poker to its holder, then pulled up to his full height as he turned to face her.

"But right now, you're soaked through and freezing because of me. I can't stop you from putting yourself unnecessarily at risk the way you did at the masquerade and tonight at Devonshire House when you eavesdropped on your brother." When she opened her mouth to protest that, he cut her off. "But I *can* save you from catching your death of cold." He put his hands on his hips in a commanding pose that showed him as the no-nonsense brigadier he'd become. "Now, take off that dress."

She refused to move and silently returned his stare. To be honest, the thought of taking off her wet clothes and finding something dry to put on tempted her. Greatly. Especially since an icy puddle was spreading around her feet at that very moment. But she'd never give him the pleasure of admitting he was right about—

A violent shiver shuddered through her so hard that her teeth chattered.

Pearce leveled an I-told-you-so gaze on her that had surely made his subordinates quake in their boots.

"Fine." With no other choice, Amelia grudgingly turned her back to him. "But I have no maid here." She tried to inject as much irritation into her voice as possible, so he wouldn't suspect how the thought of undressing in front of him twisted her belly into an aching tangle of desire. "So if you want me out of this dress, then you're going to have to help me."

Her wet hair had tumbled down from the chase, and she lifted it off her back. Her hands trembled as she smoothed it over her shoulder, out of his way.

When he reached for the row of tiny buttons on her back, she closed her eyes, willing her breath to remain steady, her pulse calm. One by one, the buttons slipped free, and her bodice loosened.

"This is necessary," he explained, misreading her protests. "You'll never warm up as long as you're in this wet thing."

She bit back a distressed laugh. "And here I thought you were simply attempting to see me naked."

She could almost hear the rueful twist of his lips. "I've undressed you before, you know."

"When I was nine." A strained quality laced through her suddenly hoarse voice. "We've changed since then. If you persist in this folly, then we'll both find out exactly how much."

"It isn't folly." He lowered his mouth over her shoulder. "And believe me, Amelia," he murmured, his breath tickling her ear, "I know exactly how much."

Foolish longing ached at the back of her weakening knees.

"All done." The last button slipped free, and her bodice drooped low down her front.

She grabbed at it with both hands to keep it in place as she whirled around to face him. "This isn't at all prop—"

Her chastisement died beneath his stare. Instantly, her anger was replaced by something else just as fierce. Something that pulsed achingly and made goose bumps spring up across her wet skin, that longed to have his hands running all over her and hers over him. His skin would be just as wet and cold as hers, she knew, but he would also be warm beneath, with smooth skin over hard muscles. The young lad she'd once loved was still there, ready for her to make love to him—

She bit her lip to fight back a groan. Damn the man for making her want him!

"Do you need me?"

Did she *need*… Yearning pulsed through her, and she squeaked, "Pardon?"

"To remove the rest of your clothes."

And *that* sent a wicked spiral of wanton desire shooting right out the top of her head.

Her hand tightened its hold on her bodice as she somehow remembered to keep breathing. "I–I can manage the rest on my own, thank you."

"Including your corset?" His gaze scorched over her, as if he could see right through her dress.

"Yes," she breathed out. Her confused brain swirled. Had she just answered his question…or given permission for him to remove even more of her clothing? To do more with her than simply look?

"All right." But he didn't turn his back to give her privacy. The rascal didn't even look away. His eyes remained on her as she stood there in the firelight, her skirts clinging to her hips and legs. "Are you certain?"

"No." She wasn't certain about anything when it came to this man…except that he made her feel beautiful. Desirable. Alive.

Was it wrong to let him stir these feelings inside her, to luxuriate in them and the memories of how wonderful their friendship had once been? After all, it was only undressing, and only to keep her from catching cold. A completely practical, not at all sexual reason. As long as nothing intimate happened between them, there was no harm in removing her dress to warm herself, no harm in letting those feelings wash over her.

Apparently, she was now lying to herself.

And she simply didn't care.

Pearce kept his distance, and she kept her gaze locked with his as her trembling fingers pulled at the cap sleeves of her dress and tugged them down her arms. The bodice came next, peeling down to her waist and then over her hips and thighs. She pushed the wet material to the floor, then stepped out of both it and her shoes. His eyes never left hers, even as she reached behind her back for her corset and tangled her shaking fingers in the lace. A tug untied the bow, and the lace came free, the stays falling loose around her. She removed the corset and let it fall to the floor, leaving her in nothing but her stockings and wet shift.

From several feet away, she saw the undulation of his throat as he swallowed. Hard. But his eyes stayed fixed on hers.

"Better?" Her voice emerged in a hoarse whisper.

A moment's hesitation…then temptation won, and he dragged a deliberate gaze over her. The wet shift clung to her body, the material surely translucent in the firelight and revealing everything underneath. This time when she shivered, it wasn't because she was cold.

He pulled in a breath so ragged that she could hear it shake into his lungs. "Much."

That rasping murmur stirred a hot throbbing between her legs. But she wasn't embarrassed to be standing in front of him like this, letting him look—encouraging his attentions, in fact, by making no attempt to cover herself. She simply stood there, her arms at her sides, the thin shift plastered over her breasts and hips. Having his gaze on her was too delicious to refuse.

"I think you have to agree," she half whispered, "that a lot's changed since I was nine."

His eyes darted up to hers, and the raw desire she saw in their depths turned her insides molten.

He took a slow step toward her, and the smooth, stalking motion spiked her pulse. Now she knew what a gazelle felt like when faced with a lion.

"What I think, Amelia," he admitted in a husky drawl that sparked across her flesh, "is that you've grown into a woman who knows her own mind and possesses the confidence not only to go after what she wants but also to know what to do with it once she has it."

Standing close in front of her, he took another deliberate sweep of his gaze over her, this time not bothering to hide his desire as his eyes lingered shamelessly on her breasts and hips. Surely, he could see the dark circles of her nipples through the shift, tightened into little points that longed to be touched, and the dark curls between her legs guarding her femininity. She might as well have been naked.

He added in a low drawl, "That includes men."

Amelia scoffed at the absurdity of that, that she of all women understood men and what they wanted—

Until he stripped off his waistcoat and tossed it to the floor to pile over her dress. The sound strangled in her throat.

He wore nothing more than black trousers and a wet shirt that clung to his sculpted chest and revealed exactly how much of a man he'd become during their years apart. Shamelessly, she let her gaze move over him, the same way he'd done to her only moments before.

Sliding the braces off his shoulders to let them dangle around his hips, he dropped his arms to his sides and let her look. The audacity of his confident stance was a clear issue of a challenge. "So the question is…what do you want?"

An anguished ache swelled inside her with such yearning need that she couldn't breathe. What she wanted was comfort and security, love, protection…*him*. God help her. Even after all these years and all that had happened, she still wanted to be with him.

Beneath her confused stare, he yanked his shirttail out of his breeches and peeled the wet shirt over his head and off. It landed on the floor at her feet.

Her lips trembled as she whispered helplessly for mercy, "Pearce…"

He cupped her cheek against his palm and slowly lowered his mouth toward hers.

"Sir!" A knock pounded at the door.

Amelia jumped just as his lips grazed hers, startled back into sanity. She quickly stepped back, putting half the room between them.

Pearce bit down a curse and ran his hand through his damp hair. His hungry gaze remained fixed on her, even as he demanded over his shoulder at the door, "What is it?"

"Mr. Hughes sent me up, sir." The high-pitched voice belonged to a boy who couldn't have been more than eleven or twelve. "You got a message you need me to run?"

"Perfect timing," Pearce bit out sarcastically in frustration as Amelia crossed her arms over her bosom to hide herself and turned away. "Wait one moment."

He snatched up the spare blanket from the foot of the bed and wrapped it around her shoulders to cover her.

"Seems that you and I never get to finish what we start," she teased, forcing a lightheartedness to ease the tension between them. "I think fate's trying to tell us something."

"I think fate can't tell time." He lowered his mouth to her ear, and his warm breath tickled over her skin as he murmured,

"Because the night's only half over, and that boy will be gone in five minutes."

Her knees turned liquid, and she reached for the bedpost to keep her balance.

He stepped past her to the little desk beneath the window and reached for a piece of paper and the quill. He scrawled out a quick message, then folded it. Not bothering with a seal, he wrote the direction on the front. Glancing at her to make certain she was covered, he opened the door.

A boy with a giant cowlick and scruffy clothes stood in the hall. The insolent look on his face belied his young age and revealed a soul who had already spent too many rough years on the streets. Amelia feared he'd have too many more harsh years of survival to come.

Pearce handed him the letter. "Can you read this direction?"

"I can read," the boy said defensively, jabbing up his chin. "And write, too." His gaze dropped to the note, and he read slowly but determinedly, sounding out every letter, "The Armory, High Holborn Street."

"The place looks abandoned but isn't. Knock hard on the door, then wait for someone to answer. You're to deliver this immediately, and the man who gets it will give you a coin." He handed over the note. "When you bring him back here, you'll get a second coin. Understand?"

"Yes, sir." The boy tucked the note under his cap, then looked curiously past him at Amelia.

"Run!"

The boy jumped and darted down the hallway, racing through the tavern toward the street.

Pearce closed the door. He grabbed the wooden chair from the corner and placed it in front of the door, sat down, and kicked out his long legs. The perfect vision of a man at leisure.

Although her head knew better, Amelia's foolish heart panged with disappointment that he wasn't attempting to pick up where they'd left off. With his lips on hers. "Why are you sitting there?"

"In case you attempt to distract me and escape."

She arched a brow. "Wearing nothing but a wet shift and a blanket?"

"I didn't say it wouldn't be thrilling to watch," he answered dryly.

She snatched up one of the pillows from the bed and threw it at him. It smacked him in the chest.

With a low chuckle, he tucked it behind him and eased back against it.

She cinched the blanket tighter around herself. "All comfy, are we?"

"Very. But a man needs to be comfortable in a situation like this."

A warning prickled at her bare toes. "What situation is that?"

"Finishing our conversation from the shop." He leaned forward, knees on elbows, and narrowed his gaze on her. "And you can start by telling me what you wanted with Charles Varnham at the masquerade."

Sixteen

PEARCE WAITED FOR HER TO BEGIN, NOT MOVING A MUSCLE. HE wasn't bluffing. She wasn't leaving this room until she told him what he wanted to know. Starting with Varnham.

"Well?" he pressed.

Amelia crossed her arms. "No."

"No what?"

"No, I'm not telling you anything."

Damnably stubborn woman. "You know, you were a lot more cooperative when I was removing your clothes."

Even in the dim light of the fire he could see her face flush. The sight was pure temptation.

Knowing she was practically naked beneath that blanket didn't help. He squirmed uncomfortably on the chair and tried again. "Why are you so interested in Varnham?"

"Why did you follow me out of the ball tonight?" she countered.

"Because rescuing you has grown into a habit. What did you want with the man?"

"Only to talk to him. Why did you follow me?"

"Because I've grown fond of your neck."

She frowned with faint bewilderment, her hand going to her throat and the old locket that hung there. "My neck?"

"I knew it was only a matter of time until you put it at risk. Again."

She angrily dropped her hand away. "Very funny."

"If those men had caught us tonight, no one would be laughing." Men he was certain were connected to Scepter. Men who'd wanted to kill her. He pinned her with a hard gaze. "Tell me, Amelia. What did you want with Varnham?"

"Well, an unmarried miss should never pass up a potential husband," she quipped. "Sometimes a woman has to take matters into her own hands."

Unease tightened in his gut. She might have been teasing about wedding Varnham, but something about the way she said it contained a deeper truth that prickled an icy warning at his nape. "It won't work."

"What won't?"

"Attempting to distract me with jealous thoughts of you with Varnham."

"Well, thank goodness for—"

"Because he'll never court you. You're not his type."

She twisted a damp curl around her finger. "Blond?"

"Intelligent." When her eyes flared, he added, "That sharp mind of yours can run circles around Varnham. He'd never let himself be shown up by a woman. Even one as beautiful and alluring as you."

Her lips parted slightly at the compliment, and for a moment, she was speechless. *Good.* The last thing he wanted to discuss was potential husbands for her.

"Is that why *you* keep embracing me?" she challenged softly once she found her voice. "Because you find me beautiful and alluring? Or are you attempting to distract me into giving you answers?"

No. *That* was the last thing. "Not at all."

"Yet you keep doing it."

A smug grin curled his lips. "Because you seem to like it."

She sniffed with mock offense. "It was the excitement of nearly being caught in Devonshire's closet, that's all."

"And in your shop? No one was there to catch us then."

"Temporary madness." Then she folded her arms over her chest, once again assuming that obstinate pose in which she'd begun this argument.

Damnation. He was getting nowhere by sparring with her like this, and time was running out. Flanking the enemy and hoping for a break in the line wasn't working. It was time for a direct assault.

He accused bluntly, "Varnham is connected to the trust, isn't he?"

She tensed, her breath catching so hard in startled surprise that he could hear it. But she managed to rasp out, "I don't know what you mean."

No, he wouldn't let her dissemble so easily and pressed, "What did you hope to gain from him? Help in delaying the trust if I turned out to be on your brother's side?"

"If I don't answer," she tossed back, once again picking a fight, "will you kiss me again in another attempt to seduce secrets from me?"

"If I kiss you, Amelia," he promised, "it won't be to uncover those kinds of secrets."

She stilled instantly, except for her cheeks which flushed bright red even in the dim firelight.

As if needing to keep herself busy, she picked up her dress from the floor and shook it out. She made a show of frowning over the ruined satin, but he knew it was really to keep from having to make eye contact with him. "What do you care about any of this?"

"I've always cared about you."

She turned toward the fireplace, ostensibly to drape the wet dress over the back of a chair to dry. But more than likely to put an even greater distance between them. Even with the blazing fire, the room had suddenly grown cold.

"I've never given you any reason to doubt that." His voice was low and controlled, but he fought the urge to clench his fists in frustration. "Even when I left Birmingham for the army, I did it to protect you. And I'll keep protecting you as long as necessary." He pushed himself out of the chair and slowly approached her. "But it would also help a great deal if you trusted me."

She held tightly to the blanket to keep it in place between them.

A desperate shield, nearly as effective in stopping him in his tracks as the look of betrayal shining in her eyes. "How can I trust you when I don't know your real motives? Or why you're so interested in what my brother has done?"

A logical question. Yet something about the way she said it implied so much more that he couldn't fathom. A defensiveness. The need to protect herself. *An old wound.* It killed him to see her in pain.

"You know that I have never done anything except act in your best interests," he assured her quietly, "even when we were children."

"But we're strangers now." Raw emotion filled her voice. "I don't know you anymore."

"You do know me. You always have." *Better than anyone else in the world.*

"But the turnpike—and the blackmail..." Her eyes glistened. "You said at the shop that Freddie was involved with a criminal group, with dangerous men." She swallowed. "How do you know that? Are you involved with them?"

"I'm set on stopping them."

"How?"

"I can't tell you."

"I see." Disappointment rang like a bell in that short response, and she turned her back to him, facing the fireplace.

Pearce raked his fingers through his hair. The last thing he wanted to do was place her in more danger by telling her about Scepter. Or betray the men of the Armory. But if he didn't tell her, if she didn't understand why he was doing this—

He'd lose her again. This time for forever.

He dragged in a deep breath. "The group is called Scepter. They're involved with smuggling, prostitution, bribery, blackmail—not just the criminal underworld, as you would expect, but penetrating all levels of society, including right up to the highest ranks of the aristocracy. And now into the government." The bitterness bit like acid on his tongue. "Thanks to your brother."

Slowly, she faced him. Her eyes still glistened in the firelight, but at least she was willing to listen. *Thank God.* "What do you mean?"

"The men your brother has placed into government appointments all have ties to Scepter. Men who now have positions all over Whitehall and the Court of St James's." He paused to punctuate the gravity of what he was confiding in her. "Men who are willing to commit murder and destroy lives to protect Scepter, to maintain its secrecy and power." He slowly approached her. "Your brother's only a pawn, but perhaps I can use him just as Scepter is. If he can help me make contacts in their organization, then I might be able to stop them."

"But a handful of government positions, mostly low-level ones…" she whispered, barely louder than a breath. "Why would a criminal organization want those?"

"We don't know."

"We?"

"The men of the Armory." He hadn't wanted to tell her about them either. But if she thought he was doing this alone, she'd most likely do something rash to try to stop him and expose everything they'd been working so hard to achieve. "We're a group of former soldiers who work out of the old armory just to the north of the City. Scepter came after one of our own and his family, and now we've pledged to stop them." He fixed his eyes on hers. "We won't let them harm the ones we love."

He couldn't tell her anything more. Not yet. But he could offer assurances, however limited.

"Believe me, Amelia." He gently touched her cheek, and she trembled at his caress. "I would never do anything to harm you. Put your trust in me, and give me the chance to prove it."

The hard stubbornness to keep him at arm's length eased from her with the sagging of her shoulders and a faint pressing of her cheek into his palm.

Yet it was a gesture of exasperation, not surrender. She still held little trust in him. Her uncertainties ran too deep to vanish so easily.

A knock came at the door, and one of the barmaids called out, "Yer hot splash an' good, as ordered."

When Pearce moved the chair aside and opened the door, the girl beamed a smile at him, which turned apologetic when she glanced past him and saw Amelia wrapped in the blanket.

Pearce bit down a grimace. What she thought had been happening here was the furthest thing from the truth. Regrettably.

The maid carried a bucket of hot water in one hand and two tankards of ale in the other, and on her arm, she balanced a plate of food. Mumbling an apology, she hurried across the small room to place the bucket by the washstand and the food and ale on the desk. Then she pulled a bottle of whiskey out of one apron pocket and a glass from the other. Those she placed on the fireplace shelf.

Pearce tossed her a coin, and she closed the door as she left.

"Hot splash and good," Amelia repeated the cant, bewilderment edging her voice. "You ordered hot water and food for us?"

Her surprise grated, that it wouldn't occur to him to think of comforts like this for her. Hadn't she learned yet? He put her first in his thoughts. Always.

"That river was filthy and freezing." He snatched up his shirt from the floor. "I thought you'd appreciate hot water to wash with and some whiskey to warm you."

"I do. I'm just…surprised, that's all."

He draped his shirt over the chair in front of the fire next to her dress and grudgingly bit out, "That I would think of that?"

"Well, yes. You're an army officer. Or used to be. For a very long time. I wouldn't think that you'd be conditioned to think of small luxuries like hot water when you're fleeing attack." She bent down to dip her fingers into the bucket to test the temperature. Thank God she didn't see the ruefulness on his face for assuming that she thought the worst of him. "Especially for a woman."

"You'd be surprised what I think about when I'm under attack," he mumbled beneath his breath, turning away from the fire. "And you're not an average woman."

Her fingers froze in midsplash. Ignoring that compliment, she gestured toward the plate on the desk. "And the food?"

Breaking the tension between them, he popped one of the grapes into his mouth. "For me."

"Of course." Her lips twisted knowingly.

He nodded toward the washstand. "Go ahead. Wash up before the water grows cold."

"So you can just stand there and eat all the food?"

He shot her a flirtatious grin. "And watch you."

"Of course," she repeated dryly.

He picked up a piece of cheese and gestured at the bucket with it. "Don't let me stop you from taking off your shift and stockings, from rubbing soapy, warm water all over your bare flesh in the fire-light." He was teasing her to lighten the tension between them, but damnation, if his words didn't make his cock ache for exactly that. "And by all means, take your time."

"How very thoughtful of you."

He trailed a lascivious gaze over her, his disappointment real that she was covered almost completely by that tent of a blanket. "I have only your best interests at heart."

"I don't think it's in your heart where your interests currently lie," she muttered, reaching down to lift the bucket and pour the steaming water into the basin.

He grinned and popped the cheese into his mouth.

She set down the bucket and circled a finger in the air. "Turn around."

He feigned wounding. "And take all the fun out of bathing?"

"Turn around, Brigadier," she ordered.

"I knew this was only a matter of time." Doing as she asked, he turned his back to her and grumbled, "In the end, all women pull rank."

A wet sponge smacked him in the middle of the back.

"That's a violation of the rules of warfare, I'll have you know." With a grin, he snatched up the sponge and threw it back at her over his head without turning around. "It's ungentlemanly to attack the enemy when he isn't looking."

She laughed. The sound came as soft and warm as the firelight, filling him with a melancholy longing to have back what her father stole from him.

But then, why shouldn't he have it? Gordon Howard was dead. The old bastard couldn't come between them any longer. More— all the man's insults that Pearce wasn't good enough for her were no longer true. He was an earl now, for God's sake. That title could at last be good for something. Like turning back time.

If given the chance, though, would she take it?

"You said before that we aren't enemies," she reminded him, just as softly as her laugh. "I'm hoping that's true."

"It is," he said quietly, distracted by the thoughts spinning through his mind, the old memories and wounds. So much had happened… How could they ever find their way back?

"Freddie has done some awful things," she began tentatively, testing the newfound trust between them. "Illegal things. And apparently not just selling his influence in Parliament."

Realization of what she meant tingled through him.

"I don't know how it was discovered or who passed along the information, but he's being blackmailed over it."

The soft rustle of fabric accompanied her quiet explanation as she dropped the blanket to the floor and removed her shift and stockings. His pulse spiked at the thought that she was standing completely naked only a few feet away.

"The blackmailer threatened to go to Sir Charles with evidence of what Freddie's done if he didn't place the men into government positions as ordered."

The water splashed gently in the basin, and Pearce envisioned Amelia reaching her arms into the air over her head, rubbing the sponge over her bare skin, droplets of water trickling down her body... *Sweet Lucifer.*

He cleared his suddenly tight throat, yet his voice still emerged as a raw rasp. "That's why you were looking for him at the masquerade." That was it—keep her talking, and keep his mind off how desirable she was. "What were you hoping to gain from him?"

"A chance to convince him of Freddie's innocence, without anyone knowing."

More soft splashes of water, more rustling movements behind him... He shifted uncomfortably. It wasn't only his throat that had grown tight. "Good. Because I'd hate to think you were planning something foolish." Madame Noir's words rushed back to him. "Like getting involved with the blackmailer yourself."

The water stilled.

Damnation. Madame hadn't lied. But he wished to hell she had.

"Only as a last resort," she admitted. "If everything else failed and Freddie was exposed."

At least she was being honest with him. Even if the thought of her becoming any more involved terrified the daylights out of him.

"But it didn't work. I still don't know Sir Charles's connection to the blackmailer." A thoughtful pause in the splashing. "There *must* be one, though. The man's in charge of the Committee of Privileges and can bring censure if laws and standards are broken, yet he would never entertain a charge against a fellow MP unless he implicitly trusted whoever made it. He wouldn't risk being made a fool of."

"It could be anyone in Parliament," he countered.

"Or any of Freddie's cronies," she added, defeat sounding in her voice. "The list is too long to consider."

The soft splashing continued then, followed by more rustling of fabric. He imagined how she must have looked, rubbing the towel over her body while she dried herself, and damn his gentleman's honor that he couldn't sneak even a single glance over his shoulder.

"Fortunately, Freddie only has three men left to place. But if he doesn't, he'll be exposed. He'll lose his seat in Parliament, perhaps even be sentenced to prison. I can't let that happen."

"He's fortunate to have your kindness." What Pearce wanted to do was pummel the bastard for putting her life in danger.

"It isn't kindness," she admitted with chagrin. "If his life is destroyed, so is mine. So are the lives of the women working at the Boutique."

More kind than she was willing to admit, based upon her answer. He knew no other society miss who would be willing to go to such lengths to help a handful of war widows.

"I owe Frederick everything." She came up behind him, close enough that her nearness sparked awareness of her across his back. "But that doesn't mean I'll let him destroy all I've worked so hard to create."

Slowly, he turned to face her.

She was once again in her shift, with the blanket now secured around her like a toga. Yet she was still bare enough to stir his desire. Which wasn't helped by the way she lifted her damp hair from her neck and shoulders, revealing the creamy smoothness of her skin as she twisted her tresses to put up her hair.

The sight of her mesmerized him. He'd watched countless women fuss with their hair. Some after they'd just left his bed, in fact. But never had the sight struck him with such visceral force as it did now, with such a fierce reminder that private, innocent moments like this still connected them. And always would.

Holding the hair pins between her lips, she twisted her damp hair into a chignon and attempted to pin it into place. She turned her lithe body this way and that, and he smiled at her antics, as if turning herself could magically make her hair do the same. But the uncooperative locks kept slipping free.

He took the pins from her, then gently turned her around. "Let me."

Her lips parted in surprise, but she obliged and didn't fight him when he carefully took her hair in his hands and loosely twisted it. Even though it was damp, her locks still slipped over his fingers like silk, and he resisted the urge to say to hell with the pins and shove his hands deep into its softness, to let the golden tresses fill his palms.

"You don't have to do that." A grudging acquiescence edged her voice that she needed his help. They'd broken down walls tonight, but they were still a long way from the trust they'd once shared. A trust he very much wanted back.

"I don't mind." No, he was grateful for any excuse to touch her, even this innocently. "Now that my stint in the army's over, I've been considering a second career," he admitted thoughtfully. "Something decidedly more dangerous."

"Home office agent?"

"Lady's maid," he said deadpan.

A mischievous smile pulled at her lips. "Well, you *are* surprisingly good at pinning up a woman's hair."

He lowered his mouth to her ear and drawled rakishly, "I'm even better at taking it down." Then he punctuated that exaggerated flirtation with a stolen kiss to her nape. *Any* excuse to touch her.

She laughed, killing whatever seduction he might have started. He would have considered that laugh as a prick to his male pride, if not for enjoying the lilting sound of it so much.

He secured the last pin, and she began to move away. "Thank you—"

He took her shoulders and stopped her. This time when he lowered his mouth to her ear, he was deadly serious. "Thank you for trusting me about your brother."

She hesitated, then gave a jerky nod. Not at all the vote of confidence he'd wanted, but he would take it. And take hope in it.

Yet he couldn't bring himself to step away from her and instead nuzzled his cheek against her exposed nape. She trembled.

"All those years, I never forgot about you," he admitted. "But I'd moved on, accepting the new life I'd been given, just as I'd hoped you had." He pulled in a deep breath. "I hated your father for what he did to us, but I also knew that he wasn't wrong. You deserved a better man for a husband than me."

"Don't say that," she scolded, but the chastisement was barely more than a breath. "It isn't true."

"It is—it *was*. The life I could have given you then would never have been enough."

He slid his hand over her shoulder, to trace delicate patterns with his fingers against the side of her neck. This time it wasn't just a tremble that he elicited from her but a quickening of her breath, a racing of her pulse beneath his fingertips. She was affected by him as much as he was by her. Her body couldn't lie.

"You deserved riches, a grand house, jewels and furs, a fine carriage…the respect of society. I couldn't have given you any of that."

Not then.

The words lingered around them, as palpably as if he'd spoken them aloud. She stood frozen beneath his hands as he slowly began to caress them up and down her arms in slow, reassuring strokes.

"But your father can't harm us any longer." He dared to place a single kiss against her ear, in hopes of stirring the same longing inside her that now pulsed through him. "And I'm no longer a man you would be ashamed to be with."

"I was *never* ashamed," she whispered between quick and

shallow breaths. "You were a good and kind man. The rest never mattered to me."

"It mattered to me." *But no longer.* Now, everything had changed. "There's no reason for us to stay apart. No reason that we can't rekindle our friendship."

"Only friendship?" The tremble in her voice undercut the challenge in her question.

"Of the very best kind." This time when he kissed her ear, he sucked gently at her earlobe in a seductive and obvious gesture that showed exactly what he hoped would happen between them.

Her answering shiver proved how much she longed to be in his arms, but except for closing her eyes, she made no move of capitulation. The past and the present warred inside her, so fiercely that he could see it in the strained expression gripping her face, could feel it in the stiff way she stood frozen against him.

If only she would let herself go, let herself have what they both wanted... He took her chin in his fingers and gently turned her around to face him so he could kiss her full on the mouth, so he could tease apart her lips and claim the decadent sweetness waiting inside.

She murmured his name in soft permission, and the tension melted away.

He tugged the blanket loose and dropped it to the floor, leaving nothing between them but her thin shift. He slipped his arms around her and drew her tightly against him to plunder her kiss in sweeping licks and thrusting plunges that made his body ache to have her beneath him, to hear soft sounds of pleasure and release falling from her lips.

She sagged bonelessly against him, her arms snaking up around his neck to keep herself from falling away.

As she clung to him, with her breasts flattened against his front, each panting breath she took rubbed her hard nipples against him and left him groaning with an aching need to possess her, with an unbearable desire for her to surrender herself completely to him. Tonight and always.

He placed his hands on her hips and lifted her onto the desk. Her hand struck the plate of food, tossing it onto the floor with a clatter. The tankards of ale tumbled away next, the bucket of remaining water kicked and spilling across the floor—

None of it mattered, because he'd grabbed her shift, lifting it up around her waist and baring her to his eyes.

"Dear God," he rasped out as he slid his hands up her inner thighs and gently parted her legs, revealing her completely to his eyes. Her feminine lips glistened in the firelight with proof of her desire. "So beautiful…"

"I'm not," she protested softly, closing her eyes in embarrassment. "Not…there."

"You have no idea how beautiful I find you, Amelia. Here." He caressed her, mesmerized as her soft folds quivered with anticipation. "And everywhere." Slowly, he circled her with his fingertip. "Every inch of you, from your toes to your soul. The most beautiful woman I've ever known."

"You're just saying that." But her hands at his shoulders shamelessly kneaded his muscles. She wanted the pleasure he could give her, so much that she shook with it.

"I mean it." With every quickening beat of his heart.

"Then…" She exhaled a deep sigh of surrender and whispered in challenge, "Prove it."

He lowered himself to his knees and brought his mouth against her.

Seventeen

AMELIA CAUGHT HER BREATH AT THE SENSATION OF HIS WARM lips between her legs. A kiss more intimate than any she'd ever been given before. Even when they were young and so very curious about each other, they'd never dared do this. Never more than a slip of his hand beneath her skirt to steal a quick touch, never his mouth on her bare flesh. But this—

She whimpered. Oh, this was simply divine!

He kissed her tenderly, careful not to frighten her, and his strong lips caressed over her with a featherlight touch that blossomed the feminine desire inside her. Liquid heat pooled between her legs, right beneath his lips.

She reached down to brush her fingers through his hair, wanting to return the same affection he was showing her, and whispered, "Brandon."

He stilled.

Her heart leapt into her throat. Had she misstepped? She'd called him by his given name only a handful of times in their entire lives. But during what they were sharing now, calling him Pearce didn't seem right somehow. Didn't seem special enough. And she longed to show him exactly how precious he was to her.

But then he placed a slow and lingering kiss to her very core, and her worry melted away. Beneath his lips, she felt how much she meant to him. All of her doubts vanished.

With a soft sigh, she draped herself backward over the desk to let herself enjoy every moment of this special kiss. But her pulse continued to pound, so strongly that she was certain he could hear it. *Hear it?* Good Lord, he would be able to *feel* it, so fiercely was the desire throbbing inside her, and right there, too, right where his lips were now teasing at her with increasingly persistent kisses—

He licked her.

She gasped, but he murmured soft reassurances against her and did it again. This time, the slow caress of his tongue rolled a shiver of pleasure through her, all the way out through the tips of her fingers and toes. And when he continued to do it, she could only bear the delicious sensation by digging her fingers into his scalp.

Then the caresses changed. No longer the sweeping, exploring licks of before. Now he simply plundered, devouring her in large, openmouthed kisses that made her body shake and her knees clench against his shoulders as she tightened like a vise around him.

A whimper of need rose from her throat. Her pulse raced beneath the relentless plunge and retreat of his wicked tongue, her blood flashing hot. Her hands grabbed at his head, and she closed her eyes against the rising desire to surrender total control.

Then he shifted, moving his mouth just a bit higher, closed his lips around the little nub there, sucked—

Her hips bucked as pure pleasure shot through her. "Brandon!"

She slammed her legs closed as the sensation became unbearable. But his shoulders between her knees and his hands stroking along her inner thighs kept her spread open wide to the sweet torture of his mouth.

Unable to hold back, she broke with a cry. The coiled spring inside her shattered, and pleasure spiraled through her in a wave of warmth that heated her from the inside out.

She collapsed bonelessly against the desk, overcome with release and emotion. Her fingers combed in gratitude through his silky hair as he rested his cheek against her thigh to catch his breath.

Slowly, he rose to his feet and gathered her into his arms, then carried her across the room to the bed. He gently placed her onto the counterpane and paused only to remove his breeches before following down over her with a heated kiss that was singular in its intention.

He was going to make love to her.

She pressed a hand to his shoulder. He stilled immediately, staring down at her in the firelight.

"Pearce…" Through the tears that heated her eyes and the tightening of her throat, she couldn't find the words to express all that needed to be said. Just as she could no longer find the resolve to keep him away.

He didn't move, but she felt the change in him, so much was he already a part of her again. Not disappointment, not anger. But understanding. "You once loved me."

God help me, I still do…

"Give me that love again, and let me love you in return." He stroked his knuckles over her cheek, and the tender touch seared pain all the way down to her soul. "There's no longer anything keeping us apart."

When he lowered his head to kiss her, her hand at his shoulder stopped pushing away and now grasped at his bicep to keep him close. This was what she had always longed for, for Pearce to make love to her. But so much had happened, so much that would keep him from her in the end…

Yet at this moment, he was here with her, asking her to allow him to love her. For now, she would let that be enough.

"Yes," she whispered, barely louder than a breath.

But he heard and deepened the kiss. On his lips, she tasted the love they shared. The certainty that he was the man to whom she wanted to give her innocence came over her as suddenly as a summer storm and just as intense, just as electrifying. She knew it with every breath she drew, with every ounce of her being— tonight was right, with him. This man she'd loved since she was a girl.

He trailed kisses down her body, across her breasts, and lower to the flat of her belly. Heat flared between her legs in anticipation, shooting up inside her in a wave of liquid desire so strong that it left her panting.

A soft chuckle rumbled against her abdomen, as if he knew the reaction he flamed inside her. Wicked man…and more wicked still for brushing his hands up her legs, pulling the chemise up her body as he went. When he reached her shoulders, she raised her arms so he could lift it over her head and toss it away, leaving her draped naked across the bed.

She shivered, but she wasn't cold. How could she be beneath the heat of his gaze as it traveled slowly over her, lingering at her breasts and hips and flaming prickly heat across her skin? There was no shame in lying bare before him, no embarrassment in letting him look his fill of her. This was Pearce, and she would never be ashamed with him.

"I knew it," he murmured longingly.

She affectionately caressed the soft hair at his temple. "Knew what?"

"That you'd be breathtaking." He trailed a fluttering hand over her bare shoulder and down across her breasts to her hip. "You were too tempting not to be."

He lowered his mouth to capture hers in a kiss born of need and desire, of twelve years of absence and loneliness. One that left her dizzy and weak and trembling. A kiss that made all the ones he'd given her before seem like whispers against the ferocity of a scream. His lips devoured hers as if he couldn't taste her deeply enough to satisfy himself. She knew he was trying to make up for every minute he'd been away from her, for all the other kisses they'd been denied.

She moaned against his mouth, verbalizing her surrender. He gently massaged her breast as if in reward for letting go of her nervousness and giving over to the yearning he created inside her. But it was easy to yield to the growing desire that gripped her, to the firm but tender caresses, the sure and delicious kisses. Because she loved him. Always had.

She knew then that she always would.

"I will make tonight perfect for you, Amelia," he whispered against her lips. "I promise you that."

She caressed her fingers along the side of his face, unable to speak. *You already have…*

He took her bottom lip between his and sucked, and the pull of his lips tugged through her from all the way down between her legs. Each deep suck seemed to pool all the blood in her body right *there,* where she throbbed and burned and longed to be touched.

She tightened her arms around his neck and pulled to bring him down on top of her. But he didn't budge. She might as well have attempted to move a mountain, but he kissed her lips with amused appreciation that she'd tried. She should have known better. He was setting the pace, every touch and kiss his to grant.

He wasn't caressing her tonight. He was discovering her. No— *rediscovering* her. And the sensation was simply exquisite.

He swept his hands over her body, along her sides and down over her thighs to her knees. Then he switched directions, moving upward along her inner thighs toward her core. She held her breath, all of her shaking as she waited to be touched at the very center of her being, as deliciously as he'd touched her before—

But his hands skirted over her hips to return to her shoulders where he'd started.

A moan of frustration poured from her. "Don't tease."

"Before this night is over, my love," he warned as he lowered himself to stretch his tall and muscular body alongside hers, "you're going to appreciate my teasing. Very." He hooked her leg over his, and his hand slid up her calf. "Very." Then along her inner thigh. "Much."

He slipped a finger into her tight warmth.

She gasped as the unfamiliar sensation of having him inside her shot through her, her eyes locking with his in the firelight as she fought to catch her breath in fast little pants. Then a second finger joined the first, and he began to caress her with slow, teasing strokes. She clasped her arms around his shoulders as each small slide of his fingers spilled a liquid warmth through her. So soft and gentle, almost sweet in his wicked ministrations, and sheer happiness thundered through her. She was lost to the sinful feel of his fingers, to the weight of his body pressing deliciously down on hers. To the joy of once more being loved by him.

When he pulled his hand away, a whimper of loss rose on her lips—only to turn into a soft mewling of anticipation when he reached between them to grasp his manhood and rub its round head against her folds. He circled her aching core until her wetness covered his tip, daring to dip deeper into her slick folds with each pass.

She squirmed beneath him, her body craving him with a primal need she couldn't restrain. The pleasure he'd given her earlier was wonderful, yet she knew there was more to come. There would be his body inside hers, her body wrapped around his—the joining they'd always been meant to share.

"Amelia," he whispered, tenderly kissing her forehead. He poised ready against the aching hollow at her core. The time for teasing was over.

"I want you." She wrapped her arms around his neck, her legs around his waist. "So very much…"

As his mouth captured hers, he lowered his hips. He pushed inside her with a single, smooth thrust that broke through the slight resistance of her maidenhead and plunged him fully inside her tight warmth.

For several long seconds he didn't move, his body lying perfectly still over hers. The fleeting pinch of pain dissolved away until she was left with only the wonderful sensation of being filled completely as she cradled him between her thighs. Then, when he began to move inside her, he stroked into her so deeply yet so carefully that his tenderness took away what little breath she'd managed to regain.

Her heart ached that he was so concerned about her, that he was careful to keep his full weight from crushing her. That a man this large, muscular, and powerful should be so very gentle— emotion overcame her, and she buried her face against his neck.

His strokes slowly increased in their pace and intensity. Closing her eyes, she breathed deep his spicy scent and brushed her lips against his skin to taste the delicious flavor of him. She wanted to impress onto her mind forever the smell and taste of him, to brand onto her body the feel of him inside her.

But even this closeness wasn't enough.

"Pearce, please." She arched herself beneath him, instinctively, knowing that there was more of him to possess. "Stop holding back."

He shook his head, his body tense with restraint as he panted out between labored breaths, "I don't...want to...hurt you."

"You won't." She wrapped her legs around him, locking her ankles at the small of his back. "Give yourself to me. I've waited too long already."

She bit his bottom lip in wanton challenge.

A growl tore from him, and he thrust into her, the single stroke so powerful and deep that she gasped. But primal pleasure also surged through her, and she clung to him, welcoming both her own overwhelming rush of passion and his capitulation to the raw desire flaming between them.

His large hands closed over her hips, and he guided her into a fast, hard rhythm, lifting her hips to meet each plunge of his. Moans of need poured from her. She was unable to stop herself from crying them out, just as she was unable to stop her body from moving with his. They were joined completely now, body to body, soul to soul, and she couldn't tell where she ended and he began.

The fire of release began to build inside her again, this time spreading out from low in her belly like a gathering storm. Each driving plunge of his hard body into hers sent a powerful jolt of yearning spinning through her, each retreat a devastating loss. She clasped her arms around his neck and simply held on as she felt herself running toward the fire, to sacrifice herself to the flames.

The storm broke over her, raining sparks and flames down upon her. Her release flashed like lightning, hot and just as electric. The pain of the past washed away until all she knew was bliss.

With one last thrust, he sank deep and held himself tightly against her. His body arched above hers as he poured himself into her, his buttocks squeezing to give up every last drop of his essence to her. Selfishly, she drank him in, refusing to surrender any part of him now that he was finally hers.

He collapsed onto the mattress beside her. She turned onto her side to continue to hold him, spent and shaking, in her arms. She couldn't bring herself to release him and end this moment, not yet. Tears gathered at her lashes in stunned appreciation of how he was capable of devastating her so completely.

He rested his forehead against her bare shoulder as he struggled to regain his breath. Slowly, he found the strength to place a tender kiss to her hot lips.

"I've never...*never*," he murmured, unable to put into words the experience they'd just shared. As if just as bewildered as she about the intensity of the passion between them, the overwhelming affection that bound them together. "You have no idea how special you are to me." He lowered his head to nuzzle his cheek against hers. "I love you, Amelia. I always have."

Her pulse spiked. *This* was the moment she wanted to remember for the rest of her life, of being held in his arms when she felt safe and protected. When she could let herself believe that the rest of the world didn't exist and tomorrow would never come.

When there was only Pearce and nothing else mattered but being loved by him.

His eyes shone intensely in the firelight. "Marry me, Amelia."

With that, her world shattered.

"We belong together… We always have." He touched his lips to hers, mistaking her shocked silence for nervous uncertainty. "Now more than ever."

"No." The single word was barely more than a breath falling lifelessly across her stunned lips. How she managed even that much effort, she had no idea. Because the pain engulfing her was blinding. Starting at the tips of her toes, it worked its way upward until it reached her chest and strangled her heart. "I can't…I can't marry you."

Confusion darkened his face. "You don't love me?"

"Of course I love you." Her fingers trembled as they reached for him, to touch his jaw and feel his strength and solidity. She breathed out the confession, "I've always loved you."

"Then why won't you marry me?"

His handsome face blurred beneath the anguished tears that welled in her eyes. "Because…I'm already married."

Eighteen

PEARCE POURED A GLASS OF WHISKEY. HE'D NEED FORTIFICATION to get through this conversation. He also needed a few minutes away from Amelia to clear his head and tamp down his shock. And his anger.

To keep a secret like this from him, and when they'd just— *Damnation.*

Crossing the small room to her, he held out the glass as she stood at the window, looking out at the dimly lit street below. But the sleeping city was still shrouded in fog and darkness and would be for another several hours. Dawn was still a long time away.

She declined the drink.

"I think you'll need it," he cajoled. Lord knew how much he did!

"And I don't think there's enough whiskey in the world to make this any easier."

Perhaps not. But whiskey would take the edge off, that was certain. And right now, he was fighting back the urge to punch his fist through the wall.

So he raised the glass to his lips with hard-won calmness. As he took a deep swallow, he studied her over the rim of the glass.

Dear God, she was beautiful, even in that ruined black gown that she'd pulled back on. Her hair had come down again during their lovemaking, and now it fell around her slender shoulders like a golden curtain and made her almost look sixteen again. Except for the womanly curves beneath. And the grief that darkened her face.

"I should have told you before," she began in a guilty whisper, so soft that it was barely more than a breath.

Yes, you should have.

"But I didn't know how." She reached to brush her fingers over the curtain framing the window. "I didn't want you to realize what an utterly stupid fool I'd been. Or worse—to pity me." Her fingertips trembled against the lacy material. "I couldn't have borne that. Not from you of all people."

"A *marriage*, Amelia." Despite his effort to keep his voice low, the frustration rang loud and clear. There was no point in attempting to hide it. "I had no idea that you…" *Christ.*

"No one does." Pulling in a deep breath, she faced him. "No one but Frederick and me…and now you."

"And your husband."

She flinched. Changing her mind, she took the glass from him and raised it to her lips for a drink. She placed the back of her hand against her mouth as she swallowed down the burning liquid and muttered through her fingers, "I wish to God that I'd never met him."

With a visible need to keep herself busy, she crossed to the desk and refilled the glass. He silently accepted it from her, although he'd lost his taste for the stuff. What he wanted was answers.

"Where is he?" he demanded as gently as possible given the anger seething inside him. "Why does no one know about him?" *Why the hell didn't I know?*

"Somewhere in America." She shook her head. "And no one knows about him because marrying him was the greatest mistake of my life. One that ruined us financially and would have destroyed us socially if not for Freddie taking charge to hide it all."

For once, she wasn't lying or keeping secrets. The grief on her face was too real to be pretense. "What happened?"

"His name is Aaron Northam, and I was almost twenty-one when I met him," she began quietly, "only weeks until my majority."

She took a few steps away, to pick up his jacket and waistcoat from the floor where he'd dropped them earlier when they'd first come into the room and carry them over to the fire. He watched her lay the waistcoat over the chair beside his drying shirt and said nothing, knowing she had to fuss with them the way she'd done with the prints at the shop. To have someplace to focus her attention other than on him while she explained.

"Papa had died two years earlier, leaving Freddie as my guardian and me an unexpected heiress." She picked up the jacket and gently shook it out, but the motion did nothing to eliminate the wrinkles puckering the kerseymere. It was completely unsalvageable. "As my guardian, Freddie controlled not only my money, but also the men who were allowed to court me. Although there hadn't been any."

"A beautiful heiress? I find that hard to believe." Pearce set the unwanted whiskey onto the fireplace mantel. "If not true gentlemen, then at least an army of fortune hunters pounding down your door to get to you."

She smiled sadly at that notion as she draped the jacket over the seat of the wooden chair. "Freddie kept the fortune hunters away, and I rejected the others."

"Because they weren't good enough?"

She slowly brushed her hand over his jacket, focusing on smoothing out the fabric and not raising her eyes to look at him. "Because they weren't you."

Her confession pierced him like a blade.

"Even then, I was still in love with you." She paused, her fingers stilling on the ruined kerseymere. "I think a part of me was still hoping you'd find your way back to me, despite the wars." Then, impossibly softer, "Somehow."

With *that*, the blade twisted and nearly killed him.

She picked up the waistcoat next and fussed over spreading it across the mantel, but she couldn't hide the shaking of her hands. "Freddie wasn't a bad guardian, you know. He looked after me quite well for someone so young." Her fingers brushed futilely at the wrinkles. "He was always concerned about my reputation, insisted that he look after my finances and spoke to all the accountants and bankers himself. And after the wedding, he protected me then, too."

"Why did he have to protect you?" Something about the way she said that gnawed at his gut in warning. "That was your husband's responsibility."

"And who protects a woman from her husband?" she challenged softly.

His blood turned cold, despite the murderously hot anger that flared into his fists. "The bastard hurt you?"

"No." She visibly steeled herself and admitted, "The bastard stole my fortune and left me."

As that information rattled inside him, she moved toward the desk and bent down to pick up one of the tankards that they'd spilled onto the floor in their earlier passion.

"I had been out walking in the park... I hadn't been feeling well, and Freddie insisted that I take some fresh air. As I walked past a little copse of trees, a young boy leapt out, grabbed my reticule, and ran. The next thing I knew, a man on horseback was galloping across the lawn in chase. The boy got away, but the man saved my reticule and brought it back to me. That was how I met Aaron." Her voice grew quiet. "He was so dashing and heroic that I was simply captivated by him. I thought he was my rescuer." She paused, bitterness filling the silence. "He proved to be anything but that."

I don't need to be rescued... Her words from the night of the masquerade came tumbling back to him. Now he knew why she'd bristled when she'd heard them, and he felt like a damned fool for not discovering sooner why she had.

She set down the tankard and slowly wiped her hands over her skirt to brush away the droplets of ale clinging to her fingertips. "I should have realized what kind of man he was, that it was all too perfect to be real…too *romantic*. But he made me feel special and beautiful—"

"Because you are."

Her bright eyes found his. "Because he reminded me of you." Her confession was barely louder than a whisper, but it rang between them like a gunshot. "He was everything I'd always loved and admired about you—strong, dashing, brilliant, protective… And you hadn't answered any of my letters." She sucked in a pained, jerking breath, as if hiding the start of a sob. "I thought you were gone from my life forever."

Turning away, she began to pace the length of the small room, wringing her hands in front of her with every step.

"When Aaron asked to court me, Freddie didn't hesitate to say yes. After all, Aaron was the son of a wealthy merchant with ties to the aristocracy through his mother. Because his parents were dead and he had no other family, the money had all come to him. There was even joking between him and Freddie about what should be included in the marriage agreement, given all the money between us, although it was far too early for that. I thought I was being careful in avoiding fortune hunters." She turned her face away, but not before he saw the self-recrimination that twisted her features. "But I wasn't as careful as I'd thought."

"What happened?" He picked up the glass of whiskey and held it out to her, stopping her in midpace.

"My brother." She stared at the glass, not yet accepting it. "That was right when he decided that he wanted a career in politics and set about maneuvering his way into the best social circles, the best clubs… He'd been called away to London, with no plans to return for at least a month, because he needed to wrangle his way into a seat in Parliament. But Aaron said he loved me, that he didn't want to wait for Freddie to return to start our life together."

Suspicion pricked the little hairs at Pearce's nape. And dread that he knew where her story was heading.

"So we married anyway." She took the glass from him, her hand trembling as she raised it to her lips. "Because he lived in York and only visited Birmingham on business, he'd already gotten a special license so that we didn't have to worry about the banns, one that let us marry in any parish. We'd planned to marry, then drive on to surprise Freddie in London with the good news. Aaron had heard there was a lovely little village three hours' drive southeast of Birmingham with a pleasant vicar and a fine inn." She smiled ruefully against the rim of the glass. "A marriage and a honeymoon, all in one. Such a romantic idea...so of course I agreed."

Pearce said nothing as she took another swallow. Drink would be good for her and give her the courage to get through this. *His* only consolation was that after tonight there could be no more secrets.

She frowned at the whiskey. "We married as planned, but never had our wedding night. He changed his mind after the ceremony, said that he wanted our first time together to be in our home, not in an inn. So we took separate rooms." She shook her head. "I should have known something was wrong right then, because what new husband finds excuses to avoid coming to his bride's bed on their wedding night, even at what turned out to be a flea-ridden tavern?" She idly traced a fingertip around the rim of the glass. "At the time, I thought it was just another example of how much he cared about me, just another example of how romantic he was. Such a damned fool I was!"

She tossed back the remaining whiskey in a gasping swallow, then stared down into the empty glass. Not all the tears glistening in her eyes came from the bite of the drink in her throat.

"When I woke, he was gone. He'd left in the night. No word, no note, just...*gone*. I waited for him there for two days, but he never returned. Finally, I took the mail coach home to Birmingham and found not Aaron at the town house but Freddie. He'd returned unexpectedly from London, only to find a message from our banker. That was when I realized that I was missing more than a husband… I was also missing a fortune." She lifted her gaze to his, and misery darkened her eyes. "Aaron had gone to the bank and withdrawn every pound and penny I possessed. He took it all, then booked passage on the first ship to Philadelphia."

"But the settlement—"

"Was never signed," she admitted with humiliation. "Frederick hadn't signed it before he left for London. I thought he had. I swear to you that I believed that!"

When she began to gesture emphatically to convince him, she realized what she was doing and stopped, her hand going to her forehead in desolation. Pearce knew not to reach for her, but it took every ounce of willpower he possessed not to go to her.

"Freddie had even taken Aaron to the bank, for heaven's sake, to introduce him to our accountant and the bank manager, to pave the way for settling the dowry and contract. We'd negotiated terms— all three of us. I put my signature to the agreement, so did Aaron. But…" Her pale face twisted with humiliation, and she sucked in a deep breath to gather the courage to continue. "But somehow, in all the excitement of the proposal and the wedding plans, Freddie hadn't signed it, and without my guardian's signature, all my property became Aaron's the moment we wed. Legally, as a minor, my signature meant nothing." She turned away, too humiliated to look at him. "Aaron told me Freddie had signed it, and I trusted him. Why wouldn't I? What woman wouldn't trust her fiancé? I loved him. We were going to share a life together… It never occurred to me that he was lying. About everything." A hoarse, bitter sound came from her throat. "The only thing he wasn't able to take in his hurry to flee was Bradenhill."

A grim realization settled over Pearce. That was why the property was so important to her, why she was fighting the trust tooth and nail. Not because of her charity, although he was certain she wanted to use it for that, but because it was all she had left.

"Did your brother go after him," he asked quietly, attempting to fill in the blanks, "try to bring him back and force him to return your money?"

She gave a jerking nod. "Freddie hired lawyers and thief-takers, went so far as to hire two men from Bow Street to find him and bring him back by force, if necessary. But it was all for nothing. Aaron had vanished, and my fortune along with him, with no way to get it back even if we found him. Because Aaron had every right to take it. He and I were legally married." A single tear slipped down her cheek and ripped open his heart as she choked back a sob. "We still are."

———

Unable to bear any look of recrimination or pity from him, Amelia turned her back and lifted her hand to her mouth to physically press down the anguish swelling inside her. How could Pearce understand all that had happened to her, when she could barely fathom it herself?

"He took everything from me," she choked out. "My fortune, my happiness...my future." Her shoulders trembled as she pulled in deep lungfuls of air to find the strength to keep from falling to the floor. "Now he's taken you."

"No, he hasn't." Pearce stepped up behind her and slipped his arms around her, to wrap her securely in his embrace. "I'll never leave you again, understand? *Never.*"

She didn't have the resolve to nod. Emotion overwhelmed her, and she simply gave up, shutting her eyes against the pain and humiliation.

"We *will* find a way out of this together, Amelia. I promise you."

Oh, he was wrong! There was no way out of her marriage. She'd pored through her lack of options so many times before that she no longer held any hope of finding one. "It takes an act of

Parliament to grant a divorce," she rasped, "and neither the courts nor the Church recognizes abandonment as grounds."

"They recognize adultery. I'm certain he hasn't been faithful to his marriage vows during the years he's been away. " His arms tightened around her, but his embrace gave her little comfort. "We'll hire new investigators, send more Bow Street runners to find him—and find evidence of what he's been doing. "

Her heart wrenched. He was trying to rescue her. Even now. "I can't ask that of you."

"You're not asking. I'm giving." He nuzzled his cheek against her hair. "We're working together now, remember? That includes this."

His kindness tore a desolate sob from her. "Even if you helped me," she whispered, the truth of her situation both undeniable and brutal, "it's not enough. A woman has to prove not only adultery on the part of her husband but cruelty as well. How do I do that when he's put an ocean between us?"

She turned in his arms and buried her face against his shoulder, desperately needing the strength of his embrace and his steadiness.

"None of it matters anyway," she murmured, slipping her arms around his waist to pull herself even closer. If she could have found a way to crawl beneath his skin, she would have done it. "Even if what he did could be considered cruelty, the divorce proceedings would be public. All of what happened would come to light." Her hands clutched at his back, her anchor in the storm. "I'd be branded as immoral for eloping, my reputation ruined. And when society learns that he took my money and left me, they'll all say that I deserved it. Just deserts for an upstart cit attempting to wheedle her way into the *ton*." A sob choked in her throat. "I'll be a laughingstock. No one will shop at my store. The charity will be ruined."

Pearce said nothing. But there *was* nothing to say. They both knew she was right.

"Freddie will be destroyed right along with me," she added, her whisper barely loud enough to reach him. "That's why we hid it, never breathing a word to anyone. Freddie only has his seat in Parliament because of his connections. He didn't buy it as everyone thinks because we didn't have the money after I eloped. But if the men who put him there ever think that his reputation has been tainted by mine, his influence limited in any way, he'll lose his seat. For all of that, we both had to keep my mistake hidden. But a divorce hearing…" An anguished sound rose from the back of her throat. "Our lives will be ruined."

"This is what you meant when you told me that your brother took care of you," he said quietly, "when you had financial trouble."

"I couldn't tell you the truth. Not then." She didn't lift her head from his shoulder, afraid of the recrimination she'd see on his face. "I was so ashamed of admitting what had happened, how stupid I'd been."

"You trusted a man you loved, one you thought loved you." He placed a kiss to her temple. "There's no fault in that."

She shook her head against his shoulder. "I can't escape him. Don't you see? I don't care about the money. I'd surrender every ha'penny just to be free of him, but I can't escape! And I can't marry anyone else." She sucked in a pained breath and confessed her darkest secret… "Do you have any idea how horrible it is to live day to day praying for a man to die just so you can be free?" She shuddered, the guilt overwhelming. "What kind of evil person does that make me? That I would be happy if he were dead?"

Pearce touched her chin and lifted her head gently to place a soothing kiss to her lips. "It doesn't make you evil. It makes you human." Another kiss, and this time, she tasted forgiveness. "But that can't be the only way out of this marriage. We *will* find another one. Together."

Oh, how she wished that were true! How desperately she wanted to claim back the life that had been denied her with Pearce.

But she knew better. She'd spent too many years desperately attempting to find a way, only to hit dead ends at every turn. There was no hope for them.

Fairy tales and wishes never came true.

"I'm *married*." She stepped back, slipping free of his arms. "Nothing can change that. Divorce, annulment—both are impossible for me."

He fixed his solemn eyes on her. "I don't care as long as you're with me."

She stilled in disbelief, stunned, as his true meaning dawned on her. What he was proposing shook through her, churning and roiling. No, he couldn't possibly be suggesting—

And she couldn't possibly accept.

"What you're proposing…" Grief threatened to overwhelm her. "A pretend marriage, never able to give you a legitimate heir, worried at every turn that someone would find out and your reputation would be ruined—" The grief spilled over, and so did her tears. "I've done it. I've lived that lie for years, and I don't ever want that for us."

"I don't give a damn about any of that."

"But I do. For you." She pressed her fist against her breast as her heart pounded eagerly at the temptation of what he was proposing. Dear God, she wanted nothing more than to be with him! But *never* like that. "You finally have the life you were meant to have, the respect you've always deserved. I won't take that away from you. I won't risk it."

He dropped his gaze pointedly down her front to her belly. "We might not have a choice if you're with child."

She placed her hand over her belly, as if a babe already grew there. A child to love and raise… *His child*.

Happiness at the thought immediately died beneath her anguish. Her hand dropped away as she whispered desolately, "I'm not that lucky."

"I won't let you go, Amelia, do you understand?" He cupped her face between his hands, and she clamped her eyes shut to hold back the flood of tears. "*Never* again. Your husband and your brother can both be damned for all I care."

He leaned in to kiss her, to prove that he meant every word. On his lips she tasted all the love he carried for her and his steely resolve to keep his promise.

But it wasn't enough. He wanted to rescue her, but in this, she would save him.

"No," she whispered, clasping his wrists to pull his hands away and break the embrace that had become torturous. "It's over for us." Once again finished before their future had the chance to even begin. "Tonight was amazing…and wonderful," she choked out, "and you have no idea how very special it is to be with you…to be loved by you."

She took a step back, to put distance between them before she lost all strength and collapsed to the floor in sobs. Or worse, before she rushed back into his arms. Because if she did, she would be lost.

"But that's all it can be—only tonight." The distraught expression that darkened his face nearly undid her. "*This* is why I didn't want to tell you about Aaron. Because I know that nothing can be done about him."

He reached for her. "Amelia—"

She pulled her arm back before his fingers could touch her. But her flesh tingled anyway, a pain as excruciating as what she'd carried with her all these years. A ghost pain. The same felt by soldiers who had lost a limb but still felt its presence. A part of them that would always be missing yet also forever with them.

"To not have you—never completely—never allowed to love with all of myself in every way as a woman and wife should, openly and proudly, without fear for ourselves and our children… I simply couldn't bear it! I want all of you, Pearce." Her voice died to barely a breath. "Or nothing at all."

Nineteen

Damnation. Pearce bit back a grimace. Amelia wouldn't look at him. Instead she stared out the carriage window at the predawn blackness as the city passed by.

In the hour since Merritt Rivers arrived to escort them from the Prospect of Whitby, with Amelia wrapped in an old army greatcoat that Pearce had instructed him to bring to cover her ruined dress, she'd not glanced at him more than a handful of times. Judging by the way she'd fixed her gaze on the black night outside, she had no intention of making it more.

A chasm had opened between them, one as deep and dark as the night around them and just as cold.

But he'd waited twelve years for the chance to have her back. He'd be damned before he let her slip away again.

"That's all you know about the men on the list?" Merritt prompted when she fell silent.

From the moment the hackney had pulled away from the tavern, she'd answered questions under Merritt's gentle interrogation. He was good, Pearce had to give him credit for that. Merritt knew exactly when to press hard and when to ease back to gain the most information, and he was able to string together bits of information that most likely Amelia didn't know were connected. That was why he was among the best barristers in all of the British Empire, certain to be appointed king's counsel at the first opportunity and eventually become a high court judge like his father. His Majesty had no idea of the brilliant mind he'd be gaining in Merritt.

Pearce frowned. Nor how much of a troubled soldier.

Like some of the other men of the Armory, Merritt had not

adapted well to being back in London. Even now, as he did his best to appear relaxed, Pearce knew he was on edge. He'd known Merritt too well for too long not to sense the man's moods. Of course, Pearce's suspicion was helped along in no small part by the way Merritt was dressed from head to boots in solid black and most likely armed to the teeth beneath his greatcoat. If Pearce were a betting man, he'd have wagered his newly acquired earldom that Merritt had been out tonight prowling the streets. Again.

Amelia answered quietly to the window, "I've told you everything."

Merritt slid Pearce a sideways glance, asking for permission to continue. They would be arriving at her shop soon, and the opportunity they'd been given to delve deeper into what she knew would end. They might never have this chance again.

Fighting down a hard breath of guilt at interrogating her like this, Pearce nodded.

Merritt leaned forward, elbows on knees. "Have you ever heard your brother mention a group called Scepter?"

"No." In the black window, her reflection shook its head.

They'd moved beyond the avenues with their gas lamps, now depending upon the lone lamp dangling off the front of the slow-moving hackney to make their way. Around them, Marylebone was asleep. The new rows of terrace houses that lined the streets were all shuttered and dark for the night, the patches of open land between wet from the drizzling rain and uninviting in the thickening fog. She could see nothing beyond the pane of glass, but she insisted on keeping her attention there, rather than on Pearce.

His punishment for daring to love her.

"And you know nothing about them?"

"Only what Pearce has told me. That they're some kind of criminal organization."

"To put it mildly," Merritt acknowledged under his breath. "Have they ever attempted to contact you?"

"No."

"Are you certain? No messages, no threats to harm you or your shop?"

That snagged her full attention, and she darted her gaze between the two men. "Why would they threaten my charity?"

"To force you into pressuring your brother to make those appointments."

"You're mistaken." She gave a short laugh. "I have no power over Freddie."

Pearce didn't doubt that. The Howard men had always treated her as little more than a burden. A doll to control and use as they wished. That her brother had helped her at all after her elopement still surprised him. Frederick Howard was nothing if not mercenary.

"Yet you're the one who's keeping the turnpike trust from going forward."

"Freddie doesn't know that. He thinks I'm willingly participating because he—" She stopped.

A chill coiled its way up Pearce's spine. "Because he's already threatened your charity himself," Pearce quietly finished for her, "so there isn't any need for Scepter to do it."

"Yes," she whispered.

He tightened his jaw. To threaten his sister to save his own hide—the more Pearce learned about the man her brother had become, the more he hated the bastard.

"You think Freddie is directly involved with them?" she asked.

A grim look from Pearce silently answered for him.

"He couldn't be. What need would there be to blackmail him if he's already working with them?"

"We don't know if your brother is part of Scepter," Merritt answered. "But we're certain that the men he's been appointing are. Home Office intelligence has confirmed it."

"We also don't know who wants them there," Pearce added.

She faintly shook her head, putting together as best she could the new puzzle pieces they were revealing to her. "If what you're saying is true, then surely Freddie's not alone. A handful of men in government positions—what good could such a small number do? Perhaps there are other MPs who are being blackmailed, others who haven't carried out their wishes, others against whom the blackmailers have actually carried out their retaliation and revealed their illegal or unethical activities." She arched an accusing brow at Merritt. "You're wasting your time, Mr. Rivers, by taking me the long way around the park just to give yourself more time to interrogate me. You should be questioning Sir Charles Varnham."

Merritt froze, caught by surprise. Most likely for the first time in his entire legal career while questioning a witness.

"Of course he won't be able to give you answers outright. He either isn't aware of the connections and so won't know what information to provide you, or he's working with the blackmailers himself and so won't cooperate. But whoever's been blackmailing my brother has the man's trust." She turned back toward the window. "So I think it might be worth investigating him, don't you?"

Pearce bit back a laugh at that sharp mind of hers. He would have admired her for it, if she didn't frustrate the daylights out of him.

"We'll keep a close eye on Varnham," Pearce assured her, "and if he has any contact with Scepter, we'll find out."

"You'll let me know what you discover?"

"*If* you promise to stay away from him."

The little minx had the nerve to look offended.

"I mean it, Amelia." She might not believe they had a future together, but he did. And he damned well planned on protecting her, whether she liked it or not. "You could have been seriously injured tonight when those men attacked your carriage." *Or killed.* He didn't dare put that into words.

"It was a small disturbance in the streets, that's all, and foot-pads who tried to take advantage after we left the carriage." She gestured at the city around them. "Uprisings have been happening all the time lately, all over London. Sir Charles couldn't possibly have had anything to do with it. For heaven's sake, he wasn't even at the Black Ball tonight to see me leave."

He didn't need to be, if other men were watching her. If other men thought she was a threat to their plans. "Stay away from Varnham," he warned. "I don't want you to have any contact with him whatsoever. If he is connected to Scepter, then he won't hesitate to silence you."

Her eyes gleamed in the shadows as brightly as jewels. "All right. I'll leave him alone."

The carriage stopped. They'd reached her shop.

The Bouquet Boutique was locked up tight against the night, but Amelia would be able to change into a clean dress here before he and Merritt took her home. After all, she couldn't go breezing into the town house looking like this. It was one thing for her to be able to explain why she'd arrived home so late, with excuses at the ready—a late-night visit to the shop, an emergency with one of the women she employed—but it was something altogether different to arrive home late in an army-issued greatcoat over a wet, ruined dress that smelled of the Thames and sour ale.

Even her self-absorbed nodcock of a brother would demand answers, if only out of concern for his own reputation.

When she rose to leave the carriage, Pearce placed a hand on her forearm. She flinched, her gaze dropping to his fingers as if he'd scorched her.

Damn it to hell. She used to crave his nearness, used to find reassurance in his touch. Now she wanted him as far away from her as possible.

Except that she didn't. Because under his fingertips at her wrist, he felt her pulse racing. He took hope in that.

"Merritt and I have to wait here," he instructed. "You can't risk that we'll be seen entering the shop with you."

"I understand." There was no anger in her reply, only regret. A world of private meaning lived in her voice when she assured him quietly, "I'll be fine on my own."

He released her, and her arm slipped from his grasp. She stepped down onto the footpath. Pearce watched through the window as she hurried through the shadows to the door.

"There was no riot tonight," Merritt said quietly. "Those men purposefully targeted her carriage. You know that."

Yes. But Pearce hadn't wanted to terrify Amelia by telling her. "She confronted her brother tonight about the trust, told him she wouldn't support it. Right there in the ballroom," he said quietly. "I think someone overheard and wanted to threaten her into changing her mind."

"Did it work?"

He watched grimly as she glanced over her shoulder at the dark, empty street before letting herself into the shop. "No."

"She lied to you, you know. She has no intention of leaving Varnham alone."

"I know."

"So what are you going to do?"

"If you race the devil for your soul," he murmured, "you'd damned well better win."

"Pardon?"

Pearce cast him a determined glance. "I'm going to beat her to him."

———————

Pearce placed his hat and coat into the attendant's arms as he strode through the front door of Boodle's that afternoon, then slapped him in the chest with his gloves as he handed them over. He didn't have membership here. Wasn't on the guest list. And didn't give a damn. The attendant was wise enough not to stop him. So was the club manager as the man nodded his greetings and let Pearce pass. Being an earl had its privileges.

He strode into the dining room, raising eyebrows of the members scattered at the tables. He didn't give a damn about them either.

He had one reason for being here, and it wasn't to play nicely with others—

Howard.

Amelia's brother sat at a small table in the corner, where he was lunching on a plate of roast pheasant and chatting with two of his cronies. Pearce stalked toward him, halting conversation at every table he passed and trailing whispers in his wake.

The man looked up, just as startled as everyone else in the club to see him there. "Sandhurst." Surprise lightened his voice. "How pleasant to—"

"I want a word with you." He narrowed his eyes at the two men flanking Howard. "In private."

"Of course." He smiled apologetically at his chums. "If you might leave us for a moment?"

The men rose from their chairs, not giving Pearce another look as they left the room to wait in the bar.

"Boodle's," Pearce muttered as he sat heavily on the chair opposite Howard and pushed the previous man's half-finished plate away. He made a disinterested gesture at the club around them. "I'm surprised that a man of your political ambitions isn't entrenched in Brooks's. That *is* where the Whigs live these days."

Howard leaned back in his chair with a twist of a smile. "My allegiance is to my country, not to a club or even to one political party."

Pearce chuckled darkly. "I didn't think you had allegiance to anyone but yourself."

Amelia's brother merely shrugged, not feeling the sting of that insult. "A man has to look after himself these days." He reached for his port. "He'd be a fool not to."

"And your sister, don't forget. You look after her, too."

He lifted the glass in a toast. "Above all else."

Pearce longed to slam his fist into the man's face. Instead, he smiled tightly. "Good. Then we're in agreement that Miss Howard's interests should be taken into consideration when it comes to the turnpike."

Howard nearly spilled his port. "Pardon?"

"Last night, after we spoke at the ball, I had the chance to spend time with your sister." Time that he would never forget. "We discussed Bradenhill." Among other things. "She's concerned about losing control of her property, that the trustees will put their interests above hers. I assured her that I would protect her." He fixed his gaze on Howard. "Always."

"Then—" Howard lowered his voice so they wouldn't be overheard. "You've come to a decision regarding the trust?"

"I have." He waved away the waiter when the man came forward to take his lunch order. He had no appetite. "I'm all in for the project."

A wide smile broke across Howard's face. "That's wond—"

"But I don't want to wait. I want to move ahead at full speed, to make certain the trust passes through Parliament before the current session closes."

"I couldn't agree more." Happiness—and relief—beamed from the man. "So we'll talk to—"

"Only one thing's holding me back."

His smile vanished, and he snapped out, "For Christ's sake!" When other members at the tables around them frowned at him, he leaned forward in exasperation and lowered his voice. "What could possibly be holding you back *now*?"

"I want to meet the other men you've chosen to be trustees."

Pearce tapped his finger against the table to punctuate his point. "I won't agree until I've had the chance to make certain that all of our interests align. I'm an experienced soldier. Character matters to me. So does trust. When the enemy has its guns pointed at you, the last thing you want to question is whether the men behind you have your back." He smiled coldly. "Or if they'll tuck tail and run."

"I assure you that these men possess exemplary character."

And Pearce was sure that he'd just lied. "Then I look forward to meeting them."

"I'll make arrangements."

"Do so quickly," he warned, shoving himself away from the table.

With that, Pearce strode from the club, pausing only to pull on his coat and hat in the foyer before stepping into the chilly rain. Howard would lead him to the last men on the blackmailer's list, and those men would lead him to Scepter. He would stop their threats, and Amelia would be safe. And once Amelia was safe, he could focus all his attention on the next battle.

Making her his wife.

Twenty

"WHO'S TO SAY THAT PANGLOSS ISN'T CORRECT, THAT THIS world—for all its capriciousness, violence, and volatility, a world in which we are utterly lost to the buffeting winds of fate—isn't in fact the best?"

Amelia rolled her eyes. And with that, the London Ladies were back to debating Voltaire. Again.

"The best of all *possible* worlds," one of the two dozen self-declared bluestockings crammed into the Countess of St James's drawing room challenged, eliciting soft *oohs* of revelation from the rest of the group. And a long-suffering sigh from Amelia. "*That* was the phrase. Not the best world—the best of all *possible* worlds, and Candide's world is clearly not the best possible."

"Possible," another repeated, defending the first woman's position. "Not imaginable. I can imagine a world created from chocolate—and surely that would be the best of all worlds." Her aside brought nods of agreement. "But imagining it does mean it's possible. Therefore, the best of all possible worlds might very well be Candide's."

That set off a firestorm of voices, all interjecting at once. And a fierce pounding at the back of Amelia's skull.

Enough! She couldn't stand one moment more of this. But she also couldn't bring herself to return home, either, where she'd be alone with reminders of all she'd lost by marrying Aaron. So she mumbled her apologies as she slid from the room, letting everyone believe she was visiting the retiring room.

Instead of turning left in the hall, however, she turned right and slipped into the music room, hoping to find a quiet moment to herself. The side garden was dark, not in use for tonight's gathering, but she opened the French doors anyway to take a deep breath and let the cool night air clear her head and ease the pain throbbing behind her eyes.

But it did little to soothe the anguish lodged around her heart. How could the foolish thing keep beating, when all she'd ever dreamed of having was now dead?

"Pearce," she breathed out as she leaned against the open door and somehow found the will to keep the gathering tears from spilling free. She could still feel the strength of his arms around her, the masculine scent of him filling up her senses, and the tender way his body had rocked into hers, bringing her such pleasures as she'd never known. She could still hear his voice... *I love you.*

Everything she'd ever wanted, all of it simply dropped in front of her like a present with a big bow, ready to be unwrapped.

But also nothing she could ever have.

"Amelia?" a voice called out from the hallway, just beyond the door. "Did you come this way?"

Amelia straightened and swiped a hand at her eyes to hide any traces of telltale tears.

"Ah yes! There you are."

She had just enough time to force a smile before Lady Agnes Sinclair swept into the room.

In a gold-edged purple gown that could have rivaled any silks found in a Turkish bazaar, capped by an orange turban decorated with a large ruby pin, the woman was simply a force of nature. The unmarried sister of the late Earl of St James and aunt to the current earl, Agnes was well known for her eccentricities and her peculiar take on the latest fashions. Possessing an air of impropriety that society only tolerated because of her age, she was gregarious, flirtatious, and amusingly inappropriate. And as Amelia had come to learn since joining the London Ladies, she also possessed an intellect that was sharp as glass.

Lady Agnes held out one of the two cups and saucers she carried. "Tea."

The woman's thoughtfulness warmed Amelia. "You followed after just to bring me tea?"

"I followed you because if I have to sit through one more declaration by Lady Houston that Voltaire possessed the greatest mind since Aristotle, I might very well strangle her." She insistently held out the tea, and Amelia had no choice but to accept, although she had no taste for the stuff. "Not the kind of catharsis Aristotle had in mind, I daresay, but *I* would surely enjoy it."

Despite the heaviness that gripped her, Amelia smiled at the image that popped into her head of Lady Agnes doing just that.

"So when I saw you slip from the room, I decided that your idea of leaving was a grand one, snatched up two teas, and followed." She took Amelia's arm and steered her through the French doors and onto the narrow terrace beyond. "Let's sit here and enjoy the fresh air."

Amelia arched a brow. "And make it harder for anyone to find us if they come looking?"

"Why, I would never suggest such a thing!" She gestured toward a nearby bench in the shadows and sat, then smiled conspiratorially with a wink as she patted the seat next to her. "Which is why I'm so glad that *you* did."

The woman laughed at her own joke, then raised the cup to her lips to take a long sip of tea. Not wanting to offend her, Amelia did the same—

She choked. Her cup clanked against the saucer as it dropped in surprise. Her fingers went to her lips at the unexpected burning that ran down her throat.

She stared down into the cup and rasped, "That's—that's—"

"The best tea in all of the British Empire, yes."

"Whiskey!" she coughed out. With just a splash of tea to disguise it.

Beside her, Agnes smiled against the rim of her cup as she took another slow sip, like the cat who'd gotten into the cream. "As I said, the best tea in the British Empire."

Amelia had always thought those stories of Lady Agnes lacing her tea with real drink were apocryphal. Until now. To think of all those long evenings of bluestocking arguments, while Agnes sat quietly in the rear of the room, sipping her tea and smiling… Amelia suddenly gained a whole new appreciation for the woman.

"Now that we've settled in with our tea," Agnes prompted, "why don't you tell me what's wrong?"

"Nothing's wrong. I just needed a few minutes' peace." Amelia took another sip to cover the lie.

Agnes rested a ring-laden hand on her arm. "Pace yourself, my dear, or that tea will go straight to your head."

Would that be so bad? Men numbed themselves in drink all the time. Why shouldn't she?

Yet she cautiously returned the whiskey to its saucer.

"Tell me your troubles." Agnes wagged a finger at her in warning. "And do not dissemble."

Amelia dropped her gaze to her cup, carefully balanced on her knee. "What makes you think anything is troubling me?"

"And do not prevaricate with me either. I *know* something is amiss. While discussing Voltaire is never a joyful experience, it certainly doesn't deserve the look of the gallows that's been darkening your face all evening." She slanted her a sideways glance, her expression softening. "A look that wretched must be the fault of love."

"*Pardon?*" Amelia startled, the air rushing from her lungs. How had Agnes guessed?

"Only love can make a woman grieve that hard." Lady Agnes's voice lowered as she added into her tea, "Believe me, I know."

"With all due respect, my lady." That Agnes Sinclair, of all women, would be a kindred spirit— "Not this you don't."

"Hmm. Perhaps not. Every love is different." Agnes thoughtfully traced a fingertip around the rim of her cup. "And mine *was* a very long time ago. I was only eighteen and incredibly foolish. Not so much younger than you."

Amelia smiled at that compliment. "I haven't been eighteen in a good while, my lady."

"But have you been foolish recently?"

Her shoulders sagged. "A great deal, it seems."

"Then we are not so different after all. Lost love and missed opportunities curse all women who lead with their hearts." She paused. "Is that what happened to you?"

With a hollow ache blossoming in her chest, Amelia confided, "Yes, missed love...twice."

"Then fate must be on your side."

A half-hysterical laugh strangled in Amelia's throat. "Fate delights in tormenting me!"

"Fate has given you a second chance, my dear. Why have you not taken it?"

Amelia lowered her gaze to her tea and whispered, "Because it's impossible."

Agnes patted Amelia's arm reassuringly. "I understand impossible love."

"Your bout of young foolishness, you mean?" Amelia changed the focus of the conversation away from herself. Gladly.

"A captain in the cavalry. The most handsome, most dashing man I'd ever seen in my life. And still is, despite over forty years of meeting all kinds of men since." Even in the shadows, her eyes sparkled at the memory of him. "Oh, he was simply marvelous! A more true gentleman was never so lowborn."

"But you didn't marry him." Amelia turned toward her on the stone bench. Perhaps Lady Agnes understood after all. "Why not?"

"Because he was utterly impossible for the daughter of an earl." She took a sip of tea to fortify herself against old wounds. "I was meant to marry well, someone possessing wealth and status. My family would never have let me marry a poor army officer, no matter how much we loved each other, no matter how good a man he was."

Emotions tightened Amelia's throat. "You never considered defying them?"

"Heavens no!" she scoffed, as if Amelia had suggested that unicorns existed. "What would have been the good in that? My father refused to give permission for us to wed."

"But you could have run away and married anyway."

Lady Agnes shook her head. "Not in those days. There were no good roads to Scotland then, no money for us to book passage on a ship. And marriage in England was out of the question. I couldn't marry here without my father's consent. If we'd have attempted it, he would have demanded the marriage be annulled on grounds of incompetency because I was too young."

"But an annulment would have scandalized you and your family." In that, at least, she and Lady Agnes were different. *Her* father had made certain that Pearce could never have wed her in the first place. "Surely, that would have been worse for your family than letting you remain married to an army officer."

"You don't know what my father was like, my dear, and my brother after him." A knowing, bitter smile pulled tightly across Lady Agnes's face. "They would have seen an annulment—and my ruination—as punishment for defying them. One they would have believed I deserved."

Amelia looked away, unable to bear seeing her own pain reflected in Lady Agnes's eyes. How many times did her father remind her of what would happen to both her and Pearce if they ever tried to contact each other? How often had Frederick blamed her for Aaron's deceit?

"You didn't wait for him?" she whispered into the darkness.

"I did, at first. But by the time I was old enough not to need my father's permission to marry, my captain had been killed in battle." She set her tea aside and reached with both hands for Amelia's. "I lost the love of my life. I wasn't given a second chance. But *you* have been." She rested her palm against Amelia's cheek.

"Do not waste this opportunity, or you will regret it for the rest of your life."

Not waste it? Laughable! She had no choice in the matter. Fate hadn't given her a second chance. Fate was laughing at her for ever daring to love in the first place.

Lady Agnes placed a kiss to Amelia's forehead, then collected her tea and stood.

"Stay here a while. I won't tell anyone where you've disappeared to." She gave a parting pat to Amelia's hand. "But don't dawdle long. I need you as an ally. Lady Helen always finds a way to steer the conversation to Montesquieu if we don't stop her, and I don't think my nerves can tolerate both him and Voltaire in the same evening." She cast a forlorn look back toward the drawing room and heaved out a long-suffering sigh. "It's like being stuck at a dinner between the world's two most narcissistic guests, only to discover that there's no pudding waiting at the end."

Amelia gave a short laugh despite the stinging of tears that threatened at her eyes.

"When fate brings us love, we have to hold on tight with both hands and never let go." Agnes looked down sympathetically at her. "Whatever you do, my dear, do *not* let go."

Amelia choked back a sob. If only being with Pearce were that simple! But she couldn't fight her father twelve years ago, and she couldn't fight the courts and the church now.

She said nothing as Lady Agnes made her way through the darkness and back into the house, but her hands trembled so badly that the whiskey from her cup sloshed over into the saucer. With a soft curse at herself, she set the unwanted drink aside, then dropped her head into her hands.

But for once, no tears came.

During the past twenty-four hours since Pearce had admitted to loving her, she'd cried enough to flood the Thames. Now, hopelessness ate at her, and she didn't have the strength to let loose another tear. What good would it have done, anyway? All the tears in the world weren't enough to dissolve her marriage. She'd given her soul to the devil the day she signed her name in the parish register.

With numb lips, she whispered into the darkness, "How could I ever have been so blind?"

Because she'd been in love. With Pearce. And needed someone to heal the wound that his absence had cut into her heart. Instead, Aaron had ended up shattering it.

Lady Agnes hadn't experienced that. She at least had a chance at being with the man she loved. Amelia had never had that with Pearce.

Not being granted permission to marry? She choked back a strangled cry. If only that were the case! Frederick would certainly grant his consent to Pearce, now that he'd become an earl and a war hero, with a fortune to accompany the fame. After all, he'd so eagerly given it to Aaron, and he was—

Her head snapped up, her chest squeezing so hard that it forced the air from her lungs. Her heart stopped.

Frederick *hadn't* given his permission. Not officially.

Oh, he'd pressed for the courtship and engagement, all right. But when it came time for the actual wedding, he'd vanished to London. The marriage settlement had been left unsigned, there was no public announcement or notification to any of their friends or distant family, no engagement party—they hadn't even had a reading of the banns because Aaron had secured a special license so that they could wed outside his home parish.

Yet she'd been only twenty and needed her guardian's consent…the same consent Frederick never publicly gave.

When her heart came back to life, the jarring thud was so violent that she cried out. This time not in pain but hope.

Shoving herself off the bench, she rushed inside the house to find Lady St James and give her apologies for having to leave so suddenly. But with the way she was shaking and fully unable to catch her breath, the countess had no reason to doubt her excuse that she'd suddenly grown ill. Neither did the hackney jarvey whom she ordered to take her home to Hill Street—"Quickly!"

She'd thrown open the carriage door and jumped to the ground before the carriage had come to a complete stop in front of the town house, then rushed inside with orders for a startled Drummond to pay the driver, leaving him in the front hall gaping after her. No explanations. No excuses.

No time.

She ran through the house to Frederick's study and his desk. Her hands pulled desperately at the drawers—*locked*.

With determination pulsing through her veins, she snatched up the letter opener.

She paused only a moment to consider what she was doing, breaking into Freddie's private study like this. Then she promptly dismissed the tiny prick of guilt as she slipped the knife-like tool into the center drawer and gave a hard twist. The lock popped free. She yanked open the drawer and grabbed up the little brass key her brother kept there.

She stalked across the room to the tallboy where Freddie kept all of his most important papers locked away from the servants and any prying guests—away from her. She slid the key into the top drawer lock and opened it with a soft click. Then the next drawer, the next after that…all the way down the front of the Chippendale cabinet, unlocking each faster than the one before. When the bottom drawer unlocked, she tossed the key to the floor and yanked it open.

She'd never dared to look through Freddie's papers before, not wanting to risk his anger. Nor had she ever had cause. As far as the law was concerned, as her closest male relative, he was still her guardian, and that was his role—to oversee all that concerned her legally, financially…*every* way.

But he'd been a good guardian. Always, he'd made things so easy for her by making all the decisions himself, taking care of all the paperwork, simply giving her an allowance to run the household and pin money for her own expenses. Never had he wanted to burden her—

That time was over.

Her fingers flew through the papers stored inside the drawer, looking for any that were dated from seven years ago. *Nothing.* Determined, she pulled open the next drawer.

"Miss!" Drummond hurried into the room, aghast at what she was doing.

"Please leave, Drummond." She didn't bother to look up. "I'll call if I need you."

Ignoring the butler, she began to pull out the files and stack them on the rug. She couldn't have cared less what she looked like to the servants, ransacking her own home like this. What mattered was finding her marriage contract. Surely, Frederick had kept it. God knew he kept everything, like a pack rat who—

There. Third drawer from the bottom, halfway through the stack.

She sank to the floor as relief flooded over her. Holding her breath, she scanned the sheet to make certain it was exactly as she remembered, with Aaron's aristocratic signature scrawled across the bottom, her worthless one beneath…and an empty space where Frederick should have signed.

Oh, thank God!

Her hands shook as she held it. *All* of her shook! For the first time in seven years, she had hope. *Real* hope. She could barely breathe beneath the sob that swelled up from the back of her throat.

So much more than a mere piece of paper. It was her freedom. The document she could use to press for an annulment. Legally, the unsigned agreement couldn't stand on its own, but when added to Aaron's abandonment of her, her minority when they'd married, and Frederick's testimony that he'd never granted permission, it would surely be enough for an annulment. *Please, God, let it be enough!*

She clutched the paper to her bosom, needing to prove to herself that it was real. Her petition would be messy and drawn out, expensive, absolutely scandalous...the verdict hanging by a thin thread, surely. But in the end, she would be free and legally entitled to remarry. She would finally be free to love Pearce, completely and openly, and his good character as a war hero and peer would prop up her charity and keep it from ruin until the scandal blew over.

If Freddie cooperated. *If* he were willing to have her sham of a marriage exposed and suffer all the damage by association that pursuing an annulment would surely bring.

A tortured sound rose from her. Even now, with freedom resting in her hands, she was trapped beneath the will of a man. Would she *ever* be free?

As she began to return the unwanted papers to the drawers, another sheet caught her attention, and she stilled. Another document with Aaron's signature.

She frowned. She didn't remember any other papers except the settlement. Fresh dread surged through her. If that sheet documented any kind of consent between Aaron and Frederick—

No. She didn't dare let herself believe that. Yet her hand trembled as she reached for it. It looked like...a receipt? No, a contract of sorts, in which Frederick promised to pay Aaron five hundred pounds for services rendered in Birmingham, England, March 1811.

She frowned. March. The same month they'd met.

"This makes no sense," she muttered, reading it again, this time much more slowly in search of any details she'd missed. Why would Freddie had been making contracts with Aaron so soon after meeting him?

"Amelia! What on God's earth are you doing?"

Her gaze darted to the doorway, where Freddie glared at the mess on the floor. And at her.

Her mind whirled to find an excuse. She couldn't tell him the truth—not yet. Not until she'd discussed it with Pearce. And not until she'd come up with a good argument to convince Freddie to go along with her plan. Or a good way to coerce him, if logic failed. After all, she still held the key to keeping the blackmailer at bay and keeping Freddie out of prison. He would owe her for that… and she was certain that he would gladly be rid of her by handing her over to an earl.

Judging from the furious look on his face, not a moment too soon either.

He stepped into the study. "You're going through my private papers. You broke into my cabinet!" His eyes narrowed on her. "What's that in your hand?"

Freedom. "My marriage settlement." She held it up. No point in attempting to hide it.

He frowned, bewildered. "What do you want with that?"

"Pearce." That was the God's honest truth.

He froze, except for his face which paled. "Sandhurst knows about your marriage?"

She swallowed. Hard. And lied. "No. The turnpike. He wanted to make certain that I had ownership rights to Bradenhill, that I could consent fully to the trust without worry that someone else might have a claim to it."

"But you refused the trust." His eyes gleamed darkly as he slowly approached her. "Quite publicly, too."

"He changed my mind." Surprisingly, no guilt accompanied lying to her brother. Only regret that they were so suspicious of each other that she couldn't even trust him with something as potentially wonderful as this. "He made me realize that I'd be able to help even more women with the revenue a turnpike would bring."

A knowing smile broke across his face. "Finally you've listened to reason."

No. Finally she'd listened to her heart. "He wanted to make certain that the decision would be completely and freely mine," she echoed his words from last night's ball. "That was when I remembered the marriage agreement. I wanted to make certain that Aaron couldn't make any claims against the property. I wanted—" She looked down at the paper in her hand and took courage in it. "I wanted to make certain that the property was listed in the agreement as part of my dower. That way, if he ever does return and attempts to take it, I can use the intent of the agreement to make my argument to keep it."

"Intent is worthless under the law. That agreement wasn't signed by both parties, and *that* was what allowed him to steal all your money. That's what all the lawyers I hired told us when we tried to retrieve your money, remember? Every last one of them." He crossed his arms and glared down at her, the look of a prefect scolding a misbehaving student. "You were impetuous and acted without thinking, and we're suffering because of it."

With a scowl, he grabbed up the papers she'd tossed onto the floor and shoved them back into the tallboy, then picked up the key from the floor and locked all the drawers. Instead of putting the key back into his desk, he slipped it into his breast pocket.

Guilt began to rise in her throat—

No. He wouldn't make her feel awful this time, as he always had before. She wouldn't let him.

Pearce was right. She'd gone into her marriage with love, and the lies and treachery Aaron committed were *not* her fault. She could never have foreseen what he'd planned. No woman could have. She wouldn't blame herself any longer.

Now, she would take back the life she'd been cheated out of.

"I found something else." She held up the other document. The contract Freddie had made with Aaron. "What is this?"

Frederick took it and heaved out a sigh as he glanced over it. "Nothing to concern yourself with." He added in an irritated mutter, "Like every other document in this cabinet that you have no right to rifle through."

Despite his anger, she held on to her resolve and pressed, "You paid Aaron five hundred pounds. Why?"

"I don't remember. That was so long ago. I'm sure I had good reason." He shoved it into his jacket breast pocket. "But you've nothing to fear about Bradenhill, I assure you." With a pleased smile, he crossed to the liquor tray and poured himself a glass of cognac from the crystal decanter. "Aaron Northam won't be able to take your land, and he won't be able to stop the trust now either. No one can."

Alarm twisted in her belly. "What do you mean?"

"Sandhurst finally agreed. Told me himself just this afternoon at Boodle's." He returned the stopper with a soft clank, punctuating the significance of the moment. "Wants to push it through as quickly as possible, in fact, before the current session of Parliament ends." He lifted the glass to her in a toast. "Congratulations, Amelia. We've got our turnpike trust."

Her breath hitched. Pearce agreed? *Impossible.* He said they were together in stopping it, in discovering who was behind the blackmail. He would never have agreed without consulting with her first…would he?

Shame heated her cheeks, and she silently castigated herself for doubting him. She'd questioned Pearce's love for her for so long that even now her first reaction was distrust.

But she wouldn't let suspicion win. Not this time. He loved her, he wanted to protect her, he wanted to marry her… That was where she'd put her trust now. In Pearce's heart.

If he'd agreed, he had good reason. Yet he'd done so without her when they were supposed to be working together. She couldn't help a prick of betrayal in her belly.

"It's all gone exactly as planned." Frederick took a long swallow of cognac, as happy as the cat who'd caught the mouse. "Now the blackmail threats will end, and my career will be saved." He gestured at her with the glass. "Your future as the sister of an MP is secure, society matrons will continue to cross the threshold of your little shop, and you don't have to pretend to like Sandhurst any longer."

"No." She gave him a smile, one Freddie completely misread. "I don't have to pretend to like him."

He finished the cognac and set the glass down. "I'm going out to a club meeting and taking Sandhurst with me. I'll be certain to tell him how happy you are about the trust."

"No need." She fought to keep the irony from her voice. "I'd be happy to tell him myself how I feel about it, the first chance I have."

"I'll be gone all night, most likely not back before dawn." He sauntered from the study. "Don't wait up."

Twenty-one

"ARE YOU SURE ABOUT THIS?"

"Not at all." Pearce flicked his gaze at Merritt Rivers in the dressing mirror as his man McTavish fussed with his cravat. The old camp aide turned valet knew practically nothing about dressing a gentleman, but Pearce hadn't hired him for his grooming skills. He'd hired him because McTavish had been a trusted and dependable soldier during the wars, only to find himself cast out upon the streets after returning home. The same story with practically all the other servants comprising his household. "That's why I want you to follow us tonight."

Merritt slid a slow look over Pearce. "Keeping you in sight won't be difficult."

Pearce frowned at his reflection in the drawing room mirror. *Most likely not.* White jacket, white breeches and stockings—white everything, except for his boots, whose black leather McTavish had shined to gleaming. But those were the instructions Howard had included in the note he'd sent over just after six o'clock. The meeting with the trustees had been arranged for that night. Be ready to be collected at half past eleven. Wear all white, including the white cap that the messenger had handed over when he'd delivered the note.

Dressed like this at midnight, he'd stand out like a beacon. Or a target. Not exactly a reassuring thought, considering Scepter's penchant for murdering people.

"And our next step after tonight?" Merritt asked.

Pearce waved McTavish out of the room with his mumbled thanks. Not that he didn't trust the man; he did, with his life. But knowing anything about Scepter, no matter how small, might put McTavish's life at risk.

When the door closed, Pearce turned away from the mirror and lifted a glass of whiskey to his lips. "We use the trustees to get closer to Scepter." He took a swallow, letting it warm down his throat. "I don't have to learn why they're being placed, just who's been pressing for it. That should lead me to Scepter's leadership."

"Charles Varnham's involved, if Miss Howard's right. Perhaps we should do as she suggested and focus on him."

Pearce shook his head. "I'm not certain. If Varnham wanted—"

A door slammed downstairs, followed by the sound of a muffled argument and pounding footsteps. Both men tensed. His gaze not leaving Pearce's, Merritt silently slid his hand into his jacket sleeve for the knife he kept there.

"No, I will not wait in the drawing room—Pearce!" The female voice shouted through the house, followed by more pounding footsteps. "Pearce! Where the devil are you?"

"Miss Howard's come calling." Merritt grimly slid the knife out of his sleeve and held it handle-first toward Pearce. "You're going to need this."

Pearce grimaced.

"Miss, stop where you are," McTavish's gruff voice climbed the stairs. "That is an order!"

His grimace turned into a wince. Oh, *that* was not going to go over well!

"An order?" Her voice rose with all the imperial haughtiness of a dowager duchess on an iceberg. "An *order*? How *dare* you think that you…"

Merritt slipped the knife back beneath his sleeve and declared, deadpan, "It's now every man for himself."

His bedroom door burst open. Amelia paused in the doorway, the hood of her cloak falling down around her shoulders and still dotted with raindrops from the drizzle falling over London. She was out of breath from racing up the stairs, her eyes blazing like a Fury's. And was simply magnificent for it.

"Apologies, sir," McTavish panted out behind her. "She slipped past me on the stairs."

"I'm sure she did." Pearce fought back a smile at the old soldier's wounded pride that the enemy had penetrated the lines. "It's all right. Miss Howard is welcome here."

She arched a brow. "You owe me an explanation."

So...her brother had told her about the trust. She was bound to have found out sooner or later, but this wasn't at all the way Pearce wanted to have this conversation. And certainly not with Merritt and McTavish listening in.

"Yes, I do." He came forward. "But not in my bedroom."

Her cheeks flushed as she looked around and realized for the first time what room they were in. "I don't care."

"I do. Gentlemen, we're finished for the evening." He called out over his shoulder as he took her arm to lead her out. "McTavish, I won't need you when I return."

He gave a sharp nod. "Yes, Brigadier."

"And Merritt, you'll do as we discussed?"

"Count on it."

"Thank you. Can you show yourself out? Miss Howard and I might have a long discussion ahead of us." He frowned down at Amelia and sensed the emotion pulsating from her. A *very* long discussion.

Merritt grinned as he slid past them and out the door, drawling, "Count on it."

Pearce's glare only made Merritt laugh.

"This way, then." He led her downstairs.

When they reached the drawing room, Pearce slid closed the pocket doors and leaned back against them, crossing his arms over his chest so he wouldn't sweep her off her feet and carry her right back upstairs to his bed.

He shot her a no-nonsense look. "You shouldn't be here."

"And you shouldn't have spoken to Freddie without me." With

her eyes flashing brightly in her pale face, she looked as determined as a green captain about to lead his first battle charge. "You said we were in this together."

"We are."

"Since when is agreeing to the trust on your own the definition of togetherness?" She waved a hand in no particular direction. A sign of how upset she was. "I *want* to trust in you, Pearce, but—"

"You can." He kept his voice even and calm, just as he kept his distance and remained where he was. He was aching to hold and reassure her, but he couldn't. Not yet. Not until she was ready. "You know me, Amelia. You know how I feel about you."

As she stared at him, biting her bottom lip, he could see her struggling with what he was telling her. She wanted to believe him, he knew. But the men in her life had taught her hard lessons about trust, had used her for their own benefit— Damn to hell every man who had ever wounded her!

But Pearce wouldn't be among them.

"I would never betray you." Keeping his distance was killing him. "In your heart, you know that."

"Then why?" Her anger deflated, along with her shoulders as they sagged beneath her cloak. "And after we…" Her voice choked off.

"Made love," he finished gently for her.

Her cheeks pinkened beautifully at the memory. "I thought we'd agreed about the turnpike."

"We did. But events have sped up, and I needed to act." Losing the battle to keep himself away from her, he shoved away from the door and stopped in front of her. "There are more lives at risk now, including yours. Delaying is no longer an option."

Her eyes widened, an expression that had him longing to kiss the confusion from her lips.

"We *are* in this together, Amelia, but I will always draw the line at protecting you." He touched her cheek to punctuate that promise. "I didn't tell you that I'd planned to agree to the trust precisely because I knew you would want to stop me. Or worse—that you'd do something foolish like go after Varnham again." When she began to protest, he cut her off with a touch of his fingertip to her lips. "But we're running out of time, and I need to get closer to Scepter." He crossed his arms before he wrapped them around her and pulled her against him. At that moment, if he did, he was certain she'd flee. "I'd like your understanding. But even without it, I'm going through with this. Starting tonight."

They stared at each other for a long while, neither speaking, neither moving. Like two adversaries staring at each other across the battlefield, each waiting for the other to give first.

Then she nodded jerkily and turned her eyes away. Not the eager endorsement he'd hoped for, yet he'd gladly accept it. With Amelia, he'd take his victories whenever he could.

Blowing out a hard breath, he sank heavily onto the settee. The posture of a man at the limits of his patience.

"We can discuss our next steps tomorrow, if you'd like, after I've learned more about the trustees. But for now, you need to leave. Your brother will be here in an hour to take me to meet them." He raked his gaze heatedly over her, so intensely that she shivered. "And if you stay, I *will* make love to you."

Her lips parted in surprise at the boldness of that declaration. *Good.* Because he wasn't teasing.

"I know how you feel about our situation. You were quite clear about it last night, and I respect your decision." Even if he hated it. He grimly leaned forward, to rest his elbows on his knees and clasp his hands between them. His gaze bore into hers. "But know that I will shamelessly seduce you if given half the chance, and I will revel in the sweetness of you, in every kiss and touch, every soft sigh and moan that falls from your lips."

When she swallowed at that wholly wanton declaration, he longed to place his mouth against her throat, to taste the soft undulation beneath his lips.

"And if that happens, you'll be in serious trouble." The warning pulsed between them with a life of its own. "Because if I make love to you a second time, Amelia, I will *never* let you go. Marriage or not."

Through her stunned expression, he couldn't read the thoughts that were surely swirling through that sharp mind of hers. But he was absolutely serious. If she knew what was good for her, she'd turn tail and run.

Instead, the minx slowly approached him, one deliberate step at a time. Her eyes never left his, not even when she reached up to untie her cloak and let it fall to the floor.

His pulse spiked, and as she came closer, he sat back to keep as much distance between them as possible. "I'm serious."

"So am I," she murmured in a throaty rasp that sent a quiver of desire arcing through him.

He caught his breath when she reached him. But she didn't stop even then. With one hand reaching for his shoulder and the other pulling her skirt up her thighs and out of the way, she climbed on top of him, straddling him right there on the settee.

He didn't dare put his hands on her. If he did, it wouldn't be to set her away. "Amelia—"

"Let me make certain that I have this right," she murmured. "If we make love a second time, you'll never let me go?"

"That's right," he forced out through gritted teeth.

Her hand slipped over the now tense muscle of his shoulder to sift tantalizingly through the short hair at his nape. Each brush of her fingers shot electricity straight down to the tip of his cock.

She lowered her head until her lips lingered just above his. Her warm breath tickled teasingly over his lips. "Promise?"

His restraint snapped. With a growl, he rose and kissed her.

She gave a soft cry of surprise when he wrapped his arms around her and pulled her down onto him. Fierce and hungry, he kissed her with greedy, openmouthed kisses that stole her breath away and left her melting into his embrace.

Rasping out her name, he reached for her hair to pull out the pins holding it in place and throw them aside to scatter across the marble floor. He shoved his hands into her golden tresses, letting them tumble down around his own head and shoulders as she leaned over him to match the ferocity of the embrace, kiss for kiss, yearning for yearning.

Gone was the sweet girl he knew from his youth. Gone, too, was the innocent woman he'd made love to in the tavern. In her place sat a goddess, the most seductive woman he'd ever known. That she was also the woman he loved—had *always* loved—rocked him to his core.

She wrapped her arms around his neck and arched herself into him, pressing her breasts flat against his chest. Then she squirmed on his lap, the desire inside her pulsing into him, and a groan tore from him. He wanted nothing more than to devour her.

"Touch me," she urged and bit tauntingly at his bottom lip.

He slipped his hands beneath her skirt and stroked up her inner thighs. The silk of her stockings gave way to bare flesh, and bare flesh gave way to—

"Yes," she panted out as his fingers found her. "There…right there."

"Jesus," he bit out as he stroked her. "You're already slick."

To prove it, he slipped a finger inside her warmth. She whimpered with need and clenched around him, her fingertips digging into the tight muscles of his shoulders.

He wanted to tease her to release. But when she threw back her head and began to thrust her hips against his hand, begging with her body to be satisfied, the time for teasing vanished. He flicked his thumb against her clit, and she jumped from a spasm of pleasure that left her folds quivering around his finger.

She was ready for him. God knew he was more than ready for her.

He reached down to open his fall and yanked his shirt out of the way to free his cock. When he teased against her folds with his tip, to slicken it with her dew, her breath came in shallow pants of anticipation that matched his own. He nestled his tip down into her folds to hold himself there and fixed his eyes on hers as his hands encircled her hips. Then with a gentle yank, he pulled her forward and slid deep inside her.

She gasped at being filled so completely, so suddenly. Then the sound transformed into a throaty moan when he moved her hips to seat her fully over him.

"Like this," he murmured as his hands at her hips began to lift and lower her over his cock in long, smooth strokes, guiding her in a wanton rhythm that left him breathless. "Sweet Jesus…just like this."

But the beautiful, independent creature in his arms had no patience and began to move against him on her own in jerking little thrusts whose unpracticed eagerness drove him wild. Her thighs shook around him as the tension mounted inside her, her fingers digging harder into his shoulders as she fought for purchase to deepen each delicious rise and fall over him.

Unable to restrain himself much longer, he leaned back as far as the settee allowed and wiggled his hand down between them to find that sensitive little bud buried in her folds. He rubbed his knuckles against her, and she bucked.

"Brandon!" Her arms grasped around his neck like iron bands, but she didn't stop the pumping of her hips over him and bore down tightly around him as she drove them both toward release.

He stroked her again, and she broke with a loud cry. He followed after, into bliss.

He nuzzled her temple. "That was a pleasant surprise."

His husky voice rumbled into her as Amelia lay draped across him, her head resting in that wonderful hollow between his neck and shoulder. Languid and satiated, the two of them were still wrapped around each other as they lay together on the settee. That was all they could bring themselves to move after making love—simply lying down right where they were.

She lazily stroked her hand over his chest, mirroring the gentle caresses he brushed over her back. She would have to leave soon, well before Frederick arrived, and Pearce would have to straighten his clothes to hide all traces of how thoroughly she'd ravished him. But for now, both were happy to remain in each other's arms.

"Yes, it was." She gave a little laugh, unable to believe the joy bubbling inside her. *Never* had she been this happy! And it was all because of Pearce. "When I came here, it was to give you a scolding for speaking to Freddie without me."

"Well then," he taunted rakishly, earning himself another one of her laughs, "scold me whenever you'd like." He growled as he nuzzled her neck. "Repeatedly. And often."

"I'm serious." She lifted her head and stared down into his eyes, the hand at his shoulder moving to caress his cheek. "I *do* trust you now. Completely."

He grinned, pleased, and placed a kiss to her shoulder where the neckline of her dress had been pulled down from their lovemaking.

"And that's why it hurt when you'd moved forward on the trust without telling me."

His smile faded. "I did it to protect you."

"I know." With a small frown, she outlined his lips with her fingertip, already missing his smile. "But if we're going to be in this together, then I need to know that we're in this *together*…completely, without doubt." She hesitated. "And not just with the trust."

His turn to frown. "What do you mean?"

Nervousness fluttered butterflies in her belly, and she couldn't look in his eyes, fixing her gaze on his chest instead as her hand lowered to rest there. Right over his heart. "After we'd made love the first time, you asked me to marry you."

He stiffened and said grimly, "I remember."

She pulled in a deep breath of courage and curled her fingers into his waistcoat. "Yes," she whispered, her voice trembling, "I will marry you."

Confusion darkened his handsome features. "You didn't think anything we could do would make a difference. If you can't end your marriage, then—"

She silenced him with a kiss, then whispered against his lips, "Everything's changed...I think."

Sitting up, he took her shoulders and set her away just far enough to search her face for answers. "What happened?"

"Agnes Sinclair."

He blinked. "Lady Agnes?"

"We had a rather revelatory conversation over tea."

"I'm sure you did," he muttered warily. "I've heard how she takes her tea with a splash of whiskey."

"Whiskey with a splash of tea, actually," she corrected at Agnes's expense. "While we were talking, she reminded me of this." She reached into the pocket of her pelisse and withdrew the folded sheet of paper. "My marriage settlement." She held it out to him. "My *unsigned* settlement." Then she added breathlessly, hope lacing through her voice, "And what I pray is my escape."

His inscrutable expression gave away none of his thoughts as he took the paper from her and read it.

Silently, he gave it back to her, then stood and moved away toward the tantalus on the side table between the windows. Ostensibly, he wanted a drink, but Amelia suspected unhappily that what he needed was distance from her.

"It's not signed." He gestured at the paper. "That was what allowed Northam to steal your money."

Her breath hitched, his words too eerily close to Freddie's. But when Pearce said them, he gave her hope. "Perhaps not."

He glanced up at her as he fastened the fall of his breeches and tucked in his shirttail, but her gaze had shamelessly gone to below his waist, staring longingly there.

"Or perhaps—" She couldn't help but lick her suddenly dry lips. "Perhaps we were never legally married in the first place, and this unsigned contract proves it."

He froze with his hand down his breeches. Disappointment panged through her that he hadn't paused like that to wantonly titillate her. But there would be time later for such play. If she had her way, they'd have a lifetime.

"Explain." He recovered himself with that brusque order and turned to pour a glass of whiskey. But every inch of him was tensed like a coiled spring.

"When we married, my twenty-first birthday was still two weeks away. I was still a minor, which meant I needed Freddie's consent to marry."

"But you had it," he said to the drink tray. "You said Howard agreed to let Northam court you, laid out the terms of the marriage agreement... He supported your marriage."

"He did." Hope spiked her pulse as she admitted, "But never in writing. Or in public."

He turned slowly toward her, raising the glass to his mouth but not drinking as he paused, waiting for her to finish.

She picked up the agreement and pointed to the blank space where her brother's signature should have gone. "No signed agreement by my guardian, no reading of the banns, no formal announcement of any kind—nothing. As far as the world knows, Freddie knew nothing about the marriage before we eloped. And without my guardian's consent—"

"Then your brother can file for an annulment on your behalf." The glass lowered away, the whiskey completely forgotten.

"Yes. On grounds of incompetency." She held her breath, a part of her yet afraid of how he would react to the full ramifications of what that meant. "But it's going to be a difficult process, with everyone from the Church and the courts attempting to make me change my mind and remain married."

His eyes sparkled. "Then they don't know the fight they have coming if they think they can make you do anything you don't want to."

She warmed at that quiet compliment, but it did little to ease her trepidation.

"I can't do it alone." She picked up the paper and tried to keep her hands from shaking as she refolded it and slipped it back into her pocket. "I have no money to hire lawyers, no status or standing to persuade the courts and Church to my side—" She cut herself off to take a deep breath as he slowly returned to her, still having no idea of what he thought about any of this. "And even if the annulment is granted, it's unlikely I'll ever see a single penny of my fortune returned to me."

He stopped in front of her but said nothing, taking a large swallow of whiskey.

She shook her head. "My first fight in this battle might very well be with Freddie. He has to agree, publicly, that he never gave consent, or the annulment won't happen." She paused. "It will also mean scandal, no matter how much we try to keep the details private. For everyone involved."

Worry tightened her belly. What she was asking would risk not only her own reputation and Freddie's but also Pearce's. Everything he'd worked so hard to achieve—his military rank, his respect as a peer, his fortune—all of it might be jeopardized if he chose to remain at her side for this fight. A fight that might take years to win, if at all. And where would he be then, tied to a woman who might be too old to give him an heir, the subject of scandalous gossip, a good chunk of his fortune gone to pay lawyers…

Judging from the grim way he looked down at her, he realized all that, too.

"Well then." He held the glass out to her, giving her the last of his drink. "It's a good thing you're not going through this alone."

Relief poured through her, and she blinked, hard, to clear her eyes of the tears that instantly blurred his handsome face. "You truly meant it, then?" she pressed breathlessly. "What you said earlier, that you have no intention of letting me go?"

He leaned down, placing his hands on the edge of the settee cushion on both sides of her and bringing his face level with hers. He reached to touch the little locket she wore around her neck. As his fingers caressed it, his eyes locked with hers. "I've got you back now, Amelia. Wild horses couldn't drag you away from me."

She fought back a smile as she teased, "What about tame ones?"

"Not those either. Or ponies, donkeys, jackasses…" He arched a brow. "Your brother."

"Pearce," she scolded, but any ferocity was lost beneath her soft laugh.

"Neither will our past, your husband, or society. Understand?"

"Then…" She inhaled a deep breath and reached to slip her hand behind his neck to tug him closer. "Will you marry me, Brandon Pearce? Do you promise to love and honor me, for richer or poorer, in sickness and health…in law courts or taverns?" He laughed, but the seriousness of the moment made her tremble as she laid her hand against his chest to feel the pulse of his strong heartbeat. "For as long as we both shall live?"

"I do." He leaned in to kiss her. "I very much do."

Twenty-two

PEARCE GLANCED OUT THE CARRIAGE WINDOW AT THE DARK city. "Where exactly are we going?"

"To a special club meeting. That's all I can tell you for now," Howard answered, pleased at the idea of mystery.

But Pearce wasn't pleased at all with the secrecy. The only consolation he had was that Merritt and his men were following behind, unseen in the darkness. In case anything went wrong.

"There are no clubs in this area." Not here. They'd long ago left those behind in the west, but they hadn't yet reached the Tower Hamlets, where less exclusive entertainments dominated. They were currently rolling through Walbrook, where the streets were unlit, the old buildings shuttered for the night, and no one was out in the cold drizzle.

"Not the usual clubs, no." Howard tugged at his white gloves. Just like Pearce, he was dressed in all white beneath his overcoat. "But this one is very private and incredibly exclusive."

"So is Brooks's," Pearce grumbled, "but I don't have to dress up like a ghost and prowl Cheapside in the dead of night to attend it."

"Far better than Brooks's. None of that St James's Street pretense. At this club, we take our traditions very seriously."

Hence the white clothes, Pearce was certain.

"But we also do whatever we like." He chuckled in private amusement. "It's our motto, you might say. I'll introduce you to the other men in the trust, of course. But I think you'll also have a good time tonight, if you let yourself."

Howard rapped his cane against the ceiling to signal to the jarvey to stop.

"You'll like our little club, Sandhurst, I'm certain." He bounded down to the street and tossed up a coin to the driver, leaving Pearce to climb out more cautiously. "You might want to consider joining."

Oh, he seriously doubted that. Especially when the hackney drove away, leaving them standing in the middle of a deserted street framed by buildings that had seen better days a hundred years ago but now lay derelict, dark, and silent.

"This way." Howard gestured toward the end of the street, in the direction of an abandoned church. He led Pearce through the rusty gate of the churchyard, down an overgrown path, and to the front door of the old stone building.

Pearce glanced around. No one else was in sight. An uneasy tingle started down his spine. "Where are we?"

"At the entrance to hell." With a grin, Howard pounded his fist against the door.

The heavy wooden door swung open with a spine-jarring creak, and a wave of cold, musty air engulfed them. A man in a friar's robe with the hood drawn low over his face stepped into the doorway and silently held up a hand, barring their way.

"The pale breast of Venus," Howard gave the password quietly, and the monk stepped aside. As they passed into the church, the monk gestured with his hand in mock blessing—an inversion of the sign of the cross.

"What the hell is this place?" Pearce demanded as he followed Howard through the abandoned church, which was lit only by a handful of offering candles at the altar.

"You know of the old Hellfire clubs that were popular fifty years ago?" Howard led him to the entrance of the crypt and down its spiral stone steps. "This is our version. Just as secret, just as exclusive, but a deuce of a lot more fun." He selected two of the white monks' robes lying over a nearby tomb and handed one to Pearce. "Put this on, along with that white cap I sent you." Howard shucked off his greatcoat and beaver hat and tossed them onto the next tomb. "We're like Almack's, you know."

Pearce arched a brow.

"We have a strict dress code. None of the brothers can go any farther without proper attire."

Apparently, they also possessed a flair for the theatrical.

But his curiosity was piqued. Donning the robe and cap, he followed Howard through the crypt which most likely hadn't seen a burial since the reign of the Stuarts. A second hooded monk guarded a narrow and short stone doorway tucked away, nearly unnoticed, at the rear of the crypt. They descended down another steep set of stone steps. When they reached the bottom, their way was blocked by a wooden door and a sign overhead that marked their arrival.

Pearce read the French inscription, "*Fais ce que tu voudras?*"

"Do what thou wilt." Howard grinned and shoved open the door.

Muted lantern light filled the old Roman ruins, along with smoke and the pungent odor of incense. The noise of loud conversation and laughter echoed off the stone, until the sounds swirled around them and Pearce couldn't tell where they were coming from. Gentlemen wearing the required white robes and caps sat on the original stone benches lining the walls, while others lay draped across Arabian-style silk mattresses scattered across the floor, all of them holding golden wine goblets. Middle Eastern music drifted through the ruins, so did feminine laughter and cries of surprise.

He followed Howard deeper into the complex, and a series of Roman chambers the size of drawing rooms unfolded, one after the other, long ago buried and forgotten as London grew above them. All of the chambers were freshly decorated with mythological figures and phallic symbols, including mosaics and paintings of men reveling in drunken debauchery. Antechambers led off the main passageway that weren't lit by lamps, although Pearce could tell by the rustle of movement in the dark shadows that each was busily occupied.

Do what thou wilt, indeed…although based on what he saw in the rooms as they passed through, most of the fifty or so men gathered in the old Roman complex couldn't have cared less for the privacy of an antechamber. Drink of all kinds was provided in an endless supply by half a dozen hooded monks, distinguished from the members by their brown robes. Exotic hookah pipes mixed the sweet scent of tobacco with the stronger odor of American cigars, and veil-clad belly dancers moved seductively to the cheers of men gathered at their feet. Prostitutes draped themselves over the laps of the seated men, wearing open green robes over flimsy, translucent gowns that hide very little of the dusky nipples and feminine curls beneath.

"The brothers share the nuns," Howard informed him when a woman slinked past, blatantly running her gaze over Pearce and lifting her finger to her red lips to suck suggestively.

"Nuns…is that what you call them?" Pearce muttered.

"What man wouldn't want to worship at that altar?" Howard grinned and turned around as he continued to stare at the woman, walking a few feet backward to let his gaze linger on her as long as possible. "If you see a nun you fancy, she's yours. Find an empty alcove and enjoy yourself. The same with any of the drink or food. You're our guest tonight. Make yourself at home."

He had no intention of doing that.

"It's all just a grand lark," Howard explained as he led Pearce through the chambers. "The church, all the religious nods, the pagan nonsense… The idea came from the old church, actually. The Duke of Raleigh owns this chunk of London, and it was a great-great-grandfather or so who donated use of the land to the Church. Raleigh took it back when the Church forfeited it into disuse. But it's put him in a pinch because he can't tear it down or build on it—it's sacred ground with a churchyard. His son is a member of the club, so he lets us meet here."

"Convenient." As they passed the opening to a dark tunnel,

Pearce gestured at it. No door blocked it—or hooded monk guarded it—and no lamps lit its darkness. "What's that?"

"The gateway to the River Styx." When Pearce arched a brow, Howard grinned. "Come on. I'll show you."

He snatched up one of the torches hanging on the wall and led Pearce down the rough-hewn passage that sloped away from the other chambers. Soon, they were surrounded by musty darkness, with water droplets falling down the narrowing walls, and the distant music from above was drowned out by the sound of running water.

They reached the end of the passageway and found a small wooden door that opened easily with a push. The two men stepped through onto a wide stone ledge above a narrow but fast-running underground river. Discarded pagan decorations from the chambers above lay on the ledge, including a large stone Egyptian sarcophagus.

Pearce glanced around, taking in the roof that must have dated from the 1400s, based on the uneven size of the bricks and the slapdash use of heavy mortar. Stinking black water spilled past, just below his boots. Everything was covered with a thin layer of mildew and slime.

"The old lost Walbrook," Howard told him, gesturing toward the river. "The club's chambers used to be part of an old Roman bastion in the city wall. The story is that diggers found the ruins when they attempted to expand the crypt of All Souls-on-the-Wall about thirty years ago. The church was closed before work on the new crypt could begin, but the workers had already opened up the Roman ruins and dug this tunnel, thinking they could undermine the old wall, only to run smack into the river. We don't use this part of the complex."

"Because of the stench?"

"Because of the rats." On that self-reminder, he waved the torch-light around at their feet. "But we occasionally use the sarcophagus for parties. The lid comes off. Makes for a fine tantalus in a pinch."

Howard guided him back out of the tunnel, carefully closing the wooden door against the stench—and the rats.

With each step back toward the chambers, Pearce became more convinced that while the Hellfire club had ties to Scepter, it wasn't part of the organization itself. No one present tonight seemed to take the club seriously enough, and too much debauchery was going on for a criminal group that existed under a veil of secrecy. Too much opportunity to be blackmailed for illicit behavior.

But he would take any opportunity that presented itself to get closer to Scepter's leaders. Including being here.

When they arrived back at the club's chambers, more men in white robes had arrived, and the smoke was even thicker.

Howard led him to the last room. "Welcome to the Inner Temple."

Pearce gazed at the large, natural cavern around them. Lanterns blazed brightly to reveal more pagan scenes decorating the walls and floor. A raised dais sat at the far end, holding up a Greek altar stone and behind it a wooden throne.

"What do you think of our little club, Sandhurst?" Howard proudly slapped him on the back. "A bit theatrical, I'll grant you, but it's all in good fun."

One of the nuns picked that moment to let out a high-pitched scream. Howard ignored it.

"The only rule involves secrecy. No one is allowed to divulge to the outside world what goes on here or who makes up the membership."

Madame Noir's words came back to Pearce, about how Howard liked to share too much. "And the punishment if he does?"

His grin faded. "The end."

"Of his membership?"

"Of him." The hard look Howard shot him proved how serious he was. "The brothers voted to allow you the privilege of a visit tonight, which means they trust you to keep our confidence about what you witness here, just as we'll keep our confidences about whatever pleasures you decide to take."

Pearce didn't believe that for a second.

"But don't cross us," Howard warned. "You'll regret it."

One of the hooded monks stepped onto the dais, lifted a large ox horn to his mouth, and blew. The horn blast carried through the subterranean complex and echoed off the walls. Pearce felt the rising tension of excitement as the music and laughter stopped and all conversation ceased. The men filed into the Inner Temple, flipping up their hoods as they entered and pulling them down over their faces. With a nudge from Howard, Pearce did the same, and soon they were indistinguishable from the crowd.

A man wearing a red robe, his hood drawn low, entered the cavern. The crowd parted to clear a path for him, and with his hands pressed together in a symbol of prayer, he went forward to the dais.

Howard leaned in to whisper, "The abbot."

The man in red held out his arms. "Brothers, you are welcome to the Temple of Bacchus."

"Thanks be to Bacchus," the crowd of men answered in unison.

"This is nonsense," Pearce half growled beneath his breath as the group recited a pledge of allegiance to their club and its pagan gods. "I'm here to meet the other trustees, not to play at fancy dress."

"The ceremony will be over soon," Howard assured him as the brothers continued their call and answer, led by the abbot. "Then we'll have dinner, and I'll introduce you to the others."

"Are you sure they're here?" Pearce could barely make out any faces in the dim shadows and smoke cast up by the lamps, cigars, and incense. Seeing was made harder by the sea of matching white hoods covering so low over everyone's faces that all he could see was a series of chins and a scattering of beards.

"Oh, Bacchus," the abbot called out, "accept our sacrifice!"

As a shout went up from the group, the abbot pushed down his hood.

Pearce's heart skipped. Arthur Varnham. Sir Charles Varnham's younger brother.

"Now let us take our feast!"

Another cheer went up, so loud that it echoed deafeningly off the stone walls. Arthur Varnham jumped from the dais and charged through the group as they parted around him, and the brothers all followed after into the connecting banqueting hall, where tables had already been laid out for a grand dinner. Two tables laden heavily with platters of food flanked a center table that was covered with a sheet. Varnham approached the table and passed his hands over it in a mock blessing.

"Enjoy this most holy of holy days, this Feast of Venus!"

He whisked the sheet away.

A blond woman lay across the table, naked except for the bunches of fruit covering her large breasts and spilling down between her thighs. A cherry rested provocatively in her navel.

Varnham folded his hands behind his back and leaned down to pick up the cherry with his teeth.

Beside Pearce, Howard stiffened, his jaw tightening as he watched Varnham eat the cherry, then lean down again to swirl his tongue into her navel to lick up the drops of juice left behind.

"Come now, brothers!" Varnham gestured at the feast laid out before them and the woman spread out like an erotic buffet, and Howard's narrowed gaze bore into the man. "Partake of the feast and satiate all of your hungers."

The men rushed forward to fill their plates. But Howard remained where he was, still staring at Varnham as the man plucked a grape from the bunch covering the woman's left breast, put it between his lips, and leaned down to decadently feed her, helping himself to a devouring, openmouthed kiss. She laughed.

Recognition snapped into Pearce's head. He knew that woman.

He'd seen her at Le Château Noir. *The brothers share the nuns*... He knew then how the blackmailer had gained information against Howard.

Amelia had been chasing after the wrong Varnham.

Twenty-three

AMELIA STOOD AT HER BEDROOM WINDOW AND WATCHED THE midmorning sunlight play across the street below. She smiled to herself as she lifted the teacup to her lips. The long case clock in the entry hall had long ago struck ten. Normally by now she'd be dressed, at the shop, and up to her elbows in problems and merchandise. But not today. Today, lazily, she still wore her dressing gown, her hair hanging freely down her back, and not one remnant of breakfast remaining on the tray she'd asked Cook to send up for her. She'd been famished.

All because of Pearce.

She laughed, the happiness inside her bubbling over. How was it possible that a man could make her feel this feminine and alive, this special? It had been over twelve hours since they made love, yet her skin still tingled from his touch. And would again, now that there was no longer any reason to deny herself the joys of being with him. In every way.

Below on the street, a hackney drawn by an old horse pulled bone-shakingly slowly to a stop in front of the house. The door opened, and a man dragged himself stiffly out of the carriage and down to the ground, as if every move pained him, no matter how small.

Amelia rolled her eyes. Freddie. Of course.

He was still in the white finery that he'd donned last night—as he did every time he headed out to those peculiar club meetings of his that he refused to tell her anything about—but his appearance was far from fresh. The worse for wear, his soiled clothes were disheveled and stained, his neckcloth askew, and his beaver hat perched precariously on his head. His cheeks were dark with morning beard, too much drink, and God only knew what else he'd done last night.

"Oh, Freddie," she muttered with a tired sigh, her shoulders slumping, "why won't you ever grow up?"

She was indebted to him. A great deal. But there was no love lost between them. She'd always known that, even when they were children.

What a relief it would be when she was no longer beneath his roof and out from under his control, with a husband who truly loved her, a house of her own, and children. Lots of children. She might even allow Freddie to visit on holidays. She smiled wryly at the idea. *If* he behaved himself.

But first, she had to tell him about the annulment.

Oh, *that* was not going to be a pleasant experience! How would he accept the scandal that was bound to result, scandal that would undoubtedly affect his career? No matter that it would mean her freedom or that she was now working to save him from prison. Given Pearce's new status as an earl, he might even be willing to—

Three men who had been lingering on the footpath began to walk toward Freddie. The men called out to him, and he stopped just before he reached the front step. Amelia could see from upstairs that her brother didn't recognize the men...but they knew *him*.

His face twisted in instant anger, and he hurried on toward the house.

Without warning, two of the men flanked him, grabbed him by the arm, and held him still while the third man reached beneath his coat—

"No!" she screamed, dropping her cup and smashing it against the floor. She ran through the house, shouting out to Drummond to help. But the butler wasn't in sight, and she couldn't wait for him.

Yanking open the front door, she raced outside. She flung herself between Frederick and the men. "Leave him alone!"

"Move out of the way, ma'am," the third man ordered. "We're with Bow Street. This doesn't concern you."

Her gaze dropped to the man's hands—not a gun as she'd feared but a pair of iron manacles. "You're arresting him?" She turned quickly back and forth between the two men behind her, still holding onto Freddie even though he wasn't struggling at all. She leveled her gaze on the more dangerous man in front. "On what charge?"

"Corruption."

"Brought by whom?"

"Sir Charles Varnham. Now step aside."

"But—but that's—" *Impossible* now that Pearce had seemingly agreed to the trust and Frederick had done all that the blackmailer had wanted. As far as anyone knew, the trust would go through, the last men would be placed—

Her blood turned to ice. No, the trust *wasn't* going through. She'd said as much herself at the Black Ball, right in front of Freddie's cronies and anyone else who might have overhead. Including the blackmailer.

Oh, she'd been so stupid! Everything she'd feared was now set in motion. All because of her.

In desperation, she jabbed a finger at Frederick and then in the general direction of Westminster. "You cannot arrest him." She needed a reason—*any* reason that would buy her time and make the men leave. Her mind spun, only to latch onto— "He's a Member of Parliament! He has Parliamentary privilege against arrest while the House is in session."

"That's only for civil charges," Frederick informed her quietly.

She whirled around to face him, then froze, struck by his expression. He was shocked by this, but also weak and defeated, with slumping shoulders and his hat knocked to the ground at his feet.

"We're arresting him on charges of smuggling, among other things," the man with the manacles explained.

But she barely heard him, her focus on her brother and her mind running rapidly through all that would now be destroyed. "No—you have to fight this." For God's sake, he wasn't even arguing in his own defense!

The man behind her roughly shoved her aside.

As she stumbled to gain her balance, he clamped the manacles over Freddie's wrists. The two men holding him hurried him to a carriage waiting down the street, opened the door, and shoved him inside. They followed after him and slammed shut the door.

The third man wordlessly doffed his hat to Amelia, then swung up onto the bench beside the driver. The whip cracked, and the team started forward at a fast clip, disappearing around the corner.

Gulping down great mouthfuls of air to keep back a scream, Amelia ran back inside the house. "Maggie!" She hurried to her room, ignoring the bewildered stare of Drummond, who had finally come to the front door to investigate the commotion. "Maggie, I need you!"

Amelia threw open the doors to her armoire and grabbed the first day dress she found.

"Miss, what on earth...?" Maggie halted in the open doorway and gaped.

"I have to dress—quickly." She yanked open the drawer and reached for a shift, tossing both it and the dress over the back of a nearby chair. "Frederick's been arrested."

Her maid closed the door and whispered, "Sir Charles?"

Amelia nodded firmly with a bite to her lip. "Just now."

"What are you going to do?" Maggie wrung her hands as she came forward.

"I'm going to speak to Sir Charles." When she reached for a corset, Maggie stopped her and selected a different one, along with a pair of stockings. "Make him understand that no good can come from prosecuting Freddie, that he'll only be hurting me and a group of innocent women." She frowned as she removed her dressing gown. "And when that doesn't work, I'll throw myself at his feet and beg."

"And when that doesn't work?"

She shook her head. "I don't know. But I won't give up."

Within minutes, Maggie had dressed her and fixed her hair in a simple but presentable chignon. Amelia hopped across the room toward her writing desk on one foot at a time as she pulled on a pair of half boots while Maggie went to ask Drummond to fetch a hackney. Amelia quickly scribbled out a note for Pearce, then sealed it.

"Deliver this to Lord Sandhurst." She handed Maggie the note as she snatched up her shawl and dashed for the door. "His town house is on St James's Square. If he isn't there, try the old armory north of the City. I'm certain that his man McTavish can give you directions."

Maggie shot her a worried look and grabbed her arm. "You shouldn't go alone, miss. Sir Charles might decide you're a party to what Mr. Howard's done and have you arrested, too."

"Which is why you have to deliver that message to Pearce. He'll meet me in Westminster and know what to do."

With a quick hug ending all protests, Amelia rushed from the house. Only to halt on the front step.

A black hackney waited on the street, its old driver doffing his hat at her as she slowly came forward. For a moment, she thought Drummond had worked quickly to find her a carriage—unusually quickly for a butler who favored laziness.

But then she noticed that the carriage wasn't empty. Two people sat inside in the shadows, just out of view of the window. Wasn't that just her luck, for the carriage to be already taken? With Drummond nowhere to be seen, she gave a frustrated curse beneath her breath and hurried down the footpath toward the square, where she could more easily wave down a hackney.

"Miss Howard!"

She stopped, startled, as a man called out to her from the waiting carriage.

"A word with you, if you please."

Slowly, she retraced her steps. The carriage door opened, and she could see inside.

"Mr. Varnham." But her heart plunged to the ground. Arthur Varnham. The *wrong* Varnham. "If you'll excuse me." She gestured apologetically down the street. "I'm in a hurry—"

"Miss Howard"—he ignored her attempt to leave—"I'd like to introduce you to my cousin, Miss Humphries. Marigold, this is Miss Howard, the woman I told you about."

Miss Humphries leaned forward from the opposite bench, her pretty and young face emerging into the slant of sunlight that fell into the compartment. The curls of her hair beneath her straw bonnet shone gold. She smiled warmly. "How do you do, Miss Howard?"

Not well. Not well at all. Anxiousness bubbled inside her until what she wanted to do was bolt down the street at a dead run. "A pleasure to meet you. But I really must go. It's urgent." She turned to leave, not caring if she were being rude. Her world was collapsing around her. "My apologies—"

"It's your brother, isn't it?" Varnham asked.

That stopped her. "Yes." She looked at him warily over her shoulder. "How do you know?"

"Because I just left Varnham House." Irritation rang in his voice. "Imagine my surprise to come home from a night out at the clubs to discover that my brother plans to arrest yours." The shadows covered his face too thickly for her to read the emotions there, but raw frustration colored his voice. "I immediately came here to stop it."

She turned slowly back toward the carriage. "Why do you care?"

"Because your brother belongs to my club, whose activities

need to be kept private. You understand, of course." He smiled a bit sheepishly. "An arrest ruins all that."

"You're too late, I'm afraid," she admitted as she glanced down the street in the direction where the men had taken Freddie, her voice choking. "The runners arrested him and took him away just a few minutes ago."

Varnham leaned out of the carriage as if searching after them. Dark fury flashed over his face for a split second, so intense that Amelia was certain he would have cursed if the two women hadn't been within earshot. Then the anger was gone, his expression easing into a troubled frown.

He leaned over to his cousin to speak quietly into her ear. The woman nodded.

"I agree. She must come with us to find your brother." Miss Humphries smiled reassuringly at Amelia. "Westminster isn't out of my way at all, and I'd be happy to accompany you."

"Good." Varnham turned his gaze onto Amelia. "Then you must come with us to speak to Charles. I insist. Perhaps you can convince him to rescind the charges." In an attempt to lighten the mood, he teased, "Can't have my brother putting all my chums into gaol. Won't have anyone interesting left to drink with at this rate." With a smile that didn't put her at ease, he gestured at the empty seat next to Miss Humphries. "Please let us help you and your brother."

Amelia hesitated. "I shouldn't impose." But she so dearly wanted to! Finding a hackney for hire at this time of day near the square would take forever, and Arthur Varnham would know exactly where to find Sir Charles. Perhaps he could even walk her past all the guards and into the offices of Parliament. If she went by herself, as a woman she wouldn't be allowed through the first doorway.

Misreading her reluctance, he added in disappointment, "I understand if you're not up to confronting Charles about this."

She nearly laughed! What other choice did she have? "Wild horses couldn't stop me," she muttered to herself, the little mantra adding to her resolve. Then she remembered Pearce's words. "Or ponies, donkeys, mules…and my jackass of a brother."

"Pardon?"

"Nothing." She pulled in a deep, determined breath and stepped up into the carriage. "Thank you for your help, both of you."

"Of course." He smiled and closed the door.

As the carriage rolled away from the house, Amelia cast a surreptitious glance at the pair sitting with her. Miss Humphries was dressed respectably in a blue muslin day dress and pelisse, but her dress was old and frayed at the hem and sleeves. Fine for average wear, but not at all what Amelia would have expected from a gentleman's cousin.

But then, Varnham's appearance wasn't exactly pristine either. From the state of his dress, he hadn't lied; he must have just returned home from a night out. Beneath cheeks darkened with morning beard and eyes red from lack of sleep, he wore red from head to toe, including an odd red cap resting on the seat beside him. All red, all white…what on earth went on at those clubs? No wonder Varnham wanted to keep secret what the men did there.

As if reading her mind, he twisted a rueful smile in her direction and stuffed the red cap into his jacket pocket.

They rode on in silence, circling the square. But just as the carriage was about to turn toward the south, Varnham pounded on the ceiling. The carriage slowed and stopped. He opened the door. Miss Humphries quickly exited with a cat-like smile for Varnham and no acknowledgment whatsoever for Amelia.

He closed the door, and the carriage moved on.

"Wait!" Amelia twisted in her seat to stare through the window after Miss Humphries, but the woman walked away, turning off the square and disappearing quickly into the tangle of narrow streets. "Miss Humphries isn't—"

"She lives nearby and is going home." His explanation did nothing to ease her wariness. "She has no need to come with us."

Yet Amelia had need of *her*. She couldn't be seen riding alone in a carriage with a man who wasn't her relative. "But she said she'd act as my companion."

"She did." His voice reverberated with mock empathy. "I'm afraid that was a lie."

A chill twisted down her spine. "I can't ride alone with you. I'm unmarried."

"Oh, but you're not, Mrs. Northam."

A piercing jolt flashed through her, momentarily freezing her heart. When it jarred back to life, it wasn't a pulse that pounded through her but fear.

She rasped out, "How do you know about my marriage?"

No one knew, except for Freddie and Pearce. And Pearce would never betray her. Which meant…Frederick. *Dear God, what have you done?*

The look Varnham gave her was one of patronizing pity. In that expression she knew—

"You," she breathed out, unable to speak above a shocked whisper. A terrifying realization slithered through her. "It's you who's been blackmailing my brother."

"Yes." He clucked his tongue, as if scolding a child. "Truly, you had no idea?"

"I thought—I thought your brother…"

"Oh, Charles is certainly after your brother. He has an overdeveloped sense of righteousness and patriotism that won't let him ignore the corruption your brother's committed. Taking bribes, selling votes, extortion, smuggling…"

"Frederick's done nothing that other MPs haven't," she answered breathlessly, blood pounding through her ears like a hammer. "Most likely including your own brother."

"That's where you're wrong. Charles is nothing if not painfully aboveboard in every way. Lord, what a dull brother! Not at all as interesting as yours." Amusement gleamed in his eyes. "But you're correct that he had nothing to do with the blackmail. My brother's arrest of yours is simply an inconvenient coincidence, the charges most certainly to be rescinded."

The way he said that was painfully polite, wholly pleasant and commonplace, as if they were two acquaintances sharing a quiet conversation about the weather— Dear heavens, he was mad! And all the more terrifying because of it.

Amelia swallowed hard to fight down the rising panic. "But if it wasn't Frederick's political corruption that you used against him, then…"

"Then what did I use? Something far worse and more lasting, I assure you." He smiled arrogantly. "I used you."

Her hand went to her stomach, as if she could physically press down the churning there. She knew— "My marriage," she rasped out, her breath growing shallow. "You threatened to reveal my marriage."

"Not your marriage." He laughed at the idea. "Your *money*."

She gave a strangled laugh. "If you know about my marriage, then you know that I have no money."

"Oh, so much more than you realize," he murmured.

The little hairs on her arms stood on end. "What do you mean?"

"Your marriage was all your brother's doing, to get his hands on your money."

"You're mistaken." After all, hadn't Frederick told her hundreds of times what a fool she was for losing her fortune, blaming her for Aaron's duplicity, castigating her for being so naive? "I eloped. My brother was in London and had nothing to do with it."

"Unfortunately for you, I'm not mistaken." He leaned back against the squabs and stretched his legs diagonally across the space between them. "He was furious, you know, that he received nothing more from your father than a pittance of an allowance and a bit of land that produced no income. It wasn't enough to keep him in cards and drink let alone afford the lifestyle of a London gentleman. Not to mention the indignation of having to manage your inheritance as your guardian." He chuckled at the irony. "A fortune at his fingertips, but not one ha'penny his."

"I know all this." She had no patience for his games. Or the alarm he rattled inside her.

"Ah, but you *don't* know that he was taking your money even before your marriage, siphoning it off little by little so that you wouldn't notice it had gone missing, blaming a decline in the accounts on falling revenues and bad investments."

The blood seeped from her cheeks. Freddie had told her exactly that whenever she'd asked to see the account books.

"But a few hundred pounds here and there wasn't nearly enough, and when you turned twenty-one, he would lose access to it completely if you asked to manage it yourself. Or if you married." He casually crossed his legs at the ankles. "Apparently, there was some old childhood friend who'd caught your interest. But as long as Howard had you with him, you see, he could live the same lifestyle as you, use your money to fund his gambling, drinking, whoring—the life of a young gentleman on the town. So he couldn't let you marry and take all that away from him."

Pearce. Bitter anger seeped up from her bones. Now she knew why her letters had never reached him. Because Frederick had never allowed them to be sent.

"But he couldn't delay the inevitable. Your majority was coming, and regardless, you were young, beautiful, and wealthy. Eventually you would have married." He traced an idle finger across the bottom of the window. "So he found a charming man with no family or ties to Birmingham for you to fall in love with, whom he could pay to pretend to court and marry you. One who would then leave for America as soon as he'd scribbled his name into the church register."

The earth dropped away beneath her, and she sank against the squabs. What he was telling her was preposterous. Absurd! But he knew about her marriage, details that no one else knew but her and Frederick. And that other document she'd found, the one tucked away with her marriage settlement—

Frederick had paid Aaron to pretend to love her.

She could barely breathe as the nauseating realization swept over her. All this time spent believing…all that pain and humiliation…

Oh God, she was going to be sick!

"You're lying," she whispered, gripping the seat beneath her so tightly that her fingertips turned white.

"I'm not. Howard planned it all out perfectly. He arranged for a special license that would allow you to marry inside England to ensure that your marriage would not be legal, then pretended to travel to London while actually shadowing you the entire time. After all, he couldn't risk that you'd elope to Scotland, where you would have been rightfully married and truly given all your money to your new husband. Where would your brother be then, if the pretender decided to keep your fortune?"

All the pieces were clicking sickeningly into place, and with each one, something ripped deep inside her. Thank God she'd already turned numb, or she would have screamed. She was barely aware of when he reached inside his jacket and withdrew his handkerchief to hold it out to her, as if he were any other gentleman wanting to comfort her. As if he hadn't just shattered her world.

"You believe that your husband hurried back to Birmingham after your wedding and absconded with all of your money, don't you? But that never happened."

"But it did," she insisted, her voice raw. "I was there!"

"No, you weren't, not for the money part of it. Howard had conveniently arrived from London at just the right moment to visit the bank manager on your behalf while you remained at home, distraught over being abandoned. Then he told you that your husband had taken everything when no such thing ever happened."

When she didn't accept the handkerchief, he shrugged and stuffed it back into his breast pocket.

"You trusted your brother, and in your humiliation, you didn't want to visit the banker and be pitied. Or laughed at. So you believed the lie." He pulled back the frayed and dirty curtain that partially covered the window. "But your fortune is still there, still sitting in the bank in Birmingham where your brother has had access to it all along as your guardian." He sadly shook his head and dropped the curtain back into place. "But unfortunately, a large part of it is now gone. He used it to purchase his seat in Parliament."

"Not true." Her numb lips struggled to form the words. "Frederick acquired that seat through his cronies, in return for political favors. There was no money for that. Aaron Northam took everything from me."

"Not everything. Not your land. Ever ask yourself why that was? If he only married you to get his hands on your money, surely he wouldn't have left valuable property behind."

"Because he didn't have time to sell it. He needed to withdraw the money and leave before I realized what he'd planned."

"But as your legally wedded husband, he would have had all the time in the world. That land—like everything else—would have become his the moment you wed. He could have sold it even from America. But the property remained yours because Howard couldn't sell it without your consent. Not even as your guardian." Varnham shook his head. "Ironic, don't you think, that in the end your brother got his hands on the land, too, by wrapping it up in that trust? I simply told him that I wanted those men placed into governmental positions. The turnpike was all his idea."

Her mind spun as fast as the world around her until a sickening nausea overcame her. Until she couldn't sort through it all. She swallowed hard to force down the swelling anguish and betrayal. "But Frederick hired lawyers and accountants to try to get the money back—Bow Street investigators, sent them all the way to America... Why would he have done that if he wanted to steal my money?"

"*Did* he hire them?" Varnham gave her another pitying look, this one so grave that his lips tightened into a thin line. "How do you know?"

Stop looking at me like that! She certainly deserved to be pitied, but *not* for what he was claiming. Because it wasn't true. None of it! It simply couldn't be.

Because if it was, then the last seven years had been nothing but a horrible, humiliating lie.

"That's what I used to blackmail your brother. Not any of those charges that Charles had him arrested for, but what he did to you. You alone have the power to destroy him, his spinster younger sister." A chuckle rose on his lips. "Your brother's more frightened of you than he is of any accusations of political corruption." He smiled tightly as he slumped against the compartment wall in a casual posture that belied the monster beneath. "Now, don't you feel like a fool for trying to save your brother, when you're the last thing in the world he cares about?"

She pulled in a deep breath of fierce resolve to keep from spilling tears. She refused to give him the satisfaction of seeing them.

"You shouldn't feel ashamed for believing his lies. After all, you're certainly not the first woman who's had her fortune swindled away by a male relative. It's just that your brother did it with so much more flair."

The smile of admiration that curled on his lips twisted her insides, and she swallowed, hard, to keep from casting up her accounts. He was a monster.

Apparently so was Frederick.

"Your brother has spine, I have to say," he muttered to himself.

"If his scheming wasn't solely directed at his own gain, he might have been a valuable asset to acquire within our ranks."

"You mean Scepter?" she challenged, fighting to keep the quavering from her voice. As if a veil of fog had been lifted, she saw how all the pieces fit together now…her marriage, the trust, Scepter.

His expression darkened to a chilling hardness. He returned her gaze for a long moment, then he began to drum his fingers against his thigh where he rested his hand. She could feel the tension radiating from him with every rotation of the carriage wheels beneath them.

"My brother has caused problems for me by having yours arrested," he told her quietly. "That wasn't at all part of my plan. I honestly did want to arrive in time to stop it."

He tugged at his neckcloth, untying the disheveled knot that he'd put there himself before he arrived home. Or by the woman he'd been with…the woman whose presence had convinced her to step inside the carriage with him. Fresh fear licked at the base of her spine. Not his cousin. A lure.

She glanced out the window. The carriage was headed in the wrong direction for Westminster, traveling east instead.

"Howard's useless to me now," he muttered, almost to himself, letting the neckcloth dangle undone around his neck. "But there's someone else of value whom I can use to put those last three men into place."

She held her terrified breath. "Who?"

"Lord Sandhurst. I'm certain he can be convinced to push through the trust in the next few days before Parliament's session ends."

"He won't." Of that, she was certain. She doubted Frederick and everything he'd told her, doubted her father and all of Papa's concern for her—but she would *never* doubt Pearce again.

"Oh, I think he will." Varnham rubbed the tight muscles at his nape. When he pulled his hand away, he slipped off the unwanted neckcloth. "After all, I have a way to make certain of it."

"What is that?"

"You." He lunged for her.

Twenty-four

PEARCE STRODE INTO THE ARMORY, NOT CARING THAT THE iron door rattled so loudly in his wake that it jarred bones all the way to Cheapside.

Merritt glanced up from the billiards table, remaining bent over the table as he lined up his shot. For once, he and Clayton Elliott were battling it out over billiards instead of with swords. Which could only mean one thing—

Marcus Braddock was here. *Thank God.*

"General!" Pearce's shout echoed off the stone walls of the old building and caught Merritt and Clayton's attention. Enough that the two men interrupted their game, waiting for an explanation.

"What is it?" Marcus stepped out of the training room, unwinding a long piece of cloth from his left hand. He wore only a pair of breeches and the cloth that protected his knuckles from cuts and bruises when he pounded them into the bags he used to keep his fighting edge. The sheen of sweat that glistened across his bare chest, shoulders, and arms gave testimony to how hard he'd been training. And how much of a threat he believed Scepter to be.

Pearce grimaced. "I have news to report."

Clayton and Merritt exchanged troubled glances. They'd parted from him that morning just as dawn was breaking over the city and just after he'd gladly left the Hellfire club, when he'd shared with them what he'd learned, including a detailed description of the other three trustees. True to his word, Howard had introduced him to them, right after dinner and right before a dozen new nuns had descended into the underworld. After that, the meeting deteriorated into little more than an orgy. Feast of Venus, indeed.

Pearce had barely gotten two hours' sleep when he was roused from bed by McTavish, with a note from Amelia delivered by her maid.

"Frederick Howard's been arrested," he informed all three men, instantly claiming their complete attention.

While they all stared at him silently, absorbing that information, he helped himself to a glass of cognac from the sideboard. One he desperately needed.

"I spent all morning trying to get him released. Nothing worked. He's still in the New Prison." Pearce splashed out the golden liquid, then put the stopper back into the crystal bottle with a small clink. "Sir Charles Varnham is determined not only to strip Howard of his seat in Parliament but also to see him either put into prison permanently or transported. I argued with him for two hours."

He'd lingered so long with the man only because Amelia's note said she was going to Westminster to confront him, and he wanted to be there when she arrived. But she never came. When he'd gone to the town house after her, Drummond informed him that she hadn't yet returned. Most likely because she'd gone to the Inns of Court, desperate to hire a lawyer to defend a brother who didn't deserve it.

Pearce tossed back a large swallow and welcomed the burn down his throat. "Varnham refuses to rescind the charges."

Marcus said nothing as he shrugged into the shirt he'd left lying over the back of one of the leather sofas. If Howard had been anyone else, Pearce knew, the general might have offered to speak to Varnham himself and leverage his newfound ducal influence, if only for Amelia's sake. But not when Howard's connection to Scepter was still unknown.

"But those charges have nothing to do with how Howard was blackmailed," Pearce added. "I'm certain of it."

"Coincidence?" Clayton laid down his cue and came forward.

Pearce shrugged. "When you do as many illegal things as

Howard, it's only a matter of time until you get caught." He dropped heavily onto a nearby settee. "I believe Varnham when he said that he's pressing charges because he wants to rout out corruption in Parliament, that he discovered Howard's illegal activities on his own. I don't think he has anything to do with blackmail or even knew that it was happening."

But his brother was a different matter.

Pearce frowned into his glass. How many men in those chambers last night belonged to Scepter? And where did Arthur Varnham fit into this?

"We can't allow Frederick Howard to be put on trial," Marcus said quietly as he fetched the decanter of cognac and a glass for himself. "If Howard testifies, he'll try to use the blackmail as justification for his actions."

"It's the only viable defense he'll have in the courtroom," Merritt agreed. "But he's damned if he does, damned if he doesn't, because that defense will also bring to light all the illegal things he's done."

"Potentially exposing his connection to Scepter in the process." Marcus grimly filled his glass and set the decanter on the low table between the men. "So he either won't say anything, in which case we're right back where we started with no leads or new information—"

"Or he tells everything he knows, including about Scepter," Pearce interjected, "and we'll lose our advantage on them."

"I can't officially be part of this conversation," Clayton reminded them, taking a seat across from Pearce. "If Howard's committed crimes against the government, I'll have to notify the Home Office."

"And *un*officially?" Merritt countered as he flopped onto the sofa next to Clayton.

"I'll do everything I can to keep Howard from testifying," he muttered, "including breaking him out of gaol myself, if necessary."

"I don't think we'll need to worry about that." Merritt passed up the cognac for one of the green apples piled in a bowl on the table. "As soon as Scepter learns that he plans on testifying, they'll make certain he can't implicate them." He shined the apple on his jacket sleeve. "He'll be found dead in his cell by morning."

Pearce couldn't let that happen. Amelia would be devastated. For all that her brother was a criminal, she was still dedicated to him. "We have to find a way to get him to safety before Scepter gets to him first."

"Agreed. And make him tell us what he knows." Marcus swirled the cognac in his glass. "But how?"

"Too bad the prison can't burn down," Clayton mused. "He could conveniently escape in the confusion."

Pearce added with a touch of sarcasm, "Where's a good riot when you need one?"

A beat of silence, then—

"I can get us a riot," Merritt said casually, kicking his feet onto the table and biting into the apple. "How big do you need it to be?"

All three men turned their heads to stare at him. And blinked.

He paused midchew to mumble around the bite of apple, "What?"

Clayton looked at him as if he'd just sprouted a second head. "What *exactly* is it that you do at night when you're not here?"

Merritt grinned and sank his teeth into the apple for a second bite.

The iron hinges of the outer courtyard door screeched, followed seconds later by the bang of the inner door as it opened. All four men jumped to their feet, with Merritt reaching for the knife in his sleeve and Clayton for the pistol beneath his jacket.

"Brigadier!" The shout echoed from the short entry hall.

Merritt and Clayton both dropped their hands away from their weapons, the sudden tension in their bodies vanishing.

McTavish hurried into the main room and halted, then stared in surprise at the transformed old building.

"Bloody hell," he spat out and turned completely around in a circle to take in the octagonal room around him. "What is this place?" Then his gaze fell on the men, and he snapped to attention. "Sirs!"

"At ease, McTavish," Pearce ordered. Unease settled like a weight onto his chest. "Why are you here?"

"This arrived at the house." He held out a sealed note. "The delivery boy said it was urgent. So I came looking for you." He slid a cautious look at the other men before lowering his voice and adding, "Thought it might have something to do with last night's visitor."

Amelia. Pearce hadn't seen her yet, but he was certain she'd been at the prison attempting to free her brother or at the Inns of Court hiring lawyers. He'd wanted to talk to Charles Varnham before he talked to her so that he would have good news for her when he did. But that didn't happen.

"What boy?" Pearce broke the wax seal and opened the note.

McTavish shrugged. "Just a messenger. Said a man paid him a coin to bring it to the house, then promised a second coin when he brought back proof that he'd delivered it."

Dread spilled through him. Street urchins were often used as anonymous messengers in the city. Their ubiquitous presence meant they largely went unnoticed, even in Mayfair. But Amelia would never have used them, instead sending her maid as she'd done that morning.

He scanned over the masculine handwriting. And his heart stopped.

Miss Howard is in my care. She'll be released unharmed when Parliament passes the trust. I advise you to hurry as it's rather difficult to feed her in her current position.

"He's got Amelia," he rasped out.

"Who?" Marcus took the note and read it.

The message was unsigned, but Pearce knew... "Arthur Varnham."

Clayton read the note over Marcus's shoulder. "Sir Charles's brother? Why would he kidnap her?"

"Because he still has three men from Scepter to place into government positions, and Howard can't do it." A murderous anger rose inside him that he had never felt before, not even in the heat of battle. "So he's using Amelia to force me into pushing the trust through."

"Parliament's session ends in less than a fortnight. The chance of passing that act now with Howard in gaol is slim at best. If it doesn't pass—"

"Then he'll let her starve to death." He took back the note and read it again, looking for any clues that would lead him to Amelia. "So we rescue her. Tonight."

Merritt shook his head. "Where do we start? Varnham could be holding her anywhere."

"I know exactly where she is." He crumpled the note in his fist. "And when she's safe, I'm going to kill the bastard."

Twenty-five

As he waited in the dark street, Pearce hunched his shoulders against the cold drizzle that fell over London. Around him, the City slept, the ward unusually dark and quiet beneath a layer of fog that had crept up from the Thames only a few streets to the south. So dark and quiet that he could hear the steady drip of rainwater falling every few seconds off the building behind him.

A figure dressed all in black emerged from the shadows and moved silently toward him, reminding Pearce of a panther on the prowl... *Merritt*.

"All set then?" Pearce tugged at his white gloves.

Merritt gave a curt nod, but his attention lay on the dark City, listening intently to the night around them. "Everyone's in place."

"Are you certain this will work?"

"Let's find out." Merritt pulled a pistol from beneath his greatcoat, pointed it into the air, and fired.

The shot split the silence of the night like cannon fire and echoed off the old brick buildings and walls lining the narrow street. A stunned silence followed. And then the streets around them came alive.

Out of the shadows of the narrow streets and back alleys emerged two dozen men and women carrying sticks, clubs, pikes, and torches. As they moved in the direction of Clerkenwell, only a mile or so away, they shouted into the night and swung their clubs at doors, at barrels and crates left in the streets—at anything that would make noise and rouse the city around them. More men came out of the buildings and joined in.

"Well, would you look at that?" Merritt grinned and tossed

Pearce the spent pistol, not wanting it on him if the authorities caught him. "Looks like we've got ourselves a riot."

He slapped Pearce on the back. Then he jogged off in pursuit of the mob.

Pearce headed in the opposite direction. His boots scuffed over the uneven pavement as he headed northeast toward the edge of the City. The noise of the riot grew dimmer the further he moved away, until he was once more wrapped in the eerie quiet of the midnight fog.

The derelict church of All Souls-on-the-Wall emerged like a ghost from the drizzle and darkness. A blanket of fog lay over its medieval churchyard, cocooning the graves and giving no sense of life anywhere nearby.

"The entrance to hell, all right," he muttered to himself as he started across the forgotten graveyard toward the door.

He paused outside the front portal to make certain no one had followed him. Then he rapped his knuckles on the wooden panel.

The door swung open slowly to reveal the waiting monk in his brown robe.

"Let me in," Pearce said quietly, not certain that true demons weren't lurking among the graves and might overhear.

The man stepped back without a word and let him pass. The door closed after him, shutting out the night.

Pearce made his way through the dusty church. Everything was in place just as before, right down to the same handful of lit candles flickering from the altar.

He descended the stone steps into the crypt where a handful of white robes had been tossed over a nearby tomb. He snatched one up and approached the second monk who guarded the door to the chambers below.

The monk made the sign of the cross.

"Wrong way," Pearce muttered.

"Apologies." Alexander Sinclair, Earl of St James, made the sign again, this time with the correct inversion.

"As long as no one else notices." Pearce slipped on the robe. "How many so far?"

"Three dozen or so."

"Has the abbot arrived yet?"

"Everyone's arrived." He added happily, "Including the nuns."

Pearce tied the robe and eyed him askance. "Monks are celibate, don't forget."

"I thought I was supposed to do everything inverted." He grinned, adding lasciviously, "*Everything.*"

"Just wait until you see what's for dinner. It's a religious experience, all right." Pearce pulled the hood down low over his face, until only his chin and jaw were visible. All teasing humor vanished. "Give me ten minutes, then blow the horn."

"Best be ready when it comes." He opened the door to the chambers and stepped back to let Pearce pass. "All hell's going to break loose."

"Then we're in a good place for it." He hurried down into the lower chambers.

When he reached the bottom, Pearce slowed his pace and moved casually through the series of rooms, not wanting to draw any attention to himself. Not that anyone would have noticed, given that the men who filled the rooms were distractedly engaged tonight in the same debauchery as before. Smoke from the same incense pots, cigars, and hookah pipes saturated the ruins, the same exotic music pulsed against the stone walls. Drink flowed into golden goblets just as quickly, and disappeared down throats just as fast. The women were there, too, wearing the same flimsy costumes as they danced or draped themselves over the laps of the members.

Pearce didn't give a damn about any of it as he slipped past, except that it had allowed the men of the Armory to take their positions inside without being noticed. Only when he reached the dark passageway that led down to the river did he pause. Trusting that no one in the room cared what he did here, he removed a lantern from its hook and started down the tunnel.

With his left hand holding up the lantern to light his way and his right hand beneath his coat on a loaded pistol, he moved carefully down the sloping tunnel in the shadows, expecting a guard to appear out of the darkness at any moment. But none materialized, the passage remaining empty.

When he reached the wooden door that barred his way, he paused to glance over his shoulder. He was alone in the tunnel. No movement, no sound. Not even muffled noise and lingering smoke from the party above. Only the dank, damp, and musty stench of the polluted river splashing quietly beyond the door.

He said a silent prayer and reached for the door handle, prepared to shoot the damn lock open if necessary. But the rusty handle gave way with a faint, metallic groan. He shoved it open just far enough to let himself into the darkness on the other side, then pushed it closed behind him.

Hanging the lantern from the door handle, he took a step toward the stone sarcophagus, and his boot sank into filthy water up to his ankle. The river had risen from the day's rain and overflowed its culvert, flooding up onto the stone ledge.

Christ! He ran to the sarcophagus, afraid that it had filled with water. The lid rested in place, but a half-inch crack had been left open at the top to let in air.

"Amelia!" His pulse pounded with dread as icy cold as the water that had surely seeped through the porous stone.

Silence.

"Amelia, can you hear me?" Panic surged through him like an electric jolt. Was he wrong? Had Arthur Varnham hidden her someplace else? "Please, Amelia, answer me!"

If the bastard had hurt her, he'd rip the man apart limb by limb with—

"Brandon." The breathless whisper came so softly that he

barely heard it over the rushing river. But her fingertips reached out tentatively through the slit between the stone lid and the case.

"I'm here, darling." With a strangled sound of relief, he grabbed her fingertips to reassure her that she was going to be all right. Dear God, she was cold as ice! "You're safe. I'm going to get you out of there."

Heart-wrenching sobs echoed from inside the stone box. Choking and guttural sounds, as if she couldn't catch her breath between cries. Each one clawed at him in agony for her.

"You're safe, my love," he repeated to reassure her. "But I need you to pull your fingers back down inside, all right?"

When she didn't let go, he reluctantly released her, only for a muffled scream to tear from the coffin. Her fingers stretched into the air as far as possible, desperately reaching for him.

"Don't leave me!" Her voice was raw from hours of screaming for help in the black darkness, now little more than a hoarse rasp of terror. "You promised—you promised you wouldn't ever leave again!"

Guilt slammed through him, and he grabbed again for her fingers to calm her. "I'm not going anywhere." He leaned over the sarcophagus to try to look inside, only to see nothing but blackness. He lowered his mouth close to the gap and promised, "I'm not leaving here without you. But you have to pull your hands down so that I can move the lid out of the way. I don't want to risk pinching your fingers against the stone."

"Then keep—keep talking to me," she begged, sobbing loudly in hysteria. "Let me hear your voice—let me know you're still there."

"All right. What should I talk about?" He forced himself to keep his voice calm, despite the rising panic. They were running out of time. "About that day we went exploring along the river in Birmingham and got caught in the storm? Or when I taught you how to shoot a bow and arrow?"

"You—you nearly shot your uncle's mule." Her fingers released their stranglehold on his, and he slowly slipped his hand away.

"Details, details." He tsked dismissively. "But you have to admit that the old beast never moved faster than when that arrow flew at him."

"I–I thought… I thought your uncle would sk-skin you alive for that." Her fingers still shook, but they'd ceased their frantic grabs for him.

"He most likely would have, too, if he hadn't blamed that group of canal workers who'd stumbled into the innyard right then, foxed to the gills."

"If you hadn't told him they did," she corrected with a forced and strained laugh. One she only gave, he knew, because she thought he'd expected it. The soft sound of her bravery nearly broke him.

"In wars and innyards, it's every man for himself." He leaned over the lid to let her touch his cheek, giving her this small reassurance that he was still there. "It's time now, love." Clayton would be blowing the horn soon, and when he did, all the men would gather in the Inner Temple, and Pearce could spirit her away. "I need you to lower your hands so I can move the lid back. Wrap them into your skirt at your sides, all right? When the lid falls away, I will be right here." He placed a kiss to her fingertips. "With you."

Tentatively, in a show of great trust, she pulled her hands down in small jerks until her fingertips slid over the edge of the slit and disappeared back into the darkness inside the stone coffin.

He placed the top of his shoulder against the lid. "Keep them down. Ready? One…two…three!"

He shoved, straining with his entire body to move the heavy stone. A fierce groan of exertion tore from him, and the lid moved with a grinding of stone on stone. Another shove and groan, more slow grinding of stone. The lid fell away, tumbling into the water on the ledge with a loud splash and thud.

"Amelia!" He yanked her out of the coffin.

Carrying her in his arms, he kicked open the door and set her down in the dry tunnel. She was soaked from the layer of icy water that had seeped through the stone, and her weak arms could barely lift to encircle his neck. She shook violently against him with both cold and terror.

"Amelia, are you all right?" He ran his hands over her to check for any sign of injury on her face and head, down her body, arms, legs—

She nodded even as she sobbed, choking on her tears as she tried to gulp in mouthfuls of air.

"You're safe. I have you now." Shedding the white robe, he wrapped it around her like a blanket to stave off the cold, then pulled her into his arms to let his body warm hers. But he couldn't hold her close enough, even as his arms held round her like iron bands, his hands fiercely rubbing her arms and legs. Her pulse pounded strong and vibrant, and finally, he let go of the terror he'd been holding in check in order to concentrate on rescuing her, finally let the rush of rage at almost losing her sweep from him. "I told you that I would never let you go. I meant every word."

"Wild horses," she whispered. Barely a sound, but his heart heard every word.

"Wild horses." He squeezed his eyes closed as relief overwhelmed him.

Twenty-six

"So very sweet you are." Arthur Varnham smiled as he dragged a fingertip across the woman's bare midriff, drawing a figure eight in the pool of golden honey puddled there.

She giggled. "That tickles!"

She lay on the table in the middle of the banqueting hall, the room closed off to the other club members while that night's dinner was being prepared. He'd attended her himself, as he always did with the women who formed the center of the feast, taking great care in the presentation. But this one was special. She'd been drizzled with honey and rolled in sugar until her skin shimmered, then finished with strategically placed dollops of jam and biscuits to just barely hide her most intimate places.

"Why am I like this?" she protested with a sticky wiggle.

"Madame Noir explained your role to you, I'm sure." She was new to the club. He'd replaced Marigold Humphries that afternoon, not needing her any longer. And anyway, he preferred this one's larger breasts and ample hips. All the more fleshy goodness to savor. "You are to be tonight's sacrifice."

That drew a wanton smile from her. "I've never been anybody's sacrifice before."

"Trust me, my pet. You'll enjoy it." But not nearly as much as he would, when dinner was over and he claimed her for his own dessert, licking off every bit of sweetness that his tongue could reach.

"But the honey and jam's all sticky! Why did you have to pour that over me?"

"Because tonight I had a craving for tea."

Then he helped himself to an early taste by taking her honeyed foot into his mouth and licking up the sugar between her toes. She squirmed, which only stirred his lust more. Perhaps there would be time before the ceremony began to—

A bleating noise shot up his spine. He cursed and released her foot. The horn blared a second time from the outer chamber, just as unsuccessfully, just as shrilly.

"What the hell is going on?" The horn signaled the start of the ritual, yet he hadn't ordered it to begin.

He looked at the two men in the room with him guarding the door, but they only shrugged. So did the footmen who carried in the platters of food from the makeshift kitchen in a hollowed-out antechamber adjoining the banqueting hall.

When the horn went off a third time, Varnham flung open the door to the Inner Chamber.

A hooded monk stood on the dais, holding the ceremonial horn in his hands. The white-robed members gathered in the room, waiting for the ritual to begin. More filtered in from the other chambers. All of their hoods were pulled down low over their faces, ready to begin the ritual, exactly as usual. Only too early.

Varnham flipped up his own red hood and walked through the crowd. They parted to let him pass. As he drew nearer to the dais, a suspicious tingle twined down his spine. Something wasn't right. The room looked the same as usual, with the same white-robed members and the scattering of guards in their brown friars' robes. But something was…off.

Pushing down his unease, he mounted the dais. "What the hell are you doing?" he demanded in a low hiss to the monk with the horn. "It's too damned early for the ritual to start."

The hooded man shrugged apologetically and lowered the horn to his side.

Biting back a frustrated curse, Varnham faced the men.

"Brothers." He spread out his arms in greeting as he always did. The smile on his face not hiding how irritated he was that the ceremony had started early. The damn man would be fired for this. "You are welcome to the Temple of Bacchus."

"Thanks be to Bacchus," the crowd of men answered in unison.

"And to the Armory," a lone voice called out from the back of the room.

On cue, a half-dozen men pulled down their hoods.

Varnham stared at the strangers who had been lost in a sea of white robes, mixed in with the members. Stunned, he wheeled to face the monk behind him who had blown the horn.

The man yanked down his hood and grinned. "Hello."

Then he pulled back his arm and swung.

———

"Now then." Clayton Elliott placed one of the chairs from the banqueting hall on the dais in front of Varnham, where he sat tied to his own mock throne. Clayton still wore that damnably silly friar's robe, but his hand now throbbed delightfully from ramming it into Varnham's face. If given half a chance, he'd gladly do it again. He straddled the chair backwards and rested his forearms over its back. "Let's have a little chat, shall we?"

Around them, the stone chambers were finally silent and empty after the fight that had broken out in the Inner Temple when the men of the Armory revealed themselves. Most of the club members had wisely rushed to leave. But a few had stood to fight and raised fists the way they'd paid Gentleman Jackson dearly to teach them to do, only to be leveled to the floor after a few swings, then physically shoved out of the chambers and deposited on the church steps on their arses. The Armory men had swiftly cleared the place of both brothers and nuns—and a naked woman who was oddly covered in honey and sugar—thankfully with no sign of Pearce or Miss Howard.

Clayton hadn't expected to see them. He was certain that

Pearce had whisked Amelia away to safety at the Armory, where Marcus and Merritt would be waiting with a riot-freed and freshly interrogated Frederick Howard. *If* all their plans had gone well.

Right now, though, Clayton's concern was Arthur Varnham.

"What do you want?" Varnham replied, surprisingly calmly for a man in his situation. "Why did you and your men invade my club?"

"Because the Home Office doesn't appreciate acts of sedition." He gestured toward the red robe and throne. "Even ones in fancy dress."

"We're just a gentlemen's club, gathering to have a good time. That's all." He laughed. "You can't take what we do here seriously."

"Here? Not at all." He shrugged dismissively. "Here was just a group of middle-aged gentlemen behaving like a bunch of randy schoolboys on their first trip to a brothel." He fixed his gaze on Varnham's. "But *you* blackmailed an MP."

Varnham smirked at the accusation. "Do you have any idea who my brother is?" He leaned as far forward as the bindings at his wrists and ankles allowed. "Not only will I be exonerated of all charges, but your own career in the Home Office will be over."

Clayton sighed patiently. "Your brother is a man so dedicated to Crown and country that he had a fellow MP arrested for corruption. Do you really think he'd come to your aid once he learns that you've criminally extorted a fellow peer and kidnapped Amelia Howard? That's enough to dangle you by the neck at Newgate, don't you think?"

Varnham paled.

"I know what you've done, and I promise that I'll argue on your behalf for leniency if you cooperate and answer my questions." He paused to let that offer settle. "What's your connection to Scepter?"

Varnham's eyes flared. "How do you know about Scepter?"

He certainly wasn't getting *that* information. "We know that you gave Howard a list of their men to be placed into government positions. What we want to know is why."

He laughed. "If you know about Scepter, then you know that they'll kill me before I have the chance to swing."

"Not if they can't find you. I can arrange for you to be exiled. You'll be halfway across the ocean before they realize you've disappeared." Blackmail was a passive act, committed by cowards who didn't have the courage to wage battle head-on. Clayton would have bet a thousand pounds that Varnham wouldn't have the spine to keep his silence and go to the gallows for Scepter. "Tell me what I want to know, and I'll take you to the Home Office tonight where you'll be kept safe. You'll be given a new identity, put on the first ship out of London, and Scepter won't be able to touch you. Neither will Brandon Pearce, who's most likely waiting outside that door right now to beat the life out of you." He paused for emphasis. "Although I'm deeply inclined to let him."

Varnham said nothing, but Clayton could see his thoughts churning, weighing his options and finding no means of escape except for cooperation. He finally answered, "Yes, I'm part of Scepter, and yes, we're seditious." His lips curled. "We'd all love nothing more than the overthrow of the British monarchy."

Icy fingers of uneasy warning slithered up Clayton's spine, but he kept his face inscrutable. Revolutionary groups existed in all corners of England these days, but none were as dangerous or powerful as Scepter. "Why?"

"You really have to ask? Take one look at Mad King George and his worthless spawn, and you'll have your answer. More useless princes God never created. Especially Prinny. Fat, arrogant, pompous, disrespectful of everyone who serves this country, and just as mentally unsound as his father. A man who wastes the hardearned money of Englishmen on palaces, food, and mistresses."

"You're talking like a Frenchman."

"Not at all. The French failed in their revolution. But we'll succeed in ours." His eyes gleamed. "Scepter will make certain of it."

The man certainly knew madness, all right. "Revolutions can't be controlled."

"Oh, but they can be." He tilted his head, studying Clayton closely. "The Americans succeeded in casting off their monarch, while the French have been forced back under the rule of one. What was the difference in the end? It was who started the revolution. The American aristocracy—businessmen like Samuel Adams, wealthy landowners like George Washington, high-ranking political figures like Thomas Jefferson and John Adams, intellectuals like Thomas Paine—*they* planted the seeds of revolution in America and guided it through to the end."

Varnham leaned back on his throne, pleased that he had Clayton's close attention

"But in Paris," he continued, "the revolution was led by a mob. The French upper class was destroyed by vindictive and jealous peasants, leaving a power vacuum in both society and government. Those few intellectuals who were left were forced to chase the mob and never gained proper control, leaving the revolution to be guided by the likes of Robespierre and Danton—part of the mob themselves, wolves who eventually devoured their own pack and helped to put not just a despotic king into power over them but an emperor."

"And Scepter thinks it has the men in place to control a revolution?" Businessmen, wealthy landowners, high-ranking political figures…the English aristocracy. The revolution Scepter planned would be top down and not at all organic. That was why Scepter wanted its men in government positions. But turnpike trustees to lead the overthrow of a monarchy? "How?"

"I can't tell you."

"Then you'll swing for—"

"I *can't* tell you," he repeated, "because I don't know. I was the one able to blackmail Howard, so I was given a list of men to pass along to him. I don't know what Scepter wants from them."

"Surely you know something about their plans."

"Generals never give their battle plan to foot soldiers." His mouth twisted wryly. "You were a former soldier. You know that better than I."

Clayton bit back a curse. Damn him, Varnham was right. "Then tell me who gave you that list."

"Would you ever be disloyal to your generals?" He shook his head. "Shot in battle by the enemy, shot after battle by your own men for retreating...either way, shot dead."

The two men stared at each other in quiet understanding. Clayton knew then that he'd get no more information from Varnham. The interrogation was over.

———

Several hours later, long after dawn had broken across London and the city was on the move into another morning, Lord Sidmouth, the Home Secretary, arrived at his office.

He stopped in the doorway and stared, blinking in bewilderment. "What the devil..."

Arthur Varnham, younger brother to Sir Charles Varnham, sat tied to his desk chair, gagged and wearing a red monk's robe. Around his neck hung a handwritten sign...

Bound for Botany Bay.

Twenty-seven

AMELIA SAID NOTHING AS PEARCE LED HER INSIDE THE ARMORY, silently letting herself take it all in, this place that had become a second home to him and to his former brothers-in-arms. He'd described the building when he'd taken her home after leaving the tunnel, explained what the men of the Armory's plans were, waited for her to bathe herself and dress, and insisted that she eat something although she had no appetite. And not leaving her side the entire time.

She knew what to expect now that they were here, yet she couldn't stop a shudder when the outer iron door banged and screeched as it opened. Or the tremble of unease as they passed beneath the twin portcullis that guarded a second inner doorway. But Pearce was at her side, and with him, she could bear anything.

Even facing down her brother.

He glanced at her fingers as they tightened on his arm. "Are you all right?"

She gave a single determined nod. "I will be."

He squeezed her hand and escorted her into the building.

The central octagonal room opened before them, its imposing size and shape taking her breath away. But so did the three men who were waiting inside, all of them on their feet and facing the door as she and Pearce entered—the Duke of Hampton, Merritt Rivers…and Frederick.

Straightening her spine, Amelia slipped her hand away from Pearce's arm. He stopped at the edge of the room and let her walk on alone.

"Amelia!" Frederick started forward. He held out his arms to embrace her. "Thank God you're all—"

She slapped him. Her hand cracked across his face so hard that the sting of the blow pulsed up her arm and the sound echoed off the stone walls.

He glared at her, rubbing at the red mark already forming on his left cheek. "What the hell—"

She slapped him again, this time with her left hand to the opposite cheek. Even harder than before. So hard that she staggered sideways from the exertion of the blow.

The duke and Merritt both stiffened. Merritt started forward a single step before stopping and shooting Pearce a look questioning whether he should intercede.

From the corner of her eye, she saw Pearce faintly shake his head, to let her confront her brother on her own.

"I know what you did," she rasped out, the feeling of betrayal in her so intense and raw that she shook.

"Damnation, Amelia!" Frederick hissed. "Control yourself. You are in the presence of a duke."

She didn't care. She'd spent too much of her life cowering in front of the Howard men. *No more.* "I know what you did."

"Of course you know." He slid a grim glance between the duke and Merritt. Apparently, they knew, too, having put him through an interrogation after freeing him from the New Prison. Most likely they were simply waiting for her and Pearce to help them decide what to do with him. "You heard the charges that Charles Varnham leveled against me when Bow Street arrested me. I told you about them when the blackmail—"

"My marriage."

The accusation hit him so forcefully that his mouth fell open, and his eyes flared wide. Shock radiated from him.

The duke and Merritt turned to leave the room. But she held up a hand and stopped them.

"No, stay," she ordered softly. "Please."

The men awkwardly exchanged glances but did as she asked and remained.

"I've had enough of secrets. I'm living my life out in the open now for all to witness. Starting immediately." She took a step forward to close the distance between her and her brother. For the first time, he wasn't at all intimidating. Up close like this, cornered by his own devices, he was simply weak and self-serving. Pathetic. "I know what you did. I know how you schemed to steal my money, the lengths you went to, all the lies and humiliations." Her voice choked, and she forced out in a rasping whisper, "Damn you…damn you to hell for what you put me through!"

"I have no idea what you're talking about," he countered, far too calmly. "Aaron Northam fooled me as much as he did you."

"Stop the lies!" Consumed by anger, she didn't step away or back down. "You hired Aaron to pretend to marry me so you could have both my money and your revenge on me for inheriting Papa's fortune. You couldn't stand that he passed you over for his daughter."

"That's absurd! For you to make those accusations, when I've done nothing but help you—" Self-righteous indignation hardened his face. "You know everything I did to pursue Northam. I hired accountants, lawyers, investigators—how I worked to keep your elopement secret so you wouldn't be ruined socially as well as financially. For God's sake, Amelia! I took care of you. I did everything I could to make you happy."

"You mean like the letters I wrote to Pearce, the ones you made certain never reached him? Did they even leave the house, or did you simply burn them in the fireplace the moment my back was turned?" Her words emerged so softly that she barely heard them herself. But if she spoke any louder, she would have screamed. "Is that what you mean by *taking care* of me?"

"Pearce was nothing then! You deserved better, Amelia. I will not apologize for keeping you from throwing your life away on an army officer."

Around her, she felt all three men stiffen at that insult. Marcus

Braddock slowly folded his arms over his chest in such an imperial posture that the air inside the room turned cold. But Frederick was too wrapped up in saving himself to notice his blunder.

"You lied to me." She blinked, her eyes burning with furious tears at all he'd cost her. "Just as you're lying now."

"I am not—"

"I saw the contract you made with Aaron! I know you paid him—and Arthur Varnham told me the rest. That's what he used to blackmail you."

He glared at her, his jaw working in anger, no longer attempting to defend himself. *Thank God.* At least he wasn't that much of a fool.

"You must have had such a great laugh at my expense when you planned out how Aaron and I would meet that day in the park, when you gave him information about all my favorites so he would know exactly how to win my affection." Fresh pain simmered inside her. But she needed to walk through the fire until it seared her heart to him and never let him inside there again. "How did you keep a straight face that day he came to the house to call on me for the first time, watching me beside myself with nervousness as I introduced you, when you'd known each other all along? Or the day you pretended to take him to our banker to introduce them?" The words strangled in her tightening throat, yet she forced them out, needing to utter them. "To go that far for money and revenge... Do you really hate me that much?"

"Yes!" he bit out. "Yes, I do."

Something deep inside her shattered. Something she knew could *never* be mended.

Slowly, she nodded, accepting this final destruction. "Then if I were you, Frederick, I would leave England and never return."

"Self-exile?" he drawled sarcastically, rubbing at the red hand-print marking his left cheek.

"Mercy," she corrected. "That you don't deserve."

He gave a scoffing laugh. "You really expect me to do that?

To walk away from the life I've created here, the power I have as an MP—"

"Yes," Pearce answered for her, still waiting on the other side of the room. "Or I'll make certain that you never see the light of day." He folded his arms over his chest. "You'll not come anywhere near her again."

Frederick leveled a murderous glare at Pearce. All the hatred and disdain he'd always held for him surged unchecked to the surface. "I won't go to prison. Varnham will protect his brother. He'll have no choice but to rescind all the accusations he's made once everything his brother has done is revealed. He'll be the one in prison, not me. He'll be at the center of talk across the empire, and no one will care what I've done."

"I never said prison." The threat in Pearce's voice cut like ice, made all the more murderous by the calm way he issued it. "I'll put you into your grave."

"Why, you worthless, arrogant brute—"

Pearce dove across the room and grabbed Frederick by the throat, pinning him to the wall. He dangled there, his feet barely touching the floor. Frederick's eyes grew wide, and gurgling sounds came from him as he tore at Pearce's arm. But Pearce never moved a muscle to release him.

"No!" Amelia placed her hand on Pearce's shoulder to hold him back. "He isn't worth it."

Pearce released him and stepped back. Frederick slumped against the wall, his hand going to his throat.

"You will swear out a statement to Mr. Rivers that you tricked me into a fraudulent marriage," Amelia ordered, her gaze darting to Merritt, who nodded his agreement to assist her. "Then you will leave on the first ship for America." She linked her arm through Pearce's, not yet trusting him not to pulp her brother right there on the Aubusson rug. Frederick deserved exactly that—and more. But she simply wanted all of this to end, as quickly as possible. "Go home and pack your trunks. Take anything from the house you want, including whatever banknotes you've hidden in your study. And *never* come back."

Defeat dimmed Freddie's eyes. His shoulders sagged.

"I'm free of you now, do you understand? You and Papa have no more power over me." A sensation she'd rarely known in her life struck her—*freedom*. "You can never hurt me again."

Frederick's jaw worked as he stared at her, wisely saying nothing. She was certain he didn't recognize the sister he knew within the woman confronting him. Most likely because that girl was gone. In her place was a strong woman who would never again let anyone control her.

He pushed himself away from the wall and hurried from the Armory. The duke and Merritt followed to make certain that he truly was gone. And to give Amelia and Pearce time alone.

Pearce turned to her and tucked a stray curl behind her ear. His eyes shone with love. "I'm so very proud of you for what you just did."

"And me of you for not hurting him."

He forced a half grin. "Only because I thought you might want to hurt him yourself."

"He isn't worth it," she repeated, then closed her eyes when Pearce placed a comforting kiss to her forehead.

She stepped into his embrace and welcomed the strength and warmth of his arms as they encircled her. She rested her cheek against his chest and felt the soothing beat of his heart. This was where she belonged, right here in his arms.

Always.

Epilogue

Three Weeks Later

"To Pearce and Amelia." Marcus Braddock stood at the head of the table in the dining room of Charlton House and lifted his glass. "May your life together be filled with happiness and love." His eyes shone, while beside him the duchess dabbed at hers with a napkin. "Congratulations on your engagement."

Around the table, the close friends whom Danielle Braddock had gathered to celebrate with them raised their glasses to join in the toast. Rounds of congratulations followed.

Beaming with more happiness than she'd ever thought possible, Amelia wrapped her arm around Pearce's as he sat beside her. She briefly rested her head against his hard bicep in a small gesture of affection, one he returned with a tender caress to her knee beneath the table.

Amelia hadn't wanted this dinner. When the duchess first proposed it, she'd declined. She wasn't eager to announce her engagement to the world when she wasn't yet officially free to remarry, when the wedding might still be a year or two away. After all, she'd willingly signed her name to the parish register when she'd married Aaron, and even though she could claim grounds of fraud, legalities had to be met, investigations made, intent publicly declared... scandal to survive. A conversation with Merritt Rivers about what was in store for her legally proved how very long she would have to wait before she could become Pearce's wife.

But Pearce had persuaded her into accepting the duchess's invitation.

He wanted this for her, a happy celebration with the people who had become family to them. Marcus and Danielle, the duke's sister Claudia and her husband, Danielle's Aunt Harriett, Clayton Elliott...even little Pippa, Marcus's niece, had joined them earlier before being whisked up to the nursery by her nanny. The only person missing was Merritt, who had suddenly left London two days ago without explanation, except to say that he'd return in time for the party. Unfortunately, he'd missed it.

Amelia hadn't realized until that evening how much this new family meant to her. Frederick was the only blood family she had, and now he was gone. America or the Continent, India or the moon—she had no idea where, but she knew he would never return. Despite the hell he'd put her through, she'd done him one last favor by convincing Charles Varnham to rescind all of his accusations and saved her brother's reputation in absentia. Varnham reluctantly agreed, his decision helped along by assurances from Marcus Braddock and Pearce that Frederick Howard would never return.

"Before we allow Miss Howard to be formally engaged," Clayton Elliott piped up, "I think she needs to know about that time in Spain when Pearce kidnapped General Pemberton's dog and held it ransom for its weight in whiskey."

Amelia stifled a laugh at Pearce's expense. All evening they'd been regaling her with stories of his army days, and she'd joined in with stories of her own from their youth in Birmingham.

"It was top-notch whiskey, I'll have you know." Pearce stretched his arm across Amelia's chair back. "And why does she need to know *that* about me, exactly?"

"Because it proves you can't be trusted with small animals," Clayton answered.

"Or whiskey," Marcus interjected.

When unchecked laughter bubbled up from her, Clayton arched an exaggerated brow in her direction. "We only want to protect you, to make certain that you know what you're getting yourself into."

"I know exactly who I'm marrying." She dared to touch Pearce's cheek. "My soul mate." Her voice softened as she looked deeply into his eyes. "And I love him with all my soul."

At that, Aunt Harriett let out a sob, and both Danielle and Claudia reached for their husbands' hands. And their handkerchiefs.

"Well then, on that happy declaration," Danielle announced as she rose to her feet, bringing everyone in the room to theirs, "shall we venture to the drawing room for coffee?"

"If you don't mind, Duchess," Pearce said as he took Amelia's arm and looped it around his, "I'd like to steal Amelia away for a moment alone."

"Of course I don't mind. The library should be lit. Join us when you're ready." Danielle's eyes gleamed knowingly as she added, "Take your time."

Amelia dug her nails into Pearce's forearm as he led her down the hall. "You said a moment alone."

"Yes, I did."

She glanced over her shoulder at the perceptive smiles the women wore as they left the dining room, the men lingering behind for a glass of port. "They all think you meant…a moment *alone*."

"Yes, they do." He grinned as he led her inside the library and closed the door, then backed her across the room until her bottom hit the back of the settee. He leaned in, his mouth lingering temptingly above hers. "But while I would love nothing more than a moment *alone*…" He kissed her heatedly and groaned against her lips. "*Several* moments, in fact…" He broke the kiss and stepped back, sucking in a deep breath of restraint. "What I need is to talk to you privately."

Dread twisted inside her. "Is something wrong? Is it Scepter?"

The men of the Armory were getting closer in their hunt for the group's leaders, but progress had been slow. Clayton Elliott and his

Home Office agents were going through the list of men Frederick had placed into government positions and those men Pearce had seen at the Hellfire club to track down any with ties to Scepter, but so far little had turned up. Arthur Varnham had covered his tracks well, as had Marigold Humphries, the prostitute who had given him the information with which to blackmail Frederick. She'd completely disappeared, in fact. The men believed that she'd fled to escape Scepter, but Amelia knew better. She'd told Frederick to take anything he wanted with him when he left. Most likely he took her, too.

The men had yet to discover Scepter's endgame, why they wanted those men in the government, why they were willing to have them placed as low-level trustees. Yet the men had succeeded in drawing attention to government appointments, which would be made more carefully at all levels going forward. In that, at least, they could claim a victory.

Scepter was still alive, but they'd succeeded in cutting off another arm from the monster. Someday, they'd kill it outright.

Pearce grinned. "I want to give you your engagement gift."

His thoughtfulness warmed her. "But I didn't get you anything."

"You've given me your heart. I don't need anything more." But then he paused. "Except your dowry. That I need from you right now."

She blinked, caught completely off guard by that. "But we've never discussed—"

"Your locket."

Her hand shot up to her neck to clasp it. "I don't—I don't understand…"

"I want it back."

She didn't stop him when he reached behind her neck to unfasten the ribbon. But she didn't like this. Not at all. When he slipped it away, she felt utterly naked and exposed.

Unease twisted her belly. "Pearce, what are you playing at?"

"Nothing. I'm perfectly serious. I'm giving you your engagement gift."

He reached into his inside breast pocket and slowly withdrew a long blue ribbon. From the end dangled a new gold locket.

Her eyes blurred with tears, and she trembled as he fastened it around her neck. To do something this thoughtful, this poignant... At that moment, she couldn't find her voice to tell him how much she loved him.

"But it's also our marriage settlement."

"Pardon?" She wasn't expecting *that*. They hadn't negotiated anything.

"I put it inside the locket." When she hesitated, he insisted gently, "Go on. Open it."

With trembling fingers, she opened the tiny clasp and revealed the slip of paper tucked within. She unfolded it to read—

She couldn't believe her eyes. Her tearful gaze darted up to his, and he smiled lovingly at her shocked reaction.

"This...can't be right," she whispered hoarsely, overcome with emotion. His masculine handwriting declared that she would keep all of her current fortune, including Bradenhill. To do with however she'd like.

"I assure you it is. Merritt told me that it can stand as a legal contract in court once you agree to it." He took the slip from her trembling fingers, refolded it, and closed it inside the locket with a soft snap. "But I warn you that none of the terms I've proposed are negotiable. Especially my pledge never to put a turnpike through your property."

"I love you." She flung her arms around him and pressed him close, as tightly as all her strength would allow. "I love you so much!"

When he kissed her, she tasted his love for her in return.

She leaned into the embrace, and desire sparked instantly between them. He kissed her possessively and hungrily, and a soft whimper of need rose from her throat. One he answered with a growl and a caress of his hand along the side of her body.

She shivered and reluctantly reminded him, "We can't...let this...get out of control."

"Oh yes, we can." He tilted her head to the side and nipped his teeth at her exposed neck.

Somehow finding enough resolve through the fog engulfing her, she slipped from his arms. "We *cannot.*" But dear heavens, how much she wanted to! Panting to catch back the breath he'd stolen, she reminded him, "We don't know how long it will take for the annulment to be formalized. No matter much I want you—and believe me, my love, I *dearly* want you"—she punctuated that with a caress of her hand down his waistcoat—"we can't risk that I might become *enceinte.* We've already taken too much risk already."

"It will be a long time, then," he agreed, raking a gaze of such heated longing over her that she ached from it. "A very, *very* long time."

Her lips parted, about to murmur terms of surrender—

"Perhaps not as long as you think," a deep voice called out from the shadows near the open terrace door.

Startled, she wheeled around with a gasp.

Merritt Rivers stepped inside the house. Dressed all in black from head to boots, he blended eerily into the night and came fresh from horseback, right down to the scent of the stable that wafted around him and the half-dried mud on his boots.

"How long were you standing there?" Pearce demanded irritably.

"Long enough." Merritt grinned at their expense and flamed the blush heating Amelia's cheeks. "Sorry to interrupt, but I stumbled across something you might like to have."

He reached up his sleeve and withdrew a rolled sheet of paper torn from a book, then held it out to her.

Frowning, she unrolled it and scanned over the page. Columns of signatures, dates, occasions, witnesses…her own signature next to Aaron's a third of the way from the bottom of the page.

Her breath rushed from her lungs. She couldn't believe… "The parish register?"

"My wedding gift," Merritt corrected with a smile. "Your name is no longer in the church records."

She didn't know what to say. Except… "And now neither is anyone else's on this page." Shaking her head against the temptation of keeping it, she handed it back. "You have to return it." She blinked rapidly to fight back the tears. To come so close to erasing everything—but she simply couldn't. "Those other couples might need proof that they were legally wed. I could never destroy that for them."

"I thought you'd say that." Merritt's eyes twinkled mischievously. "So I replaced that page with a copy that faithfully renders all the other signatures and conveniently skips over yours."

"Faithfully rendered," Pearce repeated. "Forged, you mean."

Merritt fixed a meaningful look on Pearce. "Do you really care about the difference?"

"No," Amelia replied, answering for both of them. She pressed the page against her bosom, unwilling to relinquish it. "Not at all."

With a knowing grin, Merritt nodded at Amelia and slapped Pearce on the back as he turned to leave, heading back into the night. "Congratulations."

Amelia stared down at the page. Could it be real? She could barely believe it. Now, after so many years, the thing that had cast such dread and agony over her life…the thing that was keeping her from the man she loved—the scrawl of her signature on a thin, weightless piece of paper.

"What are you going to do with it?" Pearce asked quietly.

The only official record of her marriage, the only proof that existed in the world that she'd stood in that church and pledged her life to a lie… She shook her head. "All those years," she whispered, "I thought I was married…"

She raised her gaze to his. For the first time, there was no longer any shame, no humiliation, no secrets. Now, there was only Pearce.

"But there was never a marriage. Only vows that were lies, a love that was never shared…no honoring or obeying. Only years of punishment." She stepped slowly over to the fireplace. "No one can argue that what I had was a true marriage, in the eyes of God or the Church. So no one can argue with this. This marriage gets no more of me."

She cast the page into the flames. The sheet burned, and with every black curl of the paper, a spark of freedom lit in her heart.

Pearce came up behind her and slipped his arms around her, pulling her against him.

"It's all over now," he assured her, nuzzling her hair.

"No." Her hand rose to her neck, to the little gold locket that hung there. And always would. "Our life together is just beginning."

Author's Note

I had a fabulous time writing this romance, one that proved to be a rollicking good time. As you might have guessed, I drew on several historical facts—and one literary—to bring you this adventure.

Let's begin at the end…of marriage. It was nearly impossible in Regency England to end one, even a tragically cruel one. It took an act of Parliament to secure a divorce, which was seldom granted, always scandalous, and usually a humiliating experience for both parties who had to publicly disclose their evidence, no matter how degrading. For a husband, the only grounds for divorce was adultery. But to claim so was to admit that he'd not only been cuckolded but also wasn't man enough to satisfy his wife's carnal desires. No wonder, then, that most men only sought divorce after their wives had publicly left the marriage. A woman seeking divorce had to prove not just adultery but also extreme cruelty. Not an easy task considering that husbands were legally entitled to beat their wives so long as it was done in moderation with the intent to correct their misbehavior. Further, most divorced women had to surrender all their property, all their social standing, and all their rights to their children. Obtaining an annulment was even more difficult and damning. Annulment was allowed only in cases of fraud, incompetence (in which either party was underage and married without the guardian's consent, or proven legally insane), or impotence; nonconsummation was *not* grounds for annulment. Only in 1937 were women allowed to divorce on grounds of abandonment, cruelty, and incurable insanity.

Shooting the bridge! Pearce and Amelia order the waterman to "shoot the bridge" in order to escape. That meant running the boat through the dangerously swirling waters of the Thames as it flowed beneath old London Bridge. Over the years, as the bridge grew in size, the narrow arches where the river flowed between the stone foundations—known as starlings—became narrower and fewer. The result: the river sped beneath the bridge at an astonishing rate, resulting in life-threatening rapids and a drop in water level of at least six feet. Only the brave or the very foolish attempted to guide a boat through the bridge during a flood or high tide; many drowned. Although in 1751 its two center arches were replaced by a wider, single span to make the bridge more navigable, paintings after this change still show whitewater churning around the starlings. A new bridge opened in 1831. No one knows exactly when watermen stopped shooting the bridge. During my research, none of the historians I contacted were able to provide a definitive answer, including the Museum of London, except to say that it had ended by 1832 when the old bridge was demolished. So at the slight risk of historical inaccuracy, I let Pearce and Amelia shoot the bridge. After all, I've never been able to resist a really good chase scene.

As many of you might have guessed, Amelia's sham marriage at the hand of her brother was inspired by Charles Dickens's novel, *Great Expectations.* In the Dickens book, Miss Havisham's brother tortures her for inheriting the family fortune by arranging for a man to court her, propose to her, and jilt her, destroying her life to secure his revenge. I took that idea a step further by having Frederick Howard let Amelia believe she was lawfully married and then abandoned in order to get his hands on her money. (In fact, Amelia was named after the *Dickensian* version of Miss Havisham.)

And finally, the Hellfire club. In the eighteenth century, it became fashionable for gentlemen to establish Hellfire clubs where men of "quality" could partake in immoral acts. The one in this book was based on the club established by Sir Francis Dashwood, the most infamous of the Hellfire clubs. With a motto of *Fais ce que tu voudras* ("Do what thou wilt"), the club played on religious and pagan themes, with meetings held in Medmenham Abbey, beneath which ran a series of caves carved out for meetings and decorated with mythological themes, phallic images, and other sexual symbols. The members addressed each other as brothers and the leader as the abbot, and during meetings, members wore ritual clothing—white trousers, jacket, and cap—while the abbot wore red. Prostitutes, referred to as nuns, were often present. Rumors claimed that the club sacrificed to Bacchus, Venus, and Dionysus, and meetings often included mock rituals of a pornographic nature, drinking, banqueting, and wenching.

I hope you enjoyed this historical glimpse into Regency England as much as you enjoyed spending time with Pearce and Amelia. Happy reading!

About the Author

Anna Harrington is an award-winning author of Regency romance. She writes spicy historicals with alpha heroes and independent heroines, layers of emotion, and lots of sizzle. Anna was nominated for a RITA in 2017 for her title *How I Married a Marquess*, and her debut, *Dukes Are Forever*, won the 2016 Maggie Award for Best Historical Romance. A lover of all things chocolate and coffee, when she's not hard at work writing her next book or planning her next series, Anna loves to fly airplanes, go ballroom dancing, or tend her roses. She is a terrible cook who hopes to one day use her oven for something other than shoe storage.

ONLY A DUCHESS WOULD DARE

Dazzling Regency romance from *New York Times* and *USA Today* bestselling author Amelia Grey

Alexander Mitchell, the fourth Marquis of Raceworth, is shocked when the alluring young Duchess of Brookfield accuses him of being in possession of pearls belonging to her family. The pearls in question have been in Race's family since the sixteenth century. And while Susannah Brookfield is the most beautiful, enchanting, and intelligent woman he has ever met, he's not about to hand over a family heirloom. But if he didn't steal her pearls, how exactly did he get them, and what are he and Susannah to do when they go missing once more?

"Exemplifies the very essence of what a romance novel should be...superbly written."
—Love Romance Passion

For more info about Sourcebooks's books and authors, visit:
sourcebooks.com

LADY MAGGIE'S SECRET SCANDAL

Sparkling Regency romance from *New York Times* and
USA Today bestselling author Grace Burrowes

Lady Maggie Windham has secrets…and she's been perfectly capable
of keeping them—until now. When a blackmailer threatens to expose
Maggie's parentage, she turns to investigator Benjamin Hazlit to keep
catastrophe at bay.

Benjamin Hazlit has secrets of his own, including an earldom he never
talks about. However, when Maggie comes to him with innocent eyes and
a puzzling conundrum, he feels he must offer his assistance. But with each
day that passes, Maggie begins to intrigue Benjamin more than the riddle
she's set him to solve…

**"[A] tantalizing, delectably sexy story that
is one of [Burrowes's] best yet."**
—*Library Journal* Starred Review

For more info about Sourcebooks's books and authors, visit:
sourcebooks.com